ROBERTA K

THE ASHES *of a* BROKEN LIFE

Interior Images by Sofia Santucci

Outskirts Press, Inc.
http://www.outskirtspress.com

ISBN: 978-1-4787-3950-0

PRINTED IN THE UNITED STATES OF AMERICA

To all who mourn in Israel, he will give beauty for ashes, joy instead of mourning, and praise instead of despair. For the Lord has planted them like strong and graceful oaks for his own glory.

– Isaiah 61:3

Prologue

May Second Week

Derek sighs with fatigue as he slips the keycard into his hotel room door. When the door opens, he sits his briefcase and computer case on the floor inside the door. "I'm going to enjoy my year off. No meetings, no eating restaurant meals, and most of all no travel unless it is to someplace for rest and relaxation." he said as he removes the jacket to his black suit, and hangs it in the room's closet. Because he's both famished and in need of a shower he settles for the shower, knowing it will wash some of his fatigue away with the days sweat. Kicking his fine black leather shoes off, he strips off his clothing on the way to the bathroom. Like Hansel and Gretel he leaves a path to where he can be found.

Once he is clean and dresses in jeans and a black t-shirt, he orders from the room service menu. While waiting for his meal, he checks for messages on his cell phone. Seeing no new ones he puts the phone on the lamp table next to the queen-sized bed. He has only one call to make, one that he makes every night while on the road. He will call Jack, his five year old son and his three year old daughter Lucy. "Jack and Lucy we will be able to do all the things that I have neglected." A smile wipes the tenseness from Derek's lean tanned face, a smile that also brightens his dark brown eyes. Thinking of his son and daughter always puts a smile on Derek's face.

Once his meal arrives and after he's eaten, Derek dials his son's cell phone number. When no one picks up, he decides he will try later. Maybe Jack has the phone turned off, which he has been taught to do while at school. He may have to try the land line a little later.

Not interested in any noise Derek lies on the bed on top of the quilted bedspread and closes his eyes. He figures he will rest his eyes for thirty minutes then try calling Jack again.

An hour later he is awakened from a deep sleep by the ringing of his cell phone. Rolling to his right side, he sees Jack's name flashing on the cell phone screen.

Before he can say anything he hears Jack sobbing into the phone. "Jack, buddy what's wrong? "

First he hears Jack sniff, and then his son said, "Daddy, I'm scared, I'm hungry and my bottom hurt's."

"Jack, where are you, and where are Grandpa Bing and Grandma Stella? Why does your bottom hurt?"

He hears Jack sniff again before he said, "I'm in my fort. The bus driver let us off at our house this afternoon he thought Grandpa Bing and Grandma Stella were picking us up here. They weren't here but Mommy was. I asked where Grandma and Grandpa were and she said that they told her she could watch us. I didn't believe that, but was afraid to say anything. Mommy went out and my bottom hurts because Mommy got mad at me and spanked my bottom with the pancake pan. She also hurt Lucy. Mommy pulled Lucy's hair really hard and made her cry. When Lucy said she was telling you Mommy hit her in the face and scratched Lucy when she tried to get away."

Not wanting Jack to hear his anger at Jacks admission of getting beaten, Derek shakes his head and bites his lip before he replies, "Why are you in your fort at eight at night? Where is your sister?"

"Mommy made me, Lucy, Yates, Tralee, Garfield and Odie go outside. When we came home from school Uncle Sean was here. He and Mommy got into a fight and she sent me and Lucy to our rooms. I heard Uncle Sean leave, and sneaked down to the kitchen to get food for me and Lucy and our pets. I was also making a card for you. Mommy caught me, tore the card up and called me a bad boy."

"The card was of you, me, Lucy, Aunt Flannery and the pets. When she saw the dark hair on the woman she asked who it was, when I said Aunt Flannery she was so mad she turned red and ripped the card to shreds. Daddy when she is angry like that she scares me and Lucy."

Anger at his wife Chloe is so strong that it takes a few moments before Derek can speak again. "You are a wonderful boy. Actually you are the sweetest boy I have ever known, I love you and I'm proud to be your Daddy."

"I love you too Daddy. I'm also proud of you." At his sons words Derek cannot help but smile.

"Jack, I'm going to call Grandpa Bing and Grandma Stella and have them come and get you, Lucy and your pets. The police may also come, so please stay in your fort and answer when they come for you.'

"Daddy, I can't find Odie, Mommy threw her out the door, and she ran away."

Shaking his head in disbelief, Derek said, "I'll have Grandpa Bing call someone to find Odie. Answer your phone when it rings, I will call back as soon as I talk with Grandpa."

"Ok Daddy, I'll answer. Please come home soon. I miss you."

"I'll be there when you wake up in the morning."

"Good Daddy. Good."

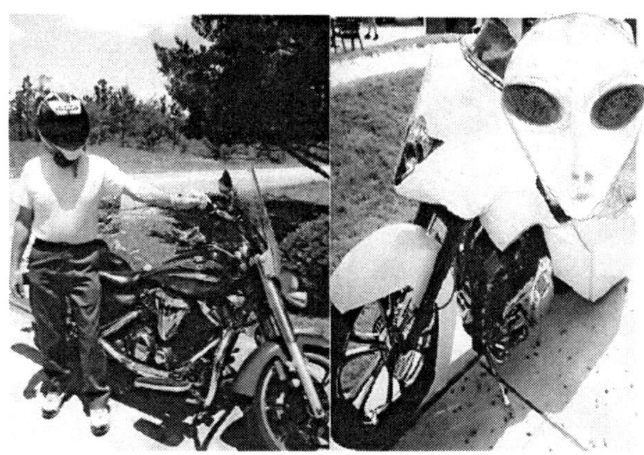

Chapter One

"Jack, Lucy, where are you? Your Grandpa Bing called us. He's on his way to get you. My partner and I are here to make sure you are ok. I'm Officer Henry and my partner is Officer Schaffer." They are surprised that there are no outside lights turned on. Everyone in the upscale area has security and motion sensor lights. Maybe the security alarms and the lights have been turned off purposely is their next thought.

"We're in our fort with our dogs and cat. We'll be right there".

With a flashlight shining on the wooden fort at the back of the large well landscaped lot, it is only seconds before the officers see the pajama clad, bare foot boy and a tiny pajama clad girl walking down the ramp of the wooden fort. With a golden retriever on their right and a border collie to their left, and a huge golden striped tabby cat in Jack's arms, they meet the officers on the lush lawn of the beautiful back yard.

"You have three wonderful friends here." said Officer Henry, as he studies the blood and dirt streaked face of the handsome little brown eyed blonde haired boy and his blonde haired brown eyed sister.

"Do you know if the alarm system and the motion sensor lights have been turned off? If so who would do so?" Officer Henry asks the little boy.

"I don't know although Mommy sometimes shuts them off. I once asked her why and she said I didn't need to know. I know from Daddy that they should remain turned on for our safety. If you ask him maybe he can tell you or maybe my Grandpa Bing. If Mommy was her she might have told you, but maybe not. She loves to be secretive?" The officers look questioning at each other. Apparently Chloe Maxwell MacDougall cares nothing for her safety or that of her children.

When the officers see Jack shiver Officer Shaffer said, "I'll take you to the police car. You will be warm there. Your pets of course can come to." Officer Shaffer is a pretty dark haired, slim woman of thirty. Officer Henry is a few years older but tall like Derek and soft spoken. Because the officers are friendly, but not overly so Jack thinks of his Daddy. Derek is also friendly, but not overly so when he and his children are out in the public eye. Derek is also soft spoken except when confronted by his wife's foolish and untrue accusations about his relationship about Flannery, his wife's half-sister.

Once Jack, Lucy and their pets are safely sitting in the back of the police car, and they feel at ease with the officers Jack said, "I'm hungry and so are Lucy and our pets, and do you know if someone will find Lucy's kitten Odie for her?"

"Someone will find Odie for you. She's probably hidden somewhere close by." said the pretty dark haired officer Shaffer while opening the glove compartment door of the car and pulling a huge Snickers bar out. "Do you like chocolate? "Officer Shaffer asked.

"Yes we do. Our Daddy always shares a huge Snickers bar with us when he's home. I love my Daddy. He always tells me I'm the sweetest boy he knows."

"I love him too. He's not mean like Mommy and he never hits us like Mommy does," adds Lucy who always takes a cue from Jack to talk with people they don't know. She knows that the officers are safe or Jack would not talk to them.

"We will share this." said Officer Shaffer, as she unwraps the candy and breaking it into three pieces hand's first a piece to Lucy and then one to Jack.

"I'm going to check the house to see if anyone is there. I'll see if I can find something for Jack, Lucy and their friends to eat." Officer Henry said once Jack, Lucy and their pets are safe in the patrol car."

"Do you know my Daddy? Jack asks while eating his part of the Snickers.

"Actually I do know Derek. He was a year ahead of me in high school I also know your Aunt Flannery. They were always together."

Officer Schaffer always thought Derek and Flannery would marry. When they became engaged in college she was happy for them. Everyone who knew them could see that they were in love. Everyone was shocked to hear that they broke off the engagement only months before the wedding, when Derek and Chloe Flannery's half-sister, got married only months later they were the fodder for the gossip monger's tongue. After Jack was born and everyone saw how much he looked like Sean, Derek's half-brother, everyone knew that Derek had been trapped in Chloe's web of deception.

. Jack nodding his head at the officers statement, chews a bite of candy before he said, "My Aunt Flannery is sweet. She's never mean. I love her whole bunch, and she loves me."

With a smile that lights his eyes, and animates the little face, now streaked with blood, dirt and chocolate, Officer Shaffer cannot help but smile back. Lost in their own thoughts, while they eat their last bit of chocolate, Officer Schaffer sees Jack finally relax. The candy may have calmed Jack, but she is certain that thinking of Derek and Flannery's love for him is the reason

"I love Aunt Flannery too." Lucy tells Officer Shaffer with her mouth full of candy.

"You're very nice and I can tell that you like children." said Jack as he wipes his mouth with the back of his hand.

Remembering that she has sanitary wipes in her pocket, Officer Shafer reaches into her uniform pocket and opening one of the packets and hands it to Jack. Jack cleans his hands and face before he said, "You have children. I can tell."

When Lucy wipes her mouth on her pajama sleeve, the officer opens another wipe, cleans Lucy's tiny hands and face, and then wipes some of the chocolate from the pajama sleeve.

When Jack hands the now soiled wipe to her she places it in a plastic bag hung on the inside door of the police car. She smiles at Jack and confirms his statement, "I have a boy your age. His name is Braden and also a daughter who will be three on Saturday. Her name is Mallory.'

"I'm three." Lucy tells the officers as she also holds three fingers up for the officer to see.

"You're a very smart girl for being only three." Officer Schaffer tells the bright eyed girl.

"When was Braden five? I was five in April." said Jack wondering how the officer knew his age. "Lucy, my sister was three in March. She was born on St. Patrick's Day. We aren't Irish but we still celebrate because it's Lucy's birthday and because Daddy takes us to the parade in Chicago. The river is green. Have you seen it?" He is correct that Lucy isn't of Irish heritage but he is unaware that Sean's mother Stella has a great deal of Irish blood flowing through her veins.

Before Officer Shaffer can answer, Jack adds, "Our Grandpa Bing is from Scotland."

"Yes, I know your Grandpa Bing is from Scotland."

"Braden was five in March. If you are wondering how I know your age, your Grandpa Bing told the dispatcher when he called the police station."

Jack thinks about her statement for a short time then replies, "My Daddy always spends lots of time with me and Lucy when he's home. He's going to take a year off work so we can hang out and do all the things we haven't had time for." A huge smile paints the little boys face and he tells Officer Shaffer, "We, Daddy, me and Lucy are going to go to Scotland."

The three talk of things to do in summer, when Officer Henry returns with a small gray striped kitten. When Officer Henry opens the back door to the police car and puts Odie in Jack's arms the smile on Jacks face is so huge it gives the offices a wonderful feeling that their work is for once truly appreciated. "Odie is Lucy's kitten. Daddy gave her to Lucy for her third birthday." Jack said before handing the kitten to his sister.

Lucy rubs her cheek against the soft kitten fur and tells Officer Henry, "Thank you sir officer. Odie is only a baby and Mommy scared her when she threw her out the back door."

When the Golden Retriever Yates and the Border collie Tralee greet the kitten with a sniff and the big golden male butt's heads with Odie, the four humans smile.

From his pants pocket Officer Henry pulls out a pack of cheese crackers and hands them to Jack, who opens them immediately and hands half to Lucy. From his shirt pocket he pulls out two broken dog treats, and from his back pants pocket he hands Jack a small pack of cat treats.

"Thank you." Jack said as he gives the hungry pets their treats.

When Officer Shaffer gives him a questioning look, Officer Henry shrugs his shoulders, and said, "That's all I could find. The refrigerator and pantry were bare."

"Mommy doesn't like to food shop. Daddy shops with us when he is home." Jack tells them innocently. "He's been out of town for two weeks because he is training someone to take his place while he is off. Because we have been at Grandpa Bings and Grandma Stella's or with Flannery's Granny Anne while he is gone no one has bought food for our house. We were going to take our pets with us but Daddy said it would be too much for those watching us so he's hired a lady to come in twice a day to feed them plus walk the dogs. Mommy isn't here much so Daddy figured that they would be safe."

The Officers look at each other with disbelief, knowing that Jack's family has plenty of money, but they have heard rumors about Jack and Lucy's mother Chloe, and know the rumors are true. Chloe Lorena Maxwell MacDougall has always been self-involved and selfish. Growing up she was spoiled and apparently she hasn't changed.

"Does your Mommy lock you outside very often?" asked Officer Schaffer while the four wait in the police car for Jack and Lucy's grandparents.

"Yes, whenever Uncle Sean comes over or when she is mad at us. I was going to tell my daddy, but was afraid to because she said she will take our pets to the pound if I do. My Daddy will make sure she doesn't do that."

“We, Lucy and I missed our pets so Grandpa and Granny Anne said that when we come there, once Daddy is home, our pets are welcome to come with us.”

Jack is so engrossed with feeding his pets that he misses the disbelief in the two adult’s eyes.

Chapter Two

It is eleven p.m. before Jack, Lucy and their grandparents arrive at the grandparent's home several miles from where Jack, Lucy and their parents live.

When the police advised Grandpa Bing and Grandma Stella that Jack and Lucy should be checked out at the hospital, their grandparent's took the advice and stopped by the emergency room.

Photos were taken of their bruises. Once they were examined thoroughly and a few tests done the two were cleared to go home with their grandparents.

Bathed and in clean pajamas, Jack and Lucy sit on their grandparent's bed eating grilled cheese sandwiches, when his Grandpa Bing walks into the room, and with a smile hands Jack his cell phone. "It's your Daddy." he said sitting near Jack and Grandma Stella.

"Thanks." said Jack as he put the last of his sandwich on the tray sitting on his outstretched legs.

"Hi Daddy, guess what?" He smiles a happy smile at hearing Derek's voice and replies "Yes Odie is ok. Officer Henry found her hiding under the bushes near the back steps."

Jack listens intently to whatever Derek is saying and said "Daddy me and Lucy are going to sleep with Grand Bing and Grandma Stella. Even our dogs and cats get to sleep in the room."

"I love you too Daddy," he said then hands the phone to his sister.

With her ear to the phone, and her sandwich half eaten in her hand, Lucy listens to whatever Derek is saying, smiles a sweet smile and said, "I love you too Daddy. We miss you." She hands the phone to Bing and finishing her sandwich, hands her plate to Stella who sits nearby, then crawls beneath the comforter and closes her eyes.

Chapter Three

With the company jet for his use, Derek is back in the Chicago area as the late spring sun washes across the city and the surrounding suburbs. With little sleep and too much worry and caffeine, he is looking forward to the coming weekend. He has two very important things to do before then. Once they are done he can begin his planned year of rest and relaxation. Most of all he will be able to give Jack and Lucy some much needed attention.

When the cab he took from the airport pulls up in front of his parent's home, he begins to relax a bit. Having said only good morning to the cabbie when he first got into the cab, the cabbie lets Derek sit in peaceful silence for the ride to his parent's home near Geneva, a suburb west of Chicago.

When the cabbie stops but leaves the cab running, he gets out and opens the back door for Derek. While the considerate driver removes Derek's suitcase, briefcase and computer case from the trunk, Derek pulls his wallet from his pants pocket and generously tips the man with a hundred dollar bill

"Do you have something smaller? You're my first run of the day and I know I don't have enough change."

The driver hands the bill back, but Derek said, "That's your tip. Here's the fare"

When the driver sees two twenties, he said, "You are very generous. Thanks a lot."

"I needed time to rest my weary brain, and you were kind enough to let me enjoy the quiet. Peace and quiet are hard to find in our busy world. For that I would pay a great deal."

The cabbie nods his head in agreement and holds his hand out for Derek to shake.

Derek watches as the cab drives through the gate to his parent's estate. He looks at the time on his cell phone screen. Because it's only six a.m. he knows everyone will probably be sleeping. He'd talked with Jack and Lucy late the night before, so figures everyone is still in bed.. As he walks up the cobblestone sidewalk to the red brick two story house, Derek smiles at the wonderful memories that he has from growing up with such caring and loving parent's. Although Stella is his step-mother she has always treated Derek as she has treated her son, his half-brother Sean.

His mother Hanna passed away from ovarian cancer when he was only four. He will never forget his mother, will always love her, but has always been thankful that his father John Binghamton MacDougal, "Bing" married his secretary Stella when Derek was five. Stella and his mom Hanna were best friends, and Hanna made Bing promise that he would marry Stella after her death. With an outgoing and sweet personality, Stella was an easy choice for Bing.

Derek walks up the six wide steps to a wide covered porch that is always inviting. With a southern exposure the house is bathed in sunny morning light. As he looks across the porch, he is surprised to find his father sitting on a glider reading the *Chicago Tribune*.

"Good morning Son. I thought I'd meet you out here. Stella is cooking some breakfast and I promised her I would bring you into the kitchen as soon as you arrived."

Bing who is tall, around six foot two inches in height and trim, looks younger than his fifty-nine years, despite his head of thick snow white hair. His dark brown eyes exactly like Derek's smile into Derek's eyes as Bing gets up from the glider and enfolds his just as tall son in a warm bear hug. Derek and Bing have the dark looks of their Romany heritage, the looks and dark hair, eyes and beautiful creamy tan complexion of Derek fraternal grandmother Charlotte.

"It's always good to see you Son. Once we've eaten and you get cleaned up we can talk. Until then we will just enjoy our time together, Jack and Lucy are still asleep. They didn't move once they fell asleep. I don't have to tell you they are extremely resilient."

"I'll carry this."Bing said as he takes Derek's suitcase from his right hand.

"Thanks Dad. Thanks for taking the suitcase and most of all thanks for bringing Jack and Lucy to stay here with you and Mom."

"There's no need to thank me. We are family above all else. We take care of those that we love and Stella and I love you and Jack and Lucy."

"Jack, Lucy and I also love you and Mom."

With this said, father and son walk through a royal blue wooden front door and into a sunny wooden floored entryway, that is large enough for an upholstered love seat, for sitting on to read the mail or to remove ones shoes if so desired. With a lamp table and lamp sitting next to the love seat, and plenty of room to sit comfortably, the sunny entryway is always a welcomed anchor to the house itself. With the mornings warm rays reaching across the floor and up the stairs to the right side of the entryway, the home of Derek's childhood is a warm and friendly place to be.

When they reach the huge country kitchen, decorated in peach, yellow, green and white, at the back of the house, they are greeted by Stella, Derek's stepmother. Still tall and slim as the day she married Bing, but with hair that is now colored a pale blonde every month, Stella turns from the stove where she is making omelets to give Derek a welcoming warm hug and kiss on the cheek. With an arm around Derek's waist she studies him for a short time then said,"I believe a year off is just what you need. Like Bing you always work much too hard."

Derek kisses her cheek and gives her a hug, before she said, "You and Bing sit, breakfast is nearly ready."

Once he's eaten his fill, Derek excuses himself and goes to take a shower and to shave. When he passes his parent's room he sees through the partially opened door his children sleeping in the center of his parent's king-sized bed. He will let them sleep while he cleans up, then he will go and let the two know that he has kept his promise to be there when they awakened. He thinks about stepping outside for a moment to smoke a cigarette, but decides smoking is definitely a habit that he needs to quit. He'd taken up the dirty, smelly habit after he married Chloe. It was his way to handle the stress of his marriage. Though he's never cared for the taste or the smell it was a way to calm his nerves, and now he is addicted. He knows he must quit for his health and his children. He wants to be a part of their life for as long as possible. Scottish Whisky is another habit he now has. At night while his children slept, he sat in the back yard and drowned his sorrows with cigarettes and whisky. Now that he is with his parents, he hopes he can get a handle on his addictions.

Stella Leigh Morgan MacDougall, his stepmother, is easy to love. Totally comfortable with her love for Bing and their sons Stella was a blessing from God and she had the foresight to give Bing and Derek time to mourn before she bravely proposed to Bing six months after he, Derek, Anne and Flannery returned from Scotland. Bing and Derek knew her because she worked for Bing, but also because she was Hanna's best friend for years. She and Hanna grew up together on Chicago's south side, near the University of Chicago. Not only were they next door neighbors, they attended the same schools, including community college and went to the same neighborhood church every Sunday.

Anne also knew Stella and liked what she saw, so she encouraged the relationship knowing that the union was also Hanna's wish. Anne knew because Hanna had told her so. When Stella told Anne that she was going to ask Bing to marry her, Anne said a prayer and the rest is history. Derek missed his Mom but was truly happy when Bing accepted the proposal and the two married six weeks later.

Stella's parents are still alive and they accepted Bing and Derek, plus Anne and Flannery as part of the Morgan family. The two now live in a retirement community not far from Bing and Stella and Derek, Sean, and Derek's parents visit them weekly. Because Stella's older brother lives in New Zealand Stella has taken complete control of their care. Bing of course is always there to help her.

They consider Derek a grandson as they do Sean.

Chapter Four

Derek, clean and shaved sits on his parents bed and brushes the dark blonde hair from his sleeping sons forehead. He will make sure that he and Jack get their hair cut on Saturday. Chloe's neglect of Jack and Lucy's needs are enormous. Without an ounce of maternal instinct his soon to be ex-wife was never interested in Jack or Lucy. Giving birth to them was the only unselfish thing she had ever done in her twenty-six years on earth. She wanted Lucy because when she was pregnant she got tons of attention, and that is what makes Chloe happy. When the babies were born and took the attention away from her she didn't handle it well.

Opening his brown eyes slowly, Jack's little boy face lights with a wide smile when he sees his father sitting next to him. "Daddy, Daddy! You're here," he said as he sits up on the bed.

Derek wraps his strong tanned arms around his son and pulls him from beneath the light-weight comforter on the bed. Looking closely at Jacks face, he sees that Jack's lower lip is still a little swollen and the right side of his nose a little bruised. So that Jack won't see his anger, at Chloe, he tells him about their plans for the day.

Lucy awakens only when Derek kisses her sweet little girl cheek. "Daddy, you're home." she says with such pleasure that Derek's heart fills with joy.

"I'll help you dress and will sit with you while you have breakfast. You'll be helping Grandma Stella today. She needs to shop for the pet's food, so you will go with her to Pets Mart."

"Grandpa Bing is going with me to our house. We are meeting the movers there and they will pack all of my things and yours. We won't be living with your Mommy anymore."

Jack thinks about his father's statement for a while then said, "Where will we live?"

"For now we'll be here and at Granny Anne's. Of course we are going to Scotland in the autumn. Remember Aunt Flannery invited us to visit when her Granny Anne goes there."

Jack nods his head and said, "That's good. I don't want to live with Mommy. She always yells at me and calls me bad boy."

Taking a cue from her brother Lucy tells them, "I don't want to live with Mommy either."

To keep his ire at Chloe from his spirit Derek kisses his son and daughter on the cheek and tells them, "You are wonderful children. Don't believe anyone who says you're not."

"Mommy is the only one who tells us that. Even Uncle Sean is nice to us. When he hears Mommy calling us names, he tells her to quit. He's always at our house when you're not there. I would have told you, but Mommy said if I did she would take our dogs and cats to the pound. I can tell you now because I know that me, Lucy and Yates, Tralee, Garfield and Odie are safe."

"Let's get you dressed." said Derek as he holds Jack's hand while Jack slips off the huge bed, to stand on the shiny oak floor. With his other hand he helps his tiny daughter from the high bed.

The three talk a little about what they will do once Derek and Bing have everything put into storage. All but their personal belongs will be stored until Derek decided where he and Jack and Lucy will live. For the next year he plans to travel with them. A good deal of that travel will be in his father's native Scotland.

Once Jack is dressed in his favorite cargo shorts with several side pockets, for carrying the things that little boys seem to collect in a day and a Chicago Cubs blue and red t-shirt and Lucy in a floral sundress of blues and reds, Derek and his children go into his parent's large master bath so that they can wash their face and hands, brush their teeth and hair.

Jack looks very thoughtful, as though he wants to say something. Once he brushes his teeth and rinses his mouth Derek decides to see what is on his sons mind.

"Jack, what do you want to ask me? You know you can ask me anything."

Jack nods his head at his father's words before asking, "Daddy, Mommy said that you are not my real Daddy. She said that Uncle Sean is my biological, real Daddy. Is Uncle Sean my real Daddy? She also said that Lucy is also Uncle Sean's."

Derek lifts his sons chin with a thumb, and tells him. "You are my son. I have loved you from the moment you entered my life. Has Uncle Sean said that he is your Daddy?"

With relief written across Jack's face he said, "No Uncle Sean never said that he is. Mommy just told me yesterday after her fight with Uncle Sean. Mommy said if I looked closely at you and then closely at Uncle Sean I would see that I look nothing like you and exactly like Uncle Sean." Jack turns to look at himself and then to look at Derek. "I have your brown eyes, don't I?"

"Yes you have my brown eyes. Let's talk about this later today. It's almost time for me and Grandpa Bing to go and meet the movers, and I want to sit with you while you have breakfast"

"Ok Daddy. We can talk about this later."

"Just one more question, "Is Uncle Sean also Lucy's father?

"I am Lucy's father." is all he said before the three leave the room to go and eat breakfast.

He believes that he is Lucy's biological father. When Jack was fourteen months old, Derek, Chloe and Jack went to Hawaii to stay with Chloe's parent's Rena and Gus for a few weeks. While there Chloe talked Derek into buying a condo in her parents building. Once she got the condo, Chloe decided that she and Derek should try for a daughter. Derek loves children and went along with the request. Lucy was born on time, so no one thought much of it. There is no doubt in his mind that she is his daughter. She has Chloe's naturally blonde hair, but his brown eyes. She also has a dimple like his in her left cheek. When she walks alone she walks with her hands clasp behind her, just like he does. She also has the habit of cocking her head when someone is talking with her, just like him. He and Chloe had sex rarely in the first years of their marriage. After Lucy was born the intimacy ended also. Derek knows that it was because she was no longer interested in him or their marriage. He also admits that he had never loved Chloe.

The main reason he agreed to having another child was because he had given up hope of ever being with Flannery, Chloe's half-sister, again. The spring before he took Chloe and Jack to Hawaii, he found out from Granny Anne that Flannery was engaged to be married to a Scottish lawyer. Stephen Ross was his name and they planned a Christmas wedding. Derek didn't find out until after Lucy's birth that Flannery called the wedding off. When he asked Granny Anne why, she said that Flannery thought it would be unfair to marry Stephen when she still loved Derek.

Once he heard that, he knew that he would not stay married to Chloe. Why he drug his feet for nearly three more years is beyond him.

Once Jack and Lucy were born and Chloe wouldn't take care of them he hired a number of nanny's. Chloe didn't want the nanny's there so he would take the two to Granny Anne on Monday and Tuesday and to his Mother Stella on Wednesday and Thursday. Because he worked a four day week he took care of the two Friday, Saturday and Sunday. The days they were with Anne and Stella, the two gracious loving ladies also cooked dinner for Derek and his children.

When Chloe found out that Granny Anne was helping take care of them she raged for days. Derek told her that Granny Anne had more love in her little finger, than Chloe had in her small hateful heart.

Because Chloe refused to lift a hand to help in anyway, Derek did hire a housekeeper. She, Nancy would come on Fridays in the afternoon with two helpers and they would have the house gleaming before they left several hours later. Derek was always there, so Chloe was out who knew where. After Lucy's birth he and the children rarely saw her. At night and on the weekends she was off somewhere with her friends. By **then Derek was relieved when she was gone.** Because she wouldn't food shop, he took the children with him on Friday mornings to MacDonald's for breakfast, where Jack and Lucy would play in the play area once they ate. He would let them play for an hour while he kept an eye on them and talked with the other parents.

Then they would go with him to the supermarket where he did the weekly shopping. Always well behaved, he would let them each choose a special treat for dessert. He is so thankful that they don't have Chloe's hateful nature. They are sweet and kind and extremely affectionate. He doesn't take all the credit for their good behavior. Bing, Stella and Granny Anne make certain that they know they are loved.

They were not supposed to be with Chloe while he was at work, or out of town. Chloe knew that he didn't trust her. His parents apparently had an emergency that day and couldn't get Derek so they left a message on his home phone. When out of town he would sometimes call home to get the messages. Because he was swamped with training the men taking over his job, he didn't check. Chloe checked the messages because she knew Sean was going to call. When she heard the message from Bing she called their preschool, where they had started going after Christmas for a few hours to socialize with other children, and pretended to be Stella and told the secretary at the school that she, Stella would pick them up at their own house, she was watching them there, so the bus driver could let them off there.

Granny Anne wasn't home when Bing called her house. He knew she would gladly pick them up from school. He called her cell phone, but apparently she didn't have it with her. He also left a message there. Even though he didn't speak directly with Anne, he assumed that she had gone to the school and picked Jack and Lucy up.

When Bing and Stella arrived home later that day they found out that the two were at home. Bing called several times, but the answering machine always picked up. When Chloe was spanking Jack and the phone rang, it was Bing. He told Derek this while they ate breakfast. Bing and Stella feel responsible for Chloe abusing Jack and Lucy, but Derek tells them they were not responsible for Chloe's actions.

Chapter Five

A moving van is parked on the curb in front of Derek's three story brick mansion. Derek never felt at home there, and is more than ready to move on with the next stage of his Jack, and Lucy's life. It was the house of Chloe's choice. Always wanting to out-do everyone that she knows, Derek bought the house in the hope that his selfish wife would settle down and become the mother that Jack and Lucy deserve. After nearly six years of marriage, Chloe has grown even more selfish and self-centered. Because she would not lift a hand to do any work, Derek has had a house keeper from day one. Because he has been on the road working for his father's telecommunications company for most of their marriage, he also had a nanny taking care of Jack while he was away. For the last year the nanny was only there when Chloe was out on the town spending their money on expensive clothes, jewelry and spa visits. Today she will be served with divorce papers. Derek doesn't worry that she won't sign them because it is in her best interest to do just that. Otherwise she will get nothing and there is still the possibility that she may be arrested for physically harming Jack and Lucy.

"Son everything is going to work in your favor. Chloe would be a fool not to sign the divorce papers." said Bing when Derek parks his Honda Odyssey van several feet in front of the moving van.

"Yes, I agree. Where Chloe is concerned who knows how she will take all of this. Although we have the proof that she physically harmed Jack and Lucy, so if she's as cunning as we know she is she will probably go to Hawaii to get away from all the accusations?"

"She told Jack that Sean is his father and Lucy's. I told Jack that I am their father. Even if Sean is Jack's biological father, something that I have suspected all along, I won't have DNA testing. No matter what the circumstances of their birth, Jack and Lucy are, and will always be my children.

"Jack finally told me that Uncle Sean is always at the house when I'm out of town. Chloe threaten him with sending his pets to the pound if he told me."

Bing shakes his head in disbelief, then said, "Jack knows he and his pets are safe, and he also trust you completely."

"It's just too bad that he and Lucy were mentally and now physically harmed by Chloe. The nanny's told me that Jack and Lucy weren't safe with Chloe, what a fool I was to try and make our sham of a marriage work."

"Son, no man or woman wants to think that they have married an evil person. You and I know that Chloe will not change. What Sean has seen in her all of these years is beyond me. I know your brother is not an innocent victim in all of this, but I also know he is extremely gullible and naïve where women are concerned."

"Yes, Chloe had us all fooled. As of today, actually as of now," Derek said as he looks at the time on his cell phone, "Chloe is finding out that she can no longer fool me."

Chapter Six

While showing the movers what he wants moved from the house, Derek's cell phone rings. Seeing that it is Chloe, he ignores the ringing. He decides he will shut the phone off, but just as he goes to do so, the phone rings again. Deciding he will have one last conversation with his soon to be ex-wife, Derek walks outside to the park-like backyard before he answers her call.

Before he can answer, Chloe immediately said with a voice full of hate, "You may think you will be free of me. Think again Derek. I want the house here and the condo in Hawaii, I also intend to ask for spousal support. If I don't get what I want I will make sure everyone knows that you and my sister have been having an affair ever since we got married."

With a calmness that surprises even him Derek tells Chloe, "I suggest that you sign the divorce papers. I am also warning you that if you ever call me, Jack, Lucy, Flannery or any of our friends and family and tell lies you will automatically forfeit what I have offered. You are getting much more than you deserve, because you deserve nothing."

"I'll see about that. You can't take Jack and Lucy. Sean is their father not you." Derek hears the ire in her voice, and is glad that he will never have to look at her again or listen to her lies again.

"I have always known Jack is Sean's biological son. As for Lucy she is mine. If you cared for Sean so much why make me believe that I got you pregnant the night you drugged my tea and I woke up the next morning with you lying nude in my bed" Derek stops for a moment to let his words sink into Chloe's thoughtless brain.

When she says nothing, Derek tells her, "I know, have known for at least the last year that Sean spends the night whenever I am out of town, so don't think for a minute that Jack and Lucy will not live with me, and that you will never see them again. You are lucky that your ass is not in jail."

"The police have photos of Jack's bruises, scratches and swollen lip and nose. They also have photos of Lucy's scratched and bruises. I have a feeling that Sean would testify that you verbally and physically abused them for several years. Why Sean had anything to do with you is beyond me. Why I married you is no secret, Jack is that reason. Why you conned me is no secret. You hate your sister because Flannery is everything that is good and kind. You on the other hand are selfish, self-centered and evil. You are not fit to wash Flannery's feet. Your sister and I have rarely seen each other since I stupidly married you. On the rare occasion that we did see each other, in Scotland or in the U.S. there was always another adult with us, usually her Grandmother Anne."

"Flannery and her grandmother would lie for you. Just because Flannery is a well-known author doesn't mean she won't lie to protect you, Jack and the disgusting MacDougall family. When I am done she won't have any fans left to buy her horrible fantasy books."

"Listen up Chloe! Remember if you bother me, Flannery, Jack, Lucy or our families and friends, you immediately forfeit what I have offered you. Most people could live a lifetime on what you are offered. If you can't manage your money, then get yourself a job. Work would be the best thing for you. I have always wondered where your evil comes from. Your parents are not unkind, and yet you have always been evil. I unfortunately did not know until after I was tricked into marrying you. Thank the Lord that after today I will no longer have anything to do with you."

"You've not seen nor heard the last of me. Jack and Lucy must be worth a great deal to you. You can pay me hush money so that your family and friends never have to know that Jack is Sean's."

"Good bye Chloe. Remember, you will get nothing but what is already offered. It would be in your best interest to move to your condo in Hawaii." Before Chloe can say anymore Derek hangs up. When the phone rings again, and he sees her name, he immediately calls his lawyer and has a restraining order placed against Chloe.

Then he shuts his phone off, and calmly tosses it into the backyard swimming pool. As he watches it sink further and further into the deep end of the pool, he smiles. He never wanted a pool, but finally had one put in the summer before. With a fence around the pool, he made certain everyone locked the gate whenever Jack and Lucy were at home. He also made sure that they can swim. Like fish in water they swim, but Jack and Lucy promised they would not go near the pool when Derek was not at home. He finds it hard to believe that a sweet boy like Jack and a sweet girl like Lucy came from an evil woman like Chloe.

It is four o'clock in the afternoon before the movers have everything packed and are ready to haul Derek and his children's things to a storage unit not far from his parent's house. The three burly movers worked nonstop, only to take a half hour lunch break at one. Even then they kept track of the time while they were taking to eat.

Derek and Bing could tell that the men were pleased by the sandwiches, drinks and chips from a Subway store a mile away. While Bing went for the food, Derek kept working right along with the movers. He made a fast trip around Chloe's room, the master suite. It was always her room and her room only. Chloe and Derek had been intimate towards each other only a hand full of times throughout their nearly six year sham of a marriage. He was never unkind to her. With a tongue full of hate Chloe made certain that he knew how she despised his touch, his kisses. They married only four months after he found her in his bed, nude and swearing that they had sex. When Jack was born only four months later, Derek knew that Chloe had lied, but once he saw Jack, he knew he would not let Chloe raise him on her own. Not only had she ruined his life, she also ruined her half-sister Flannery's.

Bing and Flannery's father James Larkin had first meet at university in Edinburgh. They were studying for a degree in business and finance. Because they hit it off from their first meeting, and planned to immigrate to the States after graduation, they formed a partnership that lasted until James was killed in a plane crash when Derek and Flannery were only four.

Flannery's parents divorced only months before James' death. James had found out that Rena totally neglected Flannery and he took his daughter to his mother's house and that is where they lived. After James' death Anne had full custody of Flannery. By then Rena was no longer a part of their lives, and Rena could have cared less.

Rena didn't like Anne because she was competition for James' attention and refused to let her live with them. James bought Anne a house on the Fox River in Geneva, where she lives most of the year. In the summer she and Flannery would go to Skye to her grandmother's small farm, or to Edinburgh and a townhome that she owned. Though he has rarely seen her since his marriage to Chloe Derek has never stopped loving her. He knows the marriage broke her heart, but it also broke his.

Chapter Seven

Derek doesn't think of Chloe until he and Bing are driving back to Bing and Stella's house. Most of his, Jack, and Lucy's clothing and personal belongings are packed and in the back of the van, though a few things they may want later went to storage with the movers. He'd taken little in the way of furniture. Most of the furnishings were Chloe's taste but not his. She's been offered whatever she wants from the house plus half the profits when the house sells. His share of the sale may be going to charity. All he desires from their union is their children. Chloe always made it clear that they were a nuisance, competition for her. Chloe always despised competition of any kind.

"Chloe's been served the divorce papers and is none too happy about what she gets. I called our lawyer and he is writing up a restraining order against her. I've told her she'll get nothing if she bothers me, Jack, Flannery or any of our friends and family."

"Good, it's time she is put in her place. Did she threaten you?"

"Yes me and Flannery. She said she is going to ruin Flannery's reputation with her fans."

Bing shakes his head and with disgust said, "It's difficult to understand women like Chloe. Her Mom and Dad have shown her only love and kindness. Although Rena was neglectful of Chloe when she was small, that was until Gus put his foot down and told her she either shaped up or they were through. She's a physically beautiful woman, and charmed James into marrying her. I have always thought that she was relieved when James took Flannery to live with his mother, Granny Anne. When he died she didn't show up at the funeral. I guess by then she had already met Gus.

"Flannery has always thought that her mother was relieved to see her with Granny Anne.. There was a time when Flannery and I could and did talk about everything." When he sees a distant light in Derek's eyes, Bing knows that Derek has never stopped loving Flannery O'Connor Larkin.

Because he and James Larkin, Flannery's father were best friends and business partners the MacDougall's and the Larkin's spent a good deal of time together.

Bing and everyone who knew the two families always thought that Flannery and Derek would marry after college graduation. They waited until the year they turned twenty five and planned a wedding in Scotland. That was the summer that Derek found a nude Chloe in his bed. Bing believed Derek when he said he didn't remember having sex with Chloe. She and Sean went to visit Derek that night. Derek was exhausted from several weeks on the road, and told them to lockup when they left his condo. He'd gone to take a shower, and then went to get a glass of iced tea from a pitcher in his refrigerator. Sean and Chloe had ordered a pizza while Derek showered. The pizza was delivered when he came out of his room. He took only one piece, that Chloe offered, and a glass of tea that she had poured."

Sean told him that he left shortly after Derek went to bed, and that Chloe was there cleaning up the kitchen. Chloe taking time to clean anything should have clued him in to her deception. When Sean was asked if he saw anything strange that night, he couldn't recall anything unusual.

Sean, of course has always been blinded to Chloe's faults. From the young age of fifteen, Sean could not pass up Chloe's advances for sex. What fifteen year old naïve teenager could?

When Chloe's parent's found the two having sex on their family room sofa they of course blamed Sean.

Her parents did their best to keep Chloe and Sean away from each other, but Chloe had other plans. Where ever Sean went Chloe would always find him, and they continued to sneak around and find many places to have sex. When Sean found out that Chloe was pregnant, he was surprised. She'd always used birth control. When he asked her about it, she said she must have forgotten the night she was with Derek. Knowing Derek, and that he and Flannery were waiting until marriage to be carnal, he had his doubts when Chloe told him she was pregnant with Derek's child. Once Derek married Chloe Sean thought his relationship with her was over. To his surprise, Chloe would call him whenever Derek was out of town and invite him over. At first they would only talk and then Chloe told him that she and Derek had a marriage in name only, so he let her charm him into her bed. He always felt guilty after, but she seemed to have a super natural hold on him. Because of his unfaithfulness to his brother, Sean and Derek rarely saw each other.

Because his conscience started to bother him, and because the housekeeper, the nannies and others who worked at Derek's saw him on numerous occasions leaving his brother's house early each morning that Derek was out of town, Sean stopped going to see her. The night she kicked Jack and Lucy out of the house was the last time he saw her. He didn't like the way she verbally abused them, and in all honesty he had finally gotten tired of her selfishness. That night he told her they were through. He also told her that Derek knew about her affair with him.

It was because his conscience began to haunt him that he went to Derek and told him everything. He and Derek haven't spoken since that horrible night in March, less than two months before but it is because of all that Sean bravely told him, that Derek filed for a divorce that was a long time coming.

Derek and Sean had always been close, despite their nearly six year age difference, and that they have different mothers. Derek would like to forgive Sean, but so far he cannot forgive the deception.

Chapter Eight

When Bing married Stella they decided to have a child, because they love children, but also because they wanted Derek to have a sibling. Derek loved having a little brother, and never minded when Sean followed him everywhere. Though Bing understands why Derek no longer talks to Sean he prays that time will heal the wound of deception. Bing and Stella miss having their two sons with them for birthdays, holidays and weekends when they once got together to watch sports on television, or go to one of the many games that the people of Chicago are blessed with.

Bing, Stella, Jack and Lucy sit on the back porch waiting for Derek to take his shower and for the pizza that they have ordered for their dinner. He and Stella love having grandchildren and pray that Derek will one day marry again. Though their hearts would love for Derek to marry Flannery, they leave that entirely up to the Lord. They also leave Sean with the Lord. Because he admitted to his affair with Chloe, they believe he is finally growing up. Derek and Sean were brought up with discipline, though not harshly. Whenever Bing thinks of his sons he is always reminded of the scripture *Ephesians* 6:1-4.

Derek, Sean, Flannery and Chloe always attended church services with their parents. At the age of fifteen Chloe stopped going entirely. Her father Gus tried everything to get her to go, but Rena would not back him, so Chloe was left to her own devises on Sundays, with disastrous results.

When Flannery's father James was alive, he was the one to take Flannery to church. Rena would go on occasion, but preferred staying in bed until noon and then going out with her friends for brunch. James didn't say much about her absence, but Bing knew that James was hurt by Rena's refusal to attend church like most families that they knew. After his death and Flannery living with Anne, Anne was the one who took Flannery to church.

That was the year that Derek's mother Hanna died from cancer, and Bing not only was left as a single parent mourning his wife, he also mourned the loss of his best friend. His heart was heavy by the mourning, but he made Anne a promise that if she or Flannery needed him, he would be there for them. Anne made the same promise to him. After the fiasco with marrying Chloe and then Jack's birth, Bing saw Anne and Flannery rarely. Anne would spend several months each year at her house on the Fox River, but Flannery had moved to Scotland full time. Now and then Flannery would show up for a few weeks here and there but she never came to Bing and Stella for fear Derek and Chloe would be there.

Flannery considers Scotland her second home for several reasons, she loves the lovely country and the Scots, plus her father's ashes were sprinkled there on The Isle of Skye where he and Granny Anne and James senior were born. Hanna Derek's mom asked to have her ashes sprinkled in Lake Geneva, Wisconsin where she spent her summers as a child and with Bing and Derek, Derek and Bing visit the town whenever they can and Bing still uses the cottage when the weather is nice.

After their first year of marriage, Chloe no longer came to their house. Derek would bring Jack over which was just fine with Bing. The times that she had come she let everyone know she was bored with them, Derek and Jack. What Chloe has done with her life has not surprised anyone. Never brainy like Flannery, though extremely cunning, Chloe was and is extremely jealous of her older half-sister. She has never worked a day in her life, but loves to spend lavishly and makes a point of flaunting her possessions and lifestyle before anyone who is or isn't interested. When Flannery became a well-known author of children's book's Chloe grew even more hateful towards her sister. Derek has bought every book that she has written, but keeps the books at Bing and Stella's. Jack and Lucy love the books and Chloe so far does not know that he has them.

Bing is brought out of his thoughts of the past when Derek walks onto the back porch and sits beside his father. Jack who has been tossing a ball for the Golden retriever Yates, and a Frisbee for his Border collie Tralee, drops both toys in the grass and comes to sit on Derek's jean clad thighs. Lucy is happily sitting in a chair next to Stella with Odie on her lap.

Derek wraps his arms around his son's warm body and kisses the top of his dark blond hair. Though Jack's hair is a little sweaty from play, Derek has always loved the earthy little boy scent. Jack will definitely need a shower before he goes to bed. Derek always helps Jack and Lucy wash their thick head of hair, so that all of the shampoo is rinsed out. When Jack was smaller, and a nanny took care of him his hair was always clean.

When Chloe no longer wanted a nanny at the house, because they were too nosey in her opinion, and Derek was on the road, Jack would try to wash his and Lucy's hair but could never get the excess of shampoo out. When Chloe refused to help Jack, Bing, Stella or Anne, when she was in Geneva would take Jack and Lucy home, wash their hair and give them the love that Chloe gave to no one. Though Sean loved Chloe, she not once told him that she cared.

"Daddy, what are we going to do tomorrow?" Jack said as he turns to look at Derek's face.

"Tomorrow is Friday. The new movies come out then, so you, Grandpa Bing, Lucy and I are going to an early movie. Then we are going to eat out. Dad and I are going to let you and Lucy chooses the restaurant."

Jack grins and before either Derek or Bing can ask where he wants to eat on Friday, Jack, with brown eyes twinkling said, "I want to go to Granny Anne's to eat. She always makes Shepherd's pie on Friday, and that is one of my favorites."

"Well, should I be offended. You never go crazy over my Shepherd's pie." said Grandma Stella with a twinkle in her own eyes.

"I like yours too, but you could use lots more ground beef, and fewer peas." Jack tells her, then slipping from Derek's lap, walks around the patio table and gives Stella a kiss on the cheek and a hug.

Stella kisses Jack in return and also hugs him. "Trying to charm me are you."

"Yeah!" is Jack's reply before he hugs her again. "The MacDougall men are always charmers." Jack tells the three adults that he trust completely. When they laugh at his statement he laughs with them.

"So, who have you been charming?" Derek asked his charmer of a son.

'I charm all the females. Women love it when I smile and tell them they are pretty."

'We must always be honest even if we are charming the ladies." Derek tells Jack as he settles in a chair at Derek's side.

Jack thinks of this for a short time before wisely saying, "If we look for the good in others we can usually find something nice about nearly everyone."

Before the adults can comment on the diplomatic statement Jack looks from one adult to the other then adds, "Mommy is always talking mean to me, Lucy and Daddy, so it is awfully hard to find something to complement her on." He stops here and cocks his head and looks seriously at Derek, before he adds, "Mommy is usually nice to Uncle Sean, and last night was the first time I heard her yell at him."

"Daddy, how's come you married Mommy, if she likes Uncle Sean better?"

Though Derek knew one day Jack would ask this question, he wasn't prepared to answer for a few more years. Now that Jack has asked he will tell him what he feels a five year old can handle.

"I married your Mommy because you were on the way, and I didn't want to miss greeting you when you came into the world. And you must know I have loved you since I first looked into your brown eyes"

"But, Daddy if Uncle Sean is my biological father, why didn't he marry Mommy instead of you?" Though the question is one Derek would rather not answer, he does because he has never lied to Jack, and he never will.

"I believed that you were my son, which you legally are. Now that I know you I have no regrets being your father. Whether I'm your biological father or Uncle Sean is, I love you and you will always be my son."

Jack sits quietly for a while taking Derek's words and letting their meaning fill his heart. When Derek leans towards his son and kisses Jack's cheek Jack smiles, and said, "It's ok Daddy. Even if you aren't my biological father, you are the best, sweetest Daddy in the world. Sean is a good Uncle, but he could never be the Daddy that you are to me.'

"And I know that you are the best and the sweetest son any man could ever have," Derek adds with a gruff voice.

Jack studies each adult closely before saying, "Grandpa Bing and Grandma Stella, I'll bet my Daddy, Derek, is the very best son also."

"Aye!" Bing said, and then Stella agrees with a yes of her own.

Lucy totally engrossed in petting Odie, finally asked her own question on paternity. "Daddy, I don't care if Uncle Sean is my bylogic daddy, I love you and I want to live with you."

"I will always be father to you and Jack. I love you and will take care of you."

Just then the dogs start barking, and Bing gets up from his wicker patio chair to collect the pizza that he ordered for their easy Friday night dinner. As Bing passes Derek's chair, he leans down and kiss his grown son on the cheek, and said, "I love you son." Next he goes to Jack and does the same. Realizing he'd left his wife and Lucy out of the love fest, Bing goes back around the table leans into Stella and lays a long kiss on her smiling lips.

When the kiss is through, Bing takes a deep bow and said, "I just want the four of you to know that I love you dearly."

Then he kisses Lucy on her sweet little girl cheek. "Thank you Grandpa." Lucy said quite pleased that she was not forgotten.

Jack grins and tells the adults, "This is how a family should be. Only a little yelling, but lots of hugs, kisses and love every day."

Because Derek, Lucy and Jack's lives have been turned around, and Derek doesn't want to think about Chloe, they talk about their plans for the following day, going to visit Granny Anne and that Aunt Flannery will be visiting in only a few weeks. Lucy, Jack, Derek and Flannery's Granny Anne had seen Flannery the previous summer on the Isle of Skye, and though the visit was restful, Flannery and Derek were never alone. The last time Derek and Flannery were alone was the heart breaking day six years before when Derek flew to Edinburgh to tell Flannery he would not be marrying her, but had to marry her half-sister Chloe because Chloe said her baby was his.

Telling Flannery that their wedding plans were off, and that they would never be together like they had planned for years, was the hardest most difficult thing Derek had ever done. Even now, nearly six years later he can see the hurt and devastation on Flannery's beautiful face and in her moss green eyes. For a brief moment Derek sees that he also married Chloe because he was hurt by Flannery's being away from him most of each year.

"Daddy, why are you so sad?" asked Jack with concern on his handsome little face.

"I'm not sad. I'm tired, but not sad. How can I be sad when I have you and Lucy?"

"Good. I don't want you to be sad.' Jack said before he pulls the cheese from his piece of pizza and puts it in his tomato sauce streaked mouth.

After dinner, Derek, Lucy and Jack take the dogs for a walk around his father and Stella's property. Because Stella also has a small Scottish terrier named Shane Bing volunteers to walk with them.

The evening is cool but refreshing. As they walk the scent of lilacs follow them. Though it is May, and the lilacs late to bloom, because of the colder than normal winter, the lilacs are beautiful to behold. The bushes were planted by Bing for Derek's mother Hanna shortly after their marriage. Lilacs had always been Hanna's favorite flower, and whenever Bing or Derek smell their sweet scent they think fondly and lovingly of Hanna. Hanna will always be young in there memory, because she was only thirty when she died.

There were many reasons why Derek and Flannery were close. True their fathers were friends and business partners, and they also lost a parent the same year, only one month apart.

Flannery's father James lost his life in a plane crash when he was only thirty-two. Two months after Hanna's death. She died in May after her lilacs bloomed. Because Bing wanted to get away from the Chicago for a while to spend time with Derek, and because Flannery had already been turned over to Granny Anne, James mother, Anne invited Bing and Derek to go with her and Flannery to Scotland. The stay there was just what the four needed. They would visit Edinburgh now and then, and stay in Granny Anne's townhouse there, so Derek and Flannery could visit the sights and get to know their Scottish heritage, but mostly they stayed at the little farm where James had grownup. There were horses to ride, hikes to enjoy and a little loch where Bing, Anne, Derek and Flannery would fish, and swim on those rare warm sunny days in Scotland.

They stayed for over a year, then they went back to the U.S. and Chicago and a house that was much too big for one man and a little boy. Six months after their return Bing married Stella and then Sean was born. The big house was once more like home and Derek and Bing settled into a good and peaceful life. Stella was never a replacement for Hanna; she is loved for the sweet woman that she is by Bing and Derek. Stella never minds when Derek and Bing reminisce about Hanna. Stella to this day loves Hanna like a sister, and misses the best friend that she ever knew.

Anne and Flannery came back with them so Flannery could go to the same school as Derek. They were born on July forth, the same year, and always celebrated their birthdays together whether in Scotland or in the Chicago area. Until Derek married Chloe he and Flannery always made a point of celebrating their special day together. She will be in Chicago this July, and Derek prays that she and he can go back to the old ways of celebration. There was always a barbecue for lunch, with hot dogs, hamburgers and all the trimmings. After they ate they would go to a carnival in the area, ride the rides and eat junk food until they feel like throwing up, which they rarely did. Then it was the fireworks and home for ice cream and cake and the gifting. Their favorite ice cream was always Rocky Road and their cake marble. Their cake was always a sheet cake with both their names on it. The candles were half royal blue, Derek's favorite color and emerald green Flannery's favorite color. The flowers were a mixture of lavender thistle, Flannery's favorite, and lilacs which Derek has always loved because of his Mother.

To this day, since he broke his and Flannery's heart Derek has not touched Rocky Road ice cream, He wonders if Flannery has also given it up.

Bing has been watching Derek as they walk the dogs. Jack and Lucy skip several feet ahead as they and Tralee his Border collie walk much fast than the two adults. When he sees a far-away glint in Derek's brown eyes, he knows Derek is remembering his times with Flannery.

"It will be wonderful to see Flannery in a few weeks. I guess she felt it was time to come here for a visit since Granny Anne has made the long trek to Scotland the past few summers."

For a moment Bing thinks Derek is still lost in the past but then Derek said, "Yes, it will be wonderful to see her. We didn't spend any time alone last summer when Jack, Lucy and I were in Scotland. I had the feeling that she was trying to avoid me for the most part. Of course I can't blame her. She had trusted me completely and I let her down in a way that is unforgiveable. I'm hoping that she and I can talk things through this summer. In her eyes I saw the old look of love. Then again, maybe I'm delusional and she doesn't love me."

Bing knows that Derek is lonely, has been so since he married Chloe. Bing prays every night that Derek and Flannery have another chance at happiness. If that means they marry as they had planned six years before he and Stella and Granny Anne will be overjoyed. If not they will have to live with not knowing how marriage between them would have turned out.

Bing has always been an optimist, and says a silent prayer while they walk. Sean is not a bad man and Bing and Stella love him, would not turn their back on him, but Derek is the son who has always excelled at everything he undertakes. Derek and Flannery have always been focused in their life choices. Sean and Chloe have never had any ambition. Derek studied business and finance as Bing and James did all those years ago and upon graduating from college, began to work at the firm Bing and James founded when the first arrived in the Chicago area.

He and James were very frugal and put all of their resources into their business. The two worked long and hard, but eventually their hard work and frugality paid off. Though James had lived long enough to reap from their hard work, Bing knows James would be amazed at how profitable and world renowned their telecommunication company is now. Derek is one of the reasons why. Derek is a born diplomat and instinctively knows how to get people interested in doing business with Larkin and MacDougall Telecommunications Inc.

Though Derek is taking a leave of absence for the next year, Bing doesn't worry that the company will suffer in Derek's absence. Derek has trained the two men who will take his accounts for the year. Derek feels that the two can handle the job, and Bing highly respects Derek's choice. Bing and Stella will miss having Derek, Lucy and Jack close by, but he knows the year off is what his son and grandchildren need. He and Stella have already purchased their tickets to spend the Christmas and New Year's holiday in Scotland with Derek, Jack, Lucy, Granny Anne and Flannery. Bing smiles to himself as he thinks of the coming year. Flannery and Derek will be together a great deal of the time, and Bing prays that they will see that life would be better if they are together.

Derek is watching Jack and Lucy who have finally slowed down to a slower pace and Bing who is smiling for some unknown reason, "It's good to see you smiling. Maybe you would like to share your happy thoughts with me." Derek said as the four turn to walk back to the big red brick house that is lit from inside with lights and outside with lights and a full moon.

"I was just thinking what a nice year you, Lucy and Jack will have. I was remembering the year that James and Hanna died, and how important our trip to Scotland was. You and me, Granny Anne and Flannery fused together by our grief, but also by the love that we shared."

"Don't forget family is a wonderful thing"

Derek nods his head at Bing's words of fact, and said, "That is definitely a true statement."

Chapter Nine

Derek, Bing, Lucy and Jack, leave Bing and Stella's at eleven a.m. The four will go to the latest Disney movie, have lunch somewhere after, and then meet Stella, the dogs and cats at Granny Anne's before dinner. Derek, Lucy and Jack have packed their bags for a stay with Anne. Her house is outside the town of Geneva, though close enough to ride a bike to get ice cream cones on a hot summer's day.

Derek has always taken his allotted vacation each year, but is happily looking forward to doing only what he, Lucy and Jack chose for the next year. When they first married Derek would let Chloe choose their vacation destination. After taking trips to New York and L.A. several times so Chloe could shop and leave Derek, Lucy and Jack to their own devices, Derek Lucy and Jack took vacations without her. Their last trip had been to Scotland. This was the trip that made Derek think about where his life was taking him. Although he knew he and Chloe would never love each other, he drug his feet at divorce. What changed his mind was his visit from Sean. Then he finally made his decision.

He knew that he would have to keep his planned divorce from Chloe until the papers were given to her. When Sean told him that Chloe was always verbally abusing Jack and Lucy, this was a no brainer. Her temper was always volatile, but until the recent incident she had not, to his knowledge physically abused them. With photos of their bruises and scratches, taken at the hospital, and with Sean's proof of the verbal abuse, Derek knows that Chloe will not try anything foolish. At least he hopes she doesn't. Where Chloe is concerned one never knows for sure. Why she had them dropped off at the house and pretended to be Stella he doesn't know. Because he has no intention of asking her why he will just have to believe that it was a way for her to get attention.

Chapter Ten

It is nearly four p.m. when Bing, Derek and the kids pull into the gravel drive in front of Granny Anne's two-story Craftsman's cottage. Large oaks shade the long driveway, and stand like sentries protecting the house and all who dwell within. Stella's small red Honda Civic sedan sits just outside the fenced and gated yard.

Jack and Lucy are out of the back seat of the gray van, and running through the royal blue wooden gate, before Bing and Derek unhook their seat belts.

"They were running so fast, I was surprised they didn't run through the gate before Jack stopped to open it" said Bing with a hearty laugh. The gate is painted the blue of the Scottish flag and when one is leaving Anne's yard to return to their car or the road there is a sign on the inside of the gate that tells one and all to "Haste Ye Back." The words are also at the Edinburgh airport when a person is leaving Scotland.

Derek laughs with his father, and replies, "They love it here. He enjoys spending time with you and Mom, but Granny Anne's place is every little child's dream."

"That's perfectly fine son. I remember how much you and Sean loved visiting Granny Anne. Although she is not related, Granny Anne has always opened her heart and home to me and mine. Because my Mam died when I was a young boy, and I have no siblings, James and I became brothers of the heart. Whenever James and I had time off from the university, he always made it clear that I was expected to go to Skye and the farm. Granny Anne accepted me right off. She even charmed my Da and John Callum MacDougall was not easy to charm."

Derek detects a bit of wistfulness in his father's voice and knows that he is remembering a man who never found it easy to express his love for Bing. Derek had seen his grandfather several times and though he found it difficult to show Bing love, Derek's grandfather always greeted Derek with open arms. After seeing photos of Bings mother Charlotte, Derek knew why his grandfather found it difficult showing Bing affection. Bing has the look of his mother. The black hair and dark eyes are hers, also his generous smile. Though he is tall like his father, Bing was a constant reminder that Charlotte had lived and died far too young. When Hanna died Bings father came to the funeral. This comforted Bing and Derek. That was the one time that Bing's father showed him the much needed affection that he needed. The year that he and Bing stayed in Scotland, after Hanna and James' death Bing and Derek saw Bings father nearly every week. If they didn't go to Edinburgh and visit, Derek's grandfather made it a point to visit Skye and stay for several days.

The driveway may be concrete, but the walkway to Anne's sky blue front door is red brick. The steps to the wide covered front porch are also red brick. Planter boxes of brick on either side of the steps are filled with red geraniums, blue Lobelia and white petunias. Because the house is surrounded by a variety of huge trees, oak, maple and a few giant Scottish pines the yard and the house are always cool, even on the hottest days.

As the two walk to the half brick and half white wooden bungalow they hear dogs barking somewhere inside the house. When they reach the front door it burst open and Jack, Lucy his dogs, Stella's dog and Granny Anne's own Scottie dog race to greet them. Derek and Bing stand still so they won't walk on or trip over one of the happily barking and jumping dogs at their feet.

Anne and Stella appear in time to rescue the men and ask about their outing. The men are greeted with kisses and hugs from Anne and Stella. With just as much affection and love Bing and Derek hug and kiss the ladies in return. Derek is grateful that his parents have always been openly affectionate with him and Sean. It is because of this that Derek has always openly shown Jack and Lucy his love.

They eat their dinner of Shepherd's pie on Anne's screened back porch. .The dogs lie nearby, but don't bother them while they eat. Their owners always make certain that they feed the dogs before they sit down to eat. Rarely are they given human food.

While the six enjoys the meal and their time together they talk about their day, the Disney movie, which Jack proclaims is the best Disney yet. Jack of course says this about every movie that he sees and that Aunt Flannery will arrive in three weeks."

"Daddy, will we stay with Granny Anne the entire time that Aunt

Flannery is here?" said Jack with a happy hopeful smile on his handsome face.

"We'll be here part of the time. We don't want to overwhelm Flannery with our rowdiness." Derek said with a far-away look in his eyes.

"Daddy I hope so." adds Lucy with hope in her voice.

The adults know that Derek's mind is on Flannery because he doesn't answer when Jack asked, "Are we rowdy?"

When Derek feels five pair of eyes on him, he returns to the present and the new life that he and Jack and Lucy have embarked upon.

"I'm sorry Jack, did you ask me something?" This he said sheepishly, because he and all the adults know that Flannery, and any mention of her name has always put Derek in another world.

"Are we rowdy?"

Derek grins and replies, "Yes, we can be, especially when the three of us are playing, swimming, or tossing Frisbees and balls for the dogs."

"So rowdy means having fun. Aunt Flannery also loves fun. Remember last summer in Scotland how she played with us and Granny Margaret's son Thomas. She is always happy and doesn't mind what we do. She is a good sport and never minds if she doesn't win."

It is several seconds before Derek said, "Yes, Aunt Flannery is a good sport." Even after Derek married Chloe, Flannery didn't turn her back on Derek and his family. The first two years after he broke her heart she rarely came to the U.S. After that she would visit at Christmas time or for the fourth of July. Those times she and Derek didn't celebrate their July Fourth birthday together though they would go to the fireworks in Chicago on July third. By them Derek and Chloe had stopped pretending they had a legitimate or caring marriage.

Most summers Chloe would be off somewhere traveling with one of her just as materialistic and vain girlfriends. Those times were a breath of fresh air for Derek. His parents, Anne or a nanny would watch Jack and Lucy while he was at work. When he was home he devoted all of his time to his children and their needs.

"Daddy will you be as happy to see Aunt Flannery? I certainly will be."

Derek looks at the loving faces around him and said truthfully, "Yes I will be very happy when Aunt Flannery comes to visit."

When dinner is through and the dishes washed the four adults, Lucy, Jack and the pack of rowdy dogs head for the back yard to toss balls, throw Frisbees and enjoy the beautiful evening on the Fox River.

Anne's house was built on a hill above the Fox River. Close enough to see from the brick back wall, yet high enough away so that never has the house been flooded. She owns several acres around the house and has a dock that gives her access to the river and boat rowing and a boathouse not far away.

The six walk to the dock once the dogs have worn themselves out with the balls and Frisbees. Anne's Scottie Charlie, named for bonnie Prince Charles, is the only pet to follow them through the back gate. Because he stumbles over his short legs as they walk down hill, Jack picks the little black dog up and carries him in his arms. Jack a lover of all the Lord's critters, laughs when Charlie kisses his face and one ear.

When they reach the dock, Jack and Lucy sit on the end of the dock with Derek close by and remove their brown sandals, so they can put their feet in the calm flowing Fox. Derek stays with Jack and Lucy while the other adults go and sit on two benches that are strategically placed to view the flowing river and both sides of the sloping river bank. The sounds of an evening coming to a close soothes each one, as they talk and remember other times in this lovely and peaceful place.

Here they sit until the light of another day is nearly gone. Because it is too early in the season for mosquitoes and bugs they truly enjoy the evening.

When they return to Anne's house Bing and Stella bid them farewell and with Derek walking them to the drive and Stella's red Honda Civic Derek's parents give him one more kiss and hug before the drive the short distance to Hundley and home.

Chapter Eleven

Because Anne has volunteered to help Jack and Lucy wash their hair and take their bath, Derek takes a few minutes and sits on the brick front steps. Anne has motion sensor lights around her house, the brick wall that surrounds the house, the two car free standing garage only feet from the house and her conservatory and garden shed at the back of the yard. A few times over the years teenagers have taken the boats from her boat house, to return in the early morning, so Anne also has lights on the boathouse and the dock. Derek knows who the teens were. Flannery and Nell, her best friend and neighbor, are the ones who took the boats out after Anne and Virginia, Anne's best friend and Nell's grandmother, were in bed. Near the same age and widowed young Anne and Virginia have much in common. When Nell's parents were killed in an auto accident when she was three Virginia took Nell, her only child's daughter and raised her.

After Flannery's father James died in the plane crash and her mother Rena was no longer part of Flannery's life, Granny Anne and Virginia formed a bond and raised their granddaughters by themselves. The two have always helped each other out, with baby sitting and anything where they needed a boost of confidence.

With the house sitting in the grove of trees and because it is not close to a main road the night is peaceful. A few birds can still be heard settling in the trees for the night, and the whistle from a train heard in the distance, but beyond those sounds that is all that Derek hears. He is tired but is relieved that the worst part of his life is coming to a close. Marriage to Chloe has taken a toll on him in many ways. In the last year his black hair has begun to show strands of silver and he is only thirty. He knows that when he is Bing's age he will more than likely have the same thatch of thick white hair, but he knows from Bing and Stella that his father's hair did not turn gray or white until Bing was in his early fifties. He has also not slept peacefully since he had to face Flannery and tell her they would not be getting married on Skye.

Although six years have changed the two of them considerably, Derek silently prays that they can have a second chance at happiness. He was never lonely with Flannery in his life. Since their breakup he has been lonely most of his nights. With his days filled with work and his children, he got through them easily. At night after Jack and Lucy were asleep, is when he would remember what might have been, and them he would miss Flannery, her love, her funny laugh and her thoughtfulness.

He once again thinks about smoking a cigarette, but remembers he left them at his parent's house. He's hoping that not having them readily available, it will help him break the habit.

He sighs and gets up from the brick steps and goes inside to read Jack and Lucy two bedtime stories, He knows that Jack will already have the books picked out. If they are short, Derek reads both. If they are long he reads only one.

After he reads to Jack and Lucy, and takes his shower, he heads downstairs to Anne's comfortable living room. The room is the largest in the house. With four windows, with white wooden shutters, looking into the front yard and four looking into the back the room is very pleasant. With a gas log fireplace and built in glassed bookcases on either side of the fireplace the room is ideal for reading and dreaming. The sofa is floral with pinks, lavenders and greens. With a rocking chair, Anne's, and a recliner, this covered in pale green tweed the room is a wonderful place to relax after a long and tedious day. The floors are oak and recently redone shine like they were waxed. The huge area rug in muted colors, pastel, like the sofa brings the space together nicely.

There is a wide screen tv and DVD player sitting inside a wooden wardrobe type chest and a top of the line stereo system sits in the bottom of the cabinet. The television is off but Anne does have an easy-listening radio station on. A Carole King oldie is playing and Derek remembers that Carole is one of Flannery's as well as his all-time favorite singer-composers.

She is there looking through a box filled with photos. When Derek enters the room, Anne pats the sofa beside her and Derek sits down. Anne has green eyes like Flannery and James Flannery's father. Whenever Derek looks into Anne's eyes he cannot but think of Flannery. Flannery is tall like her Granny Anne and her father and she also gets her thick dark brunette hair from the two. Though Anne's hair is mostly silver now, if one looks closely they will see a bit of dark brown hidden beneath the silver strands. Still a very pretty woman Derek bets she still gets propositioned by the older gents at the senior facility where she and Virginia volunteer two days a week.

She hands him a stack of snap shots and said, "Flannery has asked me to go through these so we can put them in albums by the year."

The first photo that he looks at is of his Mother Hanna. Because she died young she will forever be young to those who knew and love her. Tall, around five feet, eight inches and trim Hanna was a beautiful woman both physically and spiritually. With dark brunette hair and hazel eyes that seemed to twinkle on their own it wasn't hard to see why Bing was attracted to her at first sight. They met at Lincoln Park Zoo in Chicago Bings and James first summer in the United States. He and James had gone to the zoo because the day was gorgeous and they loved the animals and the Lincoln Park area. They shared a two bedroom apartment in the New Town area and Lincoln Park is where they would go to relax and meet new people.

Hanna was with a friend and they were enjoying the Giraffes. Bing saw Hanna smile, and that was that. He introduced himself and James and Hanna and her friend accepted their invitation to an early dinner nearby. From that meeting Bing and Hanna formed a friendship that turned to love very rapidly. Though James liked Hanna's friend Phyllis there was no spark. James met Rena only a few weeks later and he and Bing went to the park rarely after that.

As he looks at his mother's smiling face Derek feels extremely blessed that he had her in his life though only for a short time. There was no doubt that she loved him and Bing and she wasn't afraid to show her love. He believes his children have a good deal of her strength and her loving ways and the loving ways of Bing. His mother's middle name was Lucy for her own grandmother so that is why Derek's daughter is Lucy Hanna.

Derek was given his first name because Bing and Hanna loved it, Liam his middle name is for Hanna's father Liam Ryan, an American pilot who died in Viet Nam.

Derek sorts through the stack but stops to look closely at one of Flannery and himself as king and queen of their senior prom. He is mesmerized by the photo as his memories take him back to that prom and to the night when he and Flannery first proclaimed their love for each other.

Everyone always told them how wonderful they looked together. At six feet two inches, he wasn't too tall for the slim five foot nine Flannery. Their happiness at being together and their graduation only days away had the two of them smiling glorious smiles that night.

Her dress was strapless and emerald green. Though her eyes are a dark moss green, they appear to be emerald in the photo. Her earrings were emerald post, a gift from Anne on her sixteenth birthday. Her hair, a beautiful brunette like her fathers, cascades in curls from the crown on her head. The corsage on her wrist was wildflowers tied with a green satin ribbon. Her only other adornment was the gold locket that Derek had given her for Christmas the December before. Derek still remembers that he was hot because he wore a tux beneath the king's cloak, and the evening was warmer than usual.

They danced every dance an after the prom decided to skip the usual celebration with their fellow school mates. They had no interest in booze and staying up until first light. Instead they went to Granny Anne's, changed from their finery and dressed in shorts and t-shirts sat on Anne's dock and planned their future together.

They would wait until they graduated from college and worked several years before marriage. Once married, they would wait a few years before starting a family. They would have at least four children because Flannery didn't want their children to be lonely. She always felt like an only child even though she had her half-sister Chloe.

Because Flannery was raised by Granny Anne and Chloe by their mother Rena and Chloe's father Gus, the sisters were never close. Anne thought inviting Chloe to her house that Chloe and Flannery would get to know each other better. Derek and Sean also spent lots of time there as did Nell. Because Chloe had to share the attention, she only went to Anne's a few times. Those visits were extremely trying for Anne and everyone around Chloe. If Chloe didn't get everyone's undivided attention she would pout or start a ruckus. Once Anne told her she had to behave or she couldn't visit, Chloe chose to stay home with Rena and Gus. Her parents always put Chloe and her wants and needs before anyone or anything else.

"Photos are wonderful, a way to travel to the past and remember the good times." Granny said to Derek when he sits the prom photo aside to look at another small stack of photos.

Once he looks at the stack he sits them aside and tells Anne, "Photos are a treasure, although they sometimes remind us of what we've lost."

Anne takes Derek's square tanned hand in hers and said, "Humans make mistakes. The Lord knows we will make them long before we do. I honestly believe he wanted you to be Jack and Lucy's father. Even if Sean is Jack's biological father, and Sean is not a bad man, I believe they were to be your children."

Derek looks at her thoughtfully for a time and said. "Yes, the Lord knew that once I saw them and held them in my arms that I would love them in only the way a father can love a child."

Anne smiles and tells Derek, "The Lord sees your heart and yours is huge."

Derek gives Anne a smile, gets up from the sofa where they sit, and adds, "How blessed we are that the Lord takes on our troubles and carries them so we can rest."

"Yes, we are blessed" Anne adds as she watches Derek leave the living room and climbs the steps where he and his children share a room.

Anne sits on the sofa a while longer reflecting on the passing day, and then she bows her head and said a special prayer for Derek and all that he has faced since his marriage to Chloe. She knows that he is strong and a survivor but also knows humans have their limits. Knowing Chloe as she does and that Chloe can be vindictive, Anne prays that now that Derek has had their divorce papers served that Chloe is forever out of Jack, Lucy and Derek's life. As she gets up to go and let the dogs out one more time before she goes to bed Anne remembers *Psalm 9: 9-10*

For the Lord is a shelter for the oppressed, a refuge in times of trouble. Those who know your name trust in you, O Lord, have never abandoned anyone who searches for you.

She must remember to write the scripture down and show it to Derek.

Chapter Twelve

June First Week

The four days with Anne go fast and yet Derek and his children have had a much needed rest. He and they will spend Thursday through Sunday at Anne's and Monday through Wednesday with Bing and Stella until he, Jack, Lucy and Granny Anne fly to Scotland in October with Flannery. Because he didn't want Flannery to feel burdened with their stay at Anne's, he sent Flannery an email before he told Jack and Lucy of the plan. When she emailed back the same afternoon and said that she is looking forward to seeing them at Anne's and wherever else they may be, Derek emailed her a heartfelt thank you and said a prayer that he and Flannery can be friends again.

The three days with his parents were restful, but seemed to go at a snail's pace. He knows that it is because he is anxious to see Flannery, and also because he also a little anxious to know what she thinks about him being a single man again. While he waits for Granny Anne, Lucy and Jack to get ready for the trip to O'Hare airport Derek looks at a few of the snapshots that Anne has arranged in stacks on a tray that sits on one of the living room lamp tables.

He is surprised that the photos remain stacked because Odie is frisky most of the time and races around the house, up the stairs and down and across the furniture. He tried to reel the cat in several times, but Anne told him not to worry, it is just the nature of the critter. .He and the children and their pets travel together from Anne's to his parents every week, and the pets don't seem to mind. When they are at Bing and Stella's her little Scottie dog greets them like lost relatives when at Anne's her Scottie Charlie greets them in the same way.

He is looking at a photo that was taken when Flannery's first book was published. She was only nineteen at that time, in college and trying to decide if she should finish her degree in journalism or quit entirely and place her full focus on her writing. Somehow she managed to do both, and had published five children's fantasy books by the time she and Derek graduated.

Her success hadn't surprised Derek or his family and Granny Anne. Her mother Rena and her sister never acknowledged Flannery's success which surprised no one who knows the two. Gus Maxwell, Chloe's father, not only sent her a huge bouquet of wildflowers and a card to congratulate her he also took her, Granny Anne, Derek and Derek's parents to an upscale restaurant to celebrate. Even though Flannery never lived with Gus and Rena after their marriage, and that she went there only a handful of times to visit, Gus always went out of his way to let her know how wonderful she is. He always remembered her birthday as well as Derek and Sean's. At Christmas Gus always sent a card to Derek, Sean and their parents and always made a point of giving Anne gifts for those occasions and a monthly check for support of Flannery. When Anne tried to turn the support money down Gus told her it was only right because Rena is Flannery's mother and if she hadn't been so adamant that Flannery live with Anne, he would have raised her.

Flannery rarely talked about Rena or Chloe, but always had wonderful things to say about Gus. When the two found out about Gus' generosity they had a fit. Gus told them that he would always acknowledge Flannery and Anne because they deserved his consideration just as much as Chloe and Rena.

Derek knows that it is Rena who spoiled Chloe. Chloe is a younger replica of Rena with blonde hair and blue eyes and Marilyn Monroe figures. It is from Rena that Chloe acquired her taste for only the most expensive clothing, jewelry and cars.

The house that Chloe grew up in would hold several families and that is why she insisted Derek buy the three story brick mausoleum that they had spent their married life in. The house with a movie studio, swimming pool and six bedrooms and six and a half baths was never home to Derek. Most of the rooms were never used and yet Chloe insisted each had to be professionally decorated. When he was home he and the children spent their time in the huge kitchen and connecting family room. At night the two slept in connecting rooms and shared a bath. Derek's bedroom was within earshot of theirs plus he had baby monitors placed in their rooms and his. There were many nights when all three slept together in Derek's bed.

Derek lost in thought jumps when Jack comes up behind him on the sofa and said, "We're all ready to go and get Aunt Flannery."

"Did I scare you Daddy?" Jack asked as he moves in front of Derek and looks at his father's face.

"Yes. I was day dreaming."

"About Aunt Flannery I'll bet." Jack said looking from Derek to the photo of Flannery now lying on the coffee table in front of them.

"Yes, I was remembering when your Aunt Flannery and I were young."

"Aunt Flannery is fun and she never yells. Too bad Mommy isn't as nice."

Derek is not one who says negative thing about others, even when the person may deserve negative things said about them, and because he wants Jack to think the best of others, all he said is "You Mommy and Flannery are different, like Sean and I are different."

Before Jack can reply Granny Anne tells them that she and Lucy are ready to go.

Jack races out the door and is waiting by the van when Anne whispers to Derek, "I love the way you diplomatically answered Jack. Chloe doesn't deserve any positive affirmations from you but you handled it like the diplomat that you are."

"It's always easy to be diplomatic towards a person when they are no longer in your everyday life." Derek whispers back.

When Derek opens the doors, he first holds a front door for Anne. Once she is seated, he goes to the back seat to make sure Jack and Lucy are belted into booster seats.

Derek parks in the lot that's closest the terminal where Aer Lingus lands and then the three walk to the terminal where Flannery will come in.

With Derek and Anne each holding one of Jack and Lucy's hands they skips the entire distance to the baggage pickup area.

Chapter Thirteen

Their wait is not long, maybe fifteen minutes when they see tall slim Flannery walking towards them. Her hair is longer than Derek remembers; and in a high ponytail Flannery looks more like a teen than a woman who will turn thirty-one the same day as Derek. Dressed in navy capris and a long sleeved white t-shirt, she carries a navy cardigan, her purse, a case with her computer and a tote bag with a newspaper, bottle of water and a nearly finished novel peeking out.

Jack and Lucy run to her and she puts everything on the floor beside her sneaker clad feet. She picks Lucy up first and holds her on her slim hip. Then she picks Jack up to ride on her other hip. He kisses her cheek and she kisses his. Then she is kissed on the cheek by Lucy. Jack tells her with a happy voice, "I love you Aunt Flannery and I am really happy that you are here."

"Me too Aunt Flannery." said Lucy with as much happiness as Jack.

Flannery looks over Jack's head right into Derek's eyes and said, "I love you to, and I'm also happy to finally be here."

Her beautiful moss green eyes with long dark lashes seem to smile on their own as she studies him as he does her. "It's nice to see you Derek." she said before placing Jack and Lucy on the terminal floor and going to Granny Anne and giving her a hug and a kiss on the cheek.

"It's nice to see you too." Derek said as he picks up her belongings.

She smiles a beautiful smile and helps him with her few things. As she reaches for her purse her hand brushes his and the old sparks ignite. Lost in the moment and their long lost feelings they look deeply in each other's eyes until Jack, always alert said, "The luggage is coming now."

Once her bags are collected and they are in the van, Derek said, "If you are tired we will go home. If you're not we'll go in Chicago and walk around the zoo and later eat out. What's it to be?"

Flannery sees Jack and Lucy's hopeful smiles in the rearview mirror and tells the four, "I slept for several hours on the way here, and I would love to visit the Lincoln Park Zoo with you. Maybe Jack, Lucy and I will have cotton candy like the last time we were there."

The five talk of things in general and before they know it Derek is parking the van in the lot at Lincoln Park zoo. Although there is no fee to enter the zoo, there is a substantial parking fee.

Because the schools are out for the summer there are numerous children and adults at the zoo. The June weather could not be better, even if they had personally ordered it. With only a few fluffy clouds painting the vast sky, and a gentle breeze coming off Lake Michigan nearby, the seventy-five degree morning is perfect in many ways.

Jack and Lucy skip ahead of the three adults, stopping only to view each of the animal exhibits. Granny Anne and Flannery carry the majority of the conversation. Derek keeps a cautious eye on his son and daughter injects only a few thoughts into the conversation. When his eyes do stray from Jack or Lucy but only for short periods, his eyes are on Flannery. Anne also notes that Flannery has been watching Derek since they picked her up at O'Hare.

When they reach the building where the primates are housed, Jack finally slows to a normal pace. 'Daddy lets go here. I love the monkeys and the gorillas. They always make me laugh."

Jack slips his little hand into Derek's and leads him in to the cool shady building. Practically dragging Derek Jack comes to a stop in front of the Baboon display. Flannery and Anne are right behind with Lucy holding on to a hand of each lady. The five cannot help but laugh at the Baboon antics. While Jack and Lucy watch the Baboons, Anne watches Derek and Flannery sneaking peaks at each other.

They look at several displays before they stop and buy drinks and cotton candy for Jack, Lucy and Flannery. When Flannery offer Derek part of hers he takes only a small bite. She and Jack and Lucy love the pink confection, but Derek and Anne find it far too sweet for their taste.

They spend several hours enjoying the zoo and each other. When Anne sees the Chicago Conservatory close to where they stand, she asked if they would go there so she can see the new display of plants. Anne was born with a green thumb and can get everything to grow and flourish. Her gardens in Geneva, Illinois and Scotland always have something blooming, no matter what season it may be.

Jack takes one of Anne's wrinkled, long thin tanned hands and Lucy takes the other and led her around the conservatory. With its earthy and humid smell, Anne feels like she is in the tropics and loves every minute of their visit. Derek and Flannery tag behind, looking more at each other than the lovely floral display.

As they leave the Conservatory Derek asked where they would like to have lunch. Jack and Lucy whose favorite food is pizza looks hopefully from one adult face to the next and Jack said, "Uno's please Daddy. But only if everyone wants pizza as much as I do."

The adults also like Uno's on Huron street and Jack is extremely happy when everyone agrees with his choice.

Once they enter the popular pizza restaurant, and have placed their order; they each take time to write something on the restaurant's white stucco walls. "I wonder how many layers of paint these walls have." Flannery asked as she writes a quote from one of her favorite poets Emily Dickinson, Derek reads Emily's words and he tells Jack and Lucy what they say, *"If I can stop one heart from breaking, I shall not live in vain, If I can ease one life the aching or cool one pain, or help one fainting robin into his nest again, I shall not live in vain.* He knows that the words describe Flannery perfectly.

"The walls look awfully thick. So I'm guessing there are quite a few layers." Derek said while helping Jack sign his name.

"Remember all the times we came here throughout the years" Flannery said when they are walking back to their table to the just delivered pizzas.

.Derek pulls out the chairs for the ladies and Jack, and once everyone is seated he finally answers Flannery. "Yes, I remember all of our times here and anywhere we have gone."

When he sees the pleased smile on her face at his admission, Derek's heart fills with hope. He's grateful that Flannery is not one who holds a grudge. She, like Granny Anne has an extremely giving and forgiving spirit. Derek knows from Bing that James Larkin, Flannery's father also had the same spirit. He to a degree can also be giving and forgiving. Forgiving Chloe and Sean is not something he has done, but he prays that one day he will. He knows that holding unforgiveness for too long can poison a person heart and he doesn't want to become a hard-hearted man.

It is four p.m. when they head home. Derek foregoes the freeway and takes Irving Park Road home to Anne's. Flannery falls asleep as soon as they hit Irving Park road. Derek is surprised that Jack does not nod off. He does sit quietly beside Granny Anne and looks out the windows at the passing Chicago neighborhoods.

They are almost home when Jack suddenly asked Derek, "Daddy why would a person put powdered sugar on the counter or a flat surface and sniff it up their nose?"

Totally thrown by the question it is several moments before he asked, "Jack, who did you see doing that?"

Brought out of her peaceful sleep by Derek's deep voice Flannery wonders why Derek is suddenly so serious. When she hears Jack's answer she is as shocked as Derek.

"I saw Mommy doing it. She never knew I saw, but she did it several times since Christmas."

"Was Uncle Sean there? Was he also doing what your Mommy was doing?" Derek looks first at Jack in the rear view mirror, then at Anne's shocked face, and finally at Flannery's questioning expression.

'No, Uncle Sean wasn't there. One thing they fought about when Mommy spanked me and locked me, Lucy and our pets out was Mommy sniffing the powdered sugar. She didn't know I heard that. Uncle Sean said he wanted no part of her nonsense. Why was she doing that?"

Derek rubs his right earlobe several times, a habit he has had since he was young whenever he was tired or frustrated. Flannery watches his face and sees first anger and then frustration at a woman who has only given him grief since he found her naked and in his bed.

For a moment he wants to tell Jack that Chloe was using cocaine, but knows, even though Jack is extremely intelligent he must be diplomatic with his answer.

"Son, sometimes adults do extremely foolish things. They do things that can harm them and destroy their lives. Chloe was doing something dangerous when she was sniffing the white powder. It wasn't powdered sugar. Chloe apparently has decided that she would rather get high than be a Mommy."

Jack nods his head as though he understands, so Derek adds, "If you have any other questions you can always ask me." Jack nods his head yes. Derek sighs and looking first at Anne and then Flannery, shakes his head in disbelief.

The five sit in deep though at all they have learned and heard, and they say no more about Chloe and her use of Cocaine until much later.

Chapter Fourteen

After Jack and Lucy are in bed, Derek goes for a walk to the dock. There is much for him to sort out in his mind and how long has Chloe been using drugs, and how long has Sean known?

How long he sits there he is not sure. He sees the lights in Flannery's upstairs bedroom, and Granny Anne's downstairs bedrooms go off before he heads back to the house and sleep.

Flannery hears the door to the bedroom that Derek and his children's share down the hallway from hers. Then she hears the water running in the shower. She would love to talk with Derek and sooth the lines around his dark eyes but knows he is a man that needs time to sort things out for himself. She is sad that Chloe has gotten into drugs, but not surprised. Chloe never cares who she hurt as long as she gets what she wants.

Flannery is restless and hasn't slept a wink. When she looks at her bedside clock and sees that she has been trying to fall asleep for two hours, she throws back the light blanket and in short pajamas she decides to go down stairs and make some Chamomile tea. The tea usually helps. When she reaches the upstairs landing she can see as she looks over the upstairs railing, the television flickering in the nearly dark room.

When she reaches the living room, she sees Derek lying on the floral sofa with his eyes closed. When she turns to go back upstairs so she won't awaken him, he opens his eyes and sees her standing at the foot of the sofa.

"I'm not sleeping. You are welcome to sit on the sofa if you like. I can sit up or you can sit down, or you may come and lie with me.

Flannery moves towards him without a word and goes to Derek. He moves to his side, facing her and the television. Flannery lies down facing him. Eyes so dark that they look black in the light of the television and eyes deep and green look into each other. Because his complexion is olive he tans whenever they are in the sunlight. Flannery once told Derek he could pass for a pirate if only he wore a gold ring in his earlobe. Derek of course is not one who would choose anything that would change his appearance.

When Anne comes into the room at seven the next morning to find her reading glasses, she stops in her tracks when she sees Flannery and Derek sound asleep and wrapped in one another's arms. Quietly she picks up her glasses from a side table, and silently she closes her eyes and says a prayer of thanks to the Lord. Because she feels that the two need to sleep she goes upstairs to see if Jack and Lucy are awake.

They are awake and looking out the bedroom window at the dogs now in Anne's lush back yard. When Anne steps into the room she tells them that they need to be quiet because Derek and Flannery are still sleeping.

. "Where are they sleeping? I think Daddy was here for a while." said Jack with a yawn.

"They are sleeping on the sofa. We will go downstairs once you are dressed and make ourselves breakfast, which we will take out to the screened porch. We will also feed the pets. After we eat, how would you like to help me work in the garden?"

"I'll help with the breakfast, the pets and the garden. Daddy and Aunt Flannery must be tired from our trip yesterday." Jack tells Anne with such seriousness that she can't help but hug and kiss the little boy that she has always claimed as a great-grandson.

"I'll help too." said Lucy who is a morning person like Granny Anne.

It is ten a.m. before Derek and Flannery awaken. Now covered with the afghan from the back of the sofa, they are warm and cozy and Flannery and Derek lie as they fell asleep. They face each other and smile into one another's eyes.

"It's awfully quiet." said Flannery as she whispers against Derek's rough whiskered chin.

Before Derek can reply, they hear the dogs barking in the back yard, and then hear Jack say in the distance, "Shush. Daddy and Aunt Flannery are sleeping"

"I guess that is our signal to get up." Derek said with his lips against Flannery's cheek.

Flannery takes the afghan with her when she rolls away from Derek to sit up. While she folds the bright Lucas plaid of royal blue and red, Anne's family clan name, Derek sits up and sits beside her. "Now that we know what helps us sleep, where do we go from here?" Derek asked with a husky voice.

Flannery studies his tanned face, a face that she knows is etched in her heart forever and said with all the love that she feels for him, "I know this is as much a surprise to you as to me. Who knows where it will go or if it will go, but this has been nice."

Derek smiles into the lovely moss green eyes that he has gotten lost in many times.

"I wonder what time it is." Derek said looking around the room for a clock. When his eyes find an ornate white Bavarian style wooden clock on the mantle, he and Flannery are surprised that they have slept until ten a.m.

"I've not slept this late since before Jack was born."

"I sleep in once in a while, but never this late" Flannery tells him as they get up from the comfortable sofa and walk up the stairs.

When they reach the door to her room, Derek pulls her close in a warm and wonderfully inviting hug. She is so happy to be with him and Jack, Lucy and her Granny Anne that she practically glows. To her delight Derek seems to glow with happiness himself.

"Considering that the hour is late, and that Granny Anne and the kids have more than likely eaten breakfast, do you think omelets would be a good choice for us and them."

"Absolutely, I don't know many people who don't like omelets no matter what time of day it is."

"Ok, once we're cleaned up and changed you and I will make omelets." Neither takes long changing into shorts and t-shirts. They are down the stairs, and outside in the beautiful backyard in record time.

Jack and Lucy who are helping Anne weed her herb garden hear them when the screen door to the back porch squeaks. They and the dogs are surrounding Derek and Flannery in an instant. Anne smiles at the sight of dogs and people livening up her usually much too quiet life. Anne loves children and would have loved having a dozen. When she and her husband got married they'd planned a big family, but James Sr. died only after three years of marriage. James Sr. was twenty years older than Anne but the two had much in common. When he died from a weak heart, Anne was left to raise James Jr. on her own. She did many things to make a living. Because most of the jobs meant little time with her son, she used the last of the money that she and James Sr. saved and opened a bed and breakfast on the little farm where they lived.

The project was a success because Anne is not only a gracious hostess her cooking is to die for. At first Anne did all of the work. After the first season working alone she was able to hire two girls and two young men from the nearby village to help her. The four worked diligently and were faithful to Anne. She ran the bed and breakfast until James graduated from Edinburgh University and immigrated with Bing to the Chicago area. Once the two, Bing and James, got their business going and James invited her to come and live in the Chicago area. Anne closed the L and L B and B, Lucas and Larkin were what the L's stood for, and used the farm only while she was visiting Skye each summer.

Anne always tried to get along with Rena, her daughter-in-law, but Rena didn't want to share James with Anne. To make things easier for all concerned James graciously bought Anne the house by the Fox. Even then Flannery spent most of her time with Anne. James would visit often, but Rena refused to visit with him. Shortly before his death, her son asked if she would raise Flannery if anything should happen where he couldn't. He was extremely relieved when Anne told him she would be delighted to raise Flannery. Her son had named Flannery for the American author Flannery O'Connor. The name was appropriate because Flannery had a knack for storytelling even as a young girl only three and four years old.

In the last year of her sons life Anne knew that he and Rena were not getting along. They no longer slept in the same room and no longer went anywhere together. Rena acted like she was a single woman and would go out with her single friends. There were rumors that Rena had a boyfriend, which turned out to be fact. When the plane that James piloted crashed the August Flannery was four, Anne believed that her son killed himself. When the authorities proved that the plane had not been serviced properly and the fuel gauge did not register that the plane had the correct amount of fuel, it was decided that the plane ran out of fuel without registering that fact to James, the pilot and a friend Steven. .

The man who was Rena's boyfriend was out of the picture shortly thereafter and then she met Gus Maxwell. Gus, like James was swept off his feet by the voluptuous Rena. She could charm the sox off any man, especially prosperous men. The never married, charming and extremely wealthy man married her only after knowing her four months. At least James had known her six months. Both men, sweet and caring did not know what a handful they had married until Rena got tired of them. Anne has heard once again that Rena has a boyfriend. She prays for Gus and Rena that what she has heard is only rumor.

Chloe was born the first year of Gus and Rena's marriage. It was no secret why Rena had Chloe. Chloe was her way to easy street. Gus loves her with his huge generous heart and Rena has taught Chloe how to manipulate Gus and every man who is in her life. When Anne heard that Derek supposedly got Chloe pregnant she was always skeptical.

After Jack was born and Anne saw that Derek had been lied to she invited him and Jack to her house in Geneva and Scotland. At first he would come only if Flannery wasn't there. When Anne asked him why, he said he didn't want Flannery to feel uncomfortable in his presence. Anne asked Flannery how she felt about having Derek and Jack around, Flannery thought about it for a short time, and when Anne told her Derek could use her friendship, Flannery agreed to visits when Derek, Jack and Lucy were there. The two were never alone during those visits, but Anne knows that those visits helped Derek and Flannery a great deal.

Seeing them asleep in one another's arms on her sofa has Anne praying every chance she gets She knows prayers are answered and prays that Derek and Flannery will be married before Summer is through.

Chapter Fifteen

At four that afternoon, while Jack and Lucy play in his grandparents back yard with Nell's three children, who have come along from Anne's neighborhood, and while Flannery, Anne and Stella keep an eye on the five, Derek talks with his father about Chloe and her drug use,

They sit comfortably in two dark brown leather chairs in Bing's office library. With floor to ceiling bookcases filled with numerous books of many titles, this is Bing and Derek's favorite room in the house. When Derek lived with his parents he always had Bing's permission to study and read in the cool pleasant room.

With a southern exposure the room is always warm and cozy in the winter months. During the heat of a long summer's day the room is kept cool by closing the plantation shutters and using the air conditioning. Because the house has trees growing all around the summer heat is usually kept at bay by their shade. The winter sun peeks through the branches and gives the room daytime light and warmth. Although Bing no longer smokes, the room still has a faint scent of the cherry tobacco that he once favored. Stella loves to tidy the room and one can also smell a faint scent of lemon furniture polish.

"Is it Chloe you want to talk about?" Bing asked Derek while bending to tie a loose shoe lace.

"Yes. Jack told us, me Flannery and Anne that Chloe sniffs powdered sugar. She was unaware that he saw her. You and I know it was more than likely cocaine. Dad had I known I would never have left Jack and Lucy alone with her. I asked him if he saw Sean sniffing it, and he said no, that Sean and Chloe not only fought his last night in the house, because of her verbal abuse of Jack but because of the cocaine."

"I think Gus needs to know. If she listens to anyone it is him."

Bing rubs his chin several times then said, "I'll call Gus, if he can make it here tomorrow for lunch would you be free to come also? Derek nods his head yes, then Bing adds "I'll also see if Sean is willing to come by and let us know what he has seen. Chloe is her own worst enemy, but she is Gus' daughter and he loves her. We will have to remember them in our prayers."

"Yes, Flannery and Anne also pray for her."

"Where was Chloe when the divorce papers were served? I take it she wasn't at your house."

"I had them served at her Mother and Gus's house. I knew if she got them there I would be certain she was served. Knowing Chloe she would have thrown them away and then claimed she didn't receive them."

"I feel badly for Gus. He's a decent and caring man and he was charmed by Rena. Since she also charmed Flannery's father, I guess she, like Chloe should go into acting. They would more than likely win an Oscar for their performances." Derek tells his father with the shake of his head.

"I agree. It is a tragedy that one woman can destroy two kind and loving men without a bit of remorse. I remember when James first introduced me and your Mom to her. Hanna knew of Rena, although they didn't hang out in the same social circles, Hanna would see her quite often at dances and parties in the area. Apparently she never dated a man more than once. Your Mom wasn't one to spread rumors but she told me that Rena was bad news. She and James had met in a café in Chicago. He usually had his lunch there, and once she found out he was an up and coming businessman with a wonderful future she would be there when he came in. I tried to warn him without ending our friendship and our partnership. He listened and said that people just didn't understand a woman like Rena. When they flew to Vegas and eloped only after knowing each other a short time, Hanna and I and Granny Anne prayed for a good outcome."

Before the two leave the room to eat dinner with the others Bing calls first Gus and then Sean. When the two agree to meet the following day for lunch at Bing and Stella's, Derek and Bing are relieved and at the same time sorry for Gus who's only child has given him only grief and for Sean who has finally gotten over a woman who only uses the men in her life.

Chapter Sixteen

That night when Jack and Lucy are getting into clean pajamas after their bath, Jack looks from Derek to Flannery and asked, "Daddy, since you and Aunt Flannery like to sleep together, why doesn't Aunt Flannery sleep here in our room?"

He looks first at Derek, who has the old twinkle in his eyes that Flannery loves, then at Flannery who is grinning at the innocent question. Then he looks at the bed and back to them. "There's enough room even if all four of us sleep on our backs."

"Well now, Aunt Flannery do you want to lay on the bed with the three of us and see if there is enough room for one more sleeper?"

Always a good sport Flannery is the first to lie down on the blue and white quilted bed. Lucy crawls across the bed to lie beside her Aunt Flannery. Next it's Jack who is smiling a happy smile and then Derek whose eyes twinkle even more.

"See Daddy I knew we would all fit. Won't it be cozy? Because adults go to bed later than children, Lucy and I will sleep in the center, then you and Aunt Flannery can sleep on either side of us. Ok!"

"Have you been thinking about this since you saw us sleeping together on the sofa?" Derek asked his still smiling and hopeful son.

"Yeah!" is all Jack said in reply.

Derek looks hopefully at Flannery and asked, "What do you think? Do you want to have a sleep over with us, a pajama party for four? It will be only for tonight."

Flannery is now lying on her side and looks across Jack and Lucy to Derek and smiles before she said, "I would be delighted to sleep with the three of you. I think we need to let Granny Anne know, so she doesn't think I have runaway during the night."

"After we read the bedtime story we will go and give Granny Anne the message. "Derek tells a happy Lucy and an even happier Jack.

"Yeah," Jack said as he kisses first Derek, then Lucy and finally Flannery.

After their showers and dressed for bed, Flannery and Derek head downstairs to deliver the nights news to Granny Anne.

Granny Anne is sitting on the screened back porch enjoying the sounds of an early summer's night, waiting for the three dogs to do their last bathroom trip for the night. Though the light on the porch is minimal, because the light from the kitchen stove is all that aluminates the porch, Derek and Flannery don't see her sitting in one of the wooden rockers beside a porch window. The two jump with a start when she said with a laugh, "From the look on your happy faces I'm thinking something monumental must have been decided."

"Yes, you can say that." Derek tells her as he goes to sit on the glider nearby.

"Jack has decided that Derek, Lucy, Jack and I should sleep in the same bed because he saw us sleeping on the sofa, a decided we must like sleeping together." Flannery adds as she kisses her Granny Anne's cheek, before going to sit on the glider with Derek.

"Jack's an extremely smart boy. He can see, like all those who know and love the two of you that you are much happier together. I think his idea is excellent. It will give the four of you a chance to see what life together would be like." said Granny Anne with the voice of wisdom.

"The question is, will four of you fit in the bed together?"

"Jack had the four of us lying on our backs and yes we fit nicely with a bit of room to spare." Flannery tells her Grandmother with the wisp of a smile.

"I think Jack spent the day figuring it all out. He even decided that he and Lucy will sleep in the middle of the bed, so that when Flannery and I come later we can each sleep on one side."

Anne looks at the two steadily then tells them, "I agree with Jack. Nothing brings a family closer than spending the nights wrapped in one another's arms."

"What would Reverend Grant think of our arrangement?" Flannery asked because she has always tried to follow the beliefs of the Presbyterian Church that her family and Derek's have attended for years. The Reverend is young and fairly new to the church and the ministry but he and Granny Anne have gotten to know each other well in the five years that he has minister at her church.

"Keith, Reverend Grant knows the human heart well. He is not one to pass judgment on us. He is a minister who teaches by example. He and I have had many a discussion on couples and relationships in general. He'd heard all the rumors of Derek marrying Chloe after your wedding was cancelled. He is well aware of all that Derek has gone through with Chloe and that he is a wonderful father to Jack and Lucy."

Flannery looks from her grandmother to Derek who seems perfectly fine with the conversation about him and his children. "Your Grandmother invited Reverend Grant and his wife Linda here for dinner the first month they were here. Anne, my parents, Gus and I were all here and we let the Reverend know what rumors were fact and what was a lie."

"It was then that he told us he tries to live by example and that he doesn't judge others. He is well aware that the Lord is our only judge. He did say that anytime I needed a break from being father and mother to Jack and Lucy that he and Linda would happily take them for several hours or days. They were trying to have a baby back then and wanted all the experience they could get. I guess you know that after several years of trying Linda gave birth to twins, a boy and a girl in February."

Flannery nods her head at the information and said, "So your saying Reverend Grant will not put a curse on us if we sleep in the bed with Jack and Lucy?"

"That's exactly right." Granny Anne and Derek say in unison.

"Speaking of bed, I'm bringing the dogs in and heading that way myself. Good night my loves," Granny Anne tells them as she gets up from the rocker and goes to let the three dogs in.

Once Derek and Flannery greet each dog and give Granny Anne a hug and kiss, they head back into the house and up the stairs and bed. When they reach the upstairs hallway Flannery stops and tells Derek, "I better go to the bathroom then I won't be waking anyone during the night."

"I'll meet you inside. How about you sleep next to Lucy and I will sleep next to Jack. That's only if you are alright with this new arrangement."

Flannery wraps her arms around his neck, smiles into his eyes and said, "This is the best offer I have had in years. Why would I be opposed to it?"

"I am also making a big boy and girl happy." she replies as she moves from him and turns to go to the bathroom.

"Yes, you are definitely making a big boy happy. "He said as she saunters into her room for only the time it takes to pee.

As he leaves the hallway and opens the door to the room where his children sleep he remembers a quote by Robert Louis Stevenson, '*The best things in life are nearest: breath in your nostrils, light in your eyes, flowers at your feet, duties at your hand, the path of right just before you.*' Derek now knows that he would also add '*Love is the best of all that life offers, love of God and Jesus, love of family and friends, and most of all the love for and from a person who loves you in return.*'

Chapter Seventeen

It is five a.m. when Flannery opens her eyes and for a brief moment wonders where she is. She is on her right side facing the room's wide windows, and remembers she is in bed with Derek and his children. She can see from the light outside the window that it is early morning. The window is opened several inches and she can hear birds in the backyard trees beginning the new day with song. In a maple tree closest to the house she hears the many songs of the resident Mockingbird. She loves all of God's creatures, but has a special place in her heart for the Mockingbirds. Although she knows the birds die off after only a few years she always calls the talented singer Piper, and because she hopes he has a mate, she always calls the female Paisley. She knows that one reason she loves the Mocking birds is because her father James would sit in Granny Anne's backyard with her and they would whistle a variety of tunes to see if the birds would mock them. The birds never failed to memorize each and every tune that she and her father would whistle.

She listens to the early morning sounds but hears only the birds. She rolls from her side to her back for a moment and stretches her five foot nine frame as quietly as she can. From her back she rolls to her left side and there is Derek also awake and seriously studying her face. She cannot help but smile. When she agreed to Jack's request that she sleep with Derek and his two children, she thought that she would probably not sleep well, to her sweet surprise it was the most peaceful sleep she has had in the last six years. They watch each other until Flannery's eyes close once more and she goes back to sleep.

To his surprise Derek also falls back to sleep. When he awakened and saw Flannery lying beside Lucy, he'd though he was hallucinating, but then he remembered Jack's request. "Thank you Jack." he whispers under his breath. Like Flannery, the sleep was the most restful he has had in six years. He knows though that they will have to tell Jack that it was only a temporary arrangement. In fairness to all involved, he and Flannery don't know each other as they once did. Time away from each other and the circumstances as to why they were not together has changed them immeasurably. He is no longer the romantic, optimistic man that she once knew, and she is no longer the wide-eyed girl who believed he was her prince charming.

When he awakens again it is seven a.m. Derek quietly slips from the bed and the three people that have a big chunk of his heart and as quietly as possible collects his clothing for the day. He would have slept longer at least until Flannery awakened again, but he has a few thing to do before he leaves for his parent's house and the scheduled meeting with Bing, Sean and Gus.

Granny Anne, a morning person like Derek is up and preparing a pot of tea. She gives Derek a bright smile that tells him she loves his presence as much as he loves hers. Without the love and graciously given help with Jack and Lucy from Granny Anne and his parents Derek knows he would not have been able to keep his life and that of his children as normal as he did.

He walks to where she stands beside the kitchen sink and gives her a kiss on the cheek. She also gives Derek a warm hug and kiss. "Well now, it appears that you have had a good night's sleep." she tells Derek whose eyes look rested but serious.. After he and Flannery broke up she saw the same seriousness most of the time. The only time he was completely relaxed was when he played with Jack and Lucy.

"Yes, it was the most peaceful sleep I have had in six years. It was a good sleep, but I have to tell Jack and Lucy that the arrangement is only temporary, and only for the one night. I know that my kids, you, my parents and everyone who knows us would like for us to take up where were six years ago, but that is not possible. I am definitely not the same man and Flannery is also not the same woman."

Anne is thoughtful as she prepares a pot of tea and slips four slices of whole grain bread, into the four slice toaster on the counter top, then pulls two ceramic mugs, with Chicago logos, from hooks beneath one of the cabinets, opens the cream colored wooden cabinet doors and pulls out two cereal bowls and two sandwich plates. With this task complete and her thoughts clear in her mind she said, "Yes, I agree, as I know Flannery would, the two of you are not the same people, but I see in both of you a light of hope."

"The two of you have gone through a lot, especially you, but I know that you and Flannery are survivors and in my heart I feel that the Lord is offering the two of you a second chance. I know that if you ask the Lord for guidance he will show you clearly what you must do to strengthen your relationship. He will also give you the grace that you need to forgive one another."

"I know that my granddaughter doesn't pray for herself since your breakup, though I do know she has never stopped praying for others, including you. And if I am correct in my assumption, you also have stopped praying for yourself."

When the toast pops up, Derek spreads butter on it, cuts the slices crosswise and takes it to the round wooden table near the room's French doors. He and Anne fill their bowls with Cheerios and milk, a mug with tea and cream and go and sit side by side at the table.

Derek sips his tea, takes a bite of his toast and then tells Anne, "You're right about prayer. I leave it up to others to pray for me. For a while I stopped believing in prayer and God, but once Jack and Lucy became part of my life I knew that God does exist, so I have left me and my life in His hands, and I, like Flannery pray for the people in my life."

"I know, because you and my parents have told me that the three of you have never given up hope that Flannery and I will get back together. We will have this year to get to know each other, where the relationship goes from here is entirely up to the Lord."

"Time together will be a good thing. Because you will be together a great deal, I feel that you will see both the good and irritating side to your relationship." Anne smiles and the conversation ends for the moment while they eat and think about all that has been said. "

When their breakfast is over, Derek helps clear the table and rinsing the dishes places them in the dishwasher. He loves Anne, she is also like a granny to him, and he asks, because he forgot in the seriousness of their conversation, "How was your sleep."

"It was peaceful until our resident Mockingbird Piper started serenading the critters in the backyard."

"I could hear him from the bedroom. Flannery raised the window a few inches before we went to bed.

Granny Anne's heart fills with happiness every time she hears her granddaughter's name. She lost her parents, her husband and her son much too soon, but raising Flannery from the age of four was a wonderful blessing. She and Flannery may not see each other every day, as they did when she was young, but they are as close in mind, spirit and body as any two people can be.

"I guess she and the children are still sleeping." she said as she wipes the counters with a wet paper towel.

"Flannery was awake around five. I felt her when she moved from her right side to her back. When she rolled towards me and the kids she saw that I was also awake. We didn't say anything, though we did look at each other until we both fell back to sleep."

Anne hears the old happiness in Derek's voice and she thanks the Lord where she stands. Derek may have his doubts and fears of them becoming an item again, but Anne also sees a dim light of hope in Derek's dark eyes.

The two are nearly finished eating when a bright and cheerful faced Flannery walks into the sunny kitchen. Dressed in denim shorts and a white t-shirt that says *I Love Scotland*, she first goes to Anne for a morning kiss. She smiles her brightest smile for Derek, and then sits in the chair next to him.

"Well now, I see that I am not the only one who slept well."

She sits there until her stomach protests and while Derek makes another pot of tea Flannery makes herself a bowl of oatmeal and a slice of whole grain toast.

While she eats, the three talk about their plans for the day and the very important meeting that Bing and Derek will be having with Gus and Sean about Chloe and her drug use.

While Anne and Flannery feed the pets Derek goes upstairs to awaken his children. He wants to sit with them while they eat, and he always makes certain that they wear clean clothing, have their hair brushed as well as their teeth. Chloe's maternal instincts are zero. Derek's fraternal instincts are one hundred percent intact. Chloe would never win Mother of the year, but Derek could definitely win Father of the year.

"Why don't the five of us go to a movie and dinner when I get back? The four of you choose the movie and restaurant. I will be back at least by three. If I'll be later than that I will call." Derek tells an excited Jack and Lucy who love movies and eating out.

At eleven Derek tells them goodbye and heads out the door to drive the short distance to his parent's house. He hasn't talked to his brother Sean in several months, and that was not a pleasant meeting for either of them. Though Derek has not forgiven Sean for his part in Chloe's deceptions, Derek know that he will one day, just not yet.

Chapter Eighteen

Bing, as usual, sits on the front porch of his home, a place where he has lived since he married Hanna. He and Derek's mother Hanna had planned a big family because they both came from homes where they were the one and only child. The house though big by some standards is not big compared to other houses in the gated community. With five generous acres around each home, there is a country feel about the community. Although the community was built in several stages, the landscaping is beautiful with huge trees, oak, maple, cherry, plum, apple, dog wood to name a few. With pines and evergreens thrown in the mix, the community always shows the lovely colors of each season. Though some of the homes are built with the back acreage facing the community golf course, Bing and Hanna chose to be away from the eyes of the golfers and golf course groundskeepers. They had considered getting a pool but decided it was safer to take Derek to the country club pool instead. Bing loves to swim and does so several times a week, but is glad he doesn't have a pool in the yard. When he and Stella have Jack and Lucy over they don't have a pool to worry about. The two can play in their yard with the dogs without fear they or the dogs will fall into a pool.

As always, son and father greet with a warm hug and kiss on the cheek. Though Bing's father wasn't one for showing outward affection his mother Charlotte was. It was from his short time with her that Bing learned the importance of physical affection. Hanna never knew her father but was taught to be affectionate by her mother. He and Hanna made a point of being affectionate with Derek. When he married Stella, after Hanna's death and they had Sean, he and Stella made certain that both Derek and Sean knew how much they are loved. It is because of their example that Derek and Sean are extremely openly affectionate. Bing and all who know Sean could never figure out his attraction to Chloe. After they greet, Bing said as he looks at his inexpensive Timex watch. "Why don't we wait here for Sean and Gus? They should be here soon. Stella and I have the food ready and waiting in the refrigerator. Stella was generous and made club sandwiches, potato salad, a fruit salad, plus iced tea and lemonade."

"Mom is always generous. The Lord knew what he was doing when he had you hire Stella, at Mom's insistence, all those years ago."

"Yes, that was one of the many blessings the Lord has rained down on us. Of course you might not want to use the words all those years ago."

Derek laughs with Bing and they talk of the day-to-day until Sean and Gus who arrive at the same time meet them on the porch. Sean like his father and brother is tall and trim. Gus is tall but needs to lose at least fifteen pounds to be at a healthy weight. Gus and Rena eat out for most of their meals and Gus knows that is why he has packed on the unhealthy pounds. Only recently has he gone back to swimming most mornings in the pool in his back yard. His hair is thick and steel gray and his eyes a pale blue. He is a sweet and kind man and it is because of this that Rena and his daughter Chloe have him wrapped around their little finger.

Sean greets Bing, as Derek did only minutes before. Gus, Bing and Derek greet each other as they always have over the years, with friendliness and some affection. Although Derek has never felt close to Rena, he and Gus respect each other and always show affection when they meet. Derek was always surprised that Chloe had none of her father friendliness.

Sean studies Derek as Derek studies his younger brother. Sean holds his right hand out to Derek and Derek decides it is time to forgive. He takes Sean's hand and pulls him close for a hug that is a long time in coming.

Bing and Gus smile at the show of affectionate forgiveness between brothers, and Gus said, "Sean I know that we, you and I have a few issues we need to discuss and since this appears to be a day of forgiveness will you forgive me for blaming you for Chloe's waywardness."

Without hesitation Sean covers the short space between himself and Gus and once more holds his hand out in forgiveness.

Once the greetings are over, the four go into the sunny yet cool house to enjoy the wonderful lunch that Stella prepared for them.

They enjoy the meal and each other's company and decide they will leave the issue of Chloe until lunch is over. They know that stress and healthy digestion don't mix well and want to enjoy Stella's gift of the generous meal.

When lunch is over the four go to Bing's library office and sitting in the comfortable wing chairs in the room begin their discussion of Chloe and what, if anything, they can do to help her.

Derek tells the three what Jack told him about Chloe sniffing powdered sugar up her nose.

A look of sadness washes across Gus' kind face. In his late sixties Gus has aged considerably in the past fifteen years. Those who know him don't have to ask why. Chloe and Rena are why, especially Chloe, the daughter that he loves dearly, but has never been able to reel in. He knows part of the reason is Rena, his wife of twenty-seven years. Rena has not once sided with him in disciplining Chloe. Rena let Chloe do whatever made her happy and they have in the last ten years seen their daughter ruin her life, Sean's life and especially Derek and Flannery's lives. He now knows that he and Rena must join forces to save their wayward daughter from total destruction.

Gus has never faulted Derek for the way Chloe acts. He knows despite Chloe's lies and deception of Jack's conception that Derek has gone out of his way to make a go of their sham of a marriage. When Derek told him in March that he was divorcing Chloe and getting full custody of Jack and Lucy, Gus knew it was best for all their sakes. To Derek's credit he has extended a hand of friendship to Gus and Rena. Derek has told him he is Jack and Lucy's grandfather and he may spend as much time with them as he likes. Derek's only request is that Gus and Rena do not leave them alone with Chloe. Though it tears at his heart, Gus knows that his only child was a horrible wife and mother.

"Do you know where Chloe stays?" is the first of many questions that Gus answers.

"The night that she hurt Jack and Lucy, she was with me and Rena. She stayed for three days and then supposedly went to stay with her friend Mia. Where she is now is anyone's guess."

"I had no idea until Bing told me that she had abused Lucy and Jack. When I found out, several days later, she was no longer at home. Although she has called several times she won't tell us where she is. I guess she is well aware that she could still be arrested for child abuse." Gus said with tears in his voice.

The three men sitting around Gus have a good deal of empathy for the kind and generous man and know that their friendship and understanding will go a long way in helping Gus survive yet another Chloe incident.

Bing has taken it upon himself to go on the internet and get all the information on drug use and addictions and the possible recovery treatment programs. Quietly the four read all that Bing has printed and help Gus decide on a plan that may help Chloe. They know that a treatment plan will work only if Chloe agrees to get help. They also know that her agreeing to help is a huge step for Chloe. Though extremely pretty and dressed to the tees, Chloe has always felt inferior to anyone who is scholastically inclined. With a lisp since childhood, and a learning disability, she has always gone out of her way to criticize anyone who strives to succeed. Flannery has always been the biggest thorn in her side. At five foot nine to Chloe's five feet one, slim and graceful, where Chloe has always had to watch her weight, plus extremely intelligent and an A student who makes friends easily, Chloe has always felt inferior to her older half-sister.

All who know Chloe know that one reason she clung to Sean is because Sean has never strived to reach his full potential. Although he's intelligent, Sean has never applied himself to learning or keeping a job. Not until he was hired on a construction crew, remodeling houses has Sean shown his light. Chloe never belittled Sean until after he told her they were through, in March and again the night he told her to stop verbally abusing Jack and Lucy.

For some time Sean has suspected that Jack is definitely his son. He knows that Lucy belongs to Derek. True Lucy has blonde hair like him and Chloe and the brown eyes that he, Derek and Bing have, but Lucy has Derek's wide smile and Derek's deceased mother's nose and the dimple that Derek and Hanna have in their right cheek. After Derek and Chloe married and Jack was born, Sean stayed away from them out of courtesy and because he figured out that he and not Derek was Jack's father. He knows in his heart that Derek is a wonderful man and the father that Jack needs and deserves, and so he didn't tell Derek the truth until this past March, He loves Derek, and misses the closeness that they once shared, but is happy that Derek has forgiven him at least. In March is when he also told Derek that he and Chloe had restarted their affair after Lucy was born. Sean knew he was going against all that his parents had taught him, but Chloe and sex with Chloe had become his damning addiction of choice. There are things about her that he loves and things that he detests, but he is willing to help her get over her addiction if she will let him.

"I have a feeling that Chloe is either at her friend Mia's or at the condo in Hawaii." Sean tells the three thoughtful men sitting around him.

"That's a possibility. I mean she could be in Hawaii at the condo. She called me the day she received the divorce papers asking for spousal support." Derek looks at Gus after saying this and tells Chloe's father. "I guess I wasn't too diplomatic with her. I told her the best thing for her and all of us would be for her to get a job or live in Hawaii."

"I understand your anger and frustration with her. Chloe has never made it easy to love her or try to help her. My daughter is her own worst enemy. I know that you and the grandchildren had a rough time living with her. I'm not making excuses for her but I believe that she has always felt less than others because of her learning disabilities. "

"It didn't help that she was truant from school most of the time and that she finally quite at the age of sixteen."

"Yes, I could see that she tried to hide her feelings of insecurity by acting like she didn't give a darn what anyone thought of her." Derek said as he looks through the information Bing had printed on drug treatment facilities in Hawaii.

He hi-lights one that sounds promising, then hands the page to Gus. "If she's in Hawaii I will definitely check this out."

"I have Mia's phone number. I know she is actually a friend who cares about Chloe, and I bet she, if anyone, knows exactly where Chloe is. "Said Sean as he takes the paper that Gus had just looked at.

Sean pulls his cell phone from his pocket, turns it on and finding Mia's number calls her. The phone rings only once and Sean said, "Mia its Sean can you tell me where Chloe is?"

Sean asked several more questions before thanking Mia for the needed information and ending the call.

"She's in Hawaii. Mia said she left only days after Derek had the divorce papers served." Sean stops for a moment as though trying to decide if he should give all the information that Mia gave to him. With three men looking expectantly at him, he decides it is best to lay it all on the line.

"Mia caught her using cocaine and told her she would not be able to stay with her if she continued. Chloe was on a plane that evening and

Mia hasn't heard from her since she left, although one night a few days ago Mia's phone rang, but before she could answer someone hung up. A few minutes later the phone rang again, but Mia let it go to voice mail. No message was left, but then an hour later she received a text message which said only, thank you for being my friend. I love you. Don't worry. I will start a new life here and maybe once I get my act together you will come for a visit. There was no name in the text message, but Mia knew it was from Chloe because Chloe never failed to tell Mia how much she prized their friendship." Sean stops for a moment to think about this side of Chloe. Though she was never unkind to him she never told him of her feelings about their relationship.

Sean closes his eyes trying to get the memories of her from his mind. He wants to help her but also knows that he won't be in relationship with her again. The entire affair was unhealthy for both of them. When he opens his eyes he tells Gus, "Mia said to tell you that Chloe also said to tell you that she loves you. Mia also said that she wants to know how things go with Chloe."

Gus blinks his blue eyes several times and runs his finger under each and then he said, "It's good to know that Chloe has a friend like Mia. Chloe never made it easy to like her. I'll book a flight to Hawaii and Rena and I will go and see what Chloe is doing."

"You don't have to book a flight. I will call one of the pilots for our company jet and you and Rena can go whenever you want." said Bing who cannot imagine the pain and heartache Gus is going through. Although Sean has never been a model son, he is thankful that Sean has never used drugs, nor does he consume alcohol.

"Thanks. Tomorrow morning would be fine. Rena will have to find someone to keep an eye on her Fox Terriers while we're gone. We used to take them on the planes, but they are older and don't like all the noise." said Gus as he gets up from the leather chair and picking up the pages of information on drug rehabs stacks them in a tidy pile.

"You can bring the dogs here. Or if you like I can come over later tonight and bring them back here. Stella keeps telling me that her Scottie Shane is lonely and needs a friend. Keeping an eye on Rena's terriers will give us an idea of how Shane would like having a new friend." Bing tells Gus as he also rises from his chair to give Gus a much needed hug.

"That would help a great deal" Gus said as Derek and Sean stand and also give Gus a hug.

"I'd best go and tell Rena what my plan is. She may protest, but she will be on the plane even if I have to hog tie her."

The four men walk from the comfortable office and outside to Gus' car. "Thank Again." Gus said as he opens the driver side door,

"Please let us know how Chloe is. Stella and I will be over before dark to get Rena's dogs." Bing tells Gus as he sits in the driver's seat.

"I'll make sure Rena has all their supplies ready and thanks again."

Bing and his sons stand in the driveway until they can see Gus's white Ford Escape no more, and then they go inside to talk with Stella.

Bing and James knew Gus for several years before James' death. A realtor by trade and diplomatic and a people person Gus is easy to like. Like Bing and James Gus worked long and hard and has one of the most well-known real estate agencies anywhere in the U.S. He is also generous and gives numerous sums of money to several charities.

Chapter Nineteen

Later that evening after dinner out and a movie, and once Jack and Lucy are sleeping, Derek sits in Anne's living room on the sofa with Flannery, and Anne in a rocker nearby and tells them about his meeting at his parent's house with Gus, Bing and Sean.

He tells them about Sean's conversation with Chloe's friend Mia and that Gus and Rena will be flying to Hawaii the next day to try and get Chloe into a rehab on Maui.

The three sit quietly reflecting on Chloe and all that Mia has told Sean. Anne is first to speak and she tells them, "We must each say a special prayer for Chloe and getting off the drugs and also for Gus and Rena. I know it has to be difficult for them. It's too bad that Chloe has always alienated most people who know her. It is wonderful that she has a friend like Mia."

"Yes I will pray for them." Flannery tells the two with a yawn. "I'm going to get ready for bed."

"I'll be down here for a while. Jack is disappointed that you won't be sleeping with us, but I feel it is best this way."

"You're right. Good night," Flannery tells the two, kisses Anne's cheek and heads up the stairs.

The two watch her go and then Anne tells Derek good night and he goes outside to the back porch steps to smoke. While at Bing and Stella's he looked for the discarded pack of cigarettes he'd left behind, but apparently Stella had thrown them out. His Dad, Stella and Anne know of his dirty habits, though they have never said anything negative about them. He figures they know that he needs the cigarettes and whisky for the stress he's been under. On his way from his parents, he stopped to fuel the van and bought a pack of cigarettes. Normally he would buy a carton, but hopes that by buying only the pack he can get a hold on the smoking.

Though he knows Flannery always opens her bedroom window at night, and that this window is directly over the porch, whose steps he sets on, he lights up anyway. Hopefully she is asleep and won't smell the smoke.

The dogs have followed him outside and lie around at his bare feet. He sleeps in knit workout shorts and a sleeveless workout t-shirt most nights because his children usually end up in bed with him. Though they have seen him in his boxers, and think nothing of it, he feels it is only right that he is decently dressed when they climb in his bed.

He and Sean also would sleep with Bing and Stella when they were young boys, Bing always wore a t-shirt and workout short the times that they did. Stella always wore a modest nightie, like the ones Granny Anne wears. Because his parents have a loving relationship, he knows they didn't always wear proper clothing to bed. His guess is that when they have the house to themselves they forego any bed clothes at all at least he hopes they do.

As he smokes he lets his mind wonder to the future and the year ahead. Except for the trip to Scotland in the autumn he hasn't made any concrete plans. He and his children will be free to do whatever they want whenever they want. He has lived by schedules far too long, and though he wouldn't normally live on a whim he will do so for now.

Flannery is reading a novel from Anne's large collection of books, and can smell the cigarette smoke dancing into her room. The first night there she had thought she was dreaming the unpleasant odor. She puts her book aside and looks into the back yard. Seeing the dim light from the light on the back porch, and knowing that Derek is up, she goes down stairs to investigate.

When she opens the back door she sees Derek sitting on the top step and he is smoking a cigarette. She is not judgmental by nature but is surprised at his habit. While they were together neither of them tried any mind altering substances. Of course he has been under lots of stress, so maybe that is why.

"Well hello Flannery. I was wondering when you would eventually come and find out who was smoking in your backyard. I was hoping that the wind would take the smoke away, but I guess I was wrong."

When she hesitates to say anything, Derek pats the step next to him, and adds, "Take a load off Flannery. Sit and let's talk about old times."

She walks towards him and slowly sits inches away. The smoke is blowing her way, and she starts to get up. Derek crushes the stub out on the step below them and drops it into a flower pot filled with garden soil. Next he picks up a glass half filled with an amber liquid he takes a sip and offers the glass to Flannery. She shakes her head no, and frowns, then bights her lip before she bravely asks, "I'm not judging you, but I was wondering why you stayed with Chloe for nearly six years if your life was so bad that you now smoke and drink alcohol."

He takes another sip of the drink, swirls the liquid around the glass, takes another sip and answers her question. "Well since you ask, I will tell you. I stayed because of Jack and Lucy because I foolishly hoped that Chloe would change. You know, grow up and become a mother to them. When that did not happen, I threw in the preverbal towel and got my divorce."

She thinks he is finished with his answer and starts to get up from the steps. When he pushed her with force back down, she is in total shock, Although he sees the shock on her face, he is going to tell her exactly how he feels about the last few years with Chloe but also why he really broke off their engagement only months before their wedding.

"I will also tell you why I broke off our engagement. The truth is, I felt like I came second to your writing and your life in Scotland. "His voice is hard and his words fierce and Flannery doesn't know how to respond to the angry man sitting beside her.

"I felt that you didn't really love me. If you did you would have been here more instead of thousands of miles away. I know you love Scotland because your father was born there, but this is my country, our country. I also love going there, but to visit. I was on my own and missed you, but you never acted like you missed me."

"I… she begins, but he said, "Shut up Flannery, you asked me a question and I fully intend to give you the answer."

When he said shut up with force, she blinks her eyes to keep the surprise tears from falling. He sees the tears and angrily said, "Oh please, tears I'm not going to fall for that old ploy. I may have fallen for your tears when we were together, but I think your tears are a bunch of crap."

"Tell me Flannery do you have any nasty habits that you've acquired since our parting. Do you drink alcohol, smoke pot or are you still the lily white little angel that you have always been."

She refuses to give into his insults and whipping the last of the tears away sits stoically while he tells her exactly what he thinks of her.

"So nothing to say in your own defense, perhaps you shouldn't have opened the can of worms that has been my horrific life for nearly six years, those ashes that I cannot brush away with a broom or sweep under the carpet You want to talk about those ashes, let's do just that.".

This enlivens her and she immediately tells him, "You chose the life you have led. Gus didn't hold a shotgun to your head. You could have chosen to wait until Jack was born, and had a DNA testing done. I believe that you wanted that life despite your denial and the accusations that I am the reason for that choice."

This time she is up and half way across the porch when he laughs outright, not a laugh of glee, but of anger, and he tells her, "You're right. I wanted a family. I asked you several times to elope with me but no, Flannery had to have the huge wedding in Scotland. I never wanted a big wedding."

"Well you never said you didn't and I cannot read minds, thank God."

"Chloe may have lied, but at least she wasn't afraid to go after what she wanted. She was never afraid of sex and all that goes with it. I will bet you are still a virgin, still the saint who won't let a man touch her boobs, or feel her up."

With this, she walks through the door and over her shoulder said to his surprise then delight, "Derek shut the fuck up."

As she walks into the kitchen, she hears him say, "Why Flannery you have quite the potty mouth. Does your Granny know that you talk like a sailor?"

Her last words to him, as she leaves the enclosed sunroom are, "Fuck off Derek".

She takes Anne's car keys from a hook beside a kitchen cabinet, walks down the hallway to Anne's room and seeing her light on, and her Granny sitting in a recliner asks, "Granny Anne, would you mind if I borrow your car for a few hours? I need to get away for a while. "

"Certainly you may. Please drive safely and take your cell phone" Before she can turn to leave the room Derek is beside her and takes the keys from her hand.

"Granny Anne I'll drive Flannery, that way she'll be safe."

Anne cocks her head and because she heard Flannery's words of ire, said, "Just don't fight while driving." Then she looks at her extremely irritated granddaughter and tells her, "Flannery I heard you swearing at Derek. I have told you ladies do not use such language. Jack and Lucy don't need to hear that kind of language so stifle it." Flannery shrugs her shoulders, turns and walks out of the room.

She knows swearing sounds horrible, and has only started doing so in the past six years. When Derek asked if she has any vices, she'd conveniently forgotten the swearing. She has to be really frustrated or upset to use such words and Derek has definitely upset her.

She hears him call her name and stops halfway to the kitchen to see what he wants. She has absolutely no intention of riding with him, but decides to see what he wants.

"What do you want," she asked with irritation.

"I'll drive you, where are you planning to go?"

"I know for a fact that I would rather be chased by a pack of rabid dogs or stocked by a serial killer than spend even one more moment with you."

"Ah, be a sport Flannery. Let me drive you."

"No I don't need your help." With this said she is through the house and out the front door before he can catch a breath.

When he reaches the garage, she is not there and he knows she is most likely walking down the road to Geneva. He is correct in is assumption. She is nearly a mile down the road when he rolls the passenger side window and as he pulls beside her said, "Get in the car Flannery."

She refuses to look his way but said, "Shove it Derek wherever it gives you the most pleasure."

"Ah Flannery, I never thought you would hold a grudge. The next time you ask a personal question be very careful what you ask because I am not one to color coat anything. I tell it like it is even if it hurts."

Here she turns and glares at him which makes him laugh. This also irritates her and she sticks her middle finger into the air for him to see and continues to walk to Geneva.

'I guess I'll have to tell your Granny about that finger move. What will she think about that?"

She tries to ignore him, so she thinks about where she is headed at ten p.m. and knows she's going to Minnie's Restaurant. She'd eaten dinner but the anger has her famished and Minnie's is just the place to go when one is famished. As she walks, and ignores the still driving and talking

Derek she plans what she will order. She is so into her order that she fails to see Derek pull to the curb, park the car, and walk to her. She is off her feet and being hoisted over his broad shoulder before she knows it.

"Why you horses ass, put me down." She pounds his back and kicks him and all he does is laugh heartily. In a jiff he's plopping her into the front passenger seat and then hooks the seat belt around her. She goes to unhook the seat belt, but he is faster and refuses to let her. In his dark as night eyes she sees mischief and determination, so decides to stay put. She glares at him and he pats her cheek and closes the car door. He looks at her through the opened window and wags a finger in her face. She grabs his finger and goes to bite it but he pulls away, pats her head and said to her exasperation, "Stay Flannery, stay."

Nonchalantly he opens the driver's side door, sits, hooks his seatbelt, puts the car in drive and heads down the road. "Where do you want to go? I'm at your service you rowdy, dirty talking vixen."

""Minnie's." is all she said before he does just that. He hums to himself and keeps taking peeks at her and grinning. This also irritates her, but she is tired of fighting so ignores him.

Minnie's is one of his and her favorite places to eat. The food is excellent, cooked by Minnie's husband Joe. Not only is the food wonderful, so are Minnie and Joe. Derek and Flannery and their families have known them for years. Flannery, Nell, and Derek worked at Minnie's in the summer months their last two years of high school, and Derek and Flannery worked there their summers while in college. Nell wanted to become a hair stylist, but didn't have the money for cosmetology school so worked at Minnie's full time her year after high school graduation. When she became pregnant and had to stop work or lose her baby, Flannery and Anne stepped in and helped her and Virginia financially. They also paid the tuition for Nell to go to school.

Nell has told only few people who Kristen's father is and didn't want him involved in their lives, so Virginia volunteered to babysit while Nell went to school. Nell's mother was Virginias only child, and she and Anne have much in common. When Nell became pregnant again when Kristen was five and gave birth to her son Tyler, Virginia didn't hesitate to volunteer to babysit again. When Tyler was two Mary was born, and Virginia was as delighted with Mary as she is with Kristen and Tyler. Nell may not have told most people who their father is, and no one asks or cares. Her children are sweet, loving and considered a gift by Virginia and Nell.

When Kristen was no longer breast feeding, Nell started to cosmetology school and knew she'd found her calling. She was hired soon after she graduated by a woman in Geneva who had a salon in her house. Nell worked for her for two years and when Flannery found out that Nell wanted her own shop, she and Nell found the perfect spot for her business. A three story building with a basement was for sale in Geneva, on a busy street, but needed lots of renovation. Flannery wanted to give Nell the money Nell refused but did take Flannery up on a loan, which Nell has nearly paid back. The shop is modern and sleek yet a comfortable place to spend an hour or two.

The business is so successful that Nell has hired Kathy that she once worked for plus six others. The two apartments above the salon are now being renovated to rent out.

When he pulls into the parking lot it is nearly full. He has to drive to the back of the restaurant to find a spot. As he pulls into the last spot available Flannery unhooks her seatbelt, opens the door and is around the restaurant before he has the car parked. "Damn! I guess she's really upset." This he said to the night breeze because she is in the restaurant waiting for a seat before he comes in the door behind her.

Minnie sees them from the back of the dining area, walks to where they stand smiles at two of her favorite people, hugs and kisses the cheek of each, looks closely at them and said with a laugh, "I see storm clouds over Flannery's head. I wasn't aware that rain is in the forecast."

Flannery shakes her head and Derek tells Minnie. "Flannery and I have been traveling to the past and apparently the journey has been a little too bumpy for her."

She glares at him and he of course laughs, and Minnie shakes her head and asks, "Will you need menus?"

"No I know what I want." Flannery tells Minnie as Minnie leads them to a booth at the back of the dining area.

Flannery slides into the periwinkle blue vinyl booth and sits in the center. Derek sits beside her, bumps her with his slim hip and said with a wink moves over, "I need space to sit."

"Sit on the other side. I don't want you in my face."

Derek raises his dark brows at her grins and winking at Minnie said to annoy Flannery, "The woman's in need of a meal, perhaps then she will calm down."

"You're feuding huh? Perhaps food is the ticket. When Joe and I were newlyweds we had many a feud then we would eat. Of course the more we would feud the more we would eat so we were packing on the pounds. So instead of food, we decided to make love after our fights and you know what, we not only lost weight we grew closer." Her eyes travel from Derek's grinning face to Flannery's highly irritated one, and she adds, "Since neither of you is gaining weight I guess food will help for now."

"Flannery what would you like?" Flannery counts the decorative pins that Minnie wears on her apron front, and there are many, one that Flannery brought back from Scotland several years before of thistle with amethyst stones adorning it.

"I want a grilled cheese sandwich, cream of tomato soup, French fries, a large root beer, a glass of water and for dessert your yummy triple berry pie with two scoops of French vanilla ice cream, and a drizzle of chocolate syrup on everything."

Derek chuckles and Minnie smiles, then she takes Derek's order. "I'll have the same. Since Flannery is eating like a lumber jack I will too. I noticed when I had to throw her over my shoulder to make her ride in the car with me that her back side is getting a tad wide. If she continues to pound the food I will need all the strength I can get if I have to carry her butt very far."

'You are hilarious. If I weren't so hungry and irritated by your nonsense I might laugh. If you must know, I weigh exactly what I did in high school."

He looks sideways at her and gives her the once over and tells Minnie, "I guess the weight is shifting to her butt."

Minnie shakes her head and tells them she will be back with their drinks.

They watch her walk away and marvel at how well she looks. In her late fifties, Minnie looks years younger. From her Lucille Ball red spiked and moussed hair, to her ears with three piercings in each, to her curvy yet still slim figure, dressed in a periwinkle uniform with white ruffled apron, and coral lipstick, Minnie could pass for a woman in her early forties.

Flannery looks out the window near their booth, and views the tall trees that surround the cottage that has been Minnie's Restaurant for nearly thirty years. Then she looks around the cozy dining room and the other customers trying to ignore Derek and the steady look he is giving her.

The cottage was once someone's house, but Minnie and Joe bought it when the original owner put it up for sale and moved to Florida. Though they have redecorated several times, the old country charm remains. With oak floors everywhere except the kitchen, storage room and bathrooms, the place has the feel of a grandmother's country kitchen. Cookie jars, most extremely old sit on the shelves that surround the dining room and the counter at the front of the room. Colorful pieces of Depression glass adorn two china hutches across the room from where Derek and Flannery sit. Periwinkle and white are the dominant colors in the seating, the cloth table napkins and the blue and white flowered café curtains on the wide windows around the room. The Depression glass is used for special occasions, customer birthdays, holidays, anniversaries and whatever a person may want to celebrate. Sometimes Minnie will use the dishes to cheer a customer up. Some is also kept in the kitchen and this is always used before that in the china cabinets.

Flannery and Derek sit quietly enjoying the room's ambiance and their closeness. Neither will admit they are happy to be sitting side by side as they once did. He does keep looking sideways at her and finally she tells him, "Would you please quite looking at me. Why must you practically sit on me when there is plenty of room on the other side of the table?"

He thinks about this for a moment and tells her, "I would move, but you see, I drove here without my wallet. Since you have your purse I was hoping you would kindly pay for my food also. If I move, you may decide to pay for yours and leave me to wash dishes in payment."

"I'll pay on one condition that you stop being unkind to me."

"Ok, I'll call it a truce for now. Just remember, when you ask me questions about my life I fully intend to give you answers and if your feelings are hurt blame yourself."

She glares at him and watching Minnie and another waitress carrying two trays with their large order said, "I don't intend to ask you anything."

"That would probably be best." he tells her quietly.

As Minnie and the waitress sit the food, plate by plate, glass by glass and bowl by bowl on the table, Flannery and Derek see that their food is being served on Minnie's prized Depression glass. Derek's order is on the cobalt blue glassware, Flannery's the emerald green. This more than kind gesture cheers them because they know that Minnie thinks lovingly of them, as she has for has for years. It pleases them that she has not forgotten their favorite colors.

"Thanks, you are so sweet to serve us on your lovely dishes, Flannery tells the ladies as she bling back tears of happiness.

"You are wonderful remembering us this way." Derek said as he places his napkin on his lap.

"How could I forget anything about two of my favorite people?"

"Lena let me introduce you to Flannery and Derek. I have known them since they were in diapers. Actually they worked here in the summertime while in high school and college."

Derek smiles at the plump blonde waitress, dressed in periwinkle and white like Minnie and all the waitresses, and she smiles back, though she also blushes. Flannery sees the look of adoration on Lena's face for Derek and she knows how Lena feels. Derek isn't a flirt by nature but his dark, handsome looks and his gentlemanly manners always charm the ladies.

"It's nice to meet you." Flannery said with friendliness hoping to make Lena feel at ease with them.

"Yes, it is nice to meet you," adds Derek before he takes a sip of his root beer.

"We'll let you eat in peace. If you need anything else, Minnie said with a chuckle just call."

"Thanks! They say in unison which finally gives them something to laugh about.

When they return to Anne's it is two a.m. They know that they will need to be up by seven at least, they head straight for their rooms. Neither has gone to church much since their breakup. Derek usually drops his kids off at church then he would find a coffee house and read the Sunday paper until church was over. Then he and the children would join his parents and Anne at his parent's house for lunch. They would stay until four or five and then return to the huge mausoleum that was never a home to any of them.

Anne and his parents haven't said but they know in their hearts that the three would prefer that they go to church as much as possible. Though they know why Flannery and Derek have lost some of their faith they are optimistically hopeful that they will regain their old love and trust in God.

Chapter Twenty

Sunday is always a family day for the MacDougall's and the Larkin's. After church the families always eat lunch. Usually they go to Bing and Stella's though sometimes they will eat at the country club. The club chef does amazing things with whatever he cooks.

When they return to Anne's they change into everyday clothes and go outside with the dogs and the Sunday paper. Although lots of people read the daily news online, the Larkin's and MacDougall's prefer the physical paper, especially on Sunday.

Jack and Lucy entertain the three dogs. Tralee the Border collie loves her Frisbee and would catch it no matter how many times it is thrown her way. Derek keeps an eye on his kids and the active dog, and because the day is warm finally tells Jack and Lucy, "Let me have the Frisbee and the balls because Tralee is getting too hot."

Jack and Lucy hand Derek the dog toys, which he puts in a basket hanging on the back porch for this reason. Next he unfurls the backyard hose and fills to huge bowls with water. He knows Tralee is tired because she lies in front of one of the bowls and drinks her fill. Yates and Charlie played but not as much and lay under the backyard swing, where Anne and Flannery sit. They and Derek are reading the paper, but she can sense that he is not only keeping an eye on his kids and the pets but her also. Whenever she looks up he smiles at her and she smiles back. Anne has been watching the two and despite their fight of the night before she sees a spark of hope there.

When she's finished with the parts of the paper that interest her, Flannery hands them to Derek, looks at Jack and Lucy and asks, "Would you like to go down by the river. We can skip rocks."

"Sure, I'll go." said Jack who has been brushing Yates the Golden Retriever.

"Me too." adds Lucy who has been brushing Tralee.

"Anyone else," Flannery asks with hope in her voice.

"I'm going to stay put for a while." Granny Anne tells them and continues reading a newspaper article on Scotland in the travel section.

"I'll tag along. Maybe I can teach Aunt Flannery not to throw like a girl." Derek said with a teasing grin.

"Yeah, we'll see. Jack and Lucy you will be witness to how well a girl can throw."

At the water's edge they stand, each with several prime flat stones to skim across the Fox River. Derek tosses first, and gets barely a ripple in the river. Next Flannery takes a turn and her stone seems to dance across the water creating very prominent ripples.

"Daddy, Aunt Flannery doesn't throw like a girl, you do." Jack tells Derek with a furrowed brow.

"Pure luck nothing more." Derek said with a challenging grin.

"We'll see about that." said Flannery before tossing another perfect pitch across the river once more.

"Aunt Flannery, teach me. I want to beat Daddy to." Lucy tells the three with excitement.

"Me too Aunt Flannery, Daddy will have to eat his words." adds Jack with a laugh.

"Eat my words huh." Derek teases and ruffles Jack's thick blond hair.

"Yeah, eat your words." With this said Flannery shows first Jack and then Lucy just how to toss a stone properly. When the two children succeed in out doing Derek, he pretends to pout, then takes a stone of his own and out tosses all three.

"The first girlie throw was just so the rest of you wouldn't feel bad when I threw the winning toss."

"I'd say it's just pure luck." Flannery tells them and once more tosses a stone that out does the one Derek tossed.

Derek narrows his dark eyes, winds up his arm and once again throws a perfect toss.

"Your Daddy just doesn't want to be out done by a woman and two children." Flannery tells them with a pretend pout of her own.

Derek with eyes twinkling goes to Flannery pulls her flat against his chest and kisses her pouting lips. Although the kiss definitely takes her by surprise, she finds herself enjoying his lips on hers and when he pulls back to look at her face he sees both pleasure and disappoint that the kiss has ended nearly as fast as it began.

When neither says a word, Jack asks, "Aunt Flannery didn't you like Daddy's kiss?"

First she swallows a few times, then looking first at Derek and then back at Jack's and Lucy's curious face's, tells them the truth. "Yes, I enjoyed your Daddy's kiss. It took me by surprise but in all honesty I definitely enjoyed his kiss. It has been a long time since our last kiss."

Derek studies her for a moment, and then pulls her close once more and kisses her with meaning. In the kiss he pours all the years that they have been separated and all the lonely nights' that he sometimes wonders how he survived. She feels his need and returns the kiss with all the passion in her heart. The kiss deepens and then softens when Jack said, "I guess both of you like kissing each other."

Not wanting to take his eyes from her Derek tells his curious son, "I enjoyed the kiss, and from Aunt Flannery's response I believe she did also."

With time to compose herself Flannery tells the small audience, "Kissing your Daddy is always wonderful. It has been awhile but he still knows how to kiss properly."

Derek looks into her lovely moss green eyes and said, "I agree, kissing you is also wonderful and you still know how to kiss properly."

Knowing the truth of how they feel, he smiles at her she smiles back, and said, "Maybe Derek and I should spend more time kissing instead of fighting."

Jack looks puzzled by her comment, and with knitted brows ask, "Do you fight? I haven't heard you. Now when Daddy and Chloe, Mommy, fought they were loud. So loud that me and Lucy and the pets would go outside and hide until we heard Mommy's car as she pulled out of the garage an on to the road that runs by our house."

Derek knew his fights with Chloe bothered Jack and Lucy a great deal and he tried to keep the many fights away from them, but Chloe didn't care who heard them, and she would purposely start her tirade even when the kids were present.

"I'm sorry that we fought so much, and especially sorry that you and Lucy had to witness our fights. Flannery and I do argue some, and may even fight but we do so outside the house."

Flannery doesn't like to fight or argue, and there was a time when neither did Derek. Because Chloe was relentless until she got her way, she isn't surprised that Chloe and Derek fought. And as he has stated, it is just too bad that Chloe didn't consider anyone but herself when she started badgering Derek.

"Maybe you and Aunt Flannery should kiss and hug when you want to argue or fight, that way you will probably forget to fight or argue." Jack tells them with such seriousness that they cannot help but agree.

Because Granny Anne is resting in her room, it is not until she is eating dinner with the four that Jack tells her about the kisses. "Granny Anne, Daddy and Aunt Flannery were kissing by the river. They kissed twice. I think they should kiss instead of arguing or fighting. What do you think?"

Anne, with fork halfway to her mouth, tells them, "I agree with Jack, who is a really smart boy, kiss more fights less that should be your motto."

Derek, who has been watching Flannery for her response, tells all those eating at the table, "Flannery how about it, do we kiss and hug when the urge to fight grips our souls?"

Flannery, whose mouth is full of roasted chicken, nods her head yes to his words, continues to chew and then smiles and tells them, "That would be a way to solve the fighting problem, the only problem is when we fight we are far too caught up in the moment that we might not remember to kiss an hug. "

"We could put signs in all the rooms and on the porches to remind you." Lucy said to the surprise of the adults.

"Lucy that's a wonderful idea," said Jack who always goes out of his way to compliment his little sister every chance he gets.

"Yeah, thanks." Lucy said with a bright smile.

"As soon as dinner is through and the dishes washed, I will find some poster board and we can work on signs." Flannery tells all at the table, though her eyes focus mainly on Derek and his opinion.

He smiles at everyone, then with his focus entirely on Flannery said, "That's one of the best ideas I have heard since Jack's statement that we should kiss and hug instead of arguing or fighting." When she smiles at his words, he compliments his children on their wonderful ideas. He has learned from his parents and Granny Anne the importance of telling his children how wonderful they are.

With dinner and washing dishes behind them they put their best effort into designing the signs. Granny Anne helps, plus guides Lucy's tiny hand when she shows the little girl how to use a marker properly. When the signs are finished, the adults hang them in the spots that Jack chooses. When they are done, signs are taped in every room, on the porches and lastly one is hung on a tree near the dock, a tree that they must pass whenever they walk down the much uses path to the dock.

Chapter Twenty-One

Monday after breakfast Derek and the kids, plus the two dogs get ready to go to Bing and Stella's for three days. "Let's see if we can catch Odie and Garfield." Derek tells the children while looking for a cat carrier.

"Why not leave the cats here." Charlie, the Scottish terrier, and Queen Mary, Ann's huge calico cat, love the pets being here. "They aren't a problem. Dogs travel much easier than cats."

Because Derek knows this is true, he and the kids and dogs tell Flannery and Anne they will see them Thursday in the late afternoon. "If you would like to join us at the country club for swimming you are definitely invited any time you decide."

Derek has thought a good deal about Flannery's response to his kisses and knows he will kiss her again, but decides to do as their signs say, an kiss her when he feels the need to fight.

Before they leave, he does give her a warm hug and to his delight she hugs him in return.

Anne's house is extremely quiet without Derek, his kids and their dogs. Flannery and Anne are busy with everyday chores. Though Bing pays a cleaning service to clean Anne's house once a week, she still does the little things that make a house a home. The crew that cleans her house is the one that used to clean Derek and Chloe's. Derek was pleased to find out that Nancy and her efficient crew clean Anne's house.

The first week that he and his kids stayed at Anne's, after he moved them out of the mausoleum that Chloe loved, Nancy and her crew came to clean Anne's house. He and his kids were as excited to see her as she was them. He'd told her a little about getting a divorce and that he would be moving and selling the house. Nancy looked around the big house, beautifully decorated, and said, "I can understand why you want to sell. Although this is a gorgeous house, I see you and your kids in something cozy, something smaller, near families with kids for Jack and Lucy to play with."

Though he felt badly that he wouldn't need their services, at least until he found something permanent, he apologized to her an gave Nancy and the two ladies that work with her a nice bonus for the wonderful work they did to keep the house clean for him and his kids.

When Nancy saw the huge amount of the check he'd given each of them she told him it was far too generous. He told her that they deserved the bonus and to use it for something special.

When he saw her at Anne's she told him she, her husband, her mom and her two children have booked a trip to Hawaii before school resumes in September. The other ladies used theirs for vacations also. One is going to Disney World with her four kids, her mother and father. The third worker will be headed to Los Angeles and all its many tourist attractions. He'd received thank you notes from all three sent to Bing and Stella's address.

Though Derek planned to wash the covers on the bed that he shares with his kids, he forgot with the sign making and Anne and Flannery told him they would take care of it for him.

Anne has a guest room with twin beds, and Jack and Lucy sometimes start their night there, but they usually end up in bed with Derek. He is used to them by now, and lets them stay. He knows they should be in their own room and will work on the issue before they start school full time. The night that Jack conned Flannery into sleeping with them, made him rethink his plan to keep them in their own beds. He has feelings for her, wouldn't have kissed her by the river if he didn't, but he needs his freedom for now and time to dedicate solely to his kids. If the day comes when he needs a bed to himself he will have to make sure his kids are ready for a woman to share his time, and his love.

Flannery strips Derek's bed and as she holds the covers closely as she walks down the stairs to the laundry room she can faintly tell that Derek and his kids slept in the bed. They have the sweet scent of the baby shampoo and baby lotion that he still buys for them, and also the scent of Derek's Rosemary Mint shampoo. Beneath these three scents she also breaths in his Zest bar soap. She has secretly kept several unwrapped bars of Zest hidden in her dresser drawer beneath her pajamas and nighties. This habit she has kept hidden for over six years. One night he asked if she uses Zest. When she said no he looked at her questioningly. One day she may tell him her secret, but first she and he need to work on trusting each other again.

The three days with his parents seem to drag. He takes the kids swimming each day at the country club an helps his Mom cook the meals and volunteers to wash her and Bing's cars. Although he knows Bing gets the vehicles detailed every month, Bing and Stella give him and his kids the ok to wash their cars. Jack and Lucy dressed in swimwear are soaked from head to toe by the time the cars are finished, and couldn't be happier. Because Derek enjoys the time with them he lets them hose him down when the car washing is done. The day is hot and humid, so the hosing is a blessing.

Their first night back at his parent's house, while they are eating dinner, Jack and Lucy tell Bing and Stella about Derek and Flannery's kisses and the signs that they made and hung around Anne's place. Derek sees hope in his parents loving faces, and though he cares for Flannery he tells them how he feels about the future. "I care for Flannery and I believe she still has feelings for me, but we have changed, especially me. I need time just for me and my kids. Being at Anne's gives us a chance to get to know each other. Perhaps we will get back together, but I don't want to rush things."

This he tells them after Jack and Lucy are in bed. He knows his kids love Flannery and he can understand why. She is everything that Chloe is not. She is kind and not judgmental. She doesn't have a selfish bone in her body and she loves his kids as much as he, his parents and Anne do. She also loves to play with them, and is a good sport. It truly saddens his heart to know that such a caring and loving woman will never give birth to children. He remembers how she always said when she grew up and got married she would have no less than six children. Her Granny Anne told him of her visits to several doctors and that each told her that with only one ovary she would more than likely never conceive. Flannery doesn't know that Anne has told him, so he will keep the information to himself.

Chloe may be her half-sister but the two rarely saw each other. The few times that they did Chloe made it clear how much she detests Flannery. Because of their strained relationship Flannery has always felt like an only child. Nell and Flannery have always been close and Nell is more like a sister to her then Chloe ever will be. Having Virginia, Nell and her children only a stone's throw away has always been a blessing for Flannery and Anne, Virginia, Nell and her three children. And as Nancy, the cleaning lady has reminded him, it is also a blessing for him, because Nell's children and his have become wonderful friends.

While they are with his parents there aren't any children Jack and Lucy's age to play with. Most of the children are teens, though once in a while they will see grandchildren of some of the club's members. His parents live in an older established gated community, so most residences have lived here for many years. Those that Derek and Sean grew up with have moved away or live in the city of Chicago. There is also the fact that to live in Bing and Stella's community a person needs tons of money.

Gus and Rena also live in his parent's neighborhood though near the golf course and tennis courts. He's only recently seen Rena playing tennis with another club member. Rena, like Chloe loves attention, so dresses to the nines, even on the tennis court. He, Flannery and Sean once played tennis, but that was while in high school.

The area where he and Chloe lived in the humongous house is only minutes from their parent's homes, but it is much newer and doesn't have the huge trees or the friendliness. Chloe didn't want to know their neighbors, and he was on the road a great deal, so he knew his neighbors only to say hello as he and his kids were leaving the house to go to the market or to his parent's house. Because he wants Jack and Lucy to have friends and a normal life he hopes that he will be able to find a house for him and them close to Anne's and Virginias. Anne has generously told him he may stay with her forever, but he doesn't want to wear her out by staying with her too long. Geneva is also a wonderful place to raise kids.

As Thursday rolls around Derek and his children are excited to return to Anne's, Derek because of Flannery and Jack and Lucy because they love everything about living by the river.

Bing and Stella are never offended when Jack and Lucy talk excitedly about going to Anne's. He and Sean were the same at their age.

Chapter Twenty-Two

As soon as Derek walks into Anne's kitchen where she cleaning berries, he looks around for Flannery. Anne watches him looking around and knowing him well said, "Flannery took one of the row boats out around one. She has her cell phone with her and has promised to call when she is close to home. She knows that you and the children will be here and I told her dinner will be ready and waiting."

Anne hands a huge cleaned strawberry to him, which he immediately pops into his mouth to eat. "These are wonderful. Are they from your garden?"

"Yes, this is the biggest I have ever seen them. They love the sun and we have certainly been blessed with tons of that this month."

"It has been nice. Yesterday was rather warm, so Jack, Lucy and I washed all the cars. They were soaked, but had a ball." Derek's face is always happy and animated whenever he talks about his children and no one need ask if he loves them and being a father. The joy that he feels being with them softens his too serious face, and brings a beautiful smile to his lips.

Anne finishes cleaning the berries and sits them in the refrigerator and with Derek's help sits the table for dinner. "We're having meatloaf, which I baked early this morning, because I didn't want to overheat the kitchen. Flannery made her famous potato salad. We also have baked beans."

"That sound wonderful, I guess we can heat the meatloaf in the microwave or eat it cold. A meatloaf sandwich sounds good."

"Yes, that was the plan, "Anne said right before her phone rings. She answers it, and winks at Derek, She listens to the caller and said, "Derek and the kids are here and dinner is waiting, how far away are you? Ten minutes away isn't far. I'll have Derek meet you at the dock, and he can help you carry the boat back to the boathouse." Anne pauses for a moment and then smiles and adds, " I love you too sweet girl."

"I'm guessing that was Flannery. I'll head to the river right in a minute. I guess I'd better check on Jack and Lucy, their awfully quiet. They were in the living room when I walked in here. Jack forgot to take his library book to Mom and Dad's and he has to take it back tomorrow. He was reading to Lucy."

"You go and help Flannery with the boat, I'll check on Jack and Lucy."

"Thanks." Derek tells the woman who has always been a Grandmother to him, his brother and his children. He crosses the short space between them and hugs her and kisses her cheek. She smiles into his eyes and gives him a kiss and hug also.

He is at the dock waiting when Flannery comes around the bend, rowing with precision and expertise. She wears a Cubs baseball cap and sunglasses, so her face is in shadow, but she smiles when she sees him waiting, and has the boat beside the dock in record time.

"Hi!" He said as he walks to the edge of the water, to help her as she expertly steers the boat to shore. When the front of the boat scrapes land, Derek pulls it slowly to the grass covered river bank nearby. Flannery stand to get out and he stops pulling.

She pulls her glasses off and puts them in the pocket of her well-worn jeans, then smiles at him. "Thanks for coming to help with the boat. I guess I rowed too far, now that I'm on land I'm exhausted."

"So you didn't stop at Minnie' for pie?" He asks with a teasing smile.

"I rowed a good ways and then on the way back had to pee, so I pulled to the shore and went to visit Minnie and Joe. I forgot to bring some money with me but Minnie gave me iced tea, then Joe wanted me to sample a new pie he'd made. She licks her lips and smiles at the memory, which makes Derek laugh.

"Oh, the pie is to die for, its boysenberry, huckleberry and lemon. I still get excited just remembering the first delicious bite. I was going to bring one for dinner, but knew I was not to be trusted not to eat the entire pie before I reached home. Joe said he will make them again tomorrow and that he will personally save one for me. Of course I will pay for it."

Derek grins at her excitement for pie. Flannery has never found fault with any food that she has eaten. Chloe on the other hand was always sending her order back to the kitchen because something was wrong with her meal. Derek could order the exact dish and find it perfect, but Chloe wanted to be noticed and would complain just for the attention. She did this numerous times, so finally Derek refused to go out to eat with her.

This never bothered her, because he has heard from other that she is still sending her meals back.

They heft the canoe over their heads and walk the short distance to the boathouse. Derek had opened the boathouse door on his way to meet Flannery, which makes entering the structure extremely easy. Once inside, they place the boat carefully on a raised wooden structure so that the boat will dry.

With this done, they close the door, lock it with a key, from Flannery's pocket and quietly walk up the rise to Anne's and dinner. As they walk through the back gate Flannery pulls her baseball cap off and pulling an elastic band from her ponytail lets her dark waterfall of thick wavy hair fall around her shoulders.

Derek stops in his tracks at her actions and before she or he can catch another breath, he pulls her flush against his sun warmed body and kisses her until they are breathless. The kiss takes the remaining energy from Flannery, and she would have slumped to the green, green grass of the back garden, but Derek senses this and holds her close until he feels her breath again.

Neither says a word, they do hold hands once she can stand on her own, and walk into Anne's kitchen with very pleased expressions on their extremely readable faces.

Anne, Jack and Lucy are placing dinner on the table and stop for a moment to study the faces of the two happy adults. Jack with the curious wisdom of a child said, "Daddy, Aunt Flannery, did you kiss? I ask because you have the same silly look on your faces that you did the other time you kissed."

Flannery nods her head yes, Derek grins and tells his observant son, "Yes, Aunt Flannery took the elastic ponytail holder from her hair and it fell down her back, and she is so beautiful I couldn't resist." Flannery smiles happily at his admission but says nothing.

""I'm glad that you weren't fighting." Jack adds with a sigh of relief

"Sometimes adults kiss just because it feels like the thing to do, so don't worry your handsome self. One day you will know what I mean. When the right girl strikes your fancy you will more than likely kiss her just because."

"Yuck, I don't want to kiss girls. Their ok, but I'm not going to be that silly." Jack tells the grinning adults.

"Me neither. I won't kiss any boys either." Lucy tells the amused adults.

Derek narrows his dark eyes, picks Lucy up to ride his slim jeans clad hip, kisses her cheek and said, "I'm not going to let either of you kiss anyone except family until you graduate from college."

"Good luck there." Flannery teases as she helps Jack on to the wooden chair where he will eat. Flannery and Anne take their places while Derek helps Lucy sit on her bright pink booster seat on the chair next to his.

"Yes, good luck there." Adds Anne while placing a little of everything on the table on each plate as they are handed to her.

Before they eat, they bow their heads for prayer. Because they each take a turn at one meal each day, and because it is Flannery's turn, she takes Jack's tiny, warm hand on her right and Granny Anne's on her left. Jack links his hand with Lucy, and Lucy with her Dad. Because Derek and Anne are across the table from each other, they reach across the wooden table, now covered with a pretty green cloth and hold hands also. With heads bowed and eyes closed they wait for Flannery to begin. Because she has been reading her Bible much more now that she is with her Granny, Flannery quotes *Hebrews 11:6* word for word without one mistake.

So, you see, it is impossible to please God, without faith.
Anyone who wants to come to him must believe there is a God
And he rewards those who sincerely seek him.

Anne knows that Flannery said the prayer because Anne has worried that her granddaughter has lost the close relationship she once had with the Lord. Anne not only squeezes Flannery's hand lightly she also squeezes Derek's, then looks fondly from one face to the other and smiles. "That was perfect my love. It is wonderful to know that you are once again reading the word."

"I tried to live without a daily dose of wisdom from the Lord, but never felt fulfilled. I now read from my bible every evening and feel peaceful at doing so."

Jack, with fork poised over his meatloaf said, "Daddy reads the children's bible to me and Lucy every night after he reads a storybook. He said we need to know about the Lord and His goodness."

Derek who is helping Lucy cut her meatloaf looks at Flannery and then Anne and tells them with a shrug of his shoulders, "I've also started to read the word. A scripture here and there, but much more then I have done in the past six years. Like Flannery I felt an empty place in my spirit, and even though I don't read a lot of scripture I have begun to notice the emptiness leaving me.

"Yes even a small dose of scripture can fill the empty places inside us." Anne tells them with a sweet smile.

Though Derek and Flannery say nothing to her statement, they nod their heads in agreement. They know that Anne has always had their best interest at heart, and that when Derek called off their wedding, Anne's heart was also broken.

Chapter Twenty-three

Friday is always story time at the library and Anne happily takes Jack and Lucy along with Anne's friend and neighbor Virginia and Virginia's three grandchildren Kristen age ten, Tyler age five and Mary nearly three. Because Derek has the van, he always lets them drive it to the library.

When breakfast is over, and the kitchen cleaned, she, Jack and Lucy collect their rented books and head for the back door. Anne turns beside the door, holds it for Jack and Lucy and reminds Flannery and Derek that she and Virginia are also taking the kids to MacDonald's for lunch and to play in the kid's area for a while. "We also will stop at the market to buy a few things. So, stay out of mischief."

"Who, us, we'll be far too busy working in the attic to get into mischief. " Flannery tells Anne with a smile and a kiss.

"I'll keep her out of mischief. I have a whip set aside just for the purpose of keeping Flannery in line." Derek tells Anne with a mischievous laugh. He too kisses Anne's soft weathered cheek.

Flannery shakes her head at his words and rolls her eyes towards the high kitchen ceiling.

After Anne and the kids leave, Flannery and Derek, dressed in old shorts and t-shirts head upstairs to Anne's crowded attic and begin the back breaking job of sorting through many years of Anne's and Flannery's saved treasures.

They first open the attic windows to let in the breeze that is supposed to bring rain by nightfall. With two windows on either end of the long deep attic, it takes only a short time for the dusty space to cool down. Derek chooses the end of the room farthest from the stairs, and opening a huge, old and scarred trunk begins to sort through the many photo albums stored inside, Flannery chooses another old truck, this one with colorful sticker from ports around the world.

They work quietly for quite a while the only sounds being made by the three dogs that have followed them into the attic. All three dogs will need a bath after lying on the dusty wooden floor, but Flannery and Derek know the dogs are happiest when they hang out with their humans.

Flannery sorts through the clothing inside the trunk and holds Anne's dresses from her younger days to her body. Anne is only slightly shorter than Flannery, and she sets aside the dresses she is considering trying on later, in the privacy of her room. When she pulls out a tiny chiffon and satin dress the color of a mint leaf she shakes it out holds it in from of her and said excitedly to Derek, "Derek look."

He does and to her surprise said "Isn't that the dress you wore the Easter before my Mom and your Dad died?"

Truly pleased that he remembers she smiles and nods yes. "I loved this dress. My Dad bought it for me. We were at Marshall Fields in downtown Chicago. Daddy bought it because he said it went perfect with my eyes." When tears start to surface at the memory, she turns her back to Derek and wipes them away. He sees the tears and walks the short distance between them and hands her an eight by ten portrait.

She turns towards him blinks away the last tear, then taking the portrait from his hand studies the only photo that was ever taken of Flannery with her father and Rena, her biological mother. She doesn't actually remember it being taken, she was only nine months old, but she used to look at it numerous times, until she moved to Scotland and left it behind.

Derek stands closely behind her, can faintly smell her coconut shampoo and conditioner, and looks at it with her. She can feel his warmth and smell the Zest that he uses, and would normally move away, but she needs that warmth and his nearness. Her father has been dead for nearly twenty-six years, and feeling Derek's body heat and smelling his Zest lets her know that she is truly alive, and so is Derek. And as the saying goes it ain't over till the fat lady sings.

She knows prayers are answered every day, even the ones that seem impossible, and she may no longer pray for herself, but she knows others pray for her and Derek to get back together, so silently prays, "*If it be your will Lord, Derek and I will have a second chance to be together again.*"

While she prays Derek studies the portrait closely and points out the fact that she and Lucy have a chin like Rena and Rena's arched brows. He believes Lucy had his mother's nose.

"Flannery, do you see that you and Lucy have Rena's chin and arched brows?"

Flannery, now through talking with God, also studies the portrait.

"You're right, Lucy and I do have Rena's chin and arched brows. I think that if Lucy's hair was dark like mine or yours, I and you would probably have seen the close resemblance sooner. '

"Dad and Stella, Mom mentioned this fact just the other day. I couldn't see it then, but now that I see you and Rena together, the resemblance is suddenly clear."

No longer hurt and angry at her mother for not wanting her, Flannery sets the portrait aside and picks the mint green dress up once more. "Do you think…Would Lucy…"she adds.

"Would Lucy like the dress? I know she would love it. Are you certain that is what you want to do? I would make sure she doesn't play in it. Which reminds me, do you remember that Easter? Everyone, you, James, Bing and my Mom and Anne had Easter dinner here with Virginia and Nell. There were boys a little older than us who came into the front yard and egged us on to climb the trees."

"Yes, I remember it clearly. Nell had shorts under her red dress so she could climb the trees.

"Yes. Those boys challenged you and Nell to climb the trees and hang from the limbs. The boys were disappointed that they could not see Nell's panties. While they were watching Nell climb you climbed out on a limb and were hanging over, with your pretty dress over your head. I was beside you and whispered, Flannery climb down. I see your pretty green ruffled panties. Luckily the boys were teasing Nell and missed seeing you with your dress over your head."

Flannery, who remembers the incidence like it had happened only the day before, smiles a dreamy smile and tells Derek, "Yes, I remember. You were a gentleman even then. I fell in love with you that day, and prayed that one day we would marry and have a little girl who would also love the dress."

He doesn't comment on her statement but when she looks into his eyes she sees sadness there. To take the forlorn frown from his handsome face, she holds the dress in front of her and waltzes around the small cleared area of the attic.

Chapter Twenty-four

They stick to the chore until their stomach protest at not being fed lunch. Neither wears a watch, although Derek carries his cell phone in the pocket of his worn khaki shorts. He looks at the time and see it's nearly two tells her, "Let's stop for the day. We can finish tomorrow." If there's anything you want me to carry like the dress for Lucy, I'll help."

Flannery hands him the dress and she picks up the portrait and several old books, Anne's dresses and two rubber dolls. Derek remembers the dolls well and asks their names even though he remembers clearly what they are. "What were the names you gave the dolls?"

From the amusement in his eyes she knows that he remembers, but wants to hear her say their names. The boy, who has black hair and brown eyes like Derek, and the girl who has brown hair and green eyes like Flannery are the dolls that her father bought her their last Christmas together, and though she played with them every day from that point on until she was twelve, the dolls are in excellent shape. "The boy is Jamie Derek and the girl is Anne Hanna."

When he cracks a wild smile she tells him, "You remembered the names as well as I did."

"Yeah, I just wanted to hear the names from you."

"I named them for the people that I love, loved and the names maybe sound silly to an adults ears, but to a child they are perfectly fine."

When she frowns and bites her lip he pulls her close and hugs her. "So you named them for people you love, or is it loved?"

They stand only a breath away and she sees a longing in his eyes so she tells him the truth. "They were named for those that I love."

When his eyes light by degrees, she knows she has opened her heart to him, but hopefully this time not for heartbreak.

"That's good to know." he tells her as they walk down the attic stairs to the second floor.

When they get to the second floor she puts the books and portrait on the desk in her room. The dolls she sits on the loveseat at the foot of her bed, the dresses she hangs in the closet until she can try them on.

Derek carries the dress into the room he shares with his kids and hangs it on a hanger in the closet. He is certain that Lucy, his girlie girl will love it because it's pretty and also because her Aunt Flannery once wore it.

Derek knows his daughter well and later that evening when she is getting ready for bed he shows her the dress. Flannery is in her room, so Lucy and Derek go to show her how sweet Lucy looks in the dress. Lucy turns from one pose to the next, like a runway model so Flannery can see her from all angles. "You are gorgeous sweet girl." Flannery tells her and gives her a hug and kiss because she is a sweet girl.

"Thank you Aunt Flannery. Mary's birthday party is next Friday, may I wear it there?"

"Certainly you may. What's a pretty dress for except to wear for special occasions?" When Lucy goes to Flannery and kisses her cheek Flannery's heart melts and for a moment, but only that, she feels a sadness that her father never saw her grow up. Then she just as quickly shakes the sad thought away and feels the happiness that Derek and his children bring to her and her Granny Anne.

Lucy spies the dolls, walks over to them and sits beside them for a closer look. "Lucy you may pick them up. They were mine. They were my present one Christmas when I was a little older than you. Derek, your Daddy and I found them in the attic this morning."

Lucy picks each one up, sits them on her lap and asks, "What are their names?"

"The boy is Jamie Derek, for my Dad and Derek for your Dad. The girl is Anne Hanna for my Granny and Hanna of course was Derek's Mother's name."

"Hanna is like my second name." Lucy said with a smile.

"Yes Hanna like your middle name. Would you like to sleep with them?" Flannery asks knowing beforehand what Lucy will say.

"Oh yes. I would love to sleep with them. My dollies are somewhere in storage. Daddy thought he had the box in the van when we moved but he didn't. He has promised to find them but there were too many boxes to go through in the storage place. He offered to buy me more but I haven't seen any I like. If I could find two like Jamie Derek and Anne Hanna I would have him buy those."

"How would you like to keep the dollies? I think dollies are sad unless they have a little girl to love them."

Lucy looks from Flannery to her Daddy with hope in her eyes. Derek knows the dolls are one of Flannery's treasures so asks, "Are you sure you want to give them away. Lucy takes excellent care of her toys, but are you sure?"

"Yes, I'm positive. Lucy will give them the love that all dolls deserve, so from this moment on they belong to her."

Lucy sits the dolls gently on the loveseat, goes to Flannery and wrapping her arms around Flannery's thighs gives her a hug. Flannery bends down to Lucy's level and gives her a kiss on one, then two cheeks. "I love you Aunt Flannery and I will take very good care of the dollies."

"I love you too Lucy Hanna and I know you will take excellent care of the dollies."

Flannery looks over Lucy's head at Derek who gives her a smile and to lighten the moment teasingly said, "Lucy if you ever need a sitter for your Dollies Aunt Flannery and I will sit for you."

"Your silly Daddy, but that's ok because I know when your being silly you are also happy."Derek is always amassed at his children's perception of others. Jack and Lucy are always in tuned to those around them, especially those that they love.

Chapter Twenty-five

Later that evening Derek invites Flannery to walk with him to the dock to sit on the park benches nearby. The night is cool, with the promising storm only hours away. No stars can be seen through the thick clouds that have been gathering since morning, but they can see fairly clearly, because the dusk-to-dawn and motion sensor lights are on around the brick fence to the yard and the boathouse.

They talk about the past for a while and then Flannery makes the mistake of asking Derek a question about his marriage to Chloe. Because they have been getting along fairly well since their last feud, she figures it's safe to bring up the subject. "May I ask you something personal? He looks steadily at her but says nothing. This gives her the courage to ask, "Why did you buy such a hug house if it wasn't what you like? I always thought you were unafraid to tell a person when you were not interested in something. I know Chloe is good at manipulating people, but I never thought that you would let her rule the roost."

Because it is dark and his face is in shadow, she at first doesn't see the anger forming in his dark eyes, but then he is up and off the bench before she can blink an eye and with shoulders ramrod straight and his nostrils flaring, he looks at her and thunders to the dock then back to stand in front of her. When she sees the rage on his dark face and in his eyes, she realizes too late, that she is about to be chewed up and spit out by Derek's words.

"You know nothing about my marriage. I bought the house thinking that Chloe would finally settle down to marriage and motherhood. Fool that I was I still believed in a good out- come for us." He stops talking walks back down to the dock, only to walk and stand angrily in front of her. Though his words hurt she knows it is her own fault for thinking she could ask such a personal question. His eyes are filled with fire that will need a torrential downpour to put it out. So she decides she will let him stew and she gets up from the bench and goes to move past him. He grabs her shoulders and harshly shakes her until she feels like her head will spin from her shoulders. The Derek she knew rarely got angry and then only when it was justified. For a moment she feels afraid of him, and he feels her quiver beneath his strong hands. He loosens his grip and she takes advantage of this, moves to the side and starts to run up the hill to the house.

As she runs without looking down, he tells her with more anger then with their other fight, "You have the nerve to judge me. I at least have never run away from my problems. I made a huge mistake marrying Chloe, but at least I gave the marriage a chance for Jack and Lucy. You were always running away to Scotland, leaving me and our life behind. Perhaps you should wake up, take a look at yourself and the fairytale life that you live and work on changing your own life. I see why Chloe hates you. She could always see through your angelic act, and knew what a fake you are."

She doesn't want to let him see the tears working their way to her eyes, so picks up speed so she can get away from him. With tears now blinding her, she fails to see a loose flagstone in front of her. She begins to fall forward when her flip-flops fall off, and she is falling face first into the stone pathway. She tries to stop herself with her hands but is blinded by the free falling tears awash in her eyes. Her hands slip and she feels a burning against her palms, then her nose and chin are eating the stones and dirt along with her elbows, knees and two big toes on each foot. The fall stuns her for a short time, and then she feels the pain radiating from all the scrapes and bruises. Because everything is raging painfully, she sits on the path, wraps her arms around her knees and with her head bowed so Derek won't see her tears she cries as though her heart is breaking.

His anger is extinguished the moment he sees her falling, and too late to catch her, he now honkers beside her, touches her shoulder and said, as he looks at her knees, elbows and toes.

"I'm going to carry you to the house and check your wounds." With this said he tries to pick her up.

She sits where he can see her face, and with tears still flowing and her nose running she tells him "Don't touch me. I would rather bleed to death than have you do anything for me."

He sees the tears but also the scrape on her chin and the end of her nose. He feels badly that she is injured, and even though she protest he lifts her into his arms and carries her up the hill, through the gate and the yard, up the back porch steps and into the kitchen.

He sits her gently on one of the chairs, then hoping she will stay, goes to the downstairs guest bath to get what he will need to mend her wounds. As he walks away he hears her say, "I know you hate me. Why I don't know. I have always been kind to you and your family."

He turns back to the kitchen, stands before her and said in a soft voice. "I don't hate you."

"Well you could have fooled me."

Deciding it is best to let the subject lie for now he goes to the guest bath for a first aid kit.

Anne's door is opened and she has heard the exchange between the two. When Derek gives her only the shadow of a smile she decides to find out what they are fighting about this time. "Derek is everything ok. I could hear you and Flannery."

Derek loves Anne and he knows she loves him and his children and because it is Flannery's home as well he bites his lower lip and said, "We had another argument. Flannery was running up the hill from the dock trying to avoid my bombardment of cruel words and fell. She has several scrapes and I'm going to doctor them."

"I'll help." is all Anne said before going to the now sad man and giving him a warm hug.

Anne follows him into the bath and taking a washcloth from a shelf above the sink holds it under the facet and wets it to clean Flannery's wounds.

Derek finds the first aid kit in the room's small closet waits for Anne and tells her, "Maybe it would be better if my kids and I stay the summer with my parents." Although he tells her this she knows it is not what he wants to do.

"I feel that with you, Jack and Lucy staying here you and Flannery will get to know each other again. Plus she loves having you and your children here. While you were with Bing and Stella this house was far too quiet. Flannery also noted the too quiet rooms."

"Thanks. The kids and I do love being here." Knowing that he and his kids are truly welcome, Derek kisses Anne's cheek.

When they walk into the kitchen Jack and Lucy are there. They'd been in the living room reading their library books and heard Flannery and Derek.

"Maybe I can kiss your boo boos, like Daddy does for me and Jack." said a concerned Lucy who holds one of Flannery scraped hands.

Jack who is holding her other hand looks seriously at Derek and asks, "Didn't you read the sign on the boathouse. You are supposed to kiss whenever you feel like fighting."

Derek takes the wash cloth from Anne and gently cleans Flannery's face. When he wipes the end of her nose and her chin she flinches and new tears begin to form. "Sorry, I didn't mean to hurt you."

Flannery and Anne know he is not only referring to her nose and chin he is also referring to his cruel bombardment of words.

Once again Jack asks, "Daddy didn't you see the sign?"

Derek looks at his concerned son and said, "It was dark out and we were not by the boathouse."

"Oh, maybe we should use glow in the dark markers."

Derek gives Jack a little smile and agrees.

Anne, Jack, and Lucy stand quietly beside Flannery and Derek while he expertly ministers to her wounds. She flinches each time he cleans a new area that was scraped but says nothing. When Derek is finished, he tells all who are there, "I'm going to carry Flannery upstairs to her room so she can change her clothes before the blood and dirt set in. When I come back down we'll watch a movie and I'll make popcorn."

"I'll make the popcorn with Jack and Lucy's help, you and Flannery can meet us in the living room when you are ready." Anne tells him as she picks up the first aid kit from the table.

Derek picks her up and she reluctantly wraps her arms around his neck. Neither says a word until he sits her down on the area rug in her room. "Tell me what you want to wear and I will hand it to you around the bathroom door."

"That's alright I have pajamas hanging in a hook on the bathroom door." With this said Flannery hobbles the short distance into her bathroom and closes the door slightly. She winces as she removes her now stained shirt and shorts, but she finally gets them removed and hands them to Derek around the door.

"I'll wait and carry you down to the living room." When she says nothing he adds, "Of course you might prefer going to bed."

She pushes the door completely opened, and dressed in purple knit pajama bottoms and lavender knit top with a huge heart across the front with the word Love written in flowers, she tells him, "I'll go down and watch the movie, but I can walk on my own."

Because she is there standing in front of him and because he truly feels badly about her injuries, he walks the short distance to her, smiles a crooked smile and carefully taking her hands in his tells her softly, "You need a hug." Before she can respond, he pulls her close to his chest, and whispers in her ear, "I don't hate you."

Though she is still hurt by his words she wants peace so she whispers back, "I know."

With these words of truth spoken, he once again lifts her into his arms and they walk downstairs to the living room where Anne, Jack and Lucy have set a huge bowl of popcorn on the wooden coffee table in front of the comfortable sofa. They also have individual bowls stacked nearby so each person can help themselves. There are also glasses filled with drinks, tea for the adults and juice for Jack and Lucy.

Derek carries Flannery to the green tweed recliner to the right of the sofa, sits her down and lifts the lever and the footstool pops up for her comfort.

"Aunt Flannery do you want some popcorn?" asks the concerned Jack.

She considers it for only a moment and shakes her head no.

"What would you like? I'm your servant for the evening." Derek tells her while filling the smaller bowls with popcorn.

It doesn't take her long to decide and tells him with hope in her voice. "Isn't there some left over spaghetti? If so that's what I want."

"There is, but it's several days old." said Anne who is sitting in her rocker on the other side of the coffee table from Flannery. "I think it's safe to eat it though."

"I'll be back in a jiff." Derek tells them with a bow.

He not only returns with the now warmed spaghetti in a bowl on a tray that he has cut with a knife, he also has a mug of hot tea and aspirin for Flannery. He has also melted mozzarella cheese on top of the spaghetti exactly as she likes.

He goes to her, places the tray on her out stretched legs, and tells her. "When you are through I will take the tray back to the kitchen."

When the movie starts, Derek sits on the sofa between his kids and her, they and Anne eat the popcorn. While he eats and glances now and then at the family movie, a comedy, he also keeps an eye on Flannery. As soon as she is finished with her spaghetti and the tea he is beside her to take the tray.

Flannery watches the movie for a short time but cannot keeps her eyes opened for long, so gives into the need for sleep and closes her eyes and is sound asleep within seconds. The cats and dogs seem to know that Flannery was injured and anxiously keep an eye on her. Once Derek takes the tray, Garfield jumps on her lap and settles down. Odie finds just enough room near her right hip to settle in. Queen Mary, Anne's cat is lying across her slim calves. Apparently she isn't bother by their closeness because she sleeps soundly through most of the film.

"The animals are protecting her." Anne tells Derek who has been watching Flannery more than the movie.

"Yes, even the dogs are concerned." he adds as they watch Yates, Tralee and Charlie who are resting at various points around the recliner.

Imogen

Chapter Twenty-six

nnery forgoes going to church with her Granny, Der- mily. She knows they will go to Derek's parent's house for lunch, but she can use some quiet time. She needs time to think, time to reflect on Derek and his bouts of anger. He never gets angry with anyone but her and it puzzles her a great deal. She can understand that he has had tremendous stress, but she refuses to take the blame for his life with Chloe. She sits at the kitchen table with the dogs sleeping nearby. The house is extremely quiet and as she looks through the paper she makes plans. What she and they need, Derek his children and her Granny is a road trip.

When she gets to the travel section of *The Chicago Tribune* newspaper she finds an article on Galena, Illinois. She hasn't been there in years and sees that there is much one can do on a few days respite. Her middle school class had taken a field trip there. She, Derek and Nell went and had a wonderful time. She and Derek had also gone there for a weekend trip after their engagement. They'd stayed in separate rooms at the De Soto hotel, and he'd tried to get her to sleep with him, but she refused. Now she wonders, as she has many times since their breakup if having sex with him back then would have changed the outcome of their courtship. Then she remembers Jack and Lucy, and she knows that having them in the world is worth her cancelled wedding.

She will ask her Granny and Derek if they and his kids would be interested in going to Galena. If they agree she will book their rooms tonight on her laptop.

She reads the article, then folds the travel section to keep, and goes outside for some fresh summer air. All of her abrasions feel tight and hurt a little so she goes back inside to take a couple of aspirin. She walks around the house, up the stairs and back down, and is sitting on the living room sofa when she hears her cell phone ringing in the kitchen. She would let it ring without answering, but thinks it could be Derek or her Granny.

Because she moves slower than normal because of her wounds the phone stops ringing before she gets to the kitchen. The phone is on the kitchen counter. She picks it up and takes it with her into the living room.

After she sits on the sofa she checks to see whose number it is. It's one she does not recognize so figures it is a wrong number.

She sets the phone on the coffee table and closes her eyes for a while. Lost in her plans for Galena, she is startled when the phone rings again. When she picks it up she sees the same number as before, so answers it to let the person know it is the wrong number.

"Hello." she said curious to know who it is. When a woman says hello, she thinks she has heard the voice before.

While trying to remember where she has heard the voice before, the woman on the phone said, "Flannery it's me Chloe."

Yes, the voice is Chloe's, though the two haven't spoken in years, nor have they ever talked on the phone. Before she can respond Chloe said with tons of ire and hate, "Don't think that because Derek is divorced that he is yours now. He, Jack and Lucy are mine. You will never marry Derek and be a mother to our kids. Find someone else, have your own kids. Adopt if you must. Jack and Lucy belong to me and Derek and always will."

Flannery is so shocked by her statement that she can't find the words to respond to Chloe's ridiculous words. "Remember what it says in the Bible Flannery, if a man divorces his wife and marries another he is committing adultery."

With time to gather her thoughts Flannery tells Chloe exactly what she thinks of her and her absurd remark. "Adultery, you know all about that, you had an affair with Derek's brother while you were still married and you have the nerve to quote the bible to me. I want to know where you got my cell number. I do not want you calling me again."

Before she can end the call, Chloe tells her, "I've warned you. Stay away from Derek and our kids." With those words banging in her head Flannery shuts the phone off and walking across the room to a vase of silk flowers she pushes the phone to the bottom of the vase and shakes her head trying to shake Chloe's ugly hateful words loose.

She is back in the kitchen stacking the paper in a neat pile when Derek, Anne and the kids return a little after three. She for a moment wonders if she should tell Derek about the call, but just as quickly decides against it. He has had much too much of Chloe and there is no way she wants to upset him.

Jack surprises her with a bouquet of wild flower. She sits again because her knees hurt, and Jack, with a smile that could lite a dark cave said, "These are for you. Daddy let me and Lucy pick them out at the store. Aren't they beautiful?

Flannery takes the flowers and tells Jack, "They are beautiful, but not quite as beautiful as your smile."

He grins shyly and giggles when she pulls him close and kisses the end of his nose.

"These are for you too." Lucy tells her Aunt Flannery, and moves in closely for a kiss of her own.

"Cupcakes, chocolate and with sprinkles, how did you know I love chocolate cupcakes with sprinkles?"

'Daddy told us." said happy Lucy with a sweet smile.

When she finally looks at Derek he grins and reaches for her bouquet. "I'll put these in a vase of water before they wilt."

"Thank you. I thank all of you for the gifts."

Anne who is pouring a glass of iced tea smiles at her granddaughter and winks at Derek, which makes Flannery wonder just how much influence her Granny had in buying flowers and cupcakes.

Lucy who places the cupcakes on the table counts them and said, "There are six. If you share after dinner everyone can have their own' and there will be one left to share.' Flannery hears hope in the little girl voice that maybe Lucy can have the extra cupcake.

"I'll tell you what I will do with the extra one. You and Jack can share it."

"Yeah, can we?" Lucy said with glee.

"Jack we will share. Daddy can cut it in half."

Derek winks at Flannery and carries the vase of flowers to the table. "Do you want them here or somewhere else, maybe your bedroom?"

"Here on the table that way we can all enjoy them."

He sees the travel section folded and opened with the Galena article visible. He picks it up, sits on a chair nearby and opening it flat reads the article.

"I was wondering if anyone would like to take a trip to Galena that's why I have the article separated from the rest of the paper. There are lots of things to do." With hope in her eyes she looks first at Derek, then at Anne who has now set down beside Flannery.

"When do you want to go?" Anne asks with curiosity.

"If I can book the rooms this evening I was thinking this coming Thursday through Monday. We can stay two nights in Galena and two at the Chestnut lodge and drive back on Monday before the rush hour."

"Honey that would be wonderful, but I have promised Virginia I will help with Mary's party and that is Friday. Also Jack and Lucy are invited."

"I forgot the party. Maybe we can plan for another time."

"Why don't you and Derek go? I will gladly watch Jack and Lucy."

Flannery takes only a moment to think about the offer, then turns to Derek who is finished reading and asks with hope in her voice. "Would you like to go with me?"

He smiles and tells her, "I would love to go there. It's been years since my last visit."

"Ok then, after dinner I will go online and book our rooms. What if I can only get one room? If there are two beds would you be ok with the arrangement?"

"On one condition, you will have to keep your hands to yourself."

She shakes a finger at him, and with a glint in her eyes said, "I won't try to ravage you, if you don't try to ravage me."

"It's a deal no ravaging." Derek's eyes twinkle and she sees a little hint of the old less intense man that she once planned a future with.

"What does ravage mean?" asks Jack who never misses anything that adults say or do.

Flannery cracks a smile, Granny Anne covers a laugh, and Derek tells his curious son, "Ravage means to keep your hands off of a person."

"Ok." is Jack's only response before he walks to the porch and outside to play with the dogs. Lucy is not far behind the big brother that she adores.

"You handled that double edged sword nicely." Anne tells Derek before she too goes into the shady backyard.

Flannery turns her head to check the time on the kitchen clock hung above the refrigerator. Seeing that it is only three-thirty she looks at Derek and ask, "I have time before dinner. I'm going to my room to check rooms online. Would you like to come and help me choose?"

"Sure, I'd like that."

Dinner is over. Jack and Lucy are sleeping in Derek's bed. Anne has also gone into her room. Flannery and Derek are sitting in the kitchen, at the table, going over their itinerary for their Galena trip. Flannery has printed the hotel reservations and they are excited about the trip ahead.

"You and I will have to take turns in the bath." Derek tells her with a wink and a silly smile.

"It's doable or I wouldn't have reserved the rooms. We're lucky that we got a room. Apparently lots of others have the same idea."

"It will be nice. We can take our time and do whatever we want." Derek tells her with excitement.

Monday morning Derek, his kids and dogs once more go to Bing and Stella's for a few days. They will return on Wednesday instead of their usual Thursday afternoon. This way Derek and Flannery can leave right after breakfast for their trip to western Illinois.

After a busy day on Tuesday, Flannery is sitting on her bed reading when Granny Anne comes into her room carrying her cell phone. "It's Derek. He tried your number by I guess you didn't hear. He said your mailbox is filled."

Before she hands the phone to Flannery she asks, "Where is your phone?"

"It's somewhere in the living room. I had it turned off because I was getting annoying calls."

Satisfied with the answer Anne hands Flannery her phone and heads back down the stairs to watch one of her favorite mysteries on television."

"Hi. How are you? She asks because she is pleased that Derek would take the time to call her.

"I'm good. How's my patient?

"I'm good. Sorry that you couldn't get me on my phone. I have it turned off."

"I heard you telling Granny Anne that someone is annoying you. Is it someone you know?

"No. It's just someone who keeps calling the wrong number." When she thinks about Chloe she is someone that Flannery doesn't really know.

"What have you been doing? I didn't wake you did I.'

"No, I'm reading one of Dad's books that I found in the attic. It's '*The Pearl*' by John Steinbeck. It has only one hundred eighteen pages, but is excellent. Steinbeck won the Nobel for literature with '*The Pearl*'. Have you read it?"

"I've heard of it, but haven't read it."

"I'll finish it tonight and put it on the dresser in your room. You can bring it on our trip."

He hears the same excitement in her voice that he also feels.

"What have you and the kids been doing?

"Swimming every day, plus Mom and I took Jack and Lucy shopping today for Mary's birthday present. I took them to Target for new play clothes. They grow so fast that I think it wasteful to spend lots of money on all but their school and church clothes."

"I bought you a gift at Target, actually two gifts, and also a gift for Anne."

"Can I wear the gift, eat it or read it?"

"You have to wait until tomorrow. It's nice to know that some things don't change."

"I guess I am predictable but that has its merits." Flannery tells him with a yawn.

"I heard you yawn, and know it isn't because you find me boring. I'll see you tomorrow."

Chapter Twenty-seven

Third Week of June

Flannery and Derek are on the road to Galena after breakfast. The car's tank is full and they carry drinks and snack in a cooler, which sits behind the front passenger seat. Derek takes the first half of the drive and Flannery sits happily beside him humming a Scottish ditty. She sits in her seat and watches the lovely green Illinois landscape through the opened window. The morning is cool from a thunderstorm the night before and the light breeze coming through the opened window smells of soil, grass and pungent cows in the fields on the farms they pass.

Derek who is an excellent driver keeps an eye on the road but also keeps watching Flannery. When she hears him chuckling to himself, she turns and gives him a piercing gaze.

"Derek what are you thinking about? You keep looking my way and now you are chuckling to yourself. Perhaps you should share your joke, or am I the joke?"

He grins and laughing to himself tells her his thoughts. "Since you ask, I have been wondering if you ever pleasure yourself."

When she narrows her eyes to slits and frowns he thinks she won't answer, but then she tells him "Yes Derek I do. Actually I was considering pleasuring myself right where I sit. "

This makes him laugh outright and he said, "I would advise against that. Just visualizing the lovely sexy scene makes it difficult to drive."

"Hum." is her only response.

At the half-way point they stop at a gas station-convenience store to make a pit stop. When they get back in the car Flannery takes over the driving. They drive several miles when she tells Derek about her plan to help him quit smoking and drinking.

"I have been thinking of a pleasant way for you to quit smoking and drinking." She hesitates to tell him her plan so he nods his head for her to go on.

"If you will get my purse from behind my seat and open the zippered front pocket there is an envelope inside with our names on it. It's a contract of sorts. I've already signed my name and dated it with today's date." He reaches behind her seat and with the tan leather purse on his lap unzips the front pocket.

Without a word he pulls the pale blue envelope out and opens the unsealed flap. He reads the first paragraph then looks steadily at her before he continues to read to the last beautifully written line. "If you're serious about your offer I'll sign your contract. Do you have a pen?"

"Yes I'm serious and there is a pen in the same pocket." Because they wear sunglasses neither can read the others eyes.

He finds the pink pen but before he signs he ask, "What do you get out of this?"

She looks at him and softly said, "I will also benefit. There are nights when I have difficulty sleeping and I have heard and read that sex is a wonderful way to relax."

"Yes, I have heard that also." With this said Derek signs his name beneath hers and adds the days date.

They sit quietly for several miles before he returns to the contract for sex whenever he feels the need to smoke or drink. "When would you like a test drive?" He is serious when he asks this then realizes his choice of words and grins. Flannery laughs so he knows she and he will have one memorable road trip.

"Since we will share the same room, why not sometime today or night?"

"What about today and tonight? If you are wondering, I have been tested for STD's and I'm clean." He won't add that he had the test after he found out Chloe was committing adultery.

He sees her pretty face awash with color and despite the fact that she blushes big time she tells him, "Sure why not? But-what if we are not compatible physically? What if we discover we don't get a charge out of this? Do we tear the contract up and forget my plan? As for STD's, yes I have also been tested and cleared."

"Let's not be hasty here you dirty talking vixen. I instinctively know that there are untapped sparks smoldering in my libido and yours. I felt the sparks when I kissed you and I know you did also."

"Yes I felt them also."

She drives and is surprised that she can concentrate on the highway ahead. He looks at the passing scenery for a while but also keeps looking at her. "Too bad we have to drive a speed limit." he tells her with a happy laugh. "It's also too bad we can't check into our room until three."

She looks at the clock on the dash and seeing that is only ten-thirty drives a little faster.

"It's nice to know that you are as turned on and excited about our contract as I am."

"Why wouldn't I be? I wrote the contract and will get as much pleasure as you."

"Yes you will. I will make certain that you won't back out on our deal."

They drive into Geneva around noon, and decide to take their bags to the hotel desk and ask when they can check in. When the desk clerk hears anticipation for an earlier check in, he grins and asks, "Are you on your honeymoon?" If you are I can have the cleaning crew speed up and get you in around two instead."

Derek grins, Flannery blushes and turns her eyes down so the clerk can't read her much too easily read thoughts. When the clerk, Chad is the name on is I.D., badge sees her blush and Derek's grin he assumes that yes they are newlywed.

Chad winks at Derek and with a grin of his own tells them, "Leave your bags. I'll have them placed in your room. Come back at two."

They turn to leave the desk when he adds, "I see from your reservation that you have two beds. I have a cancellation for a bigger suite with one queen sized bed. Would you like that? If so you will be able to check in at one-thirty. "

Derek looks to Flannery and before he can ask if she wants the suite, she looks Chad in the eye and said with her prettiest smile, "Chad that would be perfect. I was late making our reservations and the room with two beds was all that was available. It would be extremely nice of you to give us the suite."

Though her cheeks are slightly pink from a blush Flannery doesn't hide her eyes from Chad or Derek. When she gives Chad and then Derek a sweet grin the men know that Flannery is anticipating the afternoon as much as Derek. It might not be a true honeymoon, but for her and Derek it is a honeymoon of sorts, and if she is correct in her assumption Derek feels the same.

With a new check-in time and a new room plus an earlier check in Flannery and Derek thank Chad and go out for lunch. They are suddenly famished and take little time in choosing a restaurant.

They talk about everything but their contract and their room, but do touch each other's hands and eat from each other forks. From the dreamy eyed looks that they give each other the waitress assumes, as did Chad, that they are newlyweds. When they order dessert she takes a moment to ask, "Are you here on your honeymoon?"

Derek smiles and said, "Yes we are." then kisses Flannery in front of the waitress whose name is Meg.

"I thought so I can always tell when people are in love, and the two of you have love written all over your faces."

When Meg walk away to get their berry cobbler with two scoops of vanilla ice cream Flannery ask Derek, "Do you think we will be struck by lightning for letting people believe we are newlyweds?"

He takes her hands in his, kisses her palms then tells her, "If you aren't sure that this is what you want we will figure out our sleeping arrangements later. Since the room is a suite I would guess the room also has a sofa. I can sleep there."

"Perhaps I'm just a little too prissy, but there is no way that I will back out on something that I have been wanting forever." When she leans towards him and gives him a long deep kiss he knows that what she tells him is true.

After lunch they walk around and go into a few shops. Though he wears a watch he looks at it only once while they shop. He knows that no matter when they check into their room he and she will be just fine with their new arrangement. That she would give him the ultimate gift of herself tells him that she has missed him as much as he has missed her.

When they come to a jewelry store he takes her hand and they go inside. She has no idea why they are looking at expensive jewelry but wants to be with him so follows him from case to case and looks at the sparkling diamonds and other stones with him. At the last case, at the back of the store he stops and asks the store clerk if he can see one of the rings. When the ring is sitting on the glass case he asks her if she likes it. The rings main diamond sits in a circle surrounded by dozens of smaller diamonds.

"It's beautiful. I like that the design is a circle. You know, never ending, continuing on for eternity."'

"Try it on, if it needs adjusting we do that here and you can have it by Saturday morning."

The sales clerk tells Derek and Flannery.

When the ring is slipped on her finger by Derek, neither is surprised that it fits perfectly.

"I guess it's to be yours. " The clerk tells the smiling man and woman who are most definitely in love.

"We'll take it." Derek said with a happy smile as he pulls a bank card from his wallet."

"Is it debit or credit?" the man ask Derek, who is looking at the ring and Flannery.

"Debit." is his answer before he pulls Flannery close for a hug.

"It does a heart good to see young lovers." the man tells them as he hands Derek his receipt, and a bag with the rings blue velvet box.

"Enjoy you stay in Galena and good luck."

As they walk back to the hotel Flannery keeps looking at the beautiful ring. Though she doesn't know what the price was she knows that Derek paid a large sum for her ring. She is also not sure why he bought it so decides to ask. "My ring is beautiful. Thank you. May I ask why you bought it?"

'It is our contract ring. With the ring visible on your hand you won't be able to back out on our agreement."

"A bribe of sorts, ok I agree. With this ring on my finger I will not forget my promise of sex whenever you feel the need to smoke or drink, or just whenever you may have a feeling for sex in your libido."

"He kisses her cheek and said, "That sounds great to me, sex just because I want sex. You are quite a woman Miss Flannery O'Connor Larkin."

"Yes I am, and you are quite a man Derek Liam MacDougall."

The clerk that they talked with earlier apparently has been anticipating their return, because he has their room key ready and waiting. "Everything is in ready and waiting in your room. Your bags are inside your door." He winks at Derek and gives Flannery a knowing smile, which causes her to blush deeply.

Derek signs the registry and while Flannery signs her name he pulls his bank card from his wallet and hands it to the clerk, "We'll pay for everything with this card. It will be debit."

Flannery looks up from the registry wondering why Derek just doesn't leave the room on her card, the one they used to book the room. She will eventually get around to asking him why, but wants nothing to shadow the day she and he have waited far too long for.

The clerk notes the ring on her left hand ring finger. He hadn't noticed it earlier and wondered if the two are actually married. The ring is a beauty and he knows it was extremely expensive. Perhaps they are engaged and are having a sexual fling before tying the knot. That they have different last names is not unusual, he knows numerous married women who have kept their maiden name. Whatever the circumstance he can see the love light glowing in their eyes, especially hers.

Chapter Twenty-eight

It is two-fifteen when they open the door to their beautiful suite. Their bags sit beside the door waiting to be emptied, but they walk on by and hand in hand they go to the bathroom and undressing each other, take their first shower together. When he sees her navel and that she now wears a ring there with a ruby his dark brows arch and he said, "When did you get a piercing in your navel? And if I'm correct the stone is our July birthstone. Aren't you full of wonderful surprises? Also, does Granny Anne know?"

"Full of questions aren't you. I told my Granny I was thinking about getting my navel pierced. Her only request was that I gave it some serious thought. I thought about it for a year and six months ago bravely had it done while in Edinburgh. And yes the stone is a ruby, and my Granny paid for it." For a short moment Flannery is shy and a bit embarrassed, but she wants this as much as Derek so she shoves those unwanted feeling beneath many other unwanted feelings, and loses herself in this moment with this man. For six long years she has not let herself think too much about Derek's life with Chloe, it was far too painful. When she heard from her Granny that he was getting a divorce she decided to let herself day dream of the possibilities of a relationship with him. Their time has arrived and she plans to focus on Derek and the moment. Beyond that she refuses to worry about the outcome of her very, extremely out of character move to help him quit smoking and drinking.

"Good for your Granny." he tells her as he pulls her into the shower with him.

They take their time soaping each other down, not missing even on visible area of the anatomy. Though Flannery feels a tad shy, that feeling is soon forgotten as she admires his wonderfully formed maleness. For a moment, but only that, a vision of Chloe sneaks into her mind, and that her half-sister, six years younger, had sex with Derek before she did. She shakes the image away, and because they are finally together and standing in the shower washing each other, she places her complete and total focus on the gorgeous man standing only a breath away.

No words are spoken while they minister to each other, because none are needed. Neither has to ask if the other is pleased by what they see and touch, pleasure, admiration and words yet to be spoken, they read in one another's eyes.

When he kisses her with years of pent up passion she is blown away and she would have slipped to the shower floor if his strong arms were not around her. That kiss takes away any doubts that she made the right decision when she wrote the contract for sex and then signed it. Would he have initiated having sex if she hadn't written the contract, she is certain that eventually their friendship would have brought them here. When she'd decided that he was what she wants, has always wanted, she was full of hope that he would agree with her arrangement. And no matter how it turns out she has this day, this time with the man she has always loved, and she plans to enjoy their special time immensely.

She is so caught up in the kiss and her thoughts she squeals when he shuts the shower off, throws her over his shoulder and not taking time for them to dry off, walks from the bathroom into their bedroom and lies her on the bed, then in the blink of her eye he is beside her and kissing her deeply once more.

He always knew she was a beauty, and often imagined how she would look unclothed. The beauty of her naked is far more than he imagined. Though her coloring is far lighter than his, he sees that she has the marks from a two piece swim suit, and though the tan is darker than the swim suit areas, he finds either tan or pale she stirs feelings in him that have been dormant for over six years. When he'd kissed her in the shower he could feel that she desperately wants him, as much as he wants her.

They take their time and make certain that each kiss, stroke and movement bring pleasure to the other. She doesn't have to ask if he is pleased because the glint in his eyes tells her that he is immensely so. Slowly they move enjoying the most wonderful sensation either has ever felt. At first it is slow and easy, but as the pleasure builds they move faster, and when they reach climax at the same time they are breathless and completely sated.

They hold each other tightly for a while with Derek still lying on top of her. Then he rolls to his back taking her with him. She raises her head and seeing contentment on his handsome face finally said, "I'm certainly pleased with the outcome of our mating and from your contented expression I am guessing you agree."

He gives her his gorgeous white tooth grin and tells her "Miss Flannery I am more than pleased by our pleasure. You are one gorgeous and extremely hot and sexy vixen."

She lays her cheek against broad chest and kisses the spot near her mouth. She feels him kiss the top of her head and they lay quietly for a time, when she decides she will ask about why he didn't leave the room on her debit, credit card. "Derek, why didn't you leave the hotel charge on my card? I don't mind paying."

For a moment he doesn't answer, and she moves from lying on top of him to his side. His eyes are closed and she thinks he has fallen to sleep, so she turns towards him, throws an arm across his waist and decides she will sleep also. Her eyes are closed only a short time when he finally answers her question. "I'm paying for our room and any charges that may accumulate because I'm an old fashioned man when it comes to paying for things. I have the money so want to pay to show you just how much you and this trip mean to me. I will probably pay for everything while we are here and at Chestnut lodge. So Miss Flannery do you have any more questions you need answered before you and I take our nap?"

"Not now. Maybe later." this she adds with a huge yawn. "Do you have any questions you would like to ask me?"

He thinks for a while then asks, "You said you leave your cell phone off because you are getting annoying calls." She nods yes and though she doesn't want Chloe or thoughts of her to ruin his mood, she knows she must tell him because he needs to know, even if he gets angry with her answer.

"At first the caller would leave voice mail only, which I didn't think too much about because the voice was unfamiliar. On Sunday morning when I stayed home from church the same person called. I recognized the number. When I answered a woman said my name and that is when I realized it was someone whose voice I knew but had never talked with on the phone. When I asked who they were I was in total shock."

Before she has a chance to tell him the caller's identity, he turns his head to look at her and asks, "Was it Chloe?" His voice though not hard, is staid?

"Yes it was Chloe. I have no idea where she got my cell number. I asked her and she wouldn't say. Where do you think she found my number?"

"It's hard to tell maybe she got it from my cell. I usually had it in my room when at home. There is a possibility that she found it there. Now that we have figured that out, what did she say to you?"

"She adamantly told me that you, Jack and Lucy are hers, and that I best remember that fact. She told me to find my own man and have my own children." His only reaction is to nod his head, so she tells him the rest. "She also said that because you divorced her we would be committing adultery if you marry me." He frowns at this but still says nothing.

"I told her that she was a pro at adultery considering she was having an affair with Sean in your house while you were out of town. This shut her up for a short second and then she ended the conversation by telling me that she is warning me. That she will make sure you and I are never happy together. It was then that I hung up on her. I figured she had said more than enough but she called back. I refused to talk with her, and let the phone ring. She left me a message it was nearly like our conversation but she also told me that she has warned me so I better listen, because if she hears that you or the kids are with me or my Granny she will do whatever she must to get even."

Derek shakes his head from side to side, runs his fingers through his dark, thick hair and then asks, "Why didn't you tell me. I have a restraining order on her." When Flannery raises her brows in puzzlement, he tells her why. "Chloe called me the day she received the divorce papers. Dad and I were at Castle Chloe helping the mover with the things I was keeping for me and the kids. She had the nerve to ask for spousal support. She gets the condo in Hawaii, anything from the house that she wants plus half of the profits from the sale of the house." Flannery can feel the tenseness in him and strokes his brows.

"I told her most people could live a lifetime on my offer. She had the nerve to say that since Jack and Lucy mean so much to me I should pay her hush money so she won't be telling everyone Sean is their father. That is when I hung up on her. When she called back only seconds later, I'd had enough, so I tossed the phone into the deep end of the swimming pool. That's why I had to buy a new cell phone."

The eyes that spark for only a short time become thoughtful and to ease his tension, he gives her a little shadow of his smile and he tells Flannery, "I wonder how many cell phones have been thrown away by divorced or divorcing couples. I'll bet the phone companies make a bundle on trashed phones."

"Mine isn't trashed, but I put it where it won't remind me of Chloe."

With dark brows furrowed, Derek asks, "Where did you hide it?"

She grins and tells him about the vase of silk flowers in her Granny's living room.

"I plan to buy another on Tuesday, so I will probably leave the phone hidden in the flower pot."

"Maybe you should bury it in Anne's garden," his face relaxes as they kid and he pulls her close and kisses her on the mouth. "I want you to give me the phone when we get back from Galen. How long ago did you charge it?"

She purses her lips then bites the bottom one before she tells him "It's only been a week. I charged it the night before she called."

"Tuesday I will call my lawyer and ask what I need to do to keep her from bothering us."

"I think that is far too much talking about Chloe. What I need to know is when this love fest weekend is over, where do we go to carry on. You know if I feel the need to smoke or drink I will want a private place for our rendezvous."

"Don't worry about that. We can go to my townhouse in St. Charles. I'm sure Granny and your parents won't mind babysitting now and then,"

"No, they love having Jack and Lucy with them, and I'm certain that I will need you for long periods and hopefully for overnighters."

As she brushes his hair from his forehead she tells him, "We will find a way, if we have to we can make out in your van in the garage at night."

"Now that's a pretty picture, me and you bare naked, in the van that my kids and Nell's ride in several times a week."

"If the hippies were able to turn the Beetle bus into love machines we can turn your Honda Odyssey into one also. We can buy some beads and hang them between the front and back seats, buy some incense and paint huge flowers on the outside. It will be our chance to live on the wild side."

He laughs and because neither he nor she wants to ruin their trip they make a pact to say no more about Chloe for awhile

Friday night they have make plans for dining and dancing in Dubuque, Iowa, just across the river from Galena. It has been nearly eight years since they last danced together. Flannery stands in the bath of their hotel room putting a few light touches to her barely there makeup ritual. She is dressed in a sleeveless cotton blue, green and white geometric print dress. She has a little cardigan, the same blue as the dress hanging on the doorknob. The night air is pleasantly warm but she knows that the air conditioning in the upscale restaurant will be set on cold for maximum comfort of the customers. She wears his gift from Target, a silver necklace with a turquoise heart in the center. It matches her dress perfectly and wears it to show him she is pleased with his gift. His other gift was a box of truffles, raspberry of course. Those she has in her Granny's freezer. Some were eaten when he gave them to her, plus she shared with everyone who was there on Wednesday evening.

Her Granny's gift was a frame of silver and trimmed in turquoise, in this he had placed a beautiful photo of Jack and Lucy from their yearly birthday portrait taken half way between their March 17th birthday for Lucy and the April 15th birthday for Jack. Jack wears a royal blue pullover with black slacks. Lucy wears a long sleeved knit dress of royal blue with tiny pink flowers throughout. Their smiles are sweet and they appear to be happy which makes for a gorgeous photo. It is eight by ten and Anne has it sitting on the mantel in the living room for everyone to see.

She is applying a peach lip gloss when Derek walks up behind her. She sees him in the mirror so is not surprised when he wraps his strong arms around her waist and kisses her neck. "Hello beautiful woman. You are quite a feast for the eyes. You look so amazing that I will have to keep an eye out for those who may want to move in on my territory. The necklace goes perfectly with your outfit."

"Well handsome, I will be doing the same." Dressed in black slacks and a light gray dress shirt Derek does present quite a picture. "Thanks for the compliment and this lovely gift."

Although they haven't had much sleep, because of their need to make love whenever the desire hits, the two are bright faced with happy twinkling eyes. Neither remembers the last time they were so happy and contented. They know that making love is part of the reason, but they also know that being together, alone for the first time in over six years is also the reason.

"I don't know why you bother with the gloss, I'll being kissing it off before we leave the room."

"I have no problem with that. I will slip it into my bag and apply it again later," Flannery tells him with a smile that tells him she wouldn't care if they skipped dinner and stay in their hotel room and do some special dancing of their own. Then she turns in his arms and kisses him slowly and deeply.

"Woman if you keep kissing me like that we will be spending another right in our room."

"I guess you know that wherever we are or whatever we do, I will be more than pleased because you are with me."

He smiles into her eyes, kisses her cheek, then taking her hand in one of his and her cardigan in the other walks her slowly to the hotel room door, into the hallway, down the stairs to the lobby, and out the door to the car, and over the bridge to Dubuque and their first official date since before their breakup.

"I'll pay for dinner." she tells him hopefully. "Since you're paying for the room at the De Soto I can pay here."

He studies her face, a face that needs no lip gloss or makeup at all, and taking her hand in his, he said, "Babe I know that you have an extremely generous heart, but I asked you on this date, so I will pay for our dinner."

She says nothing for a moment then deciding it is best to let him be the Man, tells him, "Thank you. Will you be letting me pay for any part of our trip?"

Without hesitation he gives her the answer she knew would come, "No Flannery I will be paying for everything. You have gone far and above in you friendship to me. Your beautiful self is worth far more than anything I can spend money on."

They eat every morsel of their seven course meal then go to the dance floor and in one another's arms dance until eleven.

Their two days in Galena are followed by two days and nights at the Chestnut Lodge high above the Mississippi not far from Galena. It's used in the winter months for skiing and a ski lift is used for the panoramic views in the warm months, When they check in Derek once more has the reservations charged to his debit card. To this Flannery says nothing. He is a proud man and she knows that she won't ruin their stay at the lodge by arguing.

Once they check into the room they have their lunch at the Lodge then changing into walking shoes they hike in the hills surrounding the lodge. They enjoy the fresh air and the peace and quiet of the area.

"Tell me a little about the adult novel that you intend to write." Derek said when they take a break from their hike.

"It's a love story that takes place in Scotland, on Skye and in the Chicago area."

He watches her face while she describes the characters that will be in the book, and he knows from their conversation that she loves what she has chosen for a career. Her creative talents are enormous and writing is all she has ever wanted to do. The passion that she puts into her writing, she is now putting into their relationship and he is delighted at this huge change. Before their breakup she never told him about her books, and she spent far more time on her writing then she ever did on him. He knows that her writing is like breathing to her, and as long as she places as much time in their romance as her writing, they will stay connected.

"I do love to write, but I have learned the hard way that I must put as much time, or more time, into my relationships."

"Good." Is all he said before taking her hand, and walking down hill to the lodge and another night of making love and getting to know one another.

Monday morning arrives far too soon, but they have made plans to take another short gaunt before summer is old. Though they have made love numerous times since they left Geneva, she is disappointed that her menstrual cycle has started early Monday morning. She goes to the bathroom to pee and the crotch of her pajama bottoms is stained with blood. "Damn it all to hell." she said forgetting her promise to Granny Anne and Derek that she would quit swearing..

Derek who is still in bed tosses the covers back and taps on the bathroom door. "Flannery is there something wrong?"

She hesitates only a moment then tells him of her dilemma, "My period has started. I forgot to pack my tampons." She opens the door a crack and gives him a ghost of a smile. With only his black boxers on he is a wonderful sight and she would have loved going back to bed and making love again. Now she can't.

"I would think that the front desk carries sanitary supplies. I'm sure you aren't the first woman to forget her tampons. I'll pull my jeans and shirt on and go down to the lobby to check. I will also take the car keys just in case I need to buy them at a pharmacy."

"Thank you. You are a life saver. My periods have always been irregular, I haven't had one in three months, but I normally make a habit of carrying tampons just in case."

He gives her a little tug and when she is standing in front of him he gives her a warm comforting hug, and then he kisses her frowning lips. "I'll be back soon. While I am gone clean yourself up and once my deed is done and you are comfortably situated we can get breakfast. You may choose where. Here in our room or in the hotel restaurant. If you'd rather eat out we can also do that." He kisses her forehead, pats her fanny and heads out on his mission.

She jumps into the shower, forgoing washing her hair and cleans herself with a shower. She is drying when Derek taps on the now closed bathroom door. "It's unlocked. Please come in."

She is standing just outside the shower totally naked and for once completely not feeling shy by her circumstance. He holds out several tampons to her and she gratefully accepts his offer. "You are a life saver. What can I do to repay your kindness?"

He grins his heart stopping grin and with dark brows arched he pulls the beautifully naked woman into his arms and looking deeply into her green eyes tells her, "Just spending my time with you is payment enough. Although I was wondering how long your periods are."

"They last only two or three days. So I will be free to romp again by Thursday." His face is contented and he gives her a kiss for the information.

"So if I desire you Thursday evening will you be available for some loving?"

"I made a deal, and I plan to stick with our contract. I enjoy our sexual tryst as much as you, though I am certain there is no need to tell you."

"It's nice to know that you enjoy are intimate times as much as me, but yes I do know that you enjoy me as much as I enjoy you. I'll give you some privacy, do you want me to bring some clean clothing. I will leave the door opened a crack and then hand your things into you."

"Yes, that would help a great deal. I have a denim skirt hanging in the closet, there's a pink t-shirt in the dresser drawer and you may choose my panties and bra." He kisses her again and goes into their room to find her clothes.

While she dresses he begins to collect their belongings and packs them into their cases. The four days have been wonderful and though Derek knows they won't be able to make love as often, he also knows that they will. Her townhouse in St. Charles isn't far from her Granny's or his parent's house and he knows that Anne and his parents will gladly babysit Jack and Lucy with short notice. He knows her Granny and his parents and everyone they know will notice the change in them. He smiles a happy smile remembering there few days together.

He needs a shower and would have loved taking one with her, but he knows there are times when women need their privacy. It doesn't take long for her to dress and join him. In her hand she carries her now washed pajama bottoms. "Is there a plastic bag here anywhere" she looks around the room then at him hoping one will materialize. He turns to his bag, pulls his few soiled pieces of clothing out and hands a bag to her

"I'll owe you big on Thursday. Be ready for a joyful sex fest."

"Hopefully the next three days won't drag." he tells her before going into the bath for his shower.

Chapter Twenty-nine

It is two in the afternoon when they pull into Anne's tree lined driveway. The dogs hear the car and bark excitedly and in only minutes Jack and Lucy are beside the car to welcome them home.

"Oh Daddy, Aunt Flannery we have missed you." Jack tells them while they give each child a kiss and a hug.

"Yes Daddy and Aunt Flannery we have missed you." Adds Lucy as Granny Anne walks through the side gate to join the welcoming party.

"Hello my loves, I guess there is no need to ask if your trip was good. I can see from your happy faces that it was."

Flannery goes to her Granny and kisses her weathered cheek, then moves aside so Derek can also give her a hug and kiss. "It's rather humid today so I'll bet everyone could use a cold drink." Anne tells them as they walk into the walled back yard closing the gate behind them.

Flannery walks holding Anne's right hand in her left. Anne feels the ring and stops at the bottom of the porch steps. Flannery looks questioning at her and stops also.

Anne turns Flannery's left hand over and smiles with delight at the sparkling beautiful ring on her granddaughter ring finger. "This is beautiful. What is the occasion for a ring so lovely?"

Derek who is behind them with Jack holding his right hand and Lucy holding the left also stops and hearing Anne's comment about the ring tells her, "I bought the ring for Flannery our first day in Galena. We were walking on the main street and I wanted to buy her something. When I saw the ring I knew it was made just for her. It is my promise to her that we will give our relationship a chance."

."Grand." is all that Granny said on the happy subject.

"We want to see." Jack tells Flannery as he and Lucy let go of Derek's hands.

Flannery smiles for Derek and holds her hand where his children can see her ring.

"It sparkles." said Lucy who holds Flannery hand so she and Jack can admire their fathers gift.

"Sparkly and very beautiful." adds Jack who looks closely at his father and Flannery.

"Daddy does this mean that you and Aunt Flannery are getting married?"

"Well son your Aunt Flannery and I have been apart for over six years and we have changed a good deal, so we will be dating and getting to know each other again. Is that alright with you, Lucy and Anne?"

"It's fine with me. Actually I think it's a good idea." Jack tells him before walking up the porch steps to the house.

"Me too Daddy, it's fine with me." Lucy adds before she follows her brother into the house.

"Granny Anne what are your thoughts on our arrangement. Do you approve me dating Flannery?"

"Of course I approve. Anytime you need a sitter I'm available." not only is her voice happy, her face smiles along with her words.

Derek winks at Flannery and said with a happy voice of his own, "Well now Miss Flannery we are officially dating. That of course means we are exclusive, so no asking guys for dates."

"Even without the ring I have no intention of dating anyone but you."

"Good or as Granny Anne and Dad say it is grand."

While Derek carries their bags up the stairs Flannery goes to the vase in the living room and pulling the silk flowers out she lifts her phone from its floral bed. She checks to see if it needs charged, but no it is working just fine. She doesn't bother to check for voice mail or text messaging. She waits for Derek and when he walks down the stairs into the living room she hands it to him. "It's ok. You may take my charger with you and I will charge yours when it needs it."

He takes the phone from her hand, slips it into the pocket of his khaki shorts and pulls her into his arms. "My phone is on the desk in your room and the charger is with it. I'll call you tonight." When her green eyes smile into his dark ones, he kisses her deeply and holds her closely for several minutes.

"How are you feeling girl friend?"

"Boyfriend I feel fat but otherwise I am as happy as a girl can be, knowing that we are an item."

"I feel deeply that God is giving us a second chance. How do you feel about this?" He asks with a tug of a smile.

"I feel the same. The first time around I apparently screwed things up by not giving you the time and attention that a relationship requires. This time I intend to give you whatever you need, but if I miss anything please let me know."

He studies her thoughtfully and tells her, "I also want you to tell me if I am neglecting any of your needs. It is true that wisdom comes with age. I am thankful that we didn't have to wait for that wisdom."

"Come, let's go and get the cold drinks that Granny Anne offered."

Chapter Thirty

Derek and his kids leave at four for his parent's house. He won't see Flannery for several days, and though he will miss her, he is at peace knowing that they are now dating. Their time alone was just what they needed. When he'd agreed to go to Galena with her he thought they would get some rest and relaxation, but the trip was far and above his expectations. When he read her contract for sex, he thought she was kidding until he saw her face. What he read in her beautiful face was hope. Signing his name beneath hers only five days before also gives him hope.

Jack and Lucy tell his parents that he and Flannery are engaged. He tells his parents what he told Granny Anne, they are dating.

"If you need a baby sitter Bing and I will gladly watch Jack and Lucy." Stella tells him with a happy smile.

"We wouldn't mind at all." Bing said to confirm her words.

"What does her ring look like?" Stella asks her now beaming son. Yes Derek is her son. She has considered him so since the day that she and Bing were married. She couldn't love him more if she'd given birth to him. He and Sean are her sons and she treats them equally.

Before Derek can tell her about the ring, Lucy describes it as sparkles in a shiny finger band. "It's beautiful and one day when I get married I will tell my husband he has to buy me one just like Aunt Flannery's."

Derek smiles at her across the kitchen table where they are eating chicken fajitas for dinner and tells her, "It going to be a long time until you get married. I think you will probably be thirty before I let you or Jack date."

"Daddy, aren't you and Aunt Flannery thirty?" Jack asks with a serious voice.

"Yes were thirty, but in a few days we'll be thirty-one."

"So me and Lucy will be old when we start dating?"

"Thirty isn't old." Bing tells Jack with a laugh. "Now day's people don't age so fast. I don't consider myself or Stella old and we are in our late fifties.'

Jack bites his lower lip thinking about Bing's statement and looking from Bing to Stella and back to Derek he said. "Ok I see that Daddy isn't all that old. When did he start dating?"

"I believe he and Flannery were dating when they were seventeen, until that time they hung out with the same crowd but didn't officially date until then."

"Daddy you don't have to worry about me. I don't think I'll ever date. There is too much kissing and hugging when you date a person and I will never kisses any girls except Lucy, Grandma Stella, Aunt Flannery and Granny Anne."

"Me either Daddy, I don't want to kiss any boys except you, Jack, Grandpa Bing and maybe Uncle Sean."

"Good, I can now stop worrying that you and Jack will start dating when you start to school next year."

"You're silly Daddy. Little kids don't date just old people."

This makes the adults laugh and thank the Lord once again for Jack and Lucy and the happiness that the two bring them.

Later that evening after Jack and Lucy are in bed, Derek and his parents are in the family room discussing the calls that Chloe has made to Flannery. Derek has counted the voice mails she's left and counted twelve of those plus several text messages. He's listened to only two voice mails and decides that is enough, the fact that she knows of the restraining order against her getting in touch with him, the kids, Flannery or their friends and Flannery aggravates him to no end. He knew there was the possibility that she would go against his wishes and do as she pleases. Though she has always done whatever pleases her at any given moment, he didn't think she would break the law.

He puts the phone on the coffee table near where they sit. "I'm thinking about talking with Gus about Chloe. If she listens to anyone it's him."

"Do you suppose she's back here in the Chicago area? The last I heard from Gus she was still in rehab on Maui. Of course she could just as easily call from there."

"Who knows where Chloe is concerned. Maybe she thinks because she isn't on the mainland the law won't touch her."

When the phone on the coffee table rings Derek picks it up and seeing the familiar number tells Bing and Stella. "Do you believe it, it's Chloe, the nerve of the woman."

He lets it ring without answering, but then it rings again and Stella takes the phone from his hand, answers it, and after hearing Chloe's voice said with a southern accent, "You apparently have the wrong number. This is the number on the phone that I bought last week. I've noticed that you have left numerous messages and several texts. I don't know who had this number before but after listening to your threatening messages if I were that person I would get the police involved." Stella listens only a short time then tells Derek and Bing, "She said go to hell and hung up, do you think that was her good bye."

"Thanks Mom. Hopefully she bought your story and will stop calling Flannery's number."

Bing shakes his head and tells them, "It is really too bad that Chloe hates Flannery. If she'd only given Flannery a chance they could have been friends. I know that Sean said Mia is her friend. I wonder if she is Chloe's only friend. That is too bad if it's so.

"If she has no friends except Mia, it is her own self-involved fault. She thinks she can say whatever she wants even if she hurts a person's feelings." Derek tells them remembering the times she told him mean things and called him horrible names.

Though he hasn't told his parents about Chloe's rants they know that she was extremely cruel to him. When he finally came to the decision to divorce her they were relieved for his sake and the sake of their grandchildren. They are not parents who interfere in their children's relationships, but they pray for them that they will make the right choices.

Derek covers a yawn with his hand, gets up from the sofa, kisses his Mom on the cheek and hugs her, then going to Bing he does the same. "I'll see you in the morning, I told Flannery I'd call tonight." He turns from them only to turn back and tells Bing, "Dad thanks for making the appointment for tomorrow morning with our lawyer. I'll give him the phone so he can listen to Chloe's rants and decide what we need to do. Once that has been settled I'll get Gus involved."

"Good night." he said before going to call Flannery as promised.

They watch him go, noting that his shoulders are back and not slumped as they have been for the past several years.

"Hopefully Gus can talk some sense into Chloe. She was lucky that Derek didn't have her arrested after she abused Jack and Lucy.

Maybe she does think that because she is in Hawaii that no one can touch her."

Stella yawns, gets up from the sofa takes Bing's hand and as they walk from the room after turning the lights off said, "Who knows, it's Chloe we're talking about here."

Bing nods yes because knowing Chloe she will do as she pleases."

Chapter Thirty-one

First week of July

Because the City of Chicago has a huge festival in Millennium Park the last week of June and the first three days of July, and because the festival ends on July third, Bing, Stella, Derek, Flannery, Jack, Lucy and Granny Anne go together in Derek's van. Sean and Nell are also going with her three children. Because his extended cab Ford truck holds six, thought tightly Virginia rides in the van which holds hold eight nicely Virginia graciously accepts the ride. They will meet Sean, Nell and her children at a designated area of the park.

Bing sits in the front with Derek though he volunteered to let Flannery sit there. Because Bing and Derek are over six foot, and have long legs Flannery insists that she will sit with Jack and Lucy. Bing notes that as he drives Derek keeps grinning in the front mirror at Flannery in the third seat in the van. Bing turns to see what her response is when she blushes he knows that his son and Flannery are silently speaking the words of lovers. Since their trip to Galen, Bing and Stella have noticed that Derek is very relaxed and extremely happy. They also see him smiling whenever he is with them plus he hums or sings, something that he hasn't done since he broke his engagement to her nearly six years before.

Though Anne, Stella and Virginia are talking about the festival, they also see Derek grinning at Flannery. When she blushes Anne is the only one in the car besides Flannery and Derek who know why he grins and her granddaughter blushes. When Derek looks at Anne and grins she shakes he head but he knows she won't tell their secret.

The night before, around midnight Flannery couldn't sleep so she wondered down stairs and goes outside to sit on the steps of the back porch. Anne is a light sleeper and hears every noise that her house or humans make. It is only a short time when she hears Derek walk through the kitchen. She knew it was him because his steps are louder when he walks across the wooden floor. When she hears the backdoor open again she knows he and Flannery are having trouble sleeping. Because her bedroom is on the first floor and her windows raised a tad for fresh air she can hear them talking. Though she hears their voices she can't make out every word with the breeze picking up and carrying their words away.

When she hears the side gate, the one they use when they go to the garage, then the squeak of the side garage door she at first thinks they are going out for a while. When she hears no car engine she knows they are in the garage. For a moment she wonders why they are sitting in a dark garage at midnight, and then it dawns on her, the van, they are in the van. She chuckles to herself and stops wondering. The two haven't ask her to babysit in several days, so she figures they are making love in the back seat of Derek's Honda Odyssey.

Though her Granny has not said anything to her or Derek about them being in the yard at midnight she know her Granny knew what they were doing in a dark garage at night. When Derek followed her to the porch steps with a blanket and the keys to his van and those to the garage she at first thought he was going to ask her to go to the townhouse in St. Charles, but when they reached his van and he opened the side door and spread the blanket on the third seat she knew they would not be going to her townhouse.

She blushed when he looked at her several times in the front mirror and grinned because she knew all the adults would probably guess why. Though she's not ashamed by what they did, and because she knows her Granny and Derek's parents are delighted that they are together she lets herself enjoy the sweet memory of their time in his van, on the seat where she and his children sit.

She had a difficult time getting to sleep only the night before, so got up from her bed and went outside to think. It was only minutes later that he walked out on the porch and sat down with a blanket and his keys beside him. "Derek why do you have a blanket and your keys?" she asks curious at what his answer will be. When he raises his dark brows and grins at her, she knows that he wants the same thing that she does. They have been to her townhouse twice and have also snuck into the boathouse like teens, where they made love in one of the canoes. She will never look at the canoe or his van without remembering their lovemaking. He is her addiction, and she hasn't sworn once since their return from Galena. She knows that she is also his addiction because he no longer needs cigarettes or whisky to calm his nerves.

The canoe was a bit hard on her backside but she was so caught up in loving him that she didn't care and apparently neither did Derek. They took their clothes off to pad the bottom of the boat but it was still hard. She wonders if anyone who lives on either side of the river heard them cry out when the explosive climaxes overtook them.

Derek is watching her in the mirror and seeing her dreamy expression he knows she is remembering their loving. Going to the townhouse was ideal except that it is in St. Charles and the last two times that they made love neither of them could wait to drive to St. Charles. Making out in the boathouse had been her wonderful idea and he was extremely pleased that she didn't mind oral sex. Though he hasn't asks, he knows she has had oral sex with only him. He knows she had sex with Stephen, the Scottish lawyer she was going to marry, because she told him so while they were in Galena. When she told him those times were rare, because she didn't love Stephen he believes her. Flannery has never told a lie, and he knows that he can trust her completely. She, unlike Chloe would not be able to hide that fact even if she tried. Chloe lied and didn't care who knew that she was lying. As quickly as Chloe comes into his mind he pushes her out. That phase of his life is over and he is truly happy that it is.

Derek and Sean park their vehicles in a downtown parking garage and everyone walks to the park on Michigan Avenue. Because everyone wants to try different food venues, they note the time on their watches or cell phones and go their separate ways for a while. They will meet later for the fireworks. B**ecause** Granny Anne, Virginia and Derek's parents volunteer to keep Jack, Lucy and Nell's three with them, Derek, Flannery, Sean and Nell walk around the park together.

Sean and Nell are exclusive also and couldn't be happier. Sean is nearly six years younger than Nell, but they have known each other for years. Sean and Derek spent lots of time at Granny Anne's when they were small and also when they were teens. Because Nell lived next door with Virginia and she and Flannery best friends Nell and Virginia are like family.

Back then Sean was like a little brother to Nell and after she, Flannery and Derek graduated from high school and Nell started working full time at Minnie' s she and Sean rarely saw each other. It wasn't until he and his crew started the work to modernize the apartments above her salon that she and he became reacquainted again. Not only had Sean grownup he is a sight for the female's wondering eye. When he and Derek are together, one can see their resemblance to Bing. They are tall and lean like their dad, and have Bing's nose and dark eyes. They also have Bing's generous smile. The difference is in their coloring. Derek has the dark gypsy coloring of his father and Charlotte his father's mother. Sean is fair with Stella's Irish coloring and her blonde hair. And though Jack has the same coloring as Sean and the blonde hair, nobody thinks of the fact that Sean is Jack's biological father. Everyone who knows and loves Derek and Jack consider that Derek is Jack's father no matter who his biological father is.

Derek and Flannery walk hand in hand as do Sean and Nell. They choose the food that they want to try from the many vendors present then find a picnic table at the back of the park and sit down to eat. It has been over eight years since Sean and Derek have been at an event at the same time, and that they are sitting at the same table and trying each other's food and talking like brothers should. "Try this." Sean said offering Derek some of his Italian beef sandwich.

Derek breaks a piece off and trying the wonderful beef said, "That is good. Remember when Dad would bring us into Chicago for a man's day out?"

"Yes, I remember and have missed those times."

Derek hears the sadness in Sean's voice when he answers Derek so Derek tells his brother, "Why don't we invite Gus and Dad to go with us to a ballgame? I'll bring Jack and you can bring Tyler. We can make a day of it."

It takes Sean only a minute to say, "That would be wonderful." Then Sean turns to Nell and asks, "Would you let me take Tyler. He and I are forming a bond and I would love to spend time with him without his sisters, although I also enjoy being with them."

Nell smiles at him and said, "Tyler would love that. You are the man in his life now and he appreciates your times with us. Last night he told me that he is very happy that you and I are dating, and that he isn't the only male anymore. He said it's a big job taking care of four women. Granny and I wanted to laugh but know that he feels it his responsibility to protect us."

"Well now Tyler and I will protect the lovely damsels in our lives." With this said Sean pulls Nell close and kisses her on the smiling lips.

Derek and Flannery, along with Nell's children and her Granny Virginia have been praying that Nell and Sean would become an item, and now that they are, Virginia and Nell's children are as happy about their relationship as Nell and Sean. Nell knows that it was fate that brought Sean and his crew to remodel her building and she thanks the Lord every night, as does Sean.

Sean and Nell have been watching Derek and Flannery closely and note the loving, happy smiles that they give to each other. Plus they sit as close as possible while they eat. When he gets food on his cheek, she lovingly wipes it off with her napkin. When she gets food on her chin he does the same for her. Sean and Nell know they are dating and that it was after their trip to Galen that they became partners again, but they wonder if the beautiful ring that she now wears is more than a promise. They know how Derek and Flannery suffered after he married Chloe and pray that they will get married as they should have six years before.

The four eat and talk like the friends and lovers that they have become. After they eat they walk around to see what things are offered this last night of the festival. The park is packed, but they don't mind. Derek brought Chloe to the festival the first summer that they were married. Jack was nearly three months old then and slept in his stroller most of that time. Stella and Bing and Gus were with them, but he knew Chloe didn't care for the festivities. She pouted and complained the entire time so Derek never took her again. A couple of summers he, Bing and Stella brought Jack and Lucy and though it was better than being with Chloe, he would leave the park depressed because of the times that he'd gone there with Flannery.

It is late when they return from Chicago and because the next day is July forth and their mutual birthday Derek and Flannery are in bed soon after his children. In the past two weeks Derek has put them to bed in the twin beds in the guest room. Because they are usually exhausted after their active days the two have remained in their room until the morning. He has also explained that they will be sleeping in their beds from now on not his.

Jack, always alert, asks, "Are we sleeping in the twin beds because you will one day be married again? I think you need to marry Aunt Flannery. The two of you seem awfully happy since your trip to Galena. Lucy and I love Aunt Flannery, and though you haven't said, we think you also love her. We also believe that she loves you. After all, why would you and she be kissing and hugging and holding hands if it isn't love. I don't see any point in all the icky hugs, kisses and hand holding if you aren't in love."

Derek is always astounded by Jack's keen perception and it is a few minutes before he comes up with a viable answer. "For a five year old you are very smart. I agree that it would be a waste of time to kiss, hug and hold hands with a person unless you feel deeply for them. Aunt Flannery and I care a great deal for each other, but we have changed since we were engaged and we need time to get to know each other. As to why I prefer that you and Lucy sleep in your own beds, well a time will come when I may remarry and you know that my wife and I will sleep together. Of course you will be allowed to join us if you are scared or not feeling well. Sean and I used to sleep with Mom and Dad only if we were afraid or sick and it worked out just fine."

Jack is thoughtful for a moment and then tells Derek, "Daddy I know that you and Chloe, Mommy didn't really like each other. If you did you and she wouldn't have had separate rooms."

"Your Mommy and I never had a loving relationship,. I tried but she wasn't interested."

"I know. I also know that you and Aunt Flannery do have one because I see how you and she look at each other with a dreamy look. I might be a little kid but I know what I know. You may fool yourself but you can't fool me. I know you Daddy and I know how sweet and loving you are."

"Yeah Daddy, Jack and I know how sweet and kind and loving you are." said Lucy taking her cue from the big brother that she trust completely.

Derek kisses them and said, "The two of you are the reason I am loving and kind and sweet but thank you for the wonderful compliment. Having you for my children, is a true blessing and I love you deeply."

"Ah, we know you love us. Lucy and I have so much sweet loving from you, Granny Anne, Aunt Flannery, Grandpa Bing and Grandma Stella, plus Grandpa Gus that I'm surprised that bees don't try to suck all that sweet nectar from our veins." Jack said with a grin.

Derek doesn't know why he was blessed with these two wonderful children but he is truly thankful that they are in his life. Without them he knows he would not have survived the last few years. He doesn't say anything to Jack's statement. Jack is right on track with his words. Derek hugs and kisses them and with a sweet peace in his heart he goes to his room and begins to read his bible, something that he has begun to do every night since his trip to Galena. A scripture that he sees as he reads brings him further peace. From his bible he reads the scripture several times, then taking a pen and small notebook from his night table begins to copy *Philippians 4:6-7,*

Don't worry about anything,
instead pray about everything,
tell God what you need
and thank him for all he has done.
If you do this you will experience God's peace
Which is more wonderful than the human mind can understand.

From time to time Derek will learn scripture and because he wants to learn Philippians 4:6-7 he knows writing it down will be a big help.

Flannery has also been reading her bible more than she has in several years. Like Derek she also keeps a small notebook beside her bed and writes down the scriptures that she wants to learn. For some odd reason she knows she must learn *Deuteronomy 31:6,* so she writes it down,

Be strong and courageous!
Do not be afraid of them!
The Lord your God will go ahead of you.
He will neither fail you nor forsake you

After reading the scripture several times, she puts her bible aside with the note pad and as she is slipping into sleep she hears Chloe's voice the day that she called Flannery and warned her to stay away from Derek and his children. Though she manages to shake those thoughts away, the scripture stays in her mind

Chapter Thirty-two

July 4th

Because they were out late the night before enjoying the festival in Chicago, the festivities for Derek and Flannery's thirty-first birthday and the July fourth celebration are planned for late afternoon.

It's nine a.m. when Flannery opens her eyes at a tapping on her door. At first she thinks she is imagining the tapping then she hears Jack and Lucy's sweet voices. "Daddy I don't think Aunt Flannery is awake" this from Jack then from Lucy, "Maybe she sneaked out while we were wrapping the gifts in our room."

She tosses her light summer blanket to the side, looks in the mirror above her dresser across the room between the rooms two wide windows, sees she doesn't look too rumpled, then goes to her bedroom door and opens it to see Derek smiling widely and his children laughing happily at seeing she is there.

"Good morning birthday girl. We've come with gifts just for you, because it is your special day and because you are special to us." Derek said before pulling her into his arms for a deep long kiss.

Jack, impatient for his Aunt Flannery to see the gifts bought just for her, pulls the sleeve of Derek's short sleeved, gray and white cotton checked shirt. Derek ends the kiss and holding Flannery with his arm around her waist, looks at his impatient son and said, "Aunt Flannery Jack and Lucy have been up since seven and could not wait to give you your gifts."

"Aunt Flannery you sleep longer than little children are you alright" Lucy said with a concerned look on her little face.

Flannery cups Lucy's little face in her hand and tells her, "Sweet Lucy, I'm fine and I guess the fun yesterday wore me out. I'm surprised that you and Jack didn't sleep longer."

"Their as excited that we have a birthday today as we are." Derek smiles happily into her eyes and she smiles back.

"Presents please let's go into your room and open your presents." Jack said as he dances around the other three.

Flannery, with Derek's arm still around her waist gestures with her hand for them to enter her room.

She sits on the unmade bed with Derek beside her. Jack and Lucy crawl across the bed to sit as close to her as possible.

"This is from me and Lucy," Jack tells her as he places a square package wrapped in gift wrap that is decorated with Disney characters and tied together with a bright green satin ribbon.

"I love the gift wrap and the ribbon," she tells them as she slowly unwraps the gift. She is sweetly surprised to see a beautiful bracelet inside the silver box that's lined in the green of the ribbon. She lifts the gift from the box and slips the Da Vinci designed charm bracelet on her arm.

"This is beautiful. How did you know I wanted one? I saw the one that Nell's kids bought her for Mother's day and told her how lovely it was. She let me try it on and told me where they bought it but I didn't think it was a gift I should buy for myself."

When her eyes become awash with tears of happiness Lucy and Jack are concerned. "Are you sure you like it? If you do why are you crying?" Jack asks with concern on his face.

"Are you sad? Don't you like our gift?" ask Lucy with much concern.

Flannery wipes her tears away with the sleeve of her pajama top, pulls them into her arms and kissing their faces tells them, "This is a wonderful gift and because it is from two of my favorite people in the entire world I will cherish it forever."

"Good." Jack tells her and his father. "Girls are so silly, they cry about everything."

"I don't." Lucy tells them with attitude.

"One day Lucy when you are with the right man, when you're thirty or older you will probably cry from happiness also." Derek tells Lucy as he musses her curly blonde hair.

"I will marry you when I'm thirty" she tells him then gives him a kiss on the cheek.

"You can't marry Daddy. You will marry someone your own age." Jack tells her with the shake of his head.

"I'm not getting married, I'm only three, and boys my age don't work so we wouldn't have money to live on." She looks at Derek and smiles then said "Daddy maybe you would let us live with you."

Flannery grins, waiting for Derek's words of wisdom for his three year old daughter. He grins when he tells Lucy, "You'll not be getting married before you finish college and work a few years. I believe a woman needs to know who she is before she settles down. I also believe the rule applies to men also."

She is pleased with his admission that women need to know who they are by living on their own before marriage. Now when she looks back at the naïve twenty-five year old engaged to Derek, she knows she wasn't ready for marriage and all that it entails. She also knows that now she wants everything that marriages and family bring to a relationship. Now she knows that she was extremely selfish and self-centered and vain. Though she hadn't wanted her fame as an established children's writer-illustrator to jade her thinking, she knows that she did. Derek was right to break off their engagement because she was so high on fame that she didn't have time for him.

"Here, this is from Daddy." said an impatient Jack who apparently thinks there is far too much talking and not enough unwrapping gifts.

Derek winks at her when she opens a C.D. of Carole King's hit songs. She knows that he also loves the music and will invite him to listen to it with her one night. "Thank you." she tells him before she kisses his smiling lips.

"Gosh, at this rate it's going to take till noon to open the gifts." Jack said with exasperation.

"Jack, Derek said sternly whose birthday is this? You need to be patient so Aunt Flannery can admire and then thank us for the gifts."

Jack, who rarely has to be reprimanded, gives his Dad and Flannery a sheepish grin and tells them, "I'm sorry. It is hard to wait and see how much Aunt Flannery likes what we bought.

"Thank you for apologizing. Flannery and I know how difficult it can be to wait for things. You will find out as you grow up that the best things are worth waiting for." Although his words are for Jack he looks deeply into her green eyes, and she agrees that the best things are definitely worth waiting for. When she smiles and kisses his cheek he knows that she agrees with him, which pleases him immensely.

Flannery opens several more beautifully wrapped gifts from Derek Jack and Lucy and remarks at how much she loves each gift. She knows that several gifts were picked out by Jack and Lucy because she remembers the gifts she once picked out for her Granny Anne. There is a huge box of truffles, which she immediately opens and offers to the gift givers. The box Derek bought for her before the Galena trip was gone in only a few days. She also eats one and sighs at the wonderful combination of chocolate and raspberry her all-time favorite combination. Derek knows she loves her raspberry and chocolate and grins when she sighs.

They have also bought her a pretty red silk bag with zipper and it is filled with at least twelve bottles of nail polish in bright psychedelic colors. "After I get dressed for the day, and eat some breakfast, why don't you and I paint our toe and fingernails?" Flannery tells a widely smiling Lucy who chose the bag and nail polish herself.

"Oh yes. Daddy said that you would let me use some too." Lucy gives Flannery a hug that warms her heart and though she does love her gifts Lucy's hug is the best gift of all.

Jack smiles happily when she opens an eight by ten box and finds one of the colored pencil drawings that he loves to give to the special people in his life. She is amazed at his talent and tells him so, which is a gift to Jack since his Aunt Flannery also draws and gets paid to do so. It is framed and matted and she knows exactly where she will hang it. She gets up from the bed, taking the framed print with her and holding the gift above her computer desk smiles and tells a very happy Jack that she will hang it where she can look at it while she works.

The print is of Jack and Lucy's pets sitting and waiting for their food bowls. The sketching is detailed and Flannery knows that Jack has a gift. "You should be proud of this. I knew you did sketches, but didn't know how amazing they are. You must show me some others."

Derek can see that she is sincere in her compliments to Jack and what has always amazed him is that Jack and Flannery are the only ones in their families who have the same talent.

Lucy who takes this all in stride has never been jealous that her big brother is a gifted artist. She stands beside Flannery with tiny hands on her hips and eyeing the spot where Flannery holds the framed print tells her, "Aunt Flannery you need to lower it a little so that when you are sitting at the computer you have a better view of Jack's sketch."

Flannery looks from a very staid and serious Lucy to a grinning Derek and trying not to laugh said, "Lucy, you are right it would be better hung lower."

"Daddy where's the other gift that you bought for Aunt Flannery?" ask a puzzled Jack who saw the gift with the others. Derek slips his hand into his shirt pocket and hands the gift to Flannery whose mouth opens in surprise when she sees ruby studs for her pierced ears. They are the exact shape as the one on her navel ring.

Derek doesn't care for tattoos or piercings per se but the sight of, and the clear memory of her beautiful stomach with the lovely navel ring with the ruby bought for her by her Granny Anne was and is extremely seductive and he knew as soon as he saw the ruby studs that he would buy them for her.

She kisses him and going to look in the mirror above her dresser she immediately hooks them in her ear lobes. She turns from side to side admiring the beautiful gift, turns to the three on the bed, gives each a hug and a kiss and tells them, "I love my gifts. Thank you for remembering."

"Aunt Flannery, where is our gifts to Daddy?" asks a once more impatient Jack.

"I've hidden them in the downstairs hall closet. Let me get dressed and then we can go downstairs and give them to your Daddy."

Derek knows that Jack will be biting at the bit while Flannery gets ready so he tells her, "We'll go downstairs and make your breakfast. Will cereal and toast be enough? I ask because we will be eating our birthday lunch in only a few hours."

"That will be great. May I also have a cup of tea?

"At your command you gorgeous woman, I still can't believe that you are thirty-one today. You could easily pass for a twenty year old. Then I remember that yes you are thirty-one, because so am I."

She crosses the short distance between them, wraps her arms around his waist and pulling him close, whispers in his ear. "After the birthday and Fourth of July festivities I will give you an extra special gift. A gift that will knock your socks off and anything else you are wearing."

He pulls back to look into twinkling eyes and he is definitely going to be anticipating her extra special birthday gift all day long. And what a long day it will be now that he knows she will definitely knock his socks and everything else off.

.He is nearly finished fixing her breakfast with Jack and Lucy's help. When the kids hear Flannery calling them from the living room they go and see what she wants.

She has pulled Derek's gifts from their closet hiding place and when they enter the room she smiles and said, "I'll need some help carrying Derek's gifts."

"Sure we'll help." said Jack who takes a big gift bag for her hand. Next she hands a gift bag of the exact size to Lucy.

"I was wondering how you would wrap these." Jack said as he opens the bag to look inside. "It's a good idea to cover the balls with tissue paper. That way Daddy won't see them until the tissue is removed."

Lucy peeks into the bag she holds and agrees with Jack.

Flannery carries two more gifts these in boxes, and gift wrapped in G.I. Joe and Hello Kitty wrap. Each package is adorned with several sticky bows of red, white and blue. She slips her new nail polish gift in the side of one of the bags, Lucy looks at her strangely then ask, "Aunt Flannery why are you giving Daddy the nail polish? Don't you want it?"

When Lucy's lower lip starts to quiver and tears pop into her brown eyes Flannery sits the gift down and pulls her into her arms and tells her, "Lucy honey, of course I want your gift. I brought it downstairs so that after Derek unwraps his gifts and I eat you and I and Granny Anne can polish each other's toe nails and finger nails. Your gift is beautiful just like you."

Lucy blinks the tears away then wrapping her arms around Flannery's long legs smiles through the tears and said "I thought you would like the pretty colors and the glitters in the polish. Daddy said that you would share with me, but since it is your gift I would have to wait for you to ask."

Flannery bends and kisses the sweet little girls soft cheek that has turned a beautiful golden tan like Derek's coloring. "I love you Lucy Hanna."

"I love you too Aunt Flannery."

"Aunt Flannery why are you so nice and kind when Chloe, Mommy is so mean?" Jack asks as the three collect the gifts and walk down the hallway to the kitchen.

"I don't really know the answer to that. I haven't seen Chloe in quite a while. Why some people are mean and others are not I don't know. Maybe if I knew Chloe better I could say."

"Maybe, I think she was meanest to Daddy. She was always saying unkind things to him. He is a wonderful Daddy and I know that all those mean things were not true."

"I knew that too. Daddy is a sweetie and if I could choose any Daddy in the world it would be my Daddy." chimes in Lucy.

When they walk into the kitchen Derek is standing at the kitchen counter spreading butter on two pieces of whole wheat bread, and Flannery can see by his expression that he has heard every word that the three have spoken. His eyes though dark study her as she walks to the table and she and his children sit his presents in the center of the table. There is a bowl of Cheerios sitting on a floral placemat at one end of the table. A small pitcher sits beside it. A ceramic mug with an Edinburgh logo across the front sits near a napkin that holds her spoon and a knife.

His gaze doesn't leave hers as he places her toast and a jar of raspberry jam near her placemat. He has also cut a red rose, only slightly opened, in a bud vase near her bowl. She smiles at him and reaches for his hand when he sits in the wooden chair next to her. "This is wonderful, a birthday breakfast. I'm sorry that I overslept or I would have eaten with you and the kids."

Though his eyes are not easily read she sees a distant light that had disappeared when they were in Galena. Hearing his kids tell her what she had only guessed, that Chloe was extremely unkind to him, hurts her heart and she knows that he apparently wasn't ready to tell her about the cruelty. And maybe he doesn't trust her enough to do so.

"Daddy why are you sad. It is your birthday and we have gifts. Open them and I'll bet you will feel better." Lucy tells him as she pushes one of the gift boxes in front of him.

He opens a gift from Flannery and his kids, he looks at the two basketball nets with hoops and the distant light disappears. "I can use these. Tomorrow I'll replace the old ones and the four of us will have to play basketball. There's only one problem we don't have a basketball."

"Daddy look in here and here." Jack tells him with excitement.

He sticks his hand into the first bag and pulls out the silk bag with nail polish. He looks at it frowns, looks at it again and said, "I guess Lucy has bought us matching bags and polish. He looks in the bag and pulls out a bottle that's cherry red with glitter mixed in. "Hum, Jack do you think you and I should wear the red or maybe the royal blue."

"Daddy you're so silly. Aunt Flannery put it in the bag so she could carry two gifts. When we're done here she, Granny Anne and me are going to polish our toe nails and finger nails. Besides, boys don't wear polish."

"Is that right? I'll have to take your word for it. Jack do you think Lucy girl is right?"

Jack shakes his head and tells Derek, "Daddy you are silly. You know that boys don't wear polish."

"Well now Flannery if Jack and Lucy tell me boys don't wear polish, I guess I won't be using the blue or the red."

"I guess I'd best open my gifts before Jack gets antsy." Derek grins at his kids and pulls the basket balls from their gift bags. At the bottom of the second bag he finds an air pump.

"Now we have everything for a game. Tomorrow after I replace the hoops why don't the boys compete against the girls? Jack of course we'll have to play like girls so we don't outdo Aunt Flannery and Lucy."

"Lucy girl don't you worry. They can play like boys and we will still stop their clocks."

Derek leans towards her kisses her cheek and grins. "I'd love to see you stop our clocks."

"Yeah Aunt Flannery we'd love to see you do that." Jack adds following Derek's lead.

"Tomorrow will be a day of defeat, so I guess it is best we don't play them today Luc. I'd hate to beat Derek on his birthday."

"Tomorrow will definitely tell who is better at basketball. And I would also hate to stop your clock today, being that it's also your birthday."

" Here are my words of advice for you don't bet on that because you sir will be defeated."

"Sure." Derek said with a laugh as he opens the one remaining box on the table. The one wrapped in Hello Kitty pink gift wrap. He opens the gift carefully and folds the paper and hands it to Lucy, as he did the G.I Joe for Jack. "Wow an I-pad, I've been thinking about getting one. My laptop is at Mom and Dad. I like this better, it's smaller and easier to carry. Thanks to all three of you. I love my gifts, and you know what is really nice. I can share my gifts."

"Daddy, will you let me and Lucy try the I-pad? There are kid's games we can play on it." Jack tells Derek with hope in his voice.

"I'll let you use it but not every day. Its summertime and I want you and Lucy to play outside as much as possible. When Aunt Flannery, Nell, Sean and I were kids we spent most of the summer days playing outside."

"Yeah we know. Granny Anne has told us."

Just then Granny Anne, dressed in navy capris, navy sandals and a short sleeved white t-shirt with an American flag on the front and the words *God Bless the USA* inscribed in black letters beneath the flag, enters the kitchen. In her hands she carries several similar shirts, one for everyone in the room. "Virginia and I had these made the other day. We thought it would be nice if everyone wears one. I've already given Bing and Stella's there's. Virginia has enough for her family including Sean." With this said she hands one to everyone around the table. Flannery who wears a tank-top pulls the t-shirt over her head, Derek who wears khaki shorts and a white polo shirt pulls his shirt over his head and replaces it with the shirt from Granny. Granny helps Lucy remove her red t-shirt, Jack removes his own. "This way if we decide to do different thing at the carnival later today we can find each other easily."

Next she pulls two envelopes from the pocket of her capris and gives one to Flannery and one to Derek. They open the envelopes and pulling out a birthday card, they open it and their mouths are agape with surprise.

"Granny Anne, tickets for Disneyland and the Disney hotel for four days. Derek I have two tickets for each, plus the tickets for the flight. Wow and the date is for next weekend." She gets up from her chair and gives her Granny a kiss on the cheek and a hug.

"I have the same, two tickets to Disneyland and tickets for the flight. Derek pushes his chair back and as Flannery did, he hugs Anne and kisses her cheek.

"Thank you," they say together and everyone laughs.

Because Jack and Lucy are totally unaffected by Anne's gift and Derek knows they love anything Disney he looks at their smiling faces and ask, "Jack and Lucy did you know about the tickets?"

They grin and nod their heads yes but say nothing. "I asked Jack and Lucy what they would buy for you and when they said Disneyland I agreed that it would be a wonderful gift."

"Yes, we chose Disneyland and not Disney World. We've been to Disney World and we think it's too big for little kids and I remember one of the kids in my pre-school talking about Disneyland, He had pictures and I ask if he'd been to the one in Florida. He'd been there and also said Disneyland is better for little kids."

"Flannery, Lucy and Jack next week at this time we will be in California. What a wonderful and generous gift."

When Derek checks the airline tickets he sees that they are only for one way. He shows Flannery and she looks at her Granny whose eyes are twinkling. "If you are wondering why the airline tickets are for only one way, it's' because Bing and Stella have the other part of your gifts.

They wait for her to clue them in on the other part of the gift, when she says nothing they know that they will have to wait until lunchtime and gift giving at Derek's parent's house.

They are cleaning the table of gifts and Flannery's breakfast dishes when the doorbell rings. The dogs were resting in the backyard, race through the doggie door on the screened porch and lead Derek and his kids into the front entryway. Derek has the kid's hold their dogs back while he picks Charlie the Scottie up before he opens the heavy wooden blue front door. Sean is standing there, dressed in a t-shirt similar to Derek's. He smiles at Derek and the kids and said as he first hugs Derek and the kids. "Happy Birthday big brother, if you're wondering why I'm here it's to tell you that I've picked Granny Virginia, Nell and the kids up." Here he turns and with his hand, gestures towards his blue extended-cab truck sitting in front of the house. Derek can see Nell in the front seat. She waves as do Virginia and Nell's kids. Derek, Jack and Lucy wave back. Apparently Virginia is going to be sitting tightly with her grandchildren but her smile tells them that she doesn't mind one bit. "I'll get everyone moving. You're welcomed to come in and wait while we get ready."

"We'd come in but Nell, Virginia and I have volunteered to help Dad and Stella, Mom with the birthday lunch. You and Flannery certainly knew how to come into this world with a bang. Being born on July fourth is one thing, but arriving between nine and nine-thirty p.m. while the fireworks are being shot off is a huge welcome into our world."

"Yes, Flannery and I wanted to be remembered. And you know how much we love to make an entrance."

Sean laughs, tells them he'll see them at Bing and Stella's and returns to his truck and a family that is becoming more precious to him every day.

Chapter Thirty-three

After lunch, which is a cookout in Bing and Stella' big backyard, a typical July fourth cookout, with hotdogs, hamburgers, potato salad and all the trimmings, the cake is lit with candles, thirty-one emerald candles for Flannery and thirty-one royal blue candles for Derek. Because it is custom of old, they blow on their candles at the same moment. When Derek blows his out with one breath, but it takes Flannery two tries, Derek grins at her and winks. She knows he is happy to beat her, because it means that her offer to help him quit smoking is apparently working.

Though Derek and Flannery have not come out and told anyone of their contract. Though those closest to them, adults only, grin because they have seen Derek and Flannery together and have seen the looks that travel between them, and note how calm they are and the once intense Derek relaxed, they know that Derek and Flannery are having regular sexual encounters.

Bing and Stella's gift also knocks their socks off. Each receives reservations for a four night stay in San Diego for four near Mission Bay, plus airfare from Los Angeles, then back to Chicago at the end of the trip. There are tickets to Sea World and the San Diego Zoo, plus the wildlife park. There is also a car rental for their San Diego stay."

"Dad, Mom, Granny Anne, your gifts are wonderful, you certainly know how to spoil us." said Derek as he hugs each parent. Flannery also thanks them and brushes the tears away.

"Aunt Flannery, don't you like the gifts? The San Diego trip was thought up by Uncle Sean and Nell. Their taking Virginia and Nell's kids there before schools starts plus they are going to Disneyland."

Before Flannery can respond to Jack's question Mary, Nell's three year old said with excitement, "Granny Virginia's going to."

"That's good. Virginia, as I recall from our trips to Six Flags, when Sean, Derek, Nell and Flannery growing up loves the roller coasters." replies Bing with a chuckle.

"Do you Granny?" ask a wide-eyed Mary.

"I do honey. Now let's let Flannery answer Jack's question."

"I love the thoughtful gifts." she tells Jack and wipes her tears on a napkin.

Derek has been watching Sean and Nell since they arrived at his parent's house, and can see that there is definitely more than just an attraction between the two. He also sees that Sean is attached to Nell's kids, plus Virginia seems to approve the relationship whole-heartedly. Nell's life has been hectic with running her salon and raising three children. Derek knows that Virginia, like Anne, has never found raising Nell and her three, or Anne raising Flannery and babysitting Jack and Lucy as anything but a gift from Heaven. How blessed they all are to share life and time together.

From Virginia, Nell and Sean they receive several gift cards for restaurants that can be found nationwide. Once Flannery and Derek hug everyone several times and thank them for the generous gifts they have enough time to play in the yard before going to the carnival nearby,.

Nell loves to dance and wants to dance with Sean so he brings a boom box into his parent's yard. The group needs to wear off a few calories from the birthday lunch so he turns it to a rock station, or disco by some standards. He and Nell dance, as well as everyone at the party. When a Gloria Gainer tune comes on Flannery and Nell take center stage on the back patio and do a fast paced rendition of "*I Will Survive.*" It is one of their signature songs for dancing and they have several trophies to attest to that. Derek knows that the two are totally uninhibited when together and grins along with Sean when the ladies dance up to them and insist that they do the routine with them. Anne and Virginia have learned the routine from their lively granddaughters and don't hesitate to join in the fun,

Jack and Lucy and Nell's children used to having fun with Nell, Virginia, Flannery and Anne don't take long to join the others.

Chapter Thirty-four

When Derek, Flannery, Anne and the kids return home everyone is ready for a quick wash, tooth brushing and bed. Anne takes care of the dogs, letting them out, then back in, and locking the doggie door, so they won't be rushing outside when the expected, unlawful fireworks are set off in the area. To her surprise the three dogs aren't as afraid of the noise as she thought they would be. Her dog Charlie, when there with only Anne had hidden under her bed at hearing the New Year's Eve fireworks. Being with the bigger Yates and Tralee seem to give him courage and for Charlie's sake she is glad.

Flannery helps Derek with Lucy and Jack. The two children are so tired that their eyes close the minute their heads hit their pillows.

Though Flannery and Derek are also tired from too much food and celebration, she knows that their celebrating has only begun. She takes Derek by the hand and into her bathroom they go. Undressing quickly they are into the shower and bathed within minutes. Redressing in only their Fourth of July and birthday shorts and t's she takes his hand again and leads him from her room.

"Will it be the boathouse or the van?" Derek asks with a happy grin.

"Neither." she tells him as they go to the end of the hallway, and opening a door she leads him upstairs to the attic. The moon is full, and peeks through the now sparkling attic windows, which gives them just enough light so they don't run into anything. She tells him to close his eyes, which he does, trusting her completely. At the top of the stairs she lets go of his hand, goes back down the stairs, and locks the door from the inside, then going to him reaches around his broad shoulders and flips a switch to a lamp that she has dusted and placed on a table in an alcove between the windows and leads him to an old, yet still usable chaise lounge.

"Was the chaise lounge here when you and I were going through the trunks several weeks ago?"

"Yes, as were the lamp and table." A beam runs across the room, close to the alcove and here she unhooks hanging beads of red, white and blue.

"I see you are a closet hippie." he tells her with a grin.

"I could be now, although when I was a teen and in my twenties I had far too many hang-ups about sex to have been a true hippy."

"And now?" he teases with a sexy grin as he pulls her close so he can see into her twinkling eyes.

"Now because I desire you, actually crave you, I believe I would be a person that the hippies of old would be proud of."

"I'm truly happy to be the recipient of your newfound sexuality. I could sense that it was hidden, but knew when the right man came along you would blossom. Thank you for making me that man."

"You have a way about you that is hard to resist. Sometimes when I am secretly watching you or at night when I am thinking of you, it takes every ounce of restraint not to go and crawl in your bed."

"I always know when you are sneaking peaks at me. Your face is dreamy and your eyes filled with desire and something that I cannot detect. Maybe you can tell me what that might be."

"Rather than tell you why don't I show you?" With this said Flannery pulls her t-shirt over her head. He is mesmerized by her nerve and her beautiful breast and happy that it is only at bedtime that she goes braless. She grins when she see him watching her, pulls her shorts off and stands before him in all her naked glory. Though he keeps his eyes on her, he also removes his shirt which is followed by his jeans. Derek also wears no underwear.

She lies on the chaise lounge that she has covered with a light summer blanket, places her head on the pillow that she brought for comfort and holds her arms out to him. With a look of passion in his dark eyes he lays on his side, with just enough room not to fall off, pulls her against his chest and kisses her deeply and long. In his kiss are the years they have been apart, and all the lonely nights before she generously offered herself to him in Galena.

With her hand holding his head she gives as much to the kiss as Derek. There are firework going off somewhere along the river, but the only fireworks that they need are the ones they are feeling in touch, strokes, kisses and loving each other. They smile into each other's eyes and lay face-to-face without saying a word. No words are needed because they have just showed how they feel about one another.

The full moon bathes the attic with its silver light, light that reach to them in the alcove. Derek had been unusually quiet for most of their day and the celebration of their countries independence. Flannery wonders if it is because of what he heard Jack and Lucy telling her while they were walking down the hallway to the kitchen with his gifts. She would like to ask him if that is the reason but doesn't want him to be upset with her, so instead of asking about what his children said, she breaches the subject of Lucy's crying when she thought Flannery didn't want her gift of the nail polish.

"Derek, I have a question, it's about an incident in the living room this morning when Jack and Lucy were helping me with your gifts." He nods his head for her to ask the question, so she does with the assurance that he won't blow his stack, as he did when she ask about his relationship with Chloe.

"I'd pulled the two gift bags with the basketballs out first, and because I had my pretty bag of nail polish with me, and didn't want to take the chance of dropping it I slipped the polish into the bag where you found it." Here she stops to see what his reaction is, when he nods again for her to continue, she adds, "Lucy's little face turned sad, her bottom lip quivered and she cried and ask, Aunt Flannery don't you like my gift."

Here she stops once more to gauge his reaction. "Continue." is all he said so she takes a leap of faith and does just that.

"I pulled her close, kissed and hugged her and said that I love her gift and was only making sure I didn't drop it on the way to the kitchen. I also told her what a wonderful little girl she is. I also said that I was going to share with her and Granny Anne and that we would polish our nails before we left the house. This cheered her up instantly and she smiled shyly and told me that her Daddy said I would probably share. Why did she think I didn't want her gift?"

Derek watches her face closely and decides that she's entitled to know why his sweet Lucy Hanna cried.

"First I will tell you a little about Chloe and gifts." Flannery nods, he continues. "Our first Christmas together after we married, I went all out and bought her gifts for Christmas and her December twenty-eighth birthday. She hadn't bothered buying gifts for anyone, her parents or me. She said she didn't feel well and I believed her. When she opened my gifts to her she frowned and said that I apparently didn't know her style and rejected each gift that I'd so thoughtfully bought." He stops with his story and kisses her cheek before he tells her more.

"Let's move ahead several months. Jack is nearly a month old, so I decide I will buy a Mother's Day gift from him. Chloe also rejected that stating that it wasn't really from Jack."

"Another of Chloe's selfish habits was that she never bought anyone, even her parent's gifts. When I ask why, she said that she was not interested in knowing what others like so she didn't feel the obligation to buy gifts." He sees the look of shock and amazement on Flannery face but continues with why Lucy cried.

"My birthday came and went without even any acknowledgement. It wasn't that I wanted gifts but a greeting of Happy Birthday would have been nice. I still foolishly went out for holidays and her birthday and bought her a gift. It was the year that Lucy was born that I stopped. When the kids were old enough to choose gifts for her, I thought that this might please her. This past Christmas the kids and I bought gifts, decorated a tree, and planned a dinner for her birthday. Her parents and mine were invited. I'd bought a cake and cooked dinner for everyone. My parent's and hers arrived on time. Chloe was home and knew about the dinner. Before our parent's came, Jack and Lucy wanted to give Chloe the gifts they had bought. She was in her room, where she spent ninety-five percent of her time getting all dolled up. Foolish me, digging my grave and almost covering it, thought she was getting ready for dinner. When we came into her fortress she frowned and said she was busy. The kids held out their wrapped gifts, which she also frowned at. She said she didn't have time to open them and if they left them in her room she would do so later. Jack and Lucy were disappointed, but thought she would open them later as promised.

He stops here remembering how angry he was at her. When he sees a concerned look on Flannery's face, he moves forward with his story. "Chloe not only didn't stay for dinner she never opened Jack and Lucy's gifts. She went out that night with friends and stayed away for several days. Jack and Lucy went into her bedroom to see if maybe she'd taken their gifts with her. They found them unwrapped and stuffed in her bathroom waste basket."

"They were devastated and cried because their Mommy didn't want their gifts. Needless to say I never brought up buying her gifts again, and neither did they."

"When I told them that they could choose gifts for you they ask if you like gifts. I said yes, that Aunt Flannery loves gifts. This brought back their joy of buying gifts for others. They are so unselfish that if I saw that they really liked something, and offered to buy them a gift they said that their birthdays are over and they only want to buy for others."

Before she thinks Flannery said, "At least they haven't inherited Chloe's selfish genes." When she realizes what she said she covers her mouth with her hand.

Derek chuckles, kisses her forehead and tells her, "A truer statement I have never heard."

His eyes hold the distant light that she saw when he'd heard his kids telling her that Chloe was mean to Derek. She puts her arm around his waist. When he doesn't push her away she knows that it is safe to comment on his sad story. "I'm so sorry that they and their gifts weren't appreciated, and also that neither were yours."

He runs his hands through his hair and gives her a kiss on the cheek. Because her concern is sincere and that she is so sweet he tells her, "After she turned down my gifts a few times and me I didn't care what she did or didn't like. What pissed me off was that she could be so cruel and cold hearted to two sweet little children who only wanted to give their Mommy gifts."

"Thank you for telling me. Now I understand fully why Lucy cried. I know I don't have to tell you, but Jack and Lucy are wonderful and you have every right to be pissed off at Chloe."

He yawns, followed by her yawn so they redress, turn the lamp off and go down the attic stairs to their rooms.

When Derek awakens he rolls towards the nightstand to look at the alarm. "Twelve p.m., goodness I've slept all morning and its lunchtime."

He tosses the light blanket back, sits on the side of the bed for a time stretches his arms above his head and goes to look out one of the windows that faces the backyard. From here he can see Flannery and Lucy cuddled together on the hammock, Flannery is apparently reading to his daughter. The beautiful sight brings a smile to his face and fills his heart with warmth. Never in the three years since Lucy was born had Chloe ever set with their children. Not once did she volunteer to read them a book.

He knew that Chloe had a learning disability and at first attributed that to her not reading to their kids. When he mentioned this to Gus, he was told that she can read to a degree but that she isn't interested in books. He bought her many books over the years but they were never read.

When Jack learned to read at the age of three Gus gave the books to him. For a while Derek worried that Jack and Lucy would have Chloe's learning disability, but Gus eased his mind when he said that when Chloe was born Rena's labor was extremely long and when Chloe was born the doctor used forceps to pull her from the birth canal. She had a huge bruise and a goose egg bump on the side of her head and wonders if that is why Chloe had trouble learning.

Once Derek is showered and dressed he goes to the kitchen to make some breakfast. After he eats he joins the others in the yard. He is immediately greeted by the three dogs, waiting patiently for a pet. Jack, whose sitting on the swing with Granny Anne reading to her, lays the book on the swing to go and greet his Dad. Flannery helps Lucy off the hammock so she can join the two. The three hug and kiss as they always do when seeing each other the first thing in the morning, the last thing at night, or whenever they feel the need to love on each other.

"You look well rested my love." Granny Anne tells Derek when he stops in front of the swing to say hello. "I'll bet you haven't had the chance to sleep in since Jack was born."

"Yes, but getting up with Jack and Lucy is always a blessing."

After he hugs Anne, he walks to where Flannery is now sitting on the side of the hammock, smiles into her eyes, kisses her and said, "Thanks for letting me sleep. Yesterday's festivities, too much food and being up late wore me out."

She grins and kisses him back. Jack looks at the two, then ask Anne with a puzzled 'expression and ask, "Granny Anne, I wonder if an animal got into the attic. Last night I thought I heard noises above me. They woke me, I listened for a while and then everything was quiet. Do you think a poor critter went up there and can't get out? Maybe we should check when we go in."

Anne looks steadily at Flannery whose eyes twinkle and who is trying not to grin, then at Derek whose eyes also twinkle. He doesn't try to hide his grin and winks at Anne.

"Jack, I'll have your Daddy and Aunt Flannery check. Flannery has been cleaning the attic and can probably tell if there is anything disturbed up there. If she and Derek find some animal, I will call the wildlife people to come and collect whatever is there."

"It appears that the two of you had an excellent birthday celebration." Anne tells them with a smile. In that smile they know that Granny Anne not only suspects but knows that Flannery and Derek are responsible for the noise that Jack heard.

Chapter Thirty-five

Once the attic is checked and shown to be critter clear Derek, Flannery and the kids go outside to the drive in front of the garage and Derek and Flannery replace the old basketball rims and nets. After a late lunch they take Jack and Lucy outside for a game of basketball.

"Jack I think we should take it easy on the girls let them have a few points so that when we whop their butts they won cry."

Flannery narrows her eyes, lifts Lucy to her shoulders and dunks the ball straight through the net near the western edge of the drive then she bounces the same ball to the basket to the east side of the drive and dunks it straight through again. "Lucy, my friend, do you see any girls playing basketball with you and me?" Lucy grins and shakes her head no.

"Daddy, you didn't tell me that Aunt Flannery plays like a pro" Jack tells Derek with awe in his voice.

"It was pure luck. Toss me the ball Michelle Jordan. I will show Jack how real men play the game." With this said, Flannery tosses Derek the ball, who hands it to Jack who is riding on his shoulders.

Jack tosses the ball which hits the rim of the basket and falls away from instead of into the basket. "Ah Daddy, I didn't toss it high enough. Please may I have a second try?"

Derek turns to face a grinning Flannery and hands the ball to Jack once more. This time Derek raises Jack off his shoulders so he is nearly as high as the basket. Jack tosses sending the ball straight through the net. "I did it. Maybe we will beat the girls." Jack tells them with a great deal of pride and happiness.

"We'll stop their clocks. We'll show them how real men play won't we Jack Larry Byrd."

"Daddy, who is Larry Byrd," Jack asks with curiosity.

"He's one of the all-time great basketball players. I think Mom still has my sports card collection, if so, I will show you Larry's card."

"Aunt Flannery I want to throw the next ball into the hoop." Derek tosses the ball to Flannery who hands it over her head to an excited Lucy. Flannery lifts Lucy above her shoulders as Derek did with Jack. Lucy tosses the ball high and she and Flannery are now scoring more points than the guys.

"Who's going to have their clock stopped? It won't be us will it Lucy Barkley."

"No it won't be the girls." Lucy said with glee.

"Daddy we better get moving or they will win." Jack said with eyes twinkling. Before Derek can hand the ball to Jack he asks, "Daddy who's Barkley. Is he the Charles who's sometimes on Sports Center?"

"Yes Jack he's the same guy. He's also one of the great basketball players. He ended his career with the Phoenix Suns. In nineteen-ninety-three Charles and the Suns tried to whoop the Chicago Bulls in the NBA finals. They did their best just like our own Michelle Jordan and Lucy Barkley."

"So Aunt Flannery is Michael Jordan, that name I do know." Jack tells Derek with pride that he would know at least one of the players. "Who are you Daddy?"

"He's Shaquille O'Neil, ya know Shaq." said Flannery who doesn't miss any of the other teams moment of letting their guard down, and tosses the ball into the basket again.

She holds onto Lucy's thighs and dances her victory dance from one end of the driveway to the other. "Lucy Barkley we rule. Hey Derek and Jack who's clock has been stopped and beaten into the concrete?"

"We'll see," he said taking the ball and dunking it without sweat.

"Pure luck Shaq, toss the ball to the real pros." When he tosses it to her over her head it goes to happy and excited Lucy. She lifts Lucy as before, only higher. So high in fact, that Lucy is right above the basket and she drops it right through the net.

Jack and Lucy are having a ball, one, because they are with Derek and Flannery and two, because they are riding on the adult's shoulders.

They play until Granny Anne comes to tell them that dinner is ready and on the table.

That night after their baths, and a bedtime story Derek is kissing them good night when Jack tells him, "Daddy why don't you marry Aunt Flannery, me and Lucy think she would be a wonderful Mommy for us and a perfect wife for you."

"Lucy is that right?" Derek asks his yawning and sleepy eyed little girl.

"Yes Daddy, I love Aunt Flannery. She's sweet and kind and lots of fun,"

"I'll have to think about that. Do you think Aunt Flannery would want to marry me?"

Jack who is also yawning looks with seriousness at Derek, and tells his Dad his thoughts on his Daddy and Flannery. "Daddy I see how she looks at you and how you look at her and everybody who knows you can tell that you and she care a great deal for each other. If you didn't, why give her the pretty ring? Also you and she kiss and hug and hold hands and go on dates."

"Jack you are a very observant and smart boy. You are right of course. It's give me something to think about."

Chapter Thirty-six

Flannery is restless and thinks that maybe she played basketball with too much enthusiasm. The game was lots of fun, and she knows that Derek and his children had fun to. She tosses from side-to-side then back again. She lies this way for a few minutes and goes to look out the bedroom window at the lightning slicing through the dark western sky, there hasn't been much rain so far and it is July. There have been a few light sprinkles here and there, but much more is needed. She walks to her bed and picking up one of her pillows goes down stairs to lie on the living room sofa.

Odie is sleeping in Granny Anne's rocker, on her chair cushion the color of a Robin's egg, and raises her head when she walks by the chair. Whenever Odie and Anne are in the living room at the same time she'll wait until Anne sits down and then she curls up on her lap to sleep. Garfield and Queen Mary, Anne's cat, have taken nicely to each other and sleep on the padded window seat in the downstairs hallway.

Tralee, the Border collie favors women and hearing Flannery walking down the steps comes to lie on the floor in front of the sofa. Charlie, Anne's Scottie, and Yates the Golden always sleep in Anne's room. The dogs rarely climb the stairs to the upstairs bedrooms and seem to prefer the downstairs room much more. At first Jack and Lucy were disappointed that their dogs don't sleep near them like they did in the big house where they lived with Chloe. Derek believes that the two loyal dogs slept near Jack and Lucy in the house they shared with Chloe because they didn't trust his ex-wife.

Flannery hears thunder rolling across the night sky and sees a few more lightning flashes before she falls asleep. She dreams that she is in the country looking at a parcel of land and doing some sketches for a house, and cries out in her sleep, when in the dream a man comes up behind

her a man whose face she cannot see. He grabs her from behind and places a cloth over her mouth, this scares her and that is why she cries out in fear and panic. This awakens her with a start, and for a moment she doesn't know where she is. She's shaking, and Tralee, concerned by her outcry goes to Flannery and licks her face.

She pets Tralee's warm head and listens to the rain dancing down the living room windows. As she listens to the comforting sound, she feels the panic subside. She sits up and reaches to turn one of the living room lamps on. It is only a short time before she sees Derek walking down the stairs faster than normal. When he sees her sitting with one arm wrapped around her pillow and the other around Tralee, he walks to the sofa and sitting beside her sees fear in her eyes.

"Flannery did I hear you cry out?" She nods yes and putting the pillow behind her wraps one arm around his waist and lays her head on his comforting shoulder. "At first I thought it was Jack or Lucy. They are sleeping soundly as they usually do. Then I saw the lamp come on down here and knew it was you."

He takes her hand in his and asks her what scared her, she tells him about her dream, and in doing so he feels the tenseness in her.

"I'll be happy to stay with you. We can stay her and sleep or wherever you want."

When she looks into his eyes she sees concern and because she doesn't want to be alone tells him, "Why don't we go to my room. I would love your company."

He kisses her cheek, stands and taking her hand he smiles a crooked smile. "Your room it is."

She pats Tralee's head, and ask the dog, "Tralee do you want to come with us?" Tralee is once more lying beside the sofa. She opens one eye in answer, sighs then closes her eye and sighs once more. "I guess her duty is over. She was licking my face when I awakened from the dream."

"She is very loyal to those that she loves. Chloe was the only person she avoided. I never saw Chloe do anything mean to her, but she kept a close eye on her when she was anywhere near me or my kids."

"She's like you, loyal and protective to those you love," Flannery tells him as he turns the lamp off and walks with her up the stairs.

"That can be said of you also. You Ms. Flannery are extremely loyal and protective."

The lamp on the bedside table is on low, the room is cool with the windows opened. When they walk into the room Derek lets go of her hand to lock her bedroom door. When he turns back to her she is laying on the bed waiting. When he reaches her she holds out her arms and he goes to her gladly.

He lies beside her then rolls to his back taking her with him. "Tomorrow is Sunday and because we are leaving for California Thursday I thought the kids and I would stay at Mom and Dad's for the night. They love having the kids there and if I go Monday instead we would have only two nights there. Also you and Granny Anne can have some quality time. With me and the kids here you don't get as much one-on-one, and I know how much the two of you cherish your time together."

She nods her head in agreement, then holds his face in her hands and kisses his eyelids, his forehead, his nose and his cheeks. When she reaches his lips she smiles against them then moves to his chin and on down his six foot, two inch frame planting kisses as she goes. When she reaches his waist she lifts her head and seeing that he is fully into the moment, she slips a finger into the waistband of his navy boxers and slowly pulls them over his flat stomach, down his thighs, pulls them over his feet and tosses them in a small heap beside her bed. Then continuing with her kisses bypasses his groin area and with her tongue runs her tongue down his thigh to the tip of his big toe. Next she runs her tongue up the missed toe, up his calve and his thigh.

After the loving he rolls off her, then to his side to face her. They study one another for a short time, and kissing each other, he pulls her to his side for sleep. "I didn't care for my dream but it brought us here so instead of it, I will remember our night of wonderful, sexy and fulfilling passion."

He kisses her neck and closing his eyes, tells her, "When I am here or anyplace that you may be with me, if you need comfort or a friend to talk with I am always available."

With her eyes now closed she nods her head and agrees that she is also available to him.

He is nearly asleep when she whispers "what will you tell Jack and Lucy if they find out you slept with me?"

It doesn't take long for him to say, "I will tell them that you had a bad dream and I came to comfort you. We fell asleep and so I spent the night in your bed."

Satisfied with his reasonable answer she sighs and completely contented fall into a dreamless sleep.

Chapter Thirty-seven

When they awaken the rain is through and the morning sun paints the walls near the bed a soft golden. Derek looks at her bedside clock and seeing that it is only six a.m. enjoys the quiet of the house and the woman smiling beside him. Her face is filled with sleep and contentment. He kisses her lips and rolling to his back said, "With me and the kids at my parents for the next three nights, and because we will be sharing a room with them in California, we will have to curtail our passion."

"I agree, it wouldn't be right for us to do the things that we do to and for each other with Jack and Lucy there. Do you think we can hold out for eight days and nights actually eleven, no twelve days and nights?"

"We will make our best effort to be celibate while in California '

She nods her head in agreement and they throw the covers back and head for her bathroom. After the shower, while brushing their teeth and combing their hair, Derek tells her that he will pay for everything that isn't covered by their generous family birthday gifts.

Chapter Thirty-eight

Flannery and Granny Anne have appointments to have their hair cut at Nell's Salon at nine on Tuesday morning. Nell is the only stylist that Anne lets near her steel gray, still thick head of hair. Once a month she goes to Nell and has the full service treatment. A wash, conditioning, cut and blow-dry are what she gets. She has thought she would one day have Nell color her hair her natural dark brunette, the color that Flannery's hair is, but chickens out every time. She is so used to her steel gray color that she believes to have it colored would make her hair look too stark.

Nell's shop is closed on Sunday and Monday, so the shop is busy though not too busy. Nell always offers tea or coffee to her clients along with a pastry. Flannery is surprised, when Anne asks for Café mocha instead of her black coffee. When her granddaughter's brows go up in amazement, Anne tells Flannery and Nell, "I've decided to branch out in my life, you know try new things. If Nell wasn't so busy I would have her color my hair."

"Flannery is getting a trim only, so Granny Anne I do have the time to color your hair. I have a color already chosen for this monumental day. I know you will like it."

Anne looks at Nell in the mirror and tells her, "Good, let's go for it. Flannery and Derek have made some changes in their relationship and so far the outcome is good, so I will join the trend."

Nell doesn't have to ask what the changes are, she knows just from looking into her friends twinkling eyes.

"Sean and I have made a few changes in our relationship also." Nell tells two of her best friends in the world.

"We noticed." Flannery tells her with a happy smile.

Hazel eyed, dark blonde short haired Nell grins at Flannery and Flannery grins in return.

Only an inch shorter than Flannery, Nell is curvy in all the right places. Having given birth to three children, her once boyish figure is definitely womanly. She has thought about doing some exercise after work two days a week so broaches the subject with Flannery and Anne.

"Granny Anne, Flannery", she said as she turns from trimming an inch from Flannery's dark hair, "I've been thinking about taking a Zumba class on Tuesdays and Thursdays and want to know if you would like to join me. We can meet here when the salon closes and go together. There is a class at six every night. This week I'll go on Wednesday, tomorrow to check it out"

"I'll go with you tomorrow evening and after our trip to California on Tuesday and Thursday nights." said Flannery who is looking at herself in the mirror above Nell's work station. Nell hands her a hand mirror so she can check and see if the trim suits her. It does so she hands the mirror back and gets up from the chair so her brave Granny can have her hair colored.

"Granny Anne what about you," Nell asks as Granny sits in the chair to have her colored for the first time in her life.

"One change at a time honey, the hair today and then I'll decide if I will Zumba."

That evening Flannery and Nell are having dinner at Virginias with Nell's three children, Kristen, Tyler, and Mary while Anne and Virginia go out for a rare ladies night to a movie and dinner. Anne's hair turned out as lovely as Nell thought it would. Instead of the dark brunette of her youth, Nell chose a color that brings out Anne's green eyes, so much like Flannery's and her late son James. With light beige blonde hair with highlights, and a little bare minimum makeup Anne was as excited about her new look as Flannery, Nell and Virginia. Virginia has always trusted Nell to color and style her hair so the Granny's may be that, but they are also pretty and vital with lots of energy and a life to live, so that is what they are doing. Though the two have been widowed for years they wouldn't mind going out with a nice man once in a while. While they were raising their granddaughters they decided that was their main goal. Now that their girls are women they may take a trip somewhere together.

Flannery and Nell are sitting in Virginia's big country kitchen, decorated in red, black and white, looking through travel brochures that Virginia and Anne have collected. They have asked the two to help them choose a trip for them to take when Anne returns from Scotland. Springtime will be the time they will go so Nell and Flannery are looking at places that are in the southern hemisphere.

"How about here?" Flannery said as she hands Nell a brochure on Australia and New Zealand. "My Granny has often talked about going here. The weather will be nice and they can take a side trip to New Zealand. The trip is for four weeks, but they would see lots of things."

Nell looks at the brochure and while she studies the itinerary she tells Flannery, "Guess who was in the salon this afternoon?" Flannery shrugs her shoulders, so Nell tells her, "Tall, dark, handsome and intense was in. He and his kids had me cut their hair,"

"Derek, Jack and Lucy I'm guessing," said Flannery with a smile. "I thought Lucy wanted to let her hair grow long."

"I trimmed hers only. Derek's hair is thick and beautiful but I've noticed he's getting more and more silver streaks in the dark hair, of course living with Chloe would turn anyone's hair gray."

"Yes, though he doesn't say a lot about his ex his kids tell me she was awfully cruel to him."

"He's changed quite a bit, but so have I. My heart goes out to him and his kids and now that he no longer sees Chloe maybe he will become less intense. We have had a few horrendous fights because I dared ask about his marriage. I asked only because I want to understand why he stayed with Chloe for nearly six years. He said because of Jack and Lucy. He did everything he could to help Chloe become the mother that they need, but it was all to no avail."

"Yes, he's a wonderful father. I've heard rumors about Chloe's treatment of Derek and the kids. How she could be so cruel has always puzzled me. I've asked Sean about her, but he said she isn't part of his life any more so he'd just rather not discuss her."

"It's wonderful that you and Sean are a couple. It always puzzled me how such a sweet guy got sucked in by Chloe, but then she also sucked Derek into her web. He has told me she wanted him only so that he wouldn't marry me."

"She's definitely a puzzle. I pray for her as does my Granny. Pray works, but Chloe is a hard one to figure out." Nell said with the shake of her head.

"So tell me my sly friend, I have heard that Derek no longer smokes or drinks the whisky. What magic are you using?"

Flannery blushes a deep rose, which makes Nell raise her chin and look closely at her sometimes secretive friend, "From the look on your face I'm guessing you are using your feminine wiles on tall, dark, handsome and intense."

Flannery gives Nell a sheepish grin and said, "Yes my feminine wiles. We have a contract. I wrote and signed it then gave it to Derek while we were in Galena, actually in the car on our way there. It is an offer for sex anytime he feels the need to smoke or drink the whisky. Of course he thought I was kidding. When he found out the offer was sincere he signed right away. Needless to say, Derek and I have started a new phase to our relationship."

"Well now girlfriend, I always knew you were creative, and I am mighty proud of all that talent. I have one question, where do you go for your pleasure?"

Flannery, over her bout of embarrassment said with a smile, "Wherever we can find a place, the boathouse, his van, the attic, the townhouse."

"Good for you and Derek." When she sees a little smile tugging at the corners of Flannery mouth she said,"I don't have to ask if it's good, I can see from your little smile that it is,"

"Not just good, it's unbelievably amazing."

"That's great. You and Derek have given up a lot and it makes everyone who knows and loves you extremely happy for the two of you."

Flannery hasn't asks but decides since they are getting personal to ask Nell about her love life.

"Sean is wonderful, thoughtful and caring. We have christened every room in the two apartments above my salon, and we have also had sex at his place and in his truck."

"Mommy, what have you and Sean done in the truck?" asked blond haired green eyed, ten year old Kristen who has just walked into the kitchen. A small replica of Nell, Kristen is always walking in on Nell's for adult ears only conversations.

Nell, used to her children's questions tells Kristen, "Sean and I love to lie in the bed of his truck and view the night sky."

Kristen, who's intelligent yet naïve said, "That would be ok. Where's the truck parked when you are in the bed?"

"In his drive way, or here in Granny Vi's driveway, or at the park."

"Hum, ok. Mommy, can Tyler, Mary and I have a little bit of ice cream. We ate all the popcorn."

"You go back to your movie and Auntie Flannery and I will make everyone root beer floats."

When Kristen is out of ear shot Flannery grins at Nell and said, "You my friend are an excellent liar."

"Storyteller, an art I have learned from you." Nell tells Flannery as she pushes back the chair she sits on, and gets up to make the promised root beer floats.

While making the promised root beer floats Nell tells Flannery about something that Derek told her while getting his hair cut, "When I told Derek that you and Granny Anne were in that morning, at the salon, he immediately asked if you got your hair cut. When I said a trim only, he smiled with relief and said, I'm certainly happy that she hasn't gotten her beautiful hair cut too short, I know she would look fantastic no matter how short or long she wears it, but I love the long hair especially in a ponytail. That is the most I have ever heard him say on any subject. You know Derek he doesn't talk much about his feelings."

"Your right, he doesn't say much, especially about his marriage to Chloe. Perhaps he would just like to forget that time." Flannery said as she scoops several scoops of vanilla bean ice cream into tall glasses.

"I know that he prefers my hair long. He's told me so, when we're in the throes of passion and when he pulls my hair aside to ravage my neck." Flannery grins a soppy grin at the memory of those precious times, and because her mind is on Derek, she pours root beer over the top of two glasses, which runs on her bare toes and the black and white tile floor.

Nell laughs, taps Flannery on the head and said, "Nell to Flannery, you have poured too much root beer in the glasses."

Flannery looks at the liquid mess on her feet and the floor and with a happy grin, takes the paper towels from Nell's hand and happily cleans her mess.

Flannery and Nell are closer than sisters and tell each other many things and because Granny Anne is the only one who knows her secret she decides she will now tell Nell. Because Nell is not one to judge others Flannery feels that Nell will hear the bit of info and keep it to herself. "There's something that I need to tell you because you are my dearest friend."

Nell knows that what Flannery is about to tell her is extremely important and personal because she can read her friend well. “I have been to several doctors, here, in London and Edinburgh. I have been told that I will never be able to conceive because I apparently was born with only one ovary and one fallopian tube. They aren’t on the same side so it will be impossible for me to get pregnant.”

Nell takes her friends hands in hers, kisses her cheek and said, “I’m truly sorry to hear that. You were meant to be a mother. Have you thought about adoption, then again hopefully you and Derek will get married and you can be Jack and Lucy’s Mom. I have heard that Chloe hasn’t a maternal bone in her body but I know that you love Jack and Lucy and they also love you.”

Flannery’s eyes lose some of the seriousness when she thinks of Jack and Lucy. She does love them and she won’t deny that she would love being their mother. “I guess that’s up to Derek. Having sex with him doesn’t guarantee a wedding. I think he needs time to be single for a while.”

“Perhaps he does, but I have seen the way he looks at you and what I see isn’t a look of lust or friendship. What I see is love and there is no denying that you have loved him since we were kids.”

“Your right, there is no denying that I love him. Of course you know that is why I didn’t marry Stephen. He’s a sweet man but he never had my heart. I did him a favor though. Remember Xena the Zumba teacher whose classes I took in Edinburgh, I introduced them after we split and they hit it off instantly. They married six months later and she is pregnant with their third child. Stephen couldn’t be happier. When I told him before our engagement that I couldn’t bear children he said he was ok with that, but when I see him with Xena and their two sons I know that marrying him wouldn’t have worked. He beamed when he told me that the newest child is a girl.”

“He seemed very nice and yet when I saw you with him on Skye I could sense that you were only settling that you liked him but didn’t love him. I do remember Xena. She must be what twenty or twenty-one.”

“She was nineteen when they married and Steven thirty but they get along amazingly well and his family is crazy about her. What’s not to like, she’s sweet and bubbly and they can see that she genuinely loves Stephen. I keep in touch with his sister Theresa and she said that when we broke up she was heartbroken but now that she knows Xena and sees how happy

Stephen is she is ok with our cancelled wedding. Xena and Stephen send me photos of each new baby and I couldn't be happier for them. Their son Cullen looks like Stephen but has Xena's exotic Italian coloring, Greg the younger son also looks like Stephen but he too has Xena's lovely dark coloring."

Nell smiles at her friend and said, "I believe you Ms. Flannery love dark looks. Could that be because one Derek Liam MacDougall also has the exotic dark looks?"

Flannery grins and said, "Yes that is why. Stephen with his reddish hair blue eyes and fair complexion is so totally different from Derek that I believe that is why I was attracted to him. You know there is no man who can compare to dark, intense Derek. I guess he will always be my heartthrob"

"There's nothing wrong with that. The ladies at the salon practically fall all over themselves when he comes for his monthly haircut. He is totally oblivious to the fact that he sets many hearts aflutter. Actually it is refreshing to see how unassuming he is. I have also noticed that with Sean and Bing. The men in the MacDougall family are to die for and yet the three don't seem to know how gorgeous they are."

"I've also noticed that about them. Speaking of which, do you suppose Chloe wanted Derek not because she hates me but because she loved him? I have wondered that for the last six years."

Nell pats her cheek with her hand considers Flannery's words and replies, "I find the MacDougall men easy to love and easy on the eye. Now that you ask I do remember the few times I saw Derek and Chloe together. That was the first year of their marriage. I saw them in Chicago at the July third fireworks. They were with her parents and his and Jack was nearly three months old. I was with my Granny, Kristen and Tyler who was two months then. Derek saw us sitting close by and brought Jack over for us to see and he just wanted to say hello. Chloe at first stayed where they were seated but then Derek called her to come and see Tyler and she can to check him out. She didn't say much but I saw her eyes and what I read there was surprising. I saw the look of love for Derek. When she realized that I was watching her closely the door on that look closed, and she turned away so that I could no longer read her expression."

"Do you think Derek also loved her? I mean she tricked him into believing Jack was his which was foolish considering he looks exactly like Sean."

"My Granny saw what I saw and we talked about it when we got home. What puzzled me was her attraction to Sean. Why would she have regular sex with Sean and know that her baby was his and then lie to Derek? That tells me that she really wanted Derek all along but since he and you were an item she felt the only way to get him was to tell her huge lie that he and she had sex even though he swore that it wasn't so. As to whether he loved her, I don't think he did but he was doing the manly thing by marrying her. Once he saw Jack he knew he would try to make their marriage work. I also believe that although Chloe loved or loves Derek she knew in her heart that he would always love you and not her. It's a sad situation all around. There are two wonderful things that came of that marriage, Jack and Lucy." Nell adds with a sigh.

"Yes Jack and Lucy are wonderful and Derek is a terrific father. He loves them dearly and I know that is why he stayed with Chloe longer than he should have. He blamed me for his marrying her. He said that I put my writing career above him and our relationship and I was never around, but always in Scotland. He also said that at least Chloe wasn't afraid to go after what she wanted. I believe as you do that she loves him but knew that he would never love her so that is why she was such a horrendous wife and mother."

"Can you imagine living with a man like Derek and then only having sex with him a hand full of times? He said the summer she got pregnant with Lucy he agreed to another child because he had heard from my Granny Anne that I was engaged to marry Stephen and he decided he had lost me forever and so he would try to be a better husband. Why they weren't closer always puzzled me. I believe Chloe always felt inadequate because of her lisp and her learning disorder. She probably felt that Derek was too intelligent to want to carry on a conversation with her so she decided to act up instead not that she would win him but that she didn't know how to relate to him intellectually."

Nell nods her head in agreement and said, "That's possible. She's certainly pretty enough and definitely sexy enough. She has a wonderful fashion sense but she also shows too much cleavage and too much thigh.

I can't see Derek approving her way of dressing. She definitely has great boobs." said Nell who also has great boobs herself.

Flannery laughs at this remark and tells Nell, "My friend you also have great boobs. You and Chloe lucked out in that department and their real."

"There are times they get in the way, but Sean gets a great deal of pleasure nuzzling my boobs so I guess they can be an asset. I do think that small boobs look best in most fashions. You for instance look great in everything that you wear."

Flannery smiles kisses Nell's soft tanned cheek and tells her, "My friend you are definitely good for my ego. Derek doesn't say much about the size of my boobs so I guess it doesn't matter to him, although I've never asked."

"As for Chloe, I pray that she will find a man that loves her for who she is and that she will actually let him see the real Chloe. I doubt that few people do see who she is because she is protecting herself from criticism. I know for fact that Gus and Rena don't criticize her, but I'll bet she has been judged harshly by others. Children can be cruel and Gus said that she tried to make friends with the kids outside special education classes but they shunned her. The students in her classes tried to befriend her but she shunned them, quite a vicious circle.

Nell remembering when they were young tells Flannery, "I don't know if you remember the times that Chloe visited Granny Anne's when we were young. She was always trying to get Derek's attention. He was never unkind to her and would always acknowledge her presence. Chloe loved that. Even then she had the look of love or adoration for him."

"Yes I remember. Even then she knew how to charm the boys and she was always dressed in the most stylish clothes. It is sad to think that all our lives were screwed up when she told Derek her lie about being Jack's father. I have forgiven her though and Derek and myself. I don't want to go through my life with hate harbored in my heart. Talking with you and my Granny and spending time with Derek and his kids has given me a new prospective on everything."

"That's good to hear. I don't guess that Derek has forgiven Chloe."

"No I don't think he has, but I pray one day that he does. I'd thought of broaching the subject of Chloe loving him, but don't want him raging again. His temper is scary and threw me a loop. It was as though he turned into a man that I had never known "

Flannery is showered and sitting on her bed reading when her phone rings. She sees that it's Derek and sets the book aside. "Hi, how are you tonight?" She asks.

'I'm good. Whenever I talk with you I always feel better. I miss you and can't wait until tomorrow afternoon to talk with you. Spending eight days with you and my kids is going to be wonderful. I know I said that we will have to curtail our romantic advances while we are in California, but I believe we will find a way, if there is a way."

"So you miss me because you like having sex with me. What about when we aren't having sex?" She said with a teasing voice.

"Flannery, you know it is much more than sex. I'm comfortable being with you. I enjoy talking with you, eating with you, sleeping with you and everything we do together."

"I feel the same about you. What are you doing right now besides talking with me?"

"I'm sitting on my bed and thinking about you, with and without clothing."

"What are you thinking about?"

"I'm thinking that I would love to have you here in my bed to love and to hold."

"Keep thinking those thoughts because tomorrow night when the kiddies are in bed we will be sharing your bed, for at least part of the night."

"May the night speed on by." she said with a little laugh.

"Yes you vixen may tomorrow be here in the blink of an eye."

"I'll see you tomorrow around three. Sleep well and may all your dreams be about us. Good night sweet and sexy."

"Good night Derek, may all your dreams be about us also."

Derek sits with his parents once Jack and Lucy are asleep. He always enjoys his times with them and sits to chat whenever he can. The three are in the kitchen and playing a game called Mexican train, a game that Derek wants to teach Jack and Lucy. He also wants to teach the game to Flannery knowing that Anne already plays the relaxing yet fun game. Derek is somewhat competitive, as is Bing. Stella, like Flannery plays for the fun of the game and the companionship. The three are discussing the California trip when Bing decides to find out exactly what Derek's future plans are with Flannery

"Son I know that you have had a few difficult years and your Mom, Granny Anne and I are pleased to see that you and Flannery are together as a couple. What we want to know is what your future intentions are toward Flannery. She's one grand lass and your Mom, Anne, and I know that you will eventually do the gentlemanly thing and propose to her. At least that is our pray for the future." Bing stops here, makes his move with the game, looks from Derek whose concentrating much too fully on Bings hands and then Bing asks. "Son, what are your intentions?"

"Flannery is not a woman that you have sex with and toss aside when the next conquest comes along. She deserves a family, a husband and children."

Derek makes his move in the game, lets Bing and Stella make theirs and then he with honesty said, "I know that Flannery is a woman that deserves a family. I also know that she isn't a woman to have sex with and toss aside for a new conquest." He loves his parents and Anne but is a little perturbed by the question.

"I care greatly for her and would not have a physical relationship with her otherwise. She has changed and I have definitely changed and I just need some time to let the past die or at least let it not ruin what Flannery and I can have together. Maybe having sex before marriage isn't what you, Mom or Anne did before marriage, but I feel it is a huge part of a marriage and I want to get things right this time. I want things to be as good as possible. I know there is no perfect marriage but I at least want it to be as good as we can possibly make it."

Bing hears the irritation in Derek words and knows that his son is a gentleman and so he tells him something that Derek has not known until this minute. First he looks at Stella, who nods her head yes, and then he said, "Stella and I aren't as squeaky clean as you think."

Derek studies his parents and when Stella grins he waits for what he knows is coming next. "The night Stella ask me to marry her, we made love for the first time. I wanted to wait but she would have none of that."

Before Bing can continue Stella takes over the story and said, "I told Bing we needed to make sure there were sparks, and yes there were and still are. I wanted a marriage like you want with Flannery and wanted to make certain the passion was there." Then she grins at Bing, and adds, "The passion is still there and neither I nor Bing regret sampling the goodies before the I Do's."

Derek sees the huge grin on his father's face also and said, "So you understand my need to sort thing out. I don't know when I'll ask Flannery to marry me, but am sure I eventually will."

Chapter Thirty-nine

As promised Derek, Jack and Lucy return to Anne's by three on Wednesday afternoon. Derek and his kids stop in their tracks when they see Anne's beige blonde highlighted hair.

"Wow look at you. You always look wonderful but the blonde is hot, said Derek with a wide grin."

"Granny Anne, if your hair is hot colored blonde why did you get it colored? Ask a puzzled Jack

Not wanting to laugh at the sweet boy's innocent question, it takes a few moments before Derek answers, "Jack my boy hot means that Granny Anne looks amazing,"

"Oh, why not just say amazing?" Jack asks with a frown.

"Daddy is Aunt Flannery hot?" asks sweet and innocent Lucy.

Flannery with hands on her hips waits for his answer, "Lucy your Aunt Flannery is definitely hot."

"Am I hot and is Jack? Lucy asks with a little smile.

"Yes Lucy Hanna you and Jack have your own kind of hotness."

"So anyone who looks good is hot?" is Jack's final question.

"You've got it son. Those who look good are hot".

It isn't until Jack and Lucy are outside in Anne's yard with Anne and the dogs that Derek gives her a proper greeting. Flannery is in her room finishing packing for their California trip when he comes in to see her. She holds up two silk camisoles, one is hot pink, the other sapphire blue, for him to see. "I'm trying to decide what to wear these with. Do I wear them with the white skirt or the black pants?"

She lays them on her bed next to the skirt and pants for him to see. He hands her the black pants and the sapphire camisole, then still holding the hot pink with the white skirt she said "Good choice. I will bring a black cardigan and a white one in case it is cool in California." When she reaches for the choices, Derek tosses them on the loveseat at the foot of her bed and pulls her into his arms for a jaw dropping kiss.

"Too much talk and not enough loving." he tells her with a sexy glint in his dark eyes. "The clothing is lovely, but I prefer you without a stitch."

Her eyes smile, she grins and said, "I guess you've missed me as much as I've missed you."

"Tonight after we put Granny Anne, Jack and Lucy to bed I will show you exactly how much I've missed you." With his arm hanging loosely around her waist she leans against him, making sure he feels her breast and with a glint in her moss green eyes, asks, "Do you think our eight days and nights together in California will cool our jets?"

"I hope not, because I like it when you've heated my jets. Tis best Miss Flannery that we go downstairs until bedtime, if we don't you can't hold me responsible for ravaging you here and now."

"You are one sweet talking man. I will be anticipating all the lovely things that we will be sharing later tonight."

He takes her hand, squeezes it lightly, kisses her cheek and as they walk from her room, down the stairs and into the living room, he stops for a moment and with a glint in his eyes said, "You must tell me about all the delicious thoughts in that creative mind of yours. Of course when it comes to loving I have some wonderful ideas of my own."

With her hand in front of her heart she grins, swoons and pretends to faint at his feet. He catches her before she hits the floor, and pulling her against his lips whispers, "I see you trust me enough that you would fall to see if I would do just that."

"Yes. I knew you would catch me."

He says nothing for a moment, then with sincerity tells her, "I'm happy that you still trust me after the Chloe fiasco."

She studies him for only a moment then replies, "That was then and I realize as you have so bluntly told me, I was also at fault. I'll admit I didn't consciously put my writing career before you, but now I know that I did, so can we put the past where it belongs, in the past?

"Yes, although the past has made us what we are, so should we gander back there please be patient and understanding."

"Alright we will let bygones be bygones until they try to side-line us."

"When they do we will have to talk our way through them. Ok?" he said with a tiny smile.

"Ok." is all she said in response before taking his hand and walking with him through the house and into the cool backyard.

Anne has the radio playing and sitting on a table on the back porch.

She has always been a music fan and she Jack and Lucy are holding hand and dancing to an old song from the sixties, Carole King's '*Up on the Roof*.' When Derek and Flannery reach the grassy lawn, Derek takes Flannery's hands in his and they dance around the yard until the song ends. When another upbeat song begins he goes to Granny Anne and taking her hands in his dances her around the yard as he did Flannery. Meanwhile Flannery is dancing with Jack and Lucy, and they are having a wonderful time.

They dance for over an hour and everyone is happily tired when it's time for bed. Jack and Lucy are asleep as soon as their heads hit the pillow. Derek watches them for a while and seeing that they are out for the night he goes to find Flannery who is showering in her bathroom. The door to her bath is unlocked so he opens it and removes his clothing before he opens the door to her shower and taking the soap from her hands begins to wash every lovely curve.

"You don't seem surprised that I have joined you." He tells her while soaping her breast.

"Did you say something? I am enjoying your hands and the grand way you manhandle me, so I missed what you said."

He laughs, kisses her and repeats what he said. "Yes, I knew you would be looking for me and wanted to make it easy for you to find me."

"Good, that is how it always should be, no looked doors between us. Also I feel that whenever we need each other, if at all possible we should be accessible to each other."

She cups his chin in her hands, kisses him and with a wide smile tells him, "I'm always available to you. Of course I am hoping when you need me I won't be in the public eye."

"I will be discreet. What we do is nobody's business but ours."

No more words are spoken because none are needed. She knows his needs and he knows hers

Chapter Forty

Though they are tired from their late night of loving, Derek and Flannery are as happy and excited as Jack and Lucy that they will be in California in only a few hours. Bing, Stella and Anne drive them to the airport by seven a.m. Their flight leaves at nine, so they have plenty of time to check their bags before they leave.

Like a family, that they are, the four talk about their plans at Disneyland and then in San Diego. An older couple that's probably in their seventies sits across from them in the airport departure lounge and listens to them talking. Derek and Flannery are sitting side-by-side with Jack beside Derek and Lucy beside Flannery. They appear to be extremely happy and the gentleman smiles at them and ask, "I take it that this is your first trip to Disneyland. We, my wife and I are going there to meet our daughter and her husband and their five children. Maybe we'll see you there."

"There's a possibility that you will." Derek tells the man with a friendly smile.

"I'm sure you've probably heard this many times but I must tell you what a beautiful family you are. Your son looks a great deal like you he tells a smiling Derek and Jack. Your daughter looks a great deal like your wife." Here he looks from Derek to Flannery, who is also smiling, to Lucy whose little face beams at the compliment.

"Thank you." is all Derek said just before the announcement that they will be boarding any minute.

Derek and Jack sit together, as do Flannery and Lucy. They are in first class so have plenty of room to stretch their legs. Derek has flown first class for years that is because he always flew on his father's corporate jets when he worked out-of-town. Flannery has flown first class only a handful of times, because she likes to talk with the passengers, and those in economy class seem to be more receptive to talking. Because she is tired, as is Derek they are hoping Jack and Lucy sleep at least part of the flight. The older gentleman and his wife smile as they head to their seats only a few rows behind Derek, Flannery and the kids.

Jack and Lucy stay awake only the first hour and then fall asleep for the remainder of the trip. Derek grins at Flannery, who yawns and stretches her arms over her head. She smiles back, winks and whispers, "I'll see you in California. I'm going to sleep while I have a chance."

"Good idea. I'm also going to get some sleep while I can. I'm looking forward to this trip and I know you are also."

"Yes I am. I believe that we are going to have a marvelous time."

He winks at her, she winks back and they close their eyes, and like Jack and Lucy sleep until the plane lands in Los Angeles.

After they collect their bags and their rental car they head for Disneyland and their hotel. They check into their connecting rooms, freshen up and go to eat lunch in the hotel dining room.

Once they have eaten the four catch the monorail from the hotel to Disneyland and an afternoon of fun. Jack's first request is to ride on Space Mountain.

"Let's check the line first. If there's a long wait I think we should do that later, ok." Derek said to an antsy Jack who has more than enough sleep and wants to have some fun.

"Ok. Let's check the line first."

Flannery and Derek hold hands as they walk through the busy amusement park. Flannery also holds Lucy's tiny hand while Derek holds Jack's Jack who is never discouraged for long skips beside Derek and sings several Disney songs, when he gets to *"A Small World"*, the other join in the happy singing.

To Derek's surprise and Jack's delight the line at Space Mountain is extremely short so the four decide Space Mountain will be their first ride of the trip.

Lucy has never been on a roller coaster, but Derek doesn't want to scare her by not letting her at least ride one time, so he rides with Lucy and Flannery rides with Jack. Lucy is fine until the ride begins its dips and dives and then she freaks out and keeps saying, "Daddy, I'm scared. I want off right now. Please let's get off."

He holds her hand and tells her, "You'll be fine, but if you don't want to ride any more roller coasters you and I will pick the rides for little kids, ok."

She squeezes his hand for reassurance and he can hear her crying softly to herself.

Meanwhile Flannery and Jack who sit together are having the time of their lives. The two love roller coasters and Derek can hear them laughing and having fun.

Finally, after what seems like eons to Derek, because he wants to get Lucy off the ride, the ride is over. Lucy's face is tear-stained, her nose is running and she finally stops crying when the ride stops and Derek picks her up to ride on his hip.

"Daddy, I don't like roller coasters. Can we ride on the teacup ride and the Small World ride instead?"

He wipes her nose with a handkerchief from his pants pocket, kisses her cheek and holds her close while waiting for Jack and Flannery. The two appear with wide smiles when they see Derek and Lucy. Flannery and Jack note right away Lucy's tear stained face, and though they love the ride, decide to keep that info hidden. When they see that the line to space Mountain is still short they grin at each other, turn to Derek and Lucy and Flannery asks, "Where do you want me and Jack to meet you. We want to ride this again while the line is short."

Flannery goes to Lucy and kisses her little face, said, "I love you sweetie pie." Then looking at Derek she kisses his lips and whispers in his ear, "Enjoy you teacup with Lucy. If you would like to ride with Jack later, I will happily ride the little kid rides with Lucy."

"Ok, Lucy and I will meet you in one hour at the Pirates of the Caribbean.'

"We'll be there. Come on Jack lets go for another round."

Derek watches them go, and standing Lucy on the ground takes her hand and said, "Sweetie lets go ride a teacup."

"Yeah Daddy, lets ride in a teacup. Daddy, Aunt Flannery is like a big kid lots of times. That is good. I think she would be a wonderful Mommy don't you?"

He smiles at her question and answers with the truth that he knows, "Yes Aunt Flannery would be a wonderful Mommy. Why do you ask?"

"Well Jack and I think you should marry Aunt Flannery. That way you would have a wife, and we would have a Mommy."

"Is that right? I will think about that, meanwhile let's go and find the teacups."

An hour later, Derek and Lucy are waiting at the Pirates of the

Caribbean ride for Flannery and Jack. The evening is cool and breezy and perfect as most evenings in southern California are. Flannery had wanted to bring cardigans or sweat shirts to the park, but he'd talked her out of it. When he sees Lucy shiver in her little pink shorts and t-shirt he knows they will be buying sweatshirt after their ride. It is only minutes later that a smiling Flannery and Jack appear in front of them.

When Flannery shivers also, Derek tells them, "We'll take this ride and then we need to find a shop and buy everyone a sweatshirt."

When Flannery raises her dark brows, but says nothing, he knows that she won't bring up his telling her not to bring cardigans or sweatshirts for everyone. Chloe on the other hand would never have shut up about his wrong decision.

Derek carries Lucy on his slim hip and holds Flannery's hand. Flannery holds Jack's hand as they go to find a store where they can buy sweatshirts.

They each choose a shirt. Jack's is royal blue, his and Derek's favorite color with an embroidered Mickey Mouse on the front. Lucy chooses a bubble gum pink shirt with Cinderella on the front. Derek's shirt of choice is black with the Disneyland logo. Flannery's choice is a lavender shirt with Tinker Bell in the center.

Derek smiles at her choice and remembers what Lucy had said about her being a wonderful Mommy. He knows in his heart his kids are right. Flannery would be an amazing Mommy for his kids. He also knows that she would be an excellent wife.

When they get to the cashier to check out, Flannery hands the cashier her credit card. Derek immediately asks for it back and hands the cashier his debit card. Flannery also says nothing about this, nor does she frown or shake her head in disagreement. She knew he said he was paying for everything that his parents and Granny Anne hadn't already paid for and for a short moment he is irritated that she would try to pay. When he turns from the cashier to look at her, she smiles so he decides to let the issue drop. She and Chloe are truly different. Chloe hasn't paid for anything her entire lifetime. Flannery has paid for everything she buys for most of her adult life and although he is fully aware that she has tons of money, he being an old fashioned man will pay when she is out with him.

When the shirts are in his possession, the four remove the price tags and Flannery helps Lucy put her shirt on. Then she helps Jack. When she gets to her shirt, Derek takes it from her and pulls it over her head. He even pulls her ponytail out of the shirt, gives her a hug, and a smile of thanks for not making a scene when he gave her card back to her. Chloe would make a scene at the least little thing. She embarrassed him and their parents numerous times when they were out together. Flannery is a wonderful breath of fresh air and he will thank her when they are back in their room.

They ride several more rides and eat dinner before they decide at eight p.m. that they need to go back to the hotel for the night.

When they reach their connecting rooms, Lucy who is riding on Derek's back is sleeping and Jack, happy because he's with three of his favorite people, is also ready for bed. Derek helps Jack get ready for bed after a quick shower and Flannery helps Lucy. Once they are in bed. Lucy in Flannery's room and Jack in Derek's Flannery decides she will take her shower also. She gathers her toiletries and her pajamas and heads for the bath. She turns the shower on to warm the water then undresses. She is taking the clip from her hair when the bathroom door opens and in walks Derek. She studies him but doesn't say anything. He removes his jeans and briefs, comes up behind her, wraps his arms around her waist and kisses her neck.

She smiles at him in the mirror over the sink where she stands. "Thank you for the sweatshirt, lunch and dinner today."

He turns her around, takes her hand and leads her into the steaming shower. He pulls her close and tells her in a whisper, "Thank you for not protesting when I returned you credit card to you. Perhaps I am an old fashioned man when it comes to paying for things but my Dad has always taught me and Sean to take care of the ladies in our lives."

"Old fashioned can be a turn on. And I want to apologize for trying to pay for the shirts."

"No problem, just don't do it again or I will have to punish you."

"Hum, what kind of punishment are we talking about?"

He sees her grin and tells her. "I will have to put you over my knee, pull your panties down and spank you."

"Then maybe I will try to pay for things, because you see tall, dark, handsome and intense I can feel my lady parts getting excited at the thought of your punishment."

"Is that right? Perhaps I will instead lock you in your room and hide all of your clothing so I can ravage you whenever I desire."

"Do you know how good you are for me? You make me feel that no matter what I do with or to you that you enjoy it all."

She smiles her sunny smile and tells him, "You are also good for me. You make me feel needed and appreciated."

"Good. Because you are needed and appreciated."

Chapter Forty-one

Friday morning the four are up by seven, so after breakfast they decide that they will go to Disneyland in the late afternoon, and will go to Santa Monica and the beach after breakfast.

Derek drives because the traffic is crazy and Flannery, though she drives in Chicago and Edinburgh, doesn't care for the crazy Los Angeles freeways. Derek who has driven in nearly every big city in the United States and Europe is totally unaffected by the fast drivers and the five lanes of traffic going each way. Actually he prefers to drive, because this too is one of his old fashioned beliefs, females should know how to drive but if they are with a male he should drive. Here too Chloe would disagree. In the early days of that marriage he found out that Chloe did whatever she wanted, when she wanted, and if he didn't like it too bad. It was rare that they went in the same car together because when he drove all she did was criticize.

When she finally decided she would drive herself wherever she went, he was relieved. She had a two year old Lexus when they married, bought by Gus and Rena, but she was tired of it and wanted him to buy her a new Corvette. That was one time that he adamantly refused her request. She said he was a cheap Scot and she didn't care for frugality.

Flannery has a small Ford in Scotland because the price of gasoline is astronomical. While in Illinois she borrows her Granny's Honda. Though she hasn't told him, he knows that Flannery bought the car for Anne, pays for the insurance and road service, plus buys a gas card for Anne to use. Anne always tells him of the wonderful things that Flannery does for her and others. Her heart is huge and she is truly unselfish or self-involved. It is difficult to believe that she and Chloe have the same biological mother. While thinking about her sweet and kind ways he turns to watch her. She enjoys life to the fullest no matter the circumstances and he never hears her complain. She feels his eyes on her, turns and gives him one of her sunny smiles, then goes back to look at the L. A. traffic. Because the morning is still early he finds a parking space easily, and that it is only a block from the beach and the pier, a miracle. Because they have left their swim suits at the hotel, where there is also a beach and pool, the four walk along the sand, leaving their sneakers on until they are near the ocean. A morning fog is slowly dissipating but they can see far enough to remove their shoes and walk into the surf, then race back to the sand. They run and jump and have a wonderful time. They even take time to build a respectable sand castle.

When they are done on the beach they put their shoes on and head for the pier and the Ferris wheel. Derek and Flannery take numerous photos of Jack and Lucy and each other. They even have another tourist, a man, take several photos of the four of them together.

They go into several shops to look for gifts for friends and family. Lucy chooses a yellow purse with kittens embroidered on it for Mary. She also chooses several hair clips for Mary's hair. The purse also comes in pink and Derek holds it up and asks Lucy, "Sweetie would you like the pink purse, you can also get some hair clips for yourself."

"Thank you daddy, I do love the pink, and the kittens on the purse look like Odie."

"Jack chose something for yourself and Tyler, and I will let Flannery choose for Kristen."

Flannery knows that Kristen loves butterflies and flowers, so chooses a bracelet, necklace and earrings with both butterflies and flowers. Then she goes to look at some books on California and the Los Angeles area, she flips through several and hands two for Derek to see. "These are great. Who are you thinking of getting them for?"

"If you like them I want to get them for you. And I would love to pay for them."

He sees the hope in her eyes that he will let her pay, so he hands them to her, kisses her cheek and said "Thanks that is very thoughtful of you."

She kisses him and looks for something for Virginia, Nell, Sean and her Granny Anne. He has already chosen gifts for his Mom and Dad, Gus and Rena. She figures the gifts are from her so she will pay for them. She is surprised that before she can take her choice to the cashier, Derek is beside her and takes all but the books she is buying for him. She doesn't protest but knows when the time is right she will have to explain to him that she feels because she chose the gifts it is only right that she pay for her choice. She is not one to embarrass a person in front of others, so lets the subject lie for now.

Jack has chosen books and little cars for himself and Tyler. Flannery spies some art books with instructions on drawing animals, vehicles and airplanes and wants to get them for Jack. She also chooses coloring books and crayons for Lucy and Mary. Because Kristen loves fairies she buys her a story book with beautiful illustrations. Knowing Jack will more than likely want to draw at the hotel she also chooses colored pencils and a pad of drawing paper. Derek has paid for all the purchases except for the books she is buying for him, When she walks up to him with her arms filled with her choice of presents, he again sees hope in her eyes that he will let her pay. For a moment he hesitates and she thinks he will refuse to let her, but he decides to make her day and lets her pay.

When they return to the car and they are ready to return to Disneyland and the hotel, he pulls a box from his shirt pocket and hands it to her, "For you, just because you are sweet and caring."

Inside the little silver box is a necklace, on a silver chain and hanging in the middle of the chain is a tiny silver fairy holding a wand with emerald green stones adorning the wand. "Thank you, this is beautiful."

He reaches for it, leans towards where she sits, has her hold her long brunette hair off her neck and he hooks the chain for her.

She kisses his hand, his cheek and his lips in thanks. Buying gifts for a woman that truly appreciates them gives his heart a jump start. After living with a woman, Chloe, who didn't like anything he bought her, Derek's spirits soar to new heights.

While she was choosing gifts, he showed the necklace to his kids, they told him it was a great gift for her and they had been right. "See Daddy, Lucy and I were right Aunt Flannery loves your gift."

"Yes Daddy, she's not like Chloe, Mommy. Chloe never likes anything and Aunt Flannery loves our gifts."

When the distant light fills his eyes for a moment, Flannery decides then and there that she will never turn him down for anything. Though he hasn't told her, or anyone how hurtful Chloe was to him, everyone suspected, and she will make sure he knows how wonderful he is. She will never intentionally hurt him.

Their time in California is restful, fun and enjoyable. Jack and Lucy love having their Daddy and Aunt Flannery with them and as always are well behaved.

Chapter Forty-two

Their four days in San Diego go much too fast and they are on the plane and headed back to Chicago much too soon. Bing, Stella and Granny Anne once more go to O'Hare to pick them up. When the three see the smiles on Flannery and Derek's faces and that they are getting along amazingly well, the three know that the trip was worth every penny that they paid.

Bing drops Granny Anne and Flannery off at home, then he Stella, Derek and his kids head back to Hundley for several days. Derek and Flannery are at a new place in their relationship and even though they will miss each other, he wants to spend time with his parents, plus wants her to have one on one with Anne.

Flannery and Anne spend the day working in the back yard. The day is gorgeous, almost as nice as the day's weather in California. Flannery checks the weather in Scotland and sees that it is only in the low fifties. The seventy degree day in Illinois is a gift to her and she is slowly getting a tan. She always uses sun screen because she like her parents and Granny Anne are fair skinned. Derek on the other hand is naturally dark, not extremely so, but he and Bing are sometimes mistaken as being of Middle Eastern heritage. Because The Gypsy in their heritage comes from Bing's maternal side of the family and Bing has had the family tree done, he knows that his Mother Charlotte's family does have some Indian heritage. This is from the northern part of India.

The two talk about her trip with Derek and his kids and Anne knows without asking that her granddaughter had a wonderful trip. When their gardening is over, they prepare a light dinner and then they go to their bedrooms to shower and rest.

Flannery is sitting on her bed reading when she hears a phone ring in the downstairs, when the ringing stops she knows that Anne has answered it. Later when she goes downstairs to prepare a cup of tea she goes to her Granny to see if she would also like some, and ask Anne who called. Anne shrugs her shoulders and said, "It was wrong number."

Flannery remembering the calls from Chloe asks, "Could it have been Chloe?"

Anne who is perfectly aware that it was Derek, and that he was asking her opinion on a very important subject, a subject that he at the moment wants to keep secret from Flannery looks at Flannery, and because she has never lied to Flannery said, “No it wasn’t Chloe. I know her voice. I wonder how she is doing in rehab.”

“I don’t know. All that Derek has told me is that she is in rehab on Maui. Things must be going well or he would know. The subject of Chloe is what caused our fights so I am reluctant to bring the subject up.”

They drink their tea and go back to their rooms. Anne is glad that Flannery believed her when she said Derek’s call was a wrong number.

Derek is working in his father’s office. His laptop is on Bing’s desk and Derek is typing. Bing walks in and asks what he is doing, Derek has Bing pull a chair beside him and Bing reads what Derek has typed. “What do you think?” Derek asks as he reaches to turn the printer on, that sits nearby.

“It sounds like a great idea. I heard you talking with Anne. Have you told her your plans?”

“Yes, she’s in total agreement and said that there is no doubt that Flannery will go along with everything. Although I don’t know if she will agree with the submissive part.”

Bing grins and tells his son about his mother Hanna and Stella and being submissive. “Stella and Hanna were in agreement with submissiveness to a point. They told me that in some ways it can work, in other it won’t. The reason is that it is no longer the Dark ages, and that women are no longer living in caves and depending on a man to meet all of their needs. I can understand you thinking, any man who is married to or has been married to a woman like Chloe may go overboard to make certain that the women they share their lives with in the future are in no way like Chloe.”

He thinks of this for a minute and adds, “I don’t see Flannery as a difficult woman. From what I see she is easy going and mostly positive about life in general.” Bing adds with a smile.

“Yes she is easy going, although she does have a temper. I saw that when we had our feuds. I know that when she asked me about my marriage I could have been a little more diplomatic in my answers, but I answered her with both barrels blazing. She of course surprised me and told me, excuse my words, to go and f--- myself."

Bing has heard from Anne that Flannery has picked up the swearing habit, and that she is trying to break her of it. He doesn't swear although Stella does from time to time, he has for years tried to get her to stop. "Son you know that Stella still has a few choice words. I have tried to reel her in, but she has said it is her only vise and a way to keep from ringing my self- righteous neck, so I leave the room when she swears. For some reason she can control the wrath when you, Jack and Lucy are here, so I would guess that this is Flannery's way of telling you she would like to ring your neck also."

"When I heard her swear I was a little surprised but then not so much considering that she to my knowledge hasn't any other vices. Without her contract I would probably still be smoking and drinking." Bing is surprised to see his grown son blush when he mentions the contract with Flannery. He has never asks what their agreement is, but from the way Derek blushes he now knows that the contract is for sex.

"Flannery is a very enterprising woman. I say that's good for her and for you. Perhaps you should add a clause at the bottom of your contract stating that her contract still must be honored under most circumstances, that is unless one of you is ill or out of town."

There is a huge grin on Bing's face and Derek cannot help but grin back. "It's a grand idea as the Scots say. I will add her contract. Do you think I should let Mom and Granny Anne read this before I present it to Flannery?"

"Sure, why not. The two will probably disagree on some of your points, but each relationship differs and if this is what you feel is needed then go for it. Flannery may find some new and colorful words to call you but your life like mine will never be boring."

"I'm sure she will. With her creative mind I am certain her repertoire of profanity will be quite colorful."

"Maybe you could have her make up her words so that only you and she will know that she is swearing."

"Good idea," Is Derek's final word on the subject.

Chapter Forty-three

Derek would love to spend every moment with Flannery, but doesn't want to overwhelm her by spending all their free time at Granny Anne's. Flannery who isn't overwhelmed easily knows that he is being considerate of her and Granny Anne's feelings and decides that when he and his kids return she will tell him that she and Anne love having them there.

Saturday is laid back for Anne and Flannery but the two miss Derek and his kids and the dogs. They know that Anne's dog Charlie misses Yates and Tralee because he is always looking for the two, in the house and the yard.

Derek hasn't called Flannery, not because he doesn't miss her nor want to talk with her, but he knows she needs her space, for now, as much as he. He has plans that will change both of their lives, and the lives of his children and that is why he has been talking in secret with her Granny, his parents, Sean, Nell and Virginia. If all goes as planned his year to relax will be suddenly enhanced by this carefully executed plan.

Flannery and Anne are in Flannery's bedroom on Saturday evening and Flannery is modeling the dress that Derek bought for her in San Diego. On their last day there he, she and his children spent the day driving around, to Coronado Island and then to Horton Square to look around. Derek saw a beautiful white sundress in one of the store displays and had her try it on. The dress is light and airy, there is an underskirt of silk with a skirt of floating white chiffon the top also is chiffon with a silk backing. The spaghetti straps are lovely, with tiny hand embroidered white roses. The dress fit her tall slim figure perfectly and he insisted that he buy it for her. The dress is beautiful but she doesn't know where she will wear it. He also insisted on buying her two inch sandals. They too are beautiful, all silvery and sparkly. Lucy loves the shoes so they found a pair of silver flats just her size. Derek also insisted that they find Lucy a dress. Her dress is also white, chiffon and silk, sleeveless with a satin placket around the waist that also has white embroidered roses. When she offers to buy him a new suit, shirt and tie plus the same for Jack, he surprised her and lets her do so.

Their suits are dark charcoal gray, their shirts white with white stripes their ties gray, white, royal blue and emerald green stripe.

After they were done shopping they went back to their hotel and Flannery thought she would wear the dress for dinner. Derek diplomatically talked her out of it and they had room service instead. His excuse was that Sean and Nell will be getting married one day and that they can wear their new clothing to the wedding.

"Granny Anne, Derek is acting secretive and unusually out of character. He buys me the dress and one for Lucy he and Jack have new suits shirts and ties. Have Nell and Sean said they are getting married?"

"Their serious, everyone can see that they are in love so maybe Sean has told Derek, but is waiting to let us know after he pops the question to Nell." Anne is fully aware why the new outfits were bought, but she isn't going to spoil Derek's surprise.

Flannery watches her Granny's face closely, she doesn't appear to be hiding anything, nor has she ever lied to Flannery so Flannery lets the subject drop.

Flannery, Anne, Nell, Virginia, Nell's kids Kristen, Tyler and Mary, Derek his kids and his parents all go to church the following day. After church they go to the country club for lunch. Derek is very attentive of Flannery but everything seems to be normal with everyone's life so Flannery decides that she will let the subject of her dress go.

Monday evening Derek calls her and asks if he can come over on Wednesday afternoon. Her Granny and Virginia are taking four days to go to Door county Wisconsin, and Flannery will be alone so of course she said yes.

Chapter Forty-four

Virginia will drive her car to The Dells and Door County because Flannery will be without a car if they take Anne's. She has considered buying one for herself because she wants to spend more time in Geneva with her Granny, Derek and his kids. She kisses her granny as they stand on the front porch waiting for Virginia. Flannery shoves her hand in her shorts pocket and pulls out a wad of hundred dollar bills, she hands it to Anne. Anne shakes her head at her granddaughters generosity then said, "Flannery you don't have to give me money, Virginia and I are splitting the cost of the trip and besides you and Nell have already paid for our rooms."

"It's a gift. I love you and Virginia and want you to have fun."

Anne sees hope in Flannery's eyes that she will accept the offer so Anne opens her cream colored leather purse and opening a zippered section inside stuffs the money there. "How much is there?"

"It's five thousand in hundred dollar bills," Is Flannery's answer to the question.

Anne opens the zippered section of the purse, counts out a thousand in bills then hands the rest back to a sad faced Flannery. "Love, you are beyond generous, but I would never carry that much cash with me."

Flannery, not easily discouraged peels another thousand from the stack and said, "This is for Virginia, that way neither of you will have too much."

"Ok I will make sure Virginia gets this. Put the rest back in your account."

Flannery nods yes, but Anne knows she won't put it back into her account. Flannery will use the cash to help someone. She is very proud of her granddaughter and tells her so just before Virginia pulls in front of the house in her blue Ford Focus.

Chapter Forty-five

July-Last Week

Flannery waits beside the garage for Derek. It is four p.m. and she has missed him. On Monday evening Virginia and Nell had a barbecue in Virginia's yard inviting Anne, Flannery, Derek and his parents, his children and Sean. When everyone arrives Derek is not with them. Needless to say Flannery is extremely disappointed that he stayed at his parent's house. Bing sees the disappointment in her eyes and taking her aside tells her, "Honey Derek is in the middle of writing and said to tell you he will need you to edit his writing for him."

She sees a twinkle in Bing's eyes which is not unusual, so accepts his excuse for Derek's absence. Bing, of course knows what Derek is writing but will keep that information to himself. To make her smile he adds," You know how it is when a person is into writing, they can write for hours."

Flannery nods yes, and gives Bing a huge hug. Derek doesn't call that night or the next, so she is hoping he hasn't changed his mind to come and stay with her for the night.

It is only five after four when he drives into Anne's long driveway driving Stella's red Civic. He smiles at her, stops the car only inches from where she stands, opens the door and she is right there to give him a toe curling kiss.

"Wow that was a kiss among kisses." Then he reaches across to the passenger seat and hands her a huge bouquet of wildflowers, "For my lady, just because you are my lady."

She holds the bouquet close to her chest so she can smell the lovely fragrance coming from them and waits while he, who also has a bottle of red wine with him, gets out of the car.

"You are a vision in your lemon yellow skirt and white t. He looks at her feet and sees that she wears sandals that are decorated with daisies. He also notes the dangling daisy earrings in her ears.

"Didn't you and Lucy buy them one day in St Charles, at the Charlestown mall?"

"Yes we did. The earrings are also Lucy's idea. She said I should buy them, and wear them until you will let her get her ears pierced. She said you told her she has to be at least twelve to do so. Why must she wait so long?"

Flannery has Charlie with her, on his leash, so Derek opens the gate to the backyard before he turns to her and tells her, "I think twelve is a good age to consider the piercing. I just pray that she and you don't get numerous piercings, and Heaven forbid, I also pray that, you, Lucy and Jack get no tattoos."

Flannery takes his explanation in but says nothing until they are eating their early dinner of turkey tacos, freshly made by Flannery. Charlie who was fed before Derek arrived lies under Flannery's chair napping, the three cats sit side-by-side on a kitchen chair that is close to the window and watch the birds in the backyard as they bathe in the always filled bird bath.

Because she has had time to think about his thoughts on tattoos and piercings, and because he appears to be extremely relaxed and happy to be with her she asks, "Derek do you know someone with tattoos and multiple piercing's? "

He is fully aware that the last time she asked him a question she was afraid of him when he got angry with her, and he had read only the night before a scripture from *Proverbs 14:7.* He remembers it word for word, *"A man of quick temper acts foolishly, but a man of discretion is patient."* He doesn't want her to be afraid to ask him questions no matter how personal, so he answers Flannery with calmness and discretion.

"Chloe went overboard with the piercings, of which she has numerous ones. Her ears are pierced almost the entire lobe. There is one in her nose, her eyebrow and her tongue. She possibly has others but I didn't ask to see for fear she would show me. She has tattoos on her ankles, her wrists, her upper back, above her right breast and on her butt cheeks. How do I know they are on her butt cheeks? She had the nerve to buy a string bikini and wear it in our pool. I refused to let her near Jack and Lucy in that getup."

Flannery looks like she has a question, but is reluctant to ask so he said, "Did she go against my wishes and wear the bikini when Jack and Lucy were swimming, no because I threw it away while she was out. She didn't ask if I'd taken it and I didn't volunteer the information."

"All rightee, I can understand your dislike for piercings and tattoos. I guess you disapprove my navel piercing?"

He sips his iced tea, eats the last bite of his taco, wipes his mouth with a napkin then smiling tells her, "I find your navel piercing extremely sexy. Please don't get any more."

"I have no plans for more piercings or for tattoos. Suppose I decide to have my head shaved, and the stylist cuts the name of a sports team in the remaining hair?"

"I will have to lock you up until your hair is as long as it is now." This he says with a little smile but she knows he is a man of his word so she will make certain she doesn't get her head shaved. She has never been controlled by a man, not even him. Of course he has changed greatly, and for a moment the thought of his control excites her. Perhaps she is losing it, but she wouldn't mind a little bit of controlling. She knows if he punished her with sex she would definitely go against his wishes. She smiles a little smile at the thought.

He watches her face closely and when she smiles to herself he wonders why. He keeps an eye on her through the meal, while they clean up the dishes and even in the car on their way to a movie. A real date as he promised. The smile comes and goes so he finally asks when they are getting out of the car at the movie theatre what is on her mind.

She grins widely, winks and taking his hand tells him how happy she is to be with him.

After the movie he ask if she would like to get some ice cream, she tells him no because she has Rocky Road in the freezer at home.

"Derek did you bring your writing for me to edit. I didn't see you carrying it into the house when you came."

"I have. It's in my bag in the back seat. When we get to Anne's I will let you see what I have been writing."

"Is it a love story?" she said kiddingly.

"It's a love story of sorts. I will let you decide for yourself the type of writing it is."

Charlie waits in the backyard for them and dances around their feet, so Flannery picks him up and carries him to the back porch where she sits him down. Derek, who carries his bag, sits it on the blue wooden table, opens the bag and hands her a folder that isn't very thick. "Here, you may start reading while I sit my bag in the kitchen. I'm going to get a glass of water. Would you like one?"

"Yes." she tells him as she flips to the first typed page of his writing. Because he wants to see her response while she reads he hurriedly leaves his bag in the kitchen, pours two glasses of cold water from the frig and goes to the porch to sit across from her.

She looks at him with surprise, happiness and a little shock as she reads the words typed on the document's front page. She reads the words several times, then reads aloud,

"These documents are an agreement for Marriage and Parenting between Derek Liam MacDougall and Flannery O'Connor Larkin. Once this document is signed and dated by the said parties, the agreement will take effect in nine days at the six p.m. marriage in Anne Marie Larkin's beautiful back yard."

She looks at him then continues to read. "*We, Derek Liam MacDougall and Flannery O'Connor Larkin will co-parent one John Binghamton MacDougall the Second "Jack" and one Lucy Hanna MacDougall. Flannery will have all the rights of parenting that I, Derek have. If Flannery wants to adopt more children, I, Derek will agree to the adoptions.*

She blinks tears that are gathering at the edges of her eyes and said in a whisper, "You want to marry me. You want me to be a mother to Jack and Lucy?"

He takes her hands across the table, squeezes them lightly and said with a soft smile painting his handsome face. "Yes, I am asking you to be my wife and a mother to Jack and Lucy. I know that you love them and that they love you. I also know that I would be proud to have you for my wife."

She looks at him for several moments and then tells him something that she has yet to do. "Derek I think it is only right that you know that I cannot have children. Then she tells him why. He studies her and said softly, "We have Jack and Lucy and if we want others we can adopt."

From his soft words and the look in his eyes she knows that her Granny has told Derek her secret. "My Granny told you, didn't she? When did she tell you?"

"She told me several months ago. She didn't think you would mind so I hope you aren't upset that she did."

"No I'm never upset with my Granny. She always has my best interest at heart. In a way I'm happy that you know, that way you won't be disappointed if I never get pregnant. Actually I I should have known that you knew." He raises his dark brows questioning, and she tells him, "You didn't ask if I was on birth control, nor did you use protection. I let the whole issue escape my mind because I figured that maybe you'd had a vasectomy."

"No Flannery I haven't had a vasectomy. Your right though, I knew that you couldn't get pregnant and decided to wait for you to tell me you story. I want you to know that it saddens me knowing what a wonderful Mother you will be, but then I realized that I wanted you to be mother to my kids. My kids keep telling me to marry you so you can be their mommy. They also have told me that I need you for my wife. Their right you know on both counts."

"Thank you for caring enough about them and me to want me in your lives. I promise that you won't be sorry that you married me. I fully intend to be the best wife and mother possible. I will always place you, Jack, Lucy and my Granny first in my life. If my writing should ever get in the way of my relationship with any of you I will stop writing."

He studies her and knows she means what she says but he also knows that her writing is a huge part of who she is and he tells her, "Honey, sweet Flannery, you will never have to put your writing aside. It is a huge part of you and I will let you know if I need more attention or our kids need more. If you think about it Jack and Lucy are already related to you." When she looks puzzled he adds, "You and Chloe have Rena's blood so the two are your relatives in a way."

She gives him a warm smile for the interesting and true information and adds. "You are right I am related to them. That's a sweet thought."

The two say nothing more for several minutes until Flannery stops her reading and asks, "I'm to be the submissive wife I see. Hum?"

"To a point, it is because in the best marriages the man makes all the important decisions. Of course if you have a more practical means to handle a situation I will certainly take that into consideration."

Satisfied with his answer she continues to read, but stops again to say, "So Scotland will be only a once a year visit?" He nods yes.

This time she reads to the end of his well-written document. When she is through she smiles at him and ask if he has a pen. He pulls one from his shirt pocket and hands it to her. "I see that the pen has water proof ink."

"Yes Flannery once you initial each clause, you will need to sign your full name at the end of my contract."

"So my contract for sex is highlighted here. Don't worry, there is no way I will not honor it. That is unless I am ill, out of town or dead." Her bright happy smile tells him that she is a woman who honors her promises and those that she makes the promises to.

"While you sign I'll go and break open the wine. This is a night of celebration."

He brings to glasses of wine to the porch, sits beside her after he places a glass near each of them.

Once she signs her name at the bottom of the last page she asks," Were you planning our wedding before we went to California? Did my Granny and your parents know, and did Virginia, Nell and Sean know?"

"Yes." is all he said to the loaded question.

"Were you and they afraid that I would high-tail it to Scotland if I knew?"

"No but I knew there was no way I would let you makes our plans. The wedding will be small, here in your Granny's beautiful back yard. The guest list is short. It will consist of you, me, my children, parents and Sean, who's agreed to be my best man. Then there's Granny Anne, who I am certain will give you away, Virginia, Nell, your maid of honor, Nell's children, Reverend Grant, his wife and their twins, Joe and Minnie, and Ned and Alice, neighbors down the road. I would have invited your agent Jean, but she will be out of the country. I have also invited Gus and Rena if they have returned from Hawaii."

He holds out his glass of wine, as does she and he toast, "To us and a happy, bright and interesting life ahead."

"Yes, to us." Flannery adds as they click glasses to their upcoming wedding only nine days away.

"I didn't think you would mind if we spend our honeymoon in Chicago. She shakes her head and he continues, we can go to the museums, eat out and enjoy our city together, as we used to."

"That will be wonderful. No plane to catch, no security to go through." she tells him with a smile.

He knows there is no perfect marriage but feels that because she is naturally easy going, unlike Chloe who was always difficult, that they may argue and disagree from time to time but for the most part they will more than likely get along reasonably well.

Thursday morning after breakfast they drive to the Charlestown Mall in St. Charles to buy their wedding rings. Flannery is extremely quiet for most of the drive and then she looks hopefully at Derek and asks, "Please let me buy your wedding ring. I feel it only fair since you have already bought me the promise ring and now you'll buy my wedding band."

Because she has a sweet and giving nature, and because he wants to compromise in their marriage he tells her, "Sweet lady, the soon to be Mrs. MacDougall, I would be honored to let you buy my wedding band."

She kisses the palm of her left hand then places the hand on his right cheek. Then she smiles and though she says nothing he knows he has made her happy. She is extremely easy to make happy. For that matter happy is her usual state. He knows that his years away from her have changed then both especially him. Although he was at one time an extremely positive and giving man, and he can still be that, but his marriage to Chloe has changed his outlook on relationships and marriage in particular. He no longer sees marriage the end all of a relationship or happiness, but he is willing once more because he cares for Flannery and his children and he has had far too much upheaval in their lives. His hope is that with his marriage to Flannery she, he and his children can have stability in their lives and many happy family times together.

When Derek thinks of Flannery's sweetness and her giving heart he remembers something that Mother Teresa once said, *"It's not how much we give but how much love we put into giving."* He knows from experience that she put lots of loving into everything that she does, and he knows her example will be just what Jack and Lucy need in a Mother. They have a sweetness of their own, but he knows living with her example they will blossom and become even sweeter and giving than they already are. He is also aware that being with her, sharing a life with her, he will no longer be the intense and serious man that he has become in the last six years.

Chapter Forty-six

On Saturday Flannery, Derek and his children want an easy day, so this day they decide to ride their bikes the two miles to Minnie's for lunch. Because Lucy is still too young to ride far Derek has a child seat just for the purpose of riding with them.

The day is breezy and sunny and in the high seventies so they wear sunglasses, baseball caps and short, t-shirts, and sneakers. Flannery leaves her wallet behind because she knows that Derek will refuse her offer to pay. She is happy that he allowed her to buy his wedding band, and the suits, shirts and ties for him and Jack to wear to their wedding.

The road that they travel has little traffic because it isn't a main road, and normally only those who live on the road use it most days. Jack rides his bike between his Dad and Flannery. He knows that they want to be sure he is safe, so he shows no opposition at the arrangement.

Minnie's is crowded but they find the booth empty, where Derek and Flannery sat the night they had their first fight. Nearly seven weeks have passed since she returned from Scotland. Those weeks have shown Derek and Flannery that they enjoy being together despite their few fights. When the waitress seats them they tell her they don't need menus they already know what they want to order.

Minnie and Joe normally work from three to eleven, but because they will be off the Friday, Saturday, and Sunday, the following weekend, for Derek and Flannery's wedding, they are filling in for the workers who will be at Minnie's while they are off.

The waitress goes into the kitchen to give Joe the order and once the food is ready, their waitress Sonja along with Joe and Minnie deliver their meal on the Depression glass dishes again.

Once the meal is set on the table first Joe then Minnie gives the four a hug and a kiss on the cheek. The two also return to eat dessert with four of their favorite people.

Flannery knows from Derek that Minnie and Joe have volunteered to make the food for the wedding, so she tells them, "It is sweet and wonderful that you are making the food for our wedding on Friday."

"Honey, you and Derek have always been like family to me and Joe and we love you and are delighted that we can share your special day." Minnie tells all at the table.

"Yes, we are extremely pleased to share your special day." adds Joe "Minnie and I were never blessed with children of own, but we have always considered the two of you family. And now there are Jack and Lucy who also count as family." For Joe, who is a man of few words and because he is also shy, this is the longest that they have ever heard him talk. Though he hasn't stayed young in appearance like Minnie, his hair has receded a lot in the past five years and he is heavier than he ever been, Joe is still a catch to Minnie who grows to love him more with each passing day.

When they return to Anne's they decide to spend a few hours in the beautiful back yard enjoying each other, the pets and the beauty of God's world. Anne and Virginia are out shopping for dresses for the wedding and plan to eat dinner out.

Derek notes how much Flannery is enjoying his children and him and he silently prays that it always be so, because he knows that Jack and Lucy, and he need her to fill the huge void of their lives.

As Lucy and Jack tell him Flannery is still a kid at heart, and when she finds two jump ropes in the back of the hall closet she shows Jack and Lucy what fun it is to play with simple toys. Athletic as a child and also as an adult, she skips rope across the back porch, down the porch steps and around the yard. Jack and Lucy do very nicely when Derek and Flannery hold the ropes between them. She is totally uninhibited by her silliness which opens Derek's heart to her even more. Rarely is she competitive, nor does she care if she wins at any game. He knows that he will no longer have to be mother and father to them, and he knows that marrying her will not only fill the huge void in him, it will also fill the void in her.

All the action has the four hungry even though their lunch at Minnie's was huge. When Derek asked for the check Joe told them that the bill was already paid. When Derek looks closely at Flannery he wonders if she snuck and paid, but the only time she left the table was to take Lucy to the ladies room. Joe knows Derek is wondering who paid, so he tells him, "There was a couple sitting nearby who heard us talking about your upcoming wedding and they paid for your lunch."

"Well, wasn't that nice."

"It's just a little gift from Heaven. They said that one day they hope you and Flannery will pay it forward". Derek knows that Flannery pays it forward a great deal of the time, because he wants his children to be giving and caring, Derek pays for the meals of all who remain in the dining room as they leave.

Everyone is hot and sweaty from jumping rope so Flannery helps Lucy take a shower while Derek helps Jack. Derek takes his and while Flannery showers he gets the grill ready for hamburgers. He also takes time to cut a bouquet of roses for Flannery. Granny Anne's roses take up one corner of the back yard and are a variety of colors. He knows that Flannery's favorites are the peach, yellow and pink, so he cuts four of each. He takes them into the kitchen and places them in a clear glass pitcher, then sits the table with green and white dishes that Flannery sent to her Granny, just because Anne likes them. She and Flannery were in Edinburgh one summer and on their walk from the Botanical Garden they walked down Dundas Street and went into *Emma Bridgestone's* home store to look around. Anne noticed the dishes straight out. Flannery wanted to buy them then but Anne turned the offer down. After Anne returned to Geneva Flannery went back to Emma Bridgstone's and ordered a set for twelve people. Anne loves the dishes and uses them every day.

When dinner is over they decide to watch a movie from Net Flex, Flannery as usual falls asleep half-way through the movie... Derek lets her rest, when the movie is over he takes Jack and Lucy upstairs and tucks them in their twin beds. One he has checked to see that the dogs and cats are down for the night he carries Flannery to her bed. She opens her eyes only long enough to kiss him good night and to thank him for carrying her up the stairs. Anne and Virginia called from the restaurant and are at a late movie.

While she sleeps he watches her in the dim light of the bedside lamp. When they were younger, in high school and college he loved her to distraction and went along with whatever she wanted. He didn't want the huge wedding in Scotland but as she said he didn't tell her that he didn't. And though the fact that she was receiving literary claim for her children's fantasies didn't bother him, that she let it go to her head did. Now that she is well known she no longer lets her talent rule her, so he knows it was because she was so young when she wrote her first books and when they was published and a huge hit, is why she let her talent rule her.

He is proud of her talent, as are all those who know and love her. He feels she will be able to write plus be an excellent mother and wife, so he at least no longer feels that she will put him, Jack and Lucy behind her writing career. The fact that she writes at home he considers a huge plus. She will always be there when needed by the children and him. That he also plans to eventually work from home is sounding better and better. He will be with his family instead of on the road, Bing knows of Derek's plan and is all for it. The two men filling in for Derek are doing a commendable job and Bing knows it is time for his son to dedicate time to Flannery and the kids.

Sunday is a mellow day with church and lunch at Bing and Stella's. Stella tells her about the plans for the evening before the wedding. The ladies, Flannery, Anne, Stella, Nell, Minnie, Lucy and Nell's girls will have a sleepover at Granny Anne's. The men, Derek, Bing, Sean, Joe, Jack and Tyler, Nell's son will have a boy's night at Bing and Stella's

At ten that night before the ladies call it a night, and are getting ready for bed, Derek calls Flannery. Because no one wants to sleep on the hard floor everyone picks a room for the night. Anne stays downstairs in her room. Virginia sleeps in the room that Derek uses, Nell and her girls sleep in the room with twin beds, Lucy, and Flannery are sharing Flannery's bed. Because Lucy fell asleep as soon as Flannery pulled the covers back, Flannery goes into her bathroom to talk with Derek. Minnie chooses the lounge in the attic once she sees how nicely Flannery cleaned and decorated it.

"How's my wife to be?" he asks in a whisper.

"I'm good. Your whispering so I'm guessing Jack is sleeping with you."

"Yes he is. Sean and Tyler are in the guest room, Joe is in the room that Lucy and Jack share when here, Dad is in his room and Gus is in the second twin bed in the room with Joe."

"So, Gus and Rena are back from Hawaii. Did he say how Chloe is doing in rehab? Also will Gus and Rena be at our wedding?"

"Yes they will be at our wedding. Gus said Rena missed ladies night because she didn't know if you would want her there. She'd also thought about missing the wedding, but Gus said it is time the two of you forgive and forget the past. Or at least the part where Rena didn't protest you living with Granny Anne after your Dad died."

"Yes, I agree. I don't believe Rena and I will ever have a mother daughter bonding, but it is time to forgive." Before he can agree she asks, "Does Chloe know that we are getting married?"

"I don't know if Gus and Rena told her. Perhaps they haven't. Gus knew about her threatening calls to you so maybe he and Rena have decided to tell her after the fact, if ever. Of course the way humans love to gossip, I'm sure she will eventually know. Why do you ask? She hasn't called you has she?"

"As to whether Chloe is doing well in rehab, yes she is. Because she is she told Gus and Rena to feel free and come back here."

"Nah, I haven't heard from her but then she doesn't have my new cell phone number."

"I'm surprised that she hasn't called the land line. Granny Anne has had that number for years. Perhaps she's listened to Gus and her lawyer and knows that even if she is in Hawaii and not on the Mainland she can be arrested for calling you, or any of us."

"I'm looking forward to our life together." he said before she hears him make a kissing sound into his cell phone.

"I'm also looking forward to tomorrow and our life together. It's been a long time coming, but this time I am ready to be a wife."

"Good. I am also ready to be a husband to you. Sweet dreams."

"Sweet dreams to you also."

Chapter Forty-Seven

Chloe sits on the balcony of her Maui condo looking out to sea. Rehab has helped her with wanting cocaine but it hasn't helped her with her hate for Flannery. She has tried to let the hate go, but because Flannery is with Derek again she feels more hate then ever whenever she thinks of her half-sister. Derek was right to say she tricked him into marrying her. The night he found her in his bed without a stitch on, she was already pregnant with Jack, she knew he was Sean's son, but didn't care. Sean was a sweet man, but not what she wanted. Derek, on the other hand was a man who stirred a desire that she'd not felt before. Tall, dark, handsome and wealthy were things that described Derek and she was going to have him no matter that he was already engaged and planning to marry Flannery.

Chloe knew that Flannery was in Scotland for most of the year and could see that Derek was a tad perturbed by that fact. She heard him talking with Sean one night about that very thing. When Sean asked him if they were going to live in Scotland Derek had given him an adamant no, then added that he also didn't want the huge over the top wedding. That is when she decided she was taking Derek from Flannery. Does she feel any remorse at her actions? No.

Because Chloe knew Derek would be a wonderful father, she knew that even if he found out that Jack was Sean's son he wouldn't end their marriage. She wanted Lucy so that she would have a second reason for him not to divorce her. When he had the divorce papers served she wasn't surprised because she knew she wasn't wife or mother material and she is certain that she never will be. At the same time the divorce has hardened her heart to Flannery and not Derek. She knows that she is foolish to think this way, but she does and she still wants to get even with Flannery.

While sitting on the balcony she makes her plan of revenge. How she will pull it off with her in Hawaii she isn't sure. The maintenance man who works at the building where her condo is comes from the Chicago area. Hopefully he will know someone in that area who will help her, that way she can stay in Hawaii while she makes her plans and has someone there carry it out.

She enjoys her reverie until she is shaken from her plan by the buzzing of her doorbell. She doesn't ask who it is because she knows. It's Diego, a man who lives on the floor beneath her. Though she had seen him many times, in the elevator or in the condo gym, it wasn't until this last trip to Maui that she has gotten to know him.

She was sunning by the condo pool her first day back and he was swimming laps. The two were the only ones at the pool, and when he was finished swimming, he nonchalantly dried with his beach towel, smiled at her and lay on the chaise lounge next to her without saying one word.

Because his eyes were closed she took advantage of her bout of luck and surveyed him from the tip of his toes to the top of his shortly cropped black hair. Though it was difficult to guess his age because he was in excellent physical shape and his complexion bronzed by the sun she knew she had to have him. Not as a permanent fixture in her life but a man to have sex with, someone who would wine and dine her. Because he seemed to be uninterested in her she takes a spray bottle of suntan lotion and sprays it his way. When he felt the spray his black eyes opened immediately.

Without a word he swiftly gets up from his lounge, picks her up and tosses her into the pool. She is so surprised that she takes in too much water and begins to cough and choke. Though her spraying him annoyed him he doesn't want to be responsible for her drowning so jumps into the pool and carries her back to the lounges. He has seen her over the years but thought that she was married. Now when he looks at her hands there is no longer a wedding band. When she is through coughing, she looks steadily at him gives him the once over again, then to his amusement said, "You certainly know how to charm the ladies don't you. I would apologize for spraying you but you were ignoring me. I knew that you were as interested in me as I was you, or you would not have set in the lounge next to mine after all there are loungers in other areas around the pool. Correct me if I am wrong."

He grins then holds out his hand to her, which she takes then he said, "I'm Diego. Yes that is my first name. Apparently I was conceived in San Diego. My last name is Robles. I'm not Hispanic, but of Portuguese, Spanish and Irish ancestry."

"Diego, I like it, it is appropriate with your bronzed beauty. My husband divorced me a few weeks ago. I guess he was tired of me not being a good wife or mother. What about you are you single?"

"At least you agree with your ex's decision to divorce you. I was married a time or two, actually four times and I have a child to each ex. I have decided never to marry again, what about you. Do you think you will marry again?"

"Absolutely not there is no way I will give up my freedom again and as to having more children, no way. I'm interested in men for one reason, and one reason only." Here she openly surveys every visible inch of him. When she grins and winks, he knows that she is inviting him to her bed.

"If your through swimming why not come to my condo, we can order some takeout. You appear to be an excellent swimmer. I can swim but prefer sunbathing instead."

Diego sees that she has a golden tan, and though it looks good with her blonde hair and blue eyes he tells her, "I hope you wear sunscreen, and did you know you need to reapply it several times a day especially if you are in the sun for many hours."

"Thanks for the info, but I have one mother and father and don't want any more."

That was the beginning of their affair. She won't call it a romance because it is sex pure and simple, and the sex is mindboggling.

She is fully aware why she is attracted to him. It is because he is tall, dark and handsome like Derek and intelligent. She has never told anyone, had not admitted it to herself, until recently, that she loves Derek. Now that she has lost him, she is remorseful that she didn't at least try to be a mother to Jack and Lucy and a wife to him, but she was fully aware from the beginning of their marriage that he loves Flannery and always will. Although he not once mentioned Flannery after their marriage, she knew that she would never have his love for herself.

When she opens the door, she is surprised that Diego is dressed up, in black slacks and a white dress shirt, and even wears a tie. She still has on her red kimono with a dragon embroidered on the back. One of his hands is behind his back and he surprises her with a bouquet of poppies. They are her favorite flower, but she wonders how he knew. She knows that she didn't tell him.

She holds the door wide for him to enter. He hands the poppies to her then pulls her close for a kiss, before he said, "I think you and I need to go out to dinner and a movie. The sex is amazing, but we need more than that in our friendship. So, while you go and get all dolled up, I will find a vase in your kitchen and place your poppies in some water."

Although they have had sex numerous times, and she enjoys those encounters she is pleased that he wants to go out. She is also pleased that he calls her a friend. She has never gone out of her way to make friends and in her lifetime can count only her friend Mia in the Chicago area as that.

This night he tells her about himself, that he is a Marine biologist and teaches at a college nearby. He if forty-six which means he is twenty years older than her. At six feet, one inch he is only an inch shorter than Derek. "I have lived in a few of the states on the mainland, but prefer it here. The four ex's live on the mainland, which means it is much easier to avoid them. My children I see at various times. The oldest Claire is twenty-two so comes to see me at least once a year. The second oldest Nicole is twenty and attends the University of Hawaii so I see her more than the others. Then there are my sons, Zane is sixteen and Seth is twelve."

"What about you, tell me what you want me to know, if there are things you prefer that I don't know, that's fine, fine for now."

"I have, or had a son Jack who's five and a daughter Lucy who's three. I don't have an ounce of maternal instinct so my ex has them. He's the far better parent so I knew he would get them anyway."

He nods his head at the information, says nothing, then she tells him that she is twenty-six, an only child and that her ex, their children and her parents live on the mainland also.

Though Diego has seen her ex, and the oldest child Jack and her parents, it has been several years since her ex and the children were in Hawaii. He would see them in the building's elevator or at the pool, but has never said more than hello. Her parents he knows fairly well, because their condo is on the same floor as his. They are friendly, especially Gus who Diego has seen in the gym many times. When he has seen Gus they talk of the day-to-day but don't get too personal. The wife Rena isn't as friendly, and Diego remembers clearly that Chloe looks a good deal like her.

Chapter Forty-eight

First Friday-August

Although she isn't nervous that her wedding is here, nor is afraid to be a wife and mother, Flannery's palms are sweaty and she will be glad to have the ceremony behind them, she stands waiting by the back door for her Granny Anne, who was nearly ready the last time Flannery talked with her. She can see her wedding guest sitting in the beautifully decorated back yard, and is happy that only their dearest friends and family are there. Even the dogs are in attendance, they are on their leashes so it is certain they will not be in the way. Each dog has a silk flower hooked to their collars. Because Granny Anne's piano is too heavy to move, the minister wife plays the wedding march on the electric keyboard. Granny Anne kisses Flannery cheek smiles at her and said, "I have waited for this day long enough. Let's go and get you married."

Flannery sees Gus and Rena sitting in one of the middle row of seats. Gus smiles at her and Rena looks at her but Flannery is unable to read her biological mother's expression. That Gus is there cheers her. That Rena is there stirs many feelings, feelings that she is addressing one by one each day. She is fully aware that God wants her to forgive Rena and she has told him many times that he will have to help her in the forgiveness. She is trying to commit everything she does to the Lord and when she has difficulty doing so she remembers *Psalm 37:5-6,*

Commit everything you do to the Lord. Trust him and He will help you.
He will make your innocence as clear as the daw,n and the justice of your
cause will shine like the noonday sun.

The distance to where Derek is standing with Sean is longer than she thought, or perhaps it isn't far at all but because she is the center of attention, along with Nell who walks only feet ahead of her, Nell's dress is simple, a cotton and rayon sundress with spaghetti straps, and green like a mint leaf. Flannery does note that Sean is admiring Nell. Like Derek and all of males attending, including Jack and Tyler, wear charcoal gray suits and white-on-white dress shirts with ties in shades of emerald, royal blue, black and white stripes. All females, no matter what age, except for Flannery and Lucy wear dresses in various shades of mint.

Flannery and Lucy wear the dresses that Derek bought for them at Horton Square in San Diego. They also wear the shoes that he bought. Flannery's the two-inch heeled silver sandals and Lucy her sparkly silver flats. Because Lucy's hair is now to her shoulders and a mass of blond curls Nell has clipped the sides back from her sweet little face with beautifully hand-painted hair clips decorated with tiny wild flowers of various colors. Lucy and Jack stand with Derek and Sean because they insist that they will marry her also. Derek wants Flannery to be able to adopt Jack and Lucy but he is waiting to get Chloe's permission.

Flannery carries her bouquet of wildflowers plus the bible that once belonged to her father James. Though she has had it since his death when she was four, and now reads from it every night, she uses it as her something old and blue because the cover is navy blue. Her something borrowed is a bracelet on her right arm. It belongs to her Granny Anne, is silver with engraved hearts and tiny sapphires which are Anne's birthstone. The bracelet is old, bought for her Granny her first year married to James Sr., her father's father.

Anne kisses Flannery's cheek as they reach the groom, his children and the best man. "I love you Granddaughter. She places Flannery's hands into Derek's, kisses his cheek and the cheeks of his children and said, "I love you grandson, meaning Derek, and I love you Jack and Lucy."

So Sean won't feel left out she also kisses his cheek and adds, "I also love you Grandson. Sean has always known that Anne considers him and Derek her grandchildren, but is extremely pleased that she acknowledged him on such a special day.

Flannery lets go of Derek's hand for a moment so that she can hug and kiss Jack, Lucy and Sean. Derek whose eyes twinkle said after she kisses Sean's cheek, "My brother may be the best man but remember that I will soon be your husband."

She heeds his words and moving in front of him she takes his face in her hands and kisses him deeply and long. Because the two seem to have forgotten that they have an audience Reverent Grant clears his throat loudly and said, "Flannery, Derek the honeymoon doesn't officially begin until after the wedding ceremony." Everyone laughs at his words. It is the laughter that brings them to the present.

Their vows are straight from the bible and they have perfect agreement on who will be submissive in their marriage. Derek tried to get Chloe to be submissive but she is definitely a free spirit. He knows that after the first year of that marriage that he gave up on her being submissive. The main reason is that he didn't care.

Derek reads his vows first. Flannery stands where he can hold her left hand. Jack and Lucy are now sitting with Granny Anne and Derek's parents.

Though he has written his vows down, Derek has managed to remember every line, he smiles at Flannery and said from *Ephesians 5:21-22*

And further you will submit to one another out of reverence for Christ.

You wives will submit to your husbands as you do to the Lord...

Next Flannery, who has also memorized her part, continues with...

And you husbands must love your wives with the same love Christ showed the church.

He gave up his life for her to make her holy and clean, washed by baptism and God's word. He did this to present her to himself as a glorious church without a spot or wrinkle or any other blemish. Instead, she will be holy, without fault. In the same way, husbands ought to love their wives as they love their own bodies, for a man is actually loving himself when he loves his wife. Ephesians 5:21-22

Derek begins to read where Flannery left off, "*In the same way, wives must accept the authority of your husbands, even those who refuse to accept the Good News. Your godly lives will speak to them better than any words. They will be won over by watching your pure, godly behavior.*

Don't be concerned with outward beauty that depends on fancy hairstyles, expensive jewelry, or beautiful clothes. You should be known for the beauty that comes from within, the unfading beauty of a gentle and quiet spirit, which is so precious to God. This is the way the holy women of old made themselves beautiful. They trusted God and accepted the authority of their husbands. For instance Sarah obeyed her husband Abraham, when she called him master. You are her daughters when you do what is right without fear or what your husbands might do.

Flannery reads as follows, *In the same way you husbands must give honor to your wives. Treat her with understanding as you live together. She may be weaker than you are, but she is your equal partner in God's gift of new life. If you don't treat her as you should, your prayers will not be heard. 1 Peter 3:1-7*

They know that the words are extremely old fashioned and considered out dated by most couples but they are serious about their union and want what's best for everyone involved. She loves him and knows for fact that he is extremely old fashioned in his ideas on marriage and she knows part of this is because of his failed marriage to Chloe.

When they chose their vows he made it clear that he will be the provider and that she must come to him before she buys any big items with their money. She wanted to put her money into their now joint account but he said he must think long and hard about that. So far he hasn't let her know his decision, so she shares his money and hers sits in the bank collecting interest. If she must she will use the money for charity. She has already opened an account for her Granny's use, but Anne has said that she will keep it for emergencies only.

Derek has no money worries. When his mother Hanna passed away she had a trust fund from her grandparents which went to Derek. He also makes money from investments started by Bing. He like Flannery has always been taught that a person must always save some, give to charity and spend wisely. It is because of this early lesson taught to Derek by Bing and Flannery by her Granny Anne that neither of them has to worry about money. Flannery also has a trust fund started by her father James and added to monthly by Bing. She knows that she and Derek are blessed in many ways, but she would gladly give her trust fund back and have her father alive, she also knows that Derek would much rather have his mother alive.

Although she knows he is old fashioned in many ways she also knows how generous and kind he can be. Whenever food is bought for Anne's house Derek foots the bill. He also pays the utilities. He has volunteered to pay Anne's property taxes but she has adamantly refused.

With many thoughts racing through her mind Flannery pushes all aside except for this moment, a moment she has wanted for six years. Now they are married and she will have to get used to his antiquated ways and focus on all that is wonderful about her, tall, dark, handsome and intense spouse.

As they walk past their friends and family they smile and receive smiles in return. When they reach the back porch Flannery stands on the top porch step and throws her bouquet of wildflowers straight into Nell's arms. Next she stands where Derek can raise her pretty dress and remove her lacy garter strewn with baby blue satin ribbon. This Derek tosses to Sean who catches it easily. The guests cheer because everyone knows that Sean and Nell will be next to wed.

Their wedding meal, prepared by Joe and some of the staff at Minnie's is served on table's set-up in the side yard. The tables are dressed in cotton table cloths of emerald or royal blue. The center pieces are wildflowers mixed with a variety of roses. The cloth napkins math the table covers. The china was given to Derek by his father who had bought it for Hanna on their first anniversary. Made in Scotland the china is white trimmed in royal blue and gold. Each plate and cup is hand painted with lilacs and thistle. When Derek was married to Chloe he didn't even ask if she would like to use the china, he knew that she would not appreciate the sentiment behind the lovely keepsake. Flannery had seen it at his parent's house in a china cabinet in their dining room. Stella never used it but loved the beauty of the design and kept it for show and safe for whenever Derek wanted to use it in his house. The china cabinet is now sitting in a nook in Anne's kitchen, safe from running children and pets, but visible to those who walk by.

Jack and Lucy sit with Nell's three children at a table near Granny Anne and Derek's parent's. Sean and Nell sit with Flannery and Derek. Sean makes the first toast to the newlyweds and smiles at his older brother when he said, "I know that this wedding has been a long time coming and I like all who gather for this celebration want to tell my brother and his lovely Flannery how happy I am for them, Derek is my role model, he is the one that I have always strived to be most like. We haven't always agreed on relationships but thank God my brother and I are once again spending time together. I have missed him greatly and am enormously happy that we are growing close again. I wish the two of you a long lasting marriage and love that grows with each passing day. Flannery and Derek may God bless this union in every way. I love you."

Others toast the newlyweds, but it is Sean's speech that warms Derek's heart. He loves his brother and agrees that their making up has helped them both. That Jack is Sean's biological son has never been mentioned by Derek. Sean has told Derek that he will always consider Jack Derek's son and Derek's son only. Because Jack has never mentioned to Sean what he knows Sean has decided to let the subject lie. If Jack should want to talk about the situation later he Sean will make certain that Derek is there with them.

After their meal Flannery makes a point of going to talk with Rena and Gus. They are sitting with Joe and Minnie and the Reverend and his family, so Flannery bravely goes right to Rena and asks if she can talk with her in private. Rena doesn't hesitate to accept Flannery's request and getting up from her chair walks with Flannery into the house and then into the living room.

Rena is aging well. Her face holds very few wrinkles but they look good on her. Flannery always thought Rena vain, but knows from Gus that she frowns on Botox or face lifts. When she looks into her biological mother's blue eyes she sees a good deal of Chloe in her. Rena is an extremely pretty woman and has also kept her weight in check. She is only a little taller than Chloe, five foot five to Chloe's five foot two and she keeps her hair beautifully styled and colored the golden blonde of her youth. She also wears a green dress and looks lovely in the color. Flannery now notes that she and Lucy do have arched brows like Rena and her chin.

"Thanks for coming to our wedding. It is nice to see you. Perhaps we can see each other more now that I am married to Derek."

Rena smiles at her grown daughter and she sees that Flannery is sincere in her words so Rena said, "I would love for you to visit with me and Gus. Not only when Derek brings Jack and Lucy over but maybe you and I can have lunch together after your honeymoon. I have a collection of teapots and cups and would love to invite you, Anne, Stella, Virginia, Nell, and Minnie over so I can get some use out of them, plus I want to get to know you. I would also like to have just you over to chat and share a meal".

"I would like that and I am sure the other ladies would love to join us for a tea party. You are also welcomed to visit us here at Granny Anne's."

"Thank you. I will make sure to visit you wherever you are. I know that I wasn't the mother that you needed or deserved and that is why I didn't protest when James decided to come here and also leave you in Granny Anne's care when he died. I know that many people thought that I was relieved not to raise you but they were wrong. I didn't know the first thing about being a good wife or mother back then. I know that is a poor excuse for not even trying to see you but I was happy when Gus made a point of bringing you to our house after Chloe was born. Growing up I had grandparents who were legalistic and very staid. They were not the role models that I needed and so I was a horrible mother to you and a horrible wife to James. I also want you to know that I love you and I loved your father. I wish I'd had the time to apologize to him for my neglect and uncaring ways. I did many unforgivable things when I was married to James and you were little. I pray that you will forgive my selfishness and that we can at least be friends."

Flannery sees the desire in Rena's blue eyes and knows that it took a lot of courage to apologize after many years of Flannery thinking she wasn't wanted. Now that she is grown and knows what selfishness and vanity can do to a relationship she holds her hand out in friendship. Rena gladly accepts.

"I would also like to apologize for Chloe and the way she has treated you. It is my fault that she is wild and does as she pleases. Derek was right to divorce her. I pray that one day you and she can sit down and talk as we are today. Her treatment for drugs seems to have helped and hopefully she won't get hooked again. She has always loved Maui and hopefully she will find happiness there."

"I'm happy that she is doing well. I would also love to get to know her. Hopefully a day will come when she can spend time alone with Jack and Lucy."

When they return to the yard everyone is waiting to eat the wedding cake.. Flannery apologizes for the delay and then the cake is served by several servers from Minnie's.

Derek gets up from his chair and pulls her chair back for her. He kisses her cheek and whispers, "How did your talk with Rena go?"

Flannery shakes her emerald green napkin out and places it on her lap then whispers back, "All is well. Rena and I have reached a new and much happier chapter in our relationship. We are going to have lunch at her house after our honeymoon. She also apologized for not seeing me more often and for being a horrible mother. We will be fine".

"I'm happy to hear the good news. She has always been kind to me."

Flannery knows that forgiving Rena is what God would want her to do. She knows that God would forgive Rena and she remembers reading only a few days ago the following,

I have swept away your sins like the morning mist. I have scattered your offenses like the clouds. Oh return to me, for I have paid the price to set you free. Isaiah 44:22

Their first dance is a waltz. The yard has a large area at the bottom of the porch steps that is paved with red brick. It is usually used as a patio extension but this night is used as a dance floor. The beautiful refrains of '*Caribbean Blue*' dances on the breeze as they dance around the patio. Their second choice is '*Walk Hand In Hand with Me*' a song made famous by Andy Williams. They chose the song because it is one that Granny Anne loves. She and Derek know how to dance with style and ease because they, Nell and Sean were given lessons when they were in grade school. She and Nell also took tap, ballet and jazz from the age of four until they were fifteen. She took the lessons to get her over her shyness. Nell took the lessons so that Flannery wouldn't feel out of place without the support of her best friend. The two loved the lessons, but knew once the reached fifteen that it was not their calling of choice. They and their dance troupe won numerous trophies, plus she and Nell won for the duo's that they always excelled at dancing. Nell's daughter Kristen goes to the same dance school. Flannery and Nell talk about Lucy and Mary going there and Flannery needs to broach the subject with Derek.

The wedding dinner is simple, yet to every ones liking. The chicken and beef shish-kabobs with veggies are perfect with rice, or potatoes, requested by Lucy. The rolls are homemade by Joe as is the entire meal. There is sorbet for dessert and the wedding cake. The cake is a sight to behold, three tiers, each beautifully decorated with white frosting and layers of Raspberry and dark chocolate between each layer. The flowers on the cake are of course a combination of thistle and lilacs. The bride and groom stand on top with the figure of a blond toddler girl and a bigger blonde boy. This was thought of by Granny Anne and everyone agrees that the two extra figures are more than appropriate. Flannery isn't marrying just Derek she is also marrying his children.

Chapter Forty-nine

Palmer House

The Palmer house is a favorite of those who live in or near Chicago. Derek has booked a suite for their four night stay and she goes to stand beside one of the rooms windows to look at the Chicago view while Derek tips the bell boy for carrying their luggage to the beautiful, comfortably decorated suite.

When he walks up behind her and wraps his arms around her waist and kisses her on the neck she turns in his arms and facing him kisses him fully on the mouth. When the long satisfying kiss is through they smile into one another's twinkling eyes. "This suite is gorgeous. I have always loved this hotel. Remember when we came here after graduation with Nell and her date. What was his name?"

Flannery knows his name but in the heat of the moment her mind is fully on her gorgeous sexy husband. Derek is listening to her but also unzipping her white dress. "His name was Greg. If I recall he was crazy about Nell, and now that I remember his face, Nell's three children look somewhat like him, or am I only imagining that?"

"Well I guess Nell won't mind if I tell you." she said while she unbuttons Derek's white on white dress shirt. "Greg is the father of Kristen, Tyler and Mary. He was, and is crazy about her, but she refused to move to Alaska where he now lives and so he is no longer in her life. I know that he sends support checks every month, plus never forgets their birthdays or Christmas. I asked why she wouldn't marry him and she said she likes him but she doesn't love him and so she felt it kinder to break their long relationship off. She has heard from his sister that he is getting married next spring. He's marrying an airline pilot named Bambi."

He nibbles her neck and asks, "Do you suppose Bambi is a dear?"

She sighs, pushes the straps of her dress from her shoulders, looks into his teasing eyes and replies, "For Gregg's sake I pray that she is dear to him. I guess he's told her about Nell and the kids, so at least there are no secrets between them."

"Um, that's good." Derek said while moving a few inches from her so he can push her dress over her slim hips where it puddles at her bare silk stocking clad feet.

She steps over the dress then bends to retrieve it from the floor. "I want to take good care of my dress. The number one reason is because it is my wedding dress and number two is because you bought it for me."

She moves from him and hangs the dress on the back of an upholstered chair at the side of their bed. When she turns he has taken all of his clothing off and lie's it on the seat of the same chair. Then he turns to her unhooks her white lacy bra and tosses it onto the same chair. Standing in only white lacy bikini panties and a garter belt also of white lace and her silk stockings he lets his eyes feast on the tall willowy brunette who is now his wife.

She gives him a come hither smile takes his hand and leads him to the beautifully covered bed. He uses his free hand to pull the comforter and top sheet to the bottom of the bed then laying down he takes her hand and pulls her flush against his now prominent and very ready erection. She wraps her arms around his neck and kisses his cheeks, his nose, his forehead and lastly his lips. Pulling her so close that not even a blade of grass would fit between their bodies he returns the kiss with gusto.

He moves back only enough to unclasp her stockings from her garter. Then he moves down her long slim thighs and with the top of a stocking between his teeth he follows the stocking down her calves, and feet where he pulls that stocking off with his teeth. Up the now bare leg he moves methodically kissing, licking and nipping each step of his way until he reaches the top of her thigh. Though her eyes are slightly closed and he cannot read them he knows that she is pleased because a smile plays at the corners of her mouth. The second stocking and her thigh receive the same consideration from the very happy and pleased Derek. When he returns to the top of this thigh he slips his thumbs inside the elastic of her white lacy bikini and with teeth and thumbs slowly pulls the garment down his wife's slender hips until he once more reaches her feet. These he tosses backwards not caring where they fall. When Flannery laughs a happy laugh he turns for a moment looks in the direction to where he tossed her panties and sees why she laughs. The panties are hanging from a floor lamp next to the chair.

He chuckles also and grins when he sees the delight in her eyes. "Hopefully my aim will be just as good when I decide to pleasure your lady parts."

"I'm not worried that you won't succeed in your goal. What I want to know is why are you taking so long to please said lady parts?"

"Well my Mrs. MacDougall, we have four nights at this lovely hotel and I don't plan to rush through any part of our honeymoon. Remember dear wife, the contract that we signed. You are the submissive one and I, your husband, am the boss. When we are in our throws of passion there will be times where we will have quickies, but for the most part our intimate times will be given special attention. Do you have any disagreement with that?"

"No my Mr. MacDougall I haven't even one disagreement with that. I know that you are an old fashioned man and that you will dominate me, especially in the bedroom so let's carry on."

With this said and that the two are in total agreement on who's submissive and who is dominant in their intimate relationship Derek joyfully does exactly what she loves. He goes far and above in pleasing her lady parts. Flannery, without even a tad of inhibition shows Derek exactly how much he means to her and how much he pleases her. Slow and easy is how they proceed and when the two are replete they lay facing each other with only an inch of well christened sheet between them.

As content as two newlyweds can be she stretches her arms over her head and said, "For some reason I'm starving. Are you also hungry? We can open the gift basket in the sitting room."

"Yes, I'm also starved. I will admit that while we were making mad passionate love that food was the last thing on my mind."

"Let's take a quick shower first, that way we will be ready for sleep after our snack."

"Do you actually believe that we will get enough sleep while we are here all alone without my Granny, or our Jack and Lucy. I find that difficult to believe."

"Perhaps I am a bit foolish to think that I won't take advantage of this lovely suite and more privacy than we have had since our Geneva sex fest."

On Saturday they sleep in until ten, have room service for breakfast then getting dressed leave their love nest for several hours to check out the new exhibit at the Chicago Art Institute. The Palmer House is ideally situated for those who don't want to drive in the busy Loop or Michigan Avenue. Although they drove Anne's Honda to the hotel, and it is parked nearby the two prefer the exercise of walking in one of their favorite cities in the World.

The two have been to the Art Institute many times, together and alone. Their trip today is their first trip here in over eight years. She loves the Monet's of which there are many, he loves these also but also enjoys the works of Vincent Van Gogh. When they get to his self-portrait Derek studies it closely. He has often wondered why extremely talented people are self-destructive and why they have mental issues. Flannery, to his knowledge, has never been self-destructive nor does she have any visible mental issues despite the loss of her father at an early age and the abandonment of her mother. He knows that Anne is the big reason why. Anne is not afraid to show affection and she lets those that she loves know that she does. Although Derek lost his mother at an early age he has had Stella's love from the day she married Bing. Bing is also an affectionate person and has always shown Derek and Sean his love.

When they get to the stained glass art, a gift to the city of Chicago, from the artist Marc Chagall, Flannery and Derek admire, and love the blues in the gorgeous piece of art.

The Art Institute gift shop is not easy to pass up, and Flannery and Derek do some shopping once their very pleasant trip around the art institute is through. They could spend most of the day there but know they will bring Jack and Lucy to visit before summers end. Granny Anne is also a lover of Claude Monet's paintings and she and Flannery have made a special trip to Giverney, France to visit his home and gardens. Nell, Virginia and Nell's three children were with them. The five had come to visit Flannery in Scotland and were pleased that Flannery and Anne had paid for their airfare and accommodations for the trip to France. Their air fare to Scotland was a birthday gift for Nell, whose birthday is July eleventh, and Virginia whose special day is July twelfth. Nell's kids travel well, like Jack and Lucy and Derek has plans to invite them to Scotland while he, Flannery, Jack, Lucy and Anne are there.

Flannery, with her generous heart, finds gifts for everyone that she loves. Because she has gone overboard in her choices she thinks it will be ok to pay for those choices. Derek has also purchased several gifts, one especially for his wife. He makes it to the cashier while she is still shopping pays for his choices and has the cashier hold his bank card so that he can pay for what she buys. Though most men don't care to spend too much time shopping Derek never complains when he and she shop together. Chloe went shopping with him only a time or two and once she found what she wanted complained until he would give up in frustration, even though he hadn't finished buying what he'd come for. Where Chloe was happy only when she was buying for herself, Flannery is happiest when she is buying for others.

Because he has his gifts bagged, and patiently allows her time to buy the perfect gifts and because two of her gifts are for him, she chooses her final gift and carries them to the cashier. First she places the gifts on the counter, then she pulls her wallet from her purse and finding her bank card hands it to the cashier. The cashier smiles, winks at Derek and said, "I'm to use this card." Here she holds up Derek's card for Flannery and Derek to see.

Derek whose been waiting nearby sees a flash of irritation in Flannery's eyes but dismisses it because she knows his rules. He pays for whatever they buy unless discussed ahead of time, and possibly agreed upon. The irritation is washed away when he walks up behind her and kisses cheek. She wants to be a fantastic wife and life partner so she gives her prettiest smile and said, "Thank you."

When they reach the stairs with the famous lions keeping watch over Michigan Avenue he stops to the side of the doorway and pulls her to stand in front of him. He smiles at her and said "Thank you for not protesting that I paid for everything."

She smiles in return and said, "You're welcome. Why would I protest? I know that you have told me several times that you will take care of our financial needs." When the honeymoon is over she fully intends to ask her new, sexy, yet at times irritating husband what she is to spend her money on if not to help pay for the things that their family will buy.

He sees the hint of irritation and knows that she is only giving into him because it is their honeymoon. He appreciates her attitude. If it had been Chloe she would have expected him to buy and pay for whatever she chose even if it didn't please him.

When they get to the hotel and enter their room they place their gifts on the table sitting near a window. "Where would you like to eat? We can have an early dinner since our breakfast was late." Derek said as he looks first at her and then the view of Chicago from the window.

"It's nearly five and I'm hungry so we can go out again, eat in the hotel dining room or have room service." Flannery loves to eat and Derek has teased her about eating more than he, but she knows he is only kidding.

"You know what would be ideal. Why don't we eat in the hotel dining room and that way we will have plenty of time to focus on our honeymoon and our lustfulness. I for a fact desire you and all your maleness. The question is do you also desire me and my femaleness?"

She is grinning when she asks her question because she is fully aware that Derek desires her femaleness and wants her as much as she wants him. He walks the short distance to where she is now sitting on the suites loveseat and sitting beside her said, "You my dear are what I am hungry for, so if you want food before our next love fest you best get our minds off sex and on something else."

She grins and kisses his slightly pouting mouth. Next she's off the sofa in a jiff and goes into the bedroom and to the bath. He follows and because the bathroom door is opened he walk to stand beside her at the sink where she is brushing her teeth.

"I think the dining room opens at five so once we're finished here lets go and have dinner. We will skip the desert because you will be my desert and I will be your desert."

"That's sounds divine, but I feel that I can handle desert and you tonight. Actually the desert will give us the extra energy that we will need after dinner."

"So my Mrs. MacDougall you are planning a long night of amore? I know that I want as much time loving you as possible."

Taking his hand she leads him from the bath, through the bedroom and to the door. "Let's get this show on the road dear husband. We have waited long enough to share our lives. I am fully ready to be an excellent wife and mother. I also plan to be a wonderful friend to you."

Before she can turn the knob on the door he pulls her flush against him and kisses her deeply, so deeply and long that the two are breathless when the kiss is over. "That's just a preview of what's to come. You better eat lots tonight because I don't plan to let you sleep for quite a while."

"That sounds like a wonderful plan and I am looking forward to everything and anything that you want us to do or try."

"Tis best that we leave this room now. If you keep making promises like that I may decide to forgo dinner and go straight for desert."

The Lockwood Restaurant is just beginning to serve dinner when they enter. Because most customers eat later Derek and Flannery are offered a choice table near the dining room windows.

Chapter Fifty

Second Week Married-Second week Aug

Flannery and Nell plan a ladies night out, which is fine with Derek. He knows that everyone needs time with friends. His only request is that she takes her cell phone with her so she can call if they will be home later than ten p.m. When ten rolls around and then eleven and finally midnight he decides to call her and see where she is. When he dials her number he gets voice mail so leaves a message on her voice mail. Because he is restless, and will be so until she calls or comes home he goes to sit on the front steps. He is there only ten minutes when he sees Nell's Ford Focus pull up in front of Anne's house.

Because the outside lights are on he can see her as she leaves the car, then he hears her tell Nell good night. Apparently she has seen him also because she walks slowly to stand on the walkway before him.

"Sorry that I didn't call. I forgot to charge my phone so left it behind."

"You are late and doesn't Nell have a cell phone, or did she leave hers behind also? Also you should have told me your phone needed charged, you could have taken mine."

She sees that he is trying not to let his temper flare, so she said, "Can we discuss my tardiness tomorrow. I'm tired and want to go to bed."

Before he has a chance to answer or move, Flannery like a marathon runner is on the porch and through the front door before he has a change to respond. She is running up the stairs to their room, and when she turns to see how close he is, he tells her," We are going to talk about this. Run away but we will talk about this."

When he reaches their room, the one that has always been hers, he hears water running in the bathroom tries the doorknob and isn't surprised that the door is locked. He knocks and she said, "I'll talk later."

Next he hears the shower go on and he waits. She has to come out eventually and he will be waiting. When he hears the bathroom window open, he thinks nothing of it and figures she is letting in some night air.

While he waits for her to come out of the bathroom he looks around their room. The queen sized bed remains, the one that was hers until they married. She asked if he would prefer a king-sized bed, but to her sweet surprise he said that the queen was ideal. They have enough room to spread out but also it isn't so big that if they aren't getting along she, or he can't have too much room between them. The room is the master suite and once Anne slept there. When Flannery started high school Granny Anne had a wing added to the downstairs where she has a bedroom, sitting room and a big bath with garden tub and walk-in shower. This wing also has a huge laundry room and a three-quarter bath with shower.

There room is still painted a soft fern green and because it is a restful color they have kept it. The bed sits between two windows that look out on the backyard and the Fox River. They each have a bedside table with lamp. There is a nice sitting area with a loveseat, a long lamp table behind it with a lamp, plus a small coffee table in front of the loveseat. They also have a rocker and an upholstered chunky, blue, green and rose striped chair with a foot stool. Each chair had a small table beside it, a place to lay a book or sit a mug. There is a floor lamp beside the striped chair and a little brass lamp on the table beside the rocker. With two long windows on either side of a long dresser the room is always bright when the sun shines. With Duet shades on all the windows they can get light even with the shades closed. He had a bachelor's chest dresser brought from the storage so that she won't have to empty any drawers in her over flowing dresser. Their sheets and comforter are new. In shades of green and sapphire blue the subtle stripes of the cover go nicely with the rest of the room. A beautiful area rug also in shades of blue and green brings the area together nicely. Anne has had all the oak floors in the house redone in the last year and they glow with a soft butterscotch prettiness. With a walk-in closet and a long row of regular closets there is more than enough room for their clothing. With a computer desk and chair in a corner near one of the backyard windows they could hole up in the room for days. All that is missing are a refrigerator and a microwave. Because Flannery has her food fetish he is surprised that she doesn't have the two appliances already installed.

Her food fetish has never bothered him. He knows that all human have some fetish to live with. His as a child was washing his hands far too much. It started shortly after his mom Hanna died and went on for several years. Even with counseling, which helped to a point he would have to wash his hands before and after everything that he did. Bing, Stella and Granny Anne were understanding and patiently helped him work through his need to practically wash the skin off his hands. He hasn't seen any fetishes in Jack and Lucy which he is grateful for.

After waiting half an hour Derek decides she has had a long enough shower and remembers that there is a key to the door, safely sitting above the door frame. There is one to each door of the house just in case his children decide to lock the adults out.

The door opens easily and he walks into the bathroom. The shower is still running, so he taps on the shower door. When no one answers, he pulls the door back and to his surprise he sees that she isn't there. Then he remembers her Granny's stories of Flannery and Nell sneaking out the bathroom window on numerous occasions after Anne and Virginia were in bed for the night. The window is above the porch so he is certain she has gone out the window, across the roof and down one of the rose arbors.

He leaves the window opened because there is a nice breeze coming into the bath and also so that the breeze will take away the mist left by the running shower. He knows that there is a backdoor key kept hidden in the flower garden and knows that she is either in the yard or somewhere in the house. When he opens their bedroom door, he listens to see if he can hear her. He decides to go downstairs when he sees that the door to the guest room is closed, where it is normally opened unless someone is sleeping there.

First he checks on Jack and Lucy who are soundly sleeping as usual then he goes to the guest room, the room where he once slept, and opens the door, flips the rooms light switch which turn the bedside lamp on. She is there lying on top of the bed in only her bikini panties and bra. She opens one eye slightly and said, "Derek please turn the light off, I'm trying to sleep."

He walks to the bed and stares down at his lovely yet irritating wife and wants to spank her. When he looks closely at her he sees numerous scratches on her lovely self. He goes to sit on the bed beside her and said, "You have scratches everywhere. You look like you were fighting with a mountain lion or a rose bush."

She opens both eyes, studies him then closes her eyes once more.

He is on her in only seconds, straddling her long thighs. She opens her eye again and with a little smile plying at the corners of her mouth, she tells him, "I guess I will have to be punished for disobeying you." He is perturbed that she was late and didn't call, but he isn't an unreasonable man so he decides he will yes punish her. From the look of amusement on her face he knows that she is likely anticipating his form of discipline.

Now that he can see her clearly in the lamplight he sees that she has several scratches on her face that are fairly deep and that they are streaked with blood. When he moves off of her and stands beside the bed again she thinks he is leaving the room and tells him with a little pout, "Aren't you going to punish me, or must I wait for that also?"

"You can bet your pretty bottom that I will punish you, but right now I'm going into the kid's bath for some ointment for your scratches. I plan to doctor you first."

Flannery knew that she should have told him her cell phone needed charged, but thought she and Nell would be home earlier than they were. She is also fully aware that she could have asked to borrow his phone. She knows that he can be controlling but this is the first time in their two week marriage that she has felt that control.

When he comes back with the Neosporin ointment, a wet wash cloth and some band aids she lies still while he gently cleans her face, her hands, arms, neck and calves. While he puts the ointment on the biggest scratch she flinches because it is apparently longer and deeper than the other scratches. "Look at your beautiful face, all scratched. I'm guessing you crawled off the roof by going down the biggest arbor by the porch. Flannery you are athletic and agile, this I know, but why would you foolishly climb out the window and down the arbor to get away from me?"

"Well I know how you can be about me listening to your rules, why are there rules once we are married but there were none before?"

As he gently cleans and puts ointment on each scratch some of which need Band aids, especially two on her face, he tells her why, "Before we married you were your own boss, now that we are married I am your boss."

"Is that so? I don't recall any words in our marriage vows stating that once we married you would be my boss."

"They were not specifically mentioned in print, but it is assumed that the woman will be submissive and listen to her husband, especially when he wants to keep you safe. I want to make sure you come to no harm. Going down the arbor was not a smart thing to do, what if the arbor broke away from the house and you fell."

"I guess my punishment will be harsh," she tells him with a huge grin and twinkling eyes.

When he is through doctoring her wounds, he caps the antibacterial ointment, lays the wash cloth on the glass topped night stand then to her delight slides his thumb down the middle of her lacy blue bra and zip snaps the bra into. Next he places his thumb under the elastic of her bikini panties, also ice blue, jerks down and the panties are now on the floor with her ruined bra.

He methodically begins to kiss, lick and use his hands to turn her into his sex slave, and she is delighted. When he stops long enough to pull his jeans off and throws them to the floor with her bra and panties she isn't a bit surprised to see that he is very ready to make passionate love with her, to her, for her, for them. When he sees her eyes light by degrees he smiles to himself. He is beginning to think that she disobeyed him purposely.

When they awaken the house is quiet and the sun is shining into the room. Flannery rolls to her side and sees from the bedside clock that it is ten a.m. Derek stretches his six foot two inch frame and then tossing the light cover aside bends from the waist to retrieve his discarded jeans. He also picks up her now torn bra and bikini panties. He turns to where he can see her face and said, "I guess I will have to buy new panties and bra to replace these. I would apologize for my action but know that you enjoy rousing me up so that I will punish you, so I won't be apologizing. In the future, when you disobey me perhaps you should forgo the undies."

When she sees a wicked glint in his eyes she pushes her side of the blanket back and on her knees moves behind him and wrapping her arms around his broad shoulders she kisses first his neck and then his cheek. He pulls his naked beauty of a wife onto his lap and studies her smiling, sleepy, yet very content scratched face. She smiles into his dark eyes then kisses his very sexy slightly parted lips. He kisses her back, and said, "How about you staying here and I will go downstairs and get us some breakfast. After we eat you and I can shower together, you know save on water."

"Save on water, sounds like a wonderful plan, and also since Granny and the kids are at the library we can take a long, long shower."

"My thoughts exactly, I am truly pleased that your sexual appetite is as huge as mine. Of course you are the reason for my appetite. Even when you piss me off I want to make love with you."

Flannery finds one of his t-shirts in the room's dresser and pulling it over her head she clears a spot on a little table near the windows so they can eat. She pulls a chair from beside a desk and one near the dresser beside the table and is bending down to pick a dropped pen up when he walks into the room with their breakfast of cereal, toast and tea. He sees her bare backside and whistles slowly.

When she turns to help him remove the food from tray to table she sees a little smile playing at the corners of his mouth. He grins and said, "Wife you are quite fetching in my t-shirt but the sight of your backside has me wanting to bypass breakfast and go back to bed.

"We've plenty of time for eating and loving and I am starved so I hope you will vote for eating first."

"You're in luck because I am also hungry. She sees an envelope with their names written in her Granny's lovely handwriting and takes it from the tray. She sips her tea while she does and grins at Derek knowing he is in total agreement with her Granny.

"So there is nothing that I do that my Granny doesn't know about."

"Apparently." is all Derek said as he eats his toast and drinks his tea.

Anne's note, on white parchment paper with a gold and blue trim said, *"Granddaughter, You must be careful coming down the rose arbor. It has been standing for over ten years so I would suggest that you or Derek check to see how sturdy it is. I wouldn't want you to fall and get injured. Also you might want to trim the roses because I am sure you have scratches from their thorns. I have clipped the roses that were bent when you climbed to the ground. I will see you this afternoon. Virginia the five children and I are going to McDonalds after reading time at the library. Enjoy your private time and no more climbing off the roof. I love the two of you. You're Granny Anne*

"I thought that once we are finished eating and showering we can do all the laundry and then go into the back yard and trim the roses on the arbor. As Granny Anne states in her note, I will check the arbor for sturdiness and make sure it is nailed properly to the wooden strips on the side of the porch. I wouldn't want you getting injured when you are trying to escape my interrogation."

Her eyes lights by degrees and she said with a come hither smile, "Your punishment is what I really need, not a lecture."

"Don't worry your pretty little head about that. I will definitely be punishing you every chance I get."

"Hum, I guess I will have to either buy a huge supply of bras and panties or just forgo wearing them at all. You wouldn't know whether I wore them until you peeked."

"Undies and bras are a must. The only time I will allow you to go without them is in the shower and our bedroom, hopefully when we were making passionate love."

"What about during my Zumba workout. The Zumba outfits are form fitting for the most part and I don't want to go out in public with the dreaded panty line."

"Even there you will dress like the lady that you are. Will I have to check before you and Nell go on Tuesday and Thursday evenings?"

"Perhaps you will. So if I don't dress with your approval you will choose my clothing? Why Derek I'm beginning to think that either you don't trust me, or you love controlling me."

'Trust you, yes I do you've given me no reason to not trust you. Actually I can read you extremely well and can tell when you are being sneaky or thinking about it. For instance, last night when I asked why you were late and didn't call you looked everywhere except at me. You also try to avoid confrontation on any issue."

And as he just stated Flannery refuses to look into his eyes, so he reaches across the small table and takes her hand in his. This action causes her to look first at his hand now holding hers, and then she looks into the dark, dark eyes that seem to see everything.

She wants to look away, but decides to prove him wrong by holding the gaze for as long as he does. She wonders how Chloe ever pulled anything over on this man, whose calm is as unavoidable as his anger. When she and Derek were a couple before the Chloe years he was also easy to read but now he no longer is.

She wants to ask him about Chloe and how she was able to do whatever she wanted even while they were married, but then decides it is probably best not to get into that part of his life again.

Because he does know her extremely well he waits for the question, when she doesn't ask he said, "Flannery what do you want to ask me. I promise I won't get upset with you."

His words give her the needed courage to ask, so she does. "How, no why was Chloe able to do whatever she wanted when you were married to her. I know that you are not afraid to put a person in their place, but I'm puzzled as to how she could avoid your control and your ire. I know that she has far more courage than I do in relationship especially with you. Did you try to reel her in without success? If that is info that is off limits please tell me, but please don't yell or ball me out, and don't be mean. Please."

He still remembers the night that he caused her to get hurt when she was running away from his cruel bombardment of words and that she was afraid of his anger. Because he doesn't want her to ever be afraid of him again he takes her hand, pats his thighs and said, "Come and sit here so we can talk."

Though the eyes are dark and not easily read she can sense that he doesn't want to scare her so trusting her instincts and his words she goes to sit on his lap. She sits stiffly with shoulders and back ram-rod straight so he tells her, "Mrs. MacDougal you don't have to be afraid of me. I may look ferocious and ready to bite when I am angry but I never bite unless you should request that I do so." His eyes twinkle at his words and she can sense that what he tells her is truth, so she relaxes and enjoys their closeness.

"That's better. Relax and enjoy our time alone. As for me and Chloe all I can say is this, Chloe is one person who will never let anyone control her. Her father can once in a while, but other than him she listens only to her own self-involved thoughts. Does she care what others think, probably not? I never tried to control her because she told me on our wedding day that we might be married but I should know that she is her only boss and that if I didn't like that too darned bad. Although Chloe would never admit it she was afraid to commit herself to any relationship because she was more than likely shunned by people for most of her life. Gus said that she didn't make friends at school because she felt incompetent with the students who weren't in special education, and superior to those in her special education classes. She wanted to fit in but didn't know how."

"As for our relationship, I trust you but I also feel that there are times when I know what would serve you better than you do." He waits for her reaction but when she said nothing he adds, "You are the most important person in my life along with our kids, and I control to keep you safe more than to keep you in line."

She studies this man that she loves and knows that what he has told her is true and because she trust him with her life she decides that she will put up with his control, at least to a point. With this decision made she takes his face in her hands smiles at him and said, "Mr. MacDougall, my dear husband, Derek Liam I know that you have my best interest at heart and I will let you be my boss most of the time, but I'm certain there will be times when I will have to go with my gut feelings and over rule you."

"Ok let's make a deal. You will wear panties even when there may be a panty line, and you always keep your cell phone charged and with you whenever you are not with me."

She runs her thumb across his arched dark as night brows, kisses his eyes his nose and his lips and then she said, "Ok I promise to wear my undies everywhere except in the shower or in the confines of our room, and I will keep my cell phone charged and on me whenever we are apart. Of course you may have to remind me about the cell phone rules. As you know my head is full of books to be written and I have a tendency to phase out when the idea for a book overcomes me."

He is fully aware that she can leave the world without a thought and spend time in her very, very creative mind, but that is what makes her the sweet child-like person that he and everyone in relationship with her knows and loves.

"It's a deal. I'll make certain that your cell is charged and with you. I love to hear your ideas for you books, so will you share them with me?"

Because she knows he loves being included in her day to day routine she smiles and said, "Derek I would love to share my ideas. Also if you have a better thought then mine, for a book, please don't hesitate to tell me."

"Sweet wife, I doubt anyone has thoughts as creative as yours, but if I should magically come up with a good idea I will share it with you."

Chapter Fifty-one

Flannery, Derek, Granny Anne, Jack and Lucy find various things to do at Anne's house and in the Geneva-St. Charles area. One day the five invite Virginia and Nell's three children to accompany them to The Museum of Science and Industry in Chicago. They arrive early so that they can view each exhibit without rushing. Because there is a place to buy snacks at the museum they take a break half-way through the museum and buy drinks and a few snacks. Derek has promised everyone a full meal when they are through, and he lets the children decide where they will eat. Uno's pizza on Huron street is chosen by the five and the adults agree that it is the perfect place to dine after a long day of learning. Derek insist that he pay for everything and because the ladies know that is what he always insist he do, they thank him and each silently thinks of a way to thank him.

Though Anne and Virginia have pensions from their husbands former employers and Virginia has social security and Anne money that her son left her from the company he owned with Bing and from his wise investments Derek knows that there are times the two need to know that they are truly loved and appreciated and so whenever he takes the two families out he insist that he pays. Nell also helps Virginia because Nell loves her Granny and because she can never give her enough thanks for helping her with her three children.

When Nell's salon became well-known and she began to make lots of money she was going to enroll her three children in a local day-care but Virginia insisted that they would do just fine with her. They have Jack and Lucy to play with and with Anne next door the two can help each other out if an emergency should arise. Kristen, age ten, is the only one of the five enrolled in school and will go back to class after Labor Day, but a bus picks her up and drops her off each day at two-thirty. She has a close friend who lives only two houses down so she either plays with Hayley or she is content hanging out with her siblings, Lucy and Jack.

Sean is a big part of their life. He and Nell will marry the Friday after Thanksgiving and Sean will become another member of Virginia's growing family.

Derek and Sean aren't as close as they once were but they are forming a bond. Many evenings before dark and after dinner Derek, Flannery, Nell, Sean and the five children play basketball in Anne's driveway. They also take the children rowing on the Fox or fishing in a nearby lake. Because Nell wants to spend more time with her kids she takes every Monday and Tuesday off and every other Saturday. Her salon is always closed on Sunday and Monday and she has several stylists who can handle the Salon easily when she isn't there. The stylist that she once worked for has been promoted to manager and because Barb sold her house and now rents one of the two apartments above the salon she doesn't mind taking over when Nell wants time off.

Flannery's St. Charles townhouse is up for sale and the realtor has told her it shouldn't take long to sell. The big mansion where Derek and the kids lived with Chloe has sold and Derek feels a sense of freedom that it is no longer his white elephant. He was going to lower the price because he hadn't gotten much interest in the house but he lucked out when his father's company hired a new executive from California and because the man has a growing family and loves the area he actually paid more for the house than Derek had asked. Apparently when the man sold his California house he made a huge profit and since Derek and Chloe's house was professionally decorated and landscaped, plus had the pool and play area with fort plus movie studio and work-out room, the man knew that even with the extra $50,000.00 above Derek's asking price he and his family were getting a bargain.

Derek has given Chloe half the profits, as promised. She didn't want any furnishings so he left them in the house. He knows that this is another reason why the new owner gave him the extra money. Though the furnishings were not his taste but Chloe's the man's wife loves Chloe's taste and he loves his wife so everyone came out a winner on the deal. Chloe's share of the money was given to Gus who put it in her bank account.

Derek would still love to find a house on the road where Anne and Virginia live but those who live there love the area so he doubts that he will find a place there. There is a parcel of land less than half a mile away and he has put a bid on it. If the owner sells to him and Flannery they can build a new house. He and Flannery have similar taste so he knows it will be easy for them to decide on what to build. There will be no movie studio or formal living and dining room, he and Flannery prefer something homey, easy to keep up and cozily decorated. Anne knows of the plan but hasn't said much about it. He knows that she would love for him, Flannery and the kids to stay with her indefinitely which they may decide to do if they can't get the parcel of land.

Anne has said that they can add on to her house, which they could. An extra bedroom and bath would be nice but he will wait to see if he can purchase the land nearby. The parcel has no access to the river which he, Flannery and the kids love living next to so he will leave his final decision until the realtor calls about the five acre parcel.

Sean has sold his condo and is staying in the second apartment above Nell's Salon, but he will be living at Virginias with Nell and the kids. He and Nell have also talked about building a house nearby so Derek has told them if he gets the five acres he will sell them half. Virginia, like Anne would prefer that they remain with her indefinitely.

Chapter Fifty-two

Sean, Nell, Virginia and Nell's children are in California for ten days so Flannery has missed several Zumba classes and has decided she will go alone. Derek has gone with Anne, Lucy and Jack to Virginias to make sure everything is alright. Virginia's dog and cat are staying at Anne's so they visit the house every evening to make sure that no one has broken in. There have never been any break-ins on the road where they live but they want to be sure. Virginia, like Anne, has motion sensor lights and a security system yet everyone still remains vigilant in their efforts to prevent break-ins in their homes.

Flannery and Nell bought Zumba attire, so that they won't look out of place when they exercise. Flannery for some reason hasn't shown Derek the four outfits because she feels he may not like them. She and Nell know that the outfits aren't overly revealing or they would not have bought them. One of her favorites is a short skort type skirt, which resembles a tennis dress. It is coral and lavender and she loves the colors. She does reveal lots of long shapely thigh when she puts it on but Nell has told her she needs to show those beauties as much as possible. The top is sleeveless and comes only beneath her breast. Because she feels Derek will refuse to let her wear it, she waits until he, Anne and the kids leave the house.

When she gets to the Zumba studio she feels good in what she wears. The instructor is tall and thin like Flannery and wears a similar outfit. Lola, the instructor compliments her on the choice as do all the other women. Because the night is warm she forgoes the long t-shirt that she arrived in. When she arrives home she goes to see her Granny and Anne also tells her the outfit looks great on her.

It is because she now feels good in the outfit that she goes upstairs where Derek is helping Jack and Lucy get ready for bed. His back is to her when she enters the bedroom, but he turns when Lucy said, "Hi mommy. Your skirt and top are beautiful." Jack agrees with Lucy, so she waits for Derek's approval. His eyes travel the length of her five foot nine figure and then back again. When he looks into her eyes she knows without asking that he does not think the outfit is cute. "We'll talk later." is all he said while trying not to let his ire show.

"I'm going to take a shower and then I will be back to tell Jack and Lucy goodnight."

"Fine, just remember we will be talking later."

She knows that she should have let him see her in the outfit, but she's an adult and isn't one to flaunt her sexuality in public. There is no way she would have bought it if lots of other women in the class weren't also wearing the same style.

They've been married for over a month and with each new week of their marriage he is finding numerous things that she does unacceptable to him. She knows he has her best interest at heart and yet she doesn't like to be treated like his child. He disciplines their children when needed, which is rare, but with her he seems to be disciplining her daily.

While showering, she goes over little scenarios that she may have with him and then decides she hasn't done anything wrong so will not feel guilty at making her own choices. Her shower is short because she wants to help him read to their kids. Where Jack and Lucy are concerned he approves of her relationship with them. She is always affectionate with them, though she can also discipline them easily. He knows that she truly loves them and that she loves being their Mommy.

She dresses demurely in long cotton pajama bottoms of teal and a tank top of aqua. The top has a built in bra so she know he will approve of the choice. The week before she was wearing a tank top that had no built in bra and he said it wasn't appropriate for her to be seen with her nipples showing. When she lived alone or was with only her Granny she often wore a regular tank top to bed. Her Granny never mentioned the fact that the shape of her nipples could be seen.

He is reading to Jack and Lucy when she reenters their shared room. He looks up when she goes to sit on the side of Lucy's twin bed. His dark as night eyes are unreadable, and he studies her for a short moment then goes back to reading again.

When he finishes the book that was Jack's choice, she takes Lucy's choice and begins to read. She can feel his dark gaze as she reads but decides she will ignore the dark eyes.

When the reading is over the adults give Lucy and Jack a huge hug and a kiss and tell them good night. In the hallway outside their bedroom door he tells her, “I’m going to shower and then we will talk.”

She waits until she hears the shower come on and then she goes to tell her Granny goodnight. When she passes the key rack in the kitchen she grabs the keys to her Granny’s car, slips her flip-flops on, the pair she always leaves beside the door and then goes out the back door to the garage. Anne’s car is still setting out in the driveway and she needs to put it in the garage. When she thinks about the balling out that will most definitely come from Derek she turns the key in the ignition and instead of parking in the garage she decides she will take a ride. Not sure where she will go she drives around Geneva with the radio on and to cheer herself up sings along with the songs on her favorite Christian radio station.

The clock on the dash shows nine p.m. and because she doesn’t want to go home so early she decides she will go and visit Minnie and Joe and order some pie, ice cream and hot tea. She knows she is blessed that she doesn’t gain weight even though she has a huge appetite. With this pleasant plan she drives to Minnie’s and orders not only her desert and tea she also orders cream of broccoli and cheese soup with lots of crackers.

Minnie is standing by the entrance to the restaurant talking with one of the waitresses. When they see Flannery they greet her with hugs and kisses. The restaurant is only half full so Minnie tells her to sit where ever she likes. Because it is vacant and gives her privacy she sits in the booth where she and Derek sat the night he got so angry that she would ask about his marriage to Chloe.

Minnie comes to wait on her and hands her a menu, and a glass of cold water. She studies the new bride and sees a strained look in the lovely moss green eyes and decides she will ask where Derek is.

“Derek’s at home. He went to take a shower and I needed to put my Granny’s car in the garage. When I got into the car and turned the key I decided I would love to have some pie, and I could also see you and Joe.”

Minnie takes Flannery’s order and goes to the kitchen to get her hot tea. Flannery looks around the pleasant room and counting on her fingers realizes it has been only two and a half months since she and Derek first came here. She’s never stopped loving him and wanted to be his wife even then. She knows that Chloe’s disrespect and disobedience in his marriage to her is one reason he is trying to control her but she doesn’t like it nor does she deserve it. Their vows were all about submission and she doesn't mind being submissive for the most part. To get her mind off her troubles she begins to plan the first chapter to her unwritten adult novel. She is so tuned into the characters and their lives that she fails to see Derek parking his van outside the window where she sits.

When Derek, dressed in faded jeans and a gray t-shirt, comes to sit beside her she jumps with a start. Afraid to ask how he knew where she was or look at him she instead looks at her hands clasped in front of her on the table.

Minnie comes back from the kitchen with a pot of tea and two white china mugs decorated with thistle. "Hi Derek I see you made it right on time."

Minnie sits the tea pot between them, sits a mug before them along with a pitcher of cream and smiling at Derek said. "I knew Flannery would be sweetly surprised to see you so that is why I called you. I thought she looked a little lonely and knew that you would come and cheer her up."

"Derek do you want the broccoli cheese soup plus the pie and ice cream?"

"Sure is that what you're having." he said to Flannery as he places his hand over hers.

She nods her head but doesn't say anything for a moment. Minnie is pleased to see them together and knows that she probably should have asked Flannery if she wanted Derek to come by, but Minnie knows that sometimes romance needs a little boost and she is sure Flannery came to the restaurant to get away from him.

When Minnie walks away Flannery turns to look at him. He smiles and kisses her cheek and this gives her the confidence to say, "I had to put Granny Anne's car away but once I got into it I decided to go for a ride which led me here. So Minnie called and told you I was here?"

He lifts the white teapot up pours them each a cup, adds cream to both and said, "Yes she called as I was getting my clothes on. I was surprised that you had left the house. I guess you aren't up for a balling out."

She sips her tea and shakes her head no.

"Ok, I won't reprimand you about the Zumba outfit, but I would rather you not wear it again and also I would like to see the other outfits that you bought."

Sipping her tea slowly she finally has the courage to look into his eyes and she sees that he's extremely calm. "It's a popular style. We sweat when dancing and I wanted to be comfortable."

"The style looks great on you, maybe a little too great. You are a beautiful woman and I don't want other men to see that much leg or that much midriff. Your mine and I don't share your lovely self."

"What if I decided I didn't want you showing your gorgeous chest with the women at the country club pool? Would you wear something that I approved?"

Before he can answer her Minnie comes with their order and smiling at the now relaxed Flannery she said, "It's good to see newlyweds talking in a peaceful and relaxing atmosphere."

Derek smiles at the happy red head and said, "Thanks for calling me to let me know my lovely wife is here."

"You're welcome. I'm happy to promote romance especially for two of my favorite people."

Flannery smiles at the two and opening a pack of crackers plops it into her soup. Then she smiles, a smile that also fills her eyes and said, "Thank Minnie, you're a true friend."

"You're welcome sweet lady. By the way, I get many compliments on the pins you brought from Scotland to wear on my apron. Many want to know where they can buy them. When I tell them they were gifts from my good friend Flannery they ask if you still live in Scotland. I tell them that you are married and settling in Geneva and they are pleased with the info. Lots of people love the thistle pin, others the Scottie with the Highland terrier. I love them all. This one, here she points to a small replica of the Edinburgh castle gives my patrons much to talk about. Scotland seems to be a place that some would love to visit and others would love to return to whenever possible."

"Are we still going to Scotland this fall?" Flannery asks with hope.

"We haven't changed our plans so we'll be leaving as planned although we won't stay for as long. Now that Flannery and I are married I'm hoping she will want to spend most of her time here"

Minnie looks at Flannery, as does Derek as they wait for her response.

"I'll go along with living here most of the year but I pray that we at least return to Scotland every year, one year for the summer and then the next for the Christmas and New Year's holidays."

"That's doable. I want Jack and Lucy to know our father's and Granny Anne's country." When she gives him a pleased smile he adds, "And Flannery's other country."

They eat quietly and it is several minutes before she asks, "Do you approve my top?" I know it shows my chest and arms are those areas of my anatomy allowed to be seen?"

He pours another cup of tea for each of them and smiling tells her, "What you are wearing now is ok. The top doesn't show any cleavage and your gorgeous legs are covered so yes I do approve. By the way aqua is definitely a color for you."

"Thank you. I have always loved pastels. That is something Lucy and I have in common."

"You and Lucy have many things in common. You loved, love, dolls and so does Lucy. The two of you are definitely girlie girls and I know if I thought about your traits long enough I would find many other ways that you are alike."

"I guess Rena's DNA is strong in us. Does Lucy have any of Chloe's traits?"

"No Lucy is thankfully nothing like Chloe. She may have Chloe's blonde hair but that is all."

Flannery sips her tea, looks at him, eats her soup, looks at him and seeing that he is calm she asks, "May I ask you something, it's about your relationship with Chloe?"

He bites his lip and tells her, "Go ahead and ask your question, although I may not give you an answer."

"Ok, Nell and I were talking the weekend that her Granny and mine took their trip to Door County. We talked of many things and then the conversation strayed to the subject of Chloe and you." He nods so she adds, "She and I believe that Chloe lied to you about Jack and said he was yours because she loves you."

His dark brows go up but he says nothing. "She may have told you she fooled you because she hates me and would do anything to make my life miserable but Nell and I honestly believe that Chloe wanted you because she's loved you for most of her life. If you think back to when we were kids and would go to Granny Anne's, the few times that she was there also there you will remember that she always hung around you. I know you thought it was because Sean hung around with you, but Nell and I remember how Chloe's face would light up whenever she saw you. Did she ever say that she loves you?"

"She had a terrible way of showing her love, if what you say is true. She went out of her way to upset me and she also never gave the impression that she loved me or anyone but herself."

"Perhaps she was afraid to tell you because she has felt rejected most of her life."

"I don't know but I went out of my way to be a good husband, but the harder I tried the more she rebelled against me."

He eats several spoonsful of soup, wipes his mouth with a napkin, looks at her then said, "I do recall an incident after my first trip to Scotland with Jack and Lucy. She no longer traveled with us but when we returned home I left the digital camera on my dresser and she looked at the photos and finding one of me, you and the kids as we walked on the beach near Leith. We were walking towards the camera and had happy smiles on our faces. Anyone who looked at that photo would know that the four of us were extremely happy."

"She showed me the photo and asked what it meant. I was puzzled at her question so I ask what she meant. She said that you and I looked like we were Jack and Lucy's parents and she did not approve of the photo. I said it was a photo and how would anyone know. She said that I apparently had never gotten over you and she could see that in my smile. I told her she was imagining things and she left the room. Later when I took the camera to have photos made she had deleted all the photos that contained any with us together. I confronted her on this and she said, too bad but she was my wife and not you."

Flannery who's eating her pie and ice cream looks at him and said, "That tells me she felt you still loved me and had never considered her feelings."

"I loved you still have strong feelings for you but I was hurt that you were always gone and marrying Chloe was my revenge for that rejection. I was a class a fool but I wanted you here and since you weren't, I figured that Chloe must really want me, no matter that she lied. I admit I hurt all of us and I am truly sorry for that but as I have said once I saw Jack's sweet face and held him, and he smiled at me I knew that no matter what

I would always take care of him. So despite my foolish reasons I married Chloe, but I not once said I loved her. It would have been a lie if I had. Her huge lie about me being Jack's father, was one lie too many.

"I wonder what would be worse, loving a person who married another, or marrying a person that would never love you." He may not tell her that he still loves her but she is sure he does because when he thinks she isn't looking he watches her and those times she can see the love there the old spark from days gone by.

"I from experience can answer part of your question, marrying a person and loving another is horrendous and no matter how hard you try you don't stop loving the one you more or less rejected."

"We are definitely our own worst enemies, aren't we?"

"Yes we certainly are, but I believe that God always shows us the right choice to make. Perhaps Chloe fooled me to get me to marry her but I know that Jack and Lucy were always supposed to have the two of us as parents. Why you were born unable to have babies I don't know, but the Lord always knows what is best for each and every one of us and my marriage to Chloe and subsequent divorce has brought us full circle. Marrying you was always in his plan for me he just went about it in an unconventional way."

"Definitely unconventional, but now we have our second chance and I for one will do all that is in my power not to screw it up." said Flannery before she eats her last bit of ice cream and pie.

She smiles a happy satisfied smile, because he and she are talking in a civil manner and because she absolutely loves the pies that Joe makes fresh each and every day.

With pie on her face and a twinkle in her happy eyes he first wipes the berry stains from her cheeks then turns her face towards him and smiling into her eyes tells her, "You are truly easy to please. I'll bet that you would take Joe's pies over anything that is bright, shiny or expensive."

"As long as I have you, Jack, Lucy and our families, friends and pets what more could I ask for or desire." Here she taps the diamonds in her wedding and promise ring and adds, "The bling is ok but it can't love nor does it taste good, so give me love and pie and I will be one happy woman."

"A woman after my own heart." he said before he gives her a long deep electrifying kiss.

"Wow kids this is a family restaurant." said Joe who always finds time to leave his kitchen to talk with friends old and new.

Derek and Flannery grin and Derek tells the smiling cook, "Blame yourself for our actions, pie, your pie excites my wife almost as much as I do."

Though Flannery grins at his statement he and Joe see the rose color of embracement wash her face.

"Flannery has always been my best food critic. If she says it's to die for she is right."

Joe sits in the booth across from them and studies the newlyweds for several minutes smiles and said, "Love is for the most part wonderful but since none of us is the same there will be times when a couple won't agree on things, but I know from my long marriage to my Minnie that compromise goes a long way in helping make and keep a marriage strong. If you put your partner's needs before your own the outcome is worth it. I know that selfishness is born into us but I also know we are never truly happy until we put others before ourselves."

Minnie free for a few minutes comes to sit beside her husband. After she sits she smiles at Joe and gives him a long sweet kiss. He kisses her in return and Derek grinning and dark brows furrowed said, "Hey you two isn't this a family establishment? You must learn to curtail your lust when in the public eye."

"This coming from the man who only minutes ago was feasting on his wife's lips." Joe tells the three with sternness and then he grins knowing that no matter where they are he and Derek and their wives will kiss whenever the urge hits."

"Joe there isn't a cook anywhere who can back pies like you but there isn't another man on this earth who can kiss like Derek. When he kisses me the rest of the world disappears."

Derek rewards her with a warm smile and a kiss on the cheek and said, "I will remember that. "

"She's correct but I must tell you that my Joe has perfected his kisses to such a degree that I would rather have his kisses than his pie and I agree with Flannery that no one can bake a pie to top Joe's."

"Where's the shovel?" Joe asks with a happy laugh.

Chapter Fifty-three

Derek, Flannery, Jack and Lucy are cleaning up the breakfast dishes. Jack and Lucy carry the dishes from the table and set them on the kitchen counter near the garbage disposal. Derek scrapes the leftovers into the disposal and turns it on for each dish. Flannery takes the dishes from him and places them in the dishwasher. When it was only her Granny Anne living alone or just her and her Granny they always washed the dishes by hand. Now that Derek and the kids are there living with them, and that they uses lots more dishes the dishwasher is used after each meal.

Derek and the kids have been living at Anne's full time since he and Flannery married only six weeks before. Because they had lived there part time before the marriage the three feel like Anne's is home. Jack and Lucy still spend a night or two with Grandpa Bing and Grandma Stella and even a night each month with Gus and Rena, but to them Granny Anne's is home. Flannery once asked them if they missed the big house where they lived with Chloe and they have said they would rather live at Anne's. They said the pool was ok but living by the Fox River is better. Because Anne was all for a tree house being built in one of the big oaks in the fenced back yard and Uncle Sean and Derek are nearly done with the construction the two no longer miss their fort at the big house.

Sean comes by every evening after his day renovating an apartment building being turned into condos and after dinner is over he and Derek go to work on the tree house. For nearly a month they have worked but tonight they will put the finishing touches to the structure and it being Friday Jack and Lucy have been given approval to stay up past their eight o'clock bedtime. Nell, Virginia and Nell's three kids will also be there so Derek and Flannery have planned a cookout in Anne's back yard.

Anne left the house shortly after breakfast because she and Virginia are helping set-up a party for some of the seniors at the nearby Senior Citizen Assisted living residence. Normally they and the kids would be headed for the library and story time but that is over for the summer and won't start again until late September. Anne and Virginia are in their seventies but no one would consider them anything but the lively vivacious women that they are. Flannery and Nell have promised their grannies that they will never place them in a senior facility but Anne and Virginia have told them that if they should need such a place they will not be upset with their granddaughters.

"Daddy what are you going to cook for tonight's party?" ask Jack who considers grilling a party even if it isn't.

"Remember the chicken and beef shish-kabobs that Joe made for our wedding, well I talked him into giving me his prized recipe. Of course he has told me not to give his secret receipt to anyone or he will make me wash dishes at Minnie's for the remainder of the year."

"What else are we having? I want some tatoes and also some bread and butter." said Lucy who sits the last of the breakfast dishes on the kitchen counter.

"We're headed to the supermarket as soon as we are through here so on the way Mommy can write down what everyone wants. Is that ok with you Mrs. MacDougal?" he said as he hands her the last scraped plate."

Flannery always smiles when he calls her Mrs. MacDougall because she loves the name and definitely loves being Mrs. MacDougall. "I can handle that. I always carry a pen and pad of paper in my purse so whatever you want I will write it down."

Because she smiles whenever he calls her his Mrs. MacDougall and because she loves being his wife he waits for her to close the dishwasher and turn it on and then he pulls her into his arms and kisses her.

Jack who is impatient and wants to get going said, "Ah you two always kissing and hugging let's get moving. Dinner will be here before we know it."

"Jack don't you know that as long as a man and his lovely wife are kissing and hugging the family is happy and home is a sweet place to be." Derek said as he musses Jack's thick dark blonde hair.

Jack thinks about this for a while and said, "Your right about that. You and Chloe never kissed or at least I don't remember that you did and you and Chloe were not a happy couple. Also the big house never felt like home. It was far too big and fancy and when you were on the road for work it seemed even bigger and unfriendly. I know when I grow up I want a house like this it's comfortable and warm and always feels like home."

"I want a house like Granny Anne's also. When I'm big I mean. I didn't like the big house either." Lucy tells them because she loves her brother and knows because he's older that he is always right.

"Well Flannery I guess we will have to build a house like Granny Anne's on the parcel of land that Sean and I are trying to buy."

"Daddy I don't want to live anywhere but here. Do we have to have another house, said Lucy with concern.

"Daddy I agree with Lucy. Why build another house when Granny Anne loves having us here. Mommy do you want to live somewhere else," ask Jack voicing the same concern as his sister.

Flannery hasn't seen the parcel of land, but knows it's only half a mile away so she will reserve judgment. If Derek thinks it best that they have their own house she will agree **even** though she would prefer staying right where they are for the rest of their lives. She hasn't told Derek that she wants to stay at her Granny's and will check out the land first.

To make it a learning experience she and Derek always split the grocery list. Derek shops with Jack and Lucy with Flannery and the adults let the children find each item when they get to the right isle. Because they won't be in school until the following year, Derek and Flannery find ways to teach the two things that will make their lives easier when they are grown.

Lucy loves cheese, as does Flannery and the two choose several kinds to add to their shopping cart. They have white cheese slices, Yellow cheddar cheese slices, string cheese, and feta cheese. They can have cheese sandwiches, put feta on their salads and the string cheese is a healthy snack. Derek was going to add cheese to the list that he and Jack are using but knows that Flannery and Lucy will get enough for everyone.

The ladies also love to make S'mores and buy the graham crackers, the marshmallows and the Hershey chocolate bars that are required to make them. They meet Derek and Jack at the checkout and Jack claps his hands with happiness when he sees that **they will be making** S'mores.

That evening when dinner is through, they, Granny Anne, Virginia, Nell, Sean and Nell's children make S'mores in the backyard. There is a fire pit which the adults use to melt toast the marshmallows. Anne has several medal forks which are used to brown the whit fluffy marshmallows.

Once the marshmallows are ready the adults take them to the table on the porch where the graham crackers and the chocolate bars are laid out on paper plates, one for everyone. Minnie and Joe are invited and arrive just before the treats are served.

Chapter Fifty-four

Mid-September

While Derek is at his parent's house dropping Jack and Lucy for a two day stay and then a night with Gus and Rena Flannery has gone to the bank to deposit the check received the day before for the sale of the St. Charles townhouse. She'd bought it for an investment and her investment has paid off nicely. Because she bought the townhouse during the recession she paid far less than it was worth. Now that it has sold she wants to help Derek with the purchase of a parcel of land nearby. He and Sean have looked at it several times with Bing and the three believe that it is ideal for two homes plus an out building or two. It sits only half a mile from Anne and Virginia's so when Sean and Nell are married they will be neighbors.

Because the parcel is off the paved road, with a dirt road leading to the property the dirt road will have to be paved. There are others expenses to consider so Flannery signs the check and happily deposits it into the joint account that she and Derek share. This account is separate from their regular account and he has already deposited the check from the sale of the big house where he and the kids once lived with Chloe. Flannery figures with her check added to the total they will have more than enough for the land and the building of their house.

Sean has sold his condo and Nell is renting the two apartments above her salon so they also have the needed funds for the future project.

When she comes home Derek has not returned yet, and Granny Anne is at Virginia's helping can some tomatoes, so she decides to ride her bike along the trail that runs near Geneva. Though she has a bike helmet she thinks of not wearing it, but wants to be a good example for Jack and Lucy so she puts in on even though the day is sunny and warm. Rain is predicted for the evening but at present the day is glorious so she pedals along the trail breathing in the earthy scent of falling leaves and somewhere she knows there is an apple tree that hasn't had the apples picked. Stopping her bicycle she put the kick stand down and goes to find the apple tree.

Following the sweet scent dancing on the breeze she finds the tree only feet from the bike trail. Bees are buzzing around the tree that still has apples to be picked and also around the apples that have fallen on the ground beneath the tree. Remembering that she has a canvas tote in the basket of her bike she goes and brings it back and fills it with as many apples as she can. Knowing that she can get more into the bike basket she empties the tote and returns to fill it again. Because the apples are making her hungry she wipes one on the leg of her jeans and bites into it. She rolls her eyes with pleasure at the sweet juicy and sun warmed fruit. The apples are Golden Delicious and one of her favorites.

Because her basket is filled and the tote is hung across the bike handles she decides she will head back home and see if Anne and Virginia would like to use the apples for baking or canning or just eating. If they want more she will have Derek go with her when he comes home. She smiles a dreamy smile that lights her eyes. Just thinking about him jump starts her heart. He can be bossy and contrary and at time arrogant and annoying but she loves him and is always excited to see him. Though they haven't made plans to do anything special while Jack and Lucy are gone she hopes that they can take the time to relax and have fun.

His van is in the driveway when she returns from Virginias and she is excited to tell him about her treasure of apples and see if he will go with her to get some more. Because she figures he will use his bike she leaves hers sitting on the road outside her Granny's walled front yard. She hangs her bike helmet by the strap from the bike handles and goes through the side gate to the back yard.

Because the house is quiet, with the dogs at Virginias she listens to see if she can hear him. She calls his name and when he replies "I'm here in the living room." She smiles as she walks towards the living room and him.

He sits in a nook that is built beneath the stairs that go up to their bedrooms. The computer monitor is on because she can see the blue light when she walks towards where he sits. "Hi." she said as she wraps her arms around his shoulders and kisses his cheek. She can still smell the Zest soap that he used that morning after they awakened before sunrise and made love.

"Hi, I have a question for you, when did you put the check from the sale of the town house in the account for the building of our house?"

"I deposited it this morning. I'm surprised that it shows on the account so soon."

"Why did you deposit it in this account? The money is yours so you need to withdraw it tomorrow. You are fully aware that I will take care of the finances for our family."

"I thought we could use it for the purchase of the land or the road surfacing or for the house itself."

"We need to talk. Apparently you don't listen when I tell you things or you conveniently forget them and do as you please. Come sit here next to me." There is a wooden chair sitting beside him and she knows that he purposely moved it there from the hallway. She hates confrontation of any kind and instead of sitting as he asked she turns walks like a race walker across the living room, through the entryway and out the door, across the porch and is down the steps and through the wooden gate before he can stop her. With helmet forgotten, though hanging in her handle bars she puts her purse, conveniently kept by the front door, into the bike basket and pedals away from Derek and the confrontational speech that she isn't in the mood to listen to.

When she reaches Virginia's house she considers going there but knows he will find her so as fast as she can she begins to pedal away from home and Derek and towards St. Charles. For a second she thinks she hears him call her name but she refuses to stop.

She doesn't like being treated like a child nor does she want to be interrogated by Derek. It has been several weeks since their last confrontation about her Zumba outfits and she was beginning to feel that he finally sees her as an intelligent adult rather than the air head that he has accused her of being. Because she has always been creative and has many stories in her head she knows she comes across as an air head at times, but she knows that she isn't. Not sure where she is going she pedals for at least an hour. She is surprised that he didn't try to follow her in the van.

The wind has picked up and dark clouds move across the sky above so she decides she will find shelter. Seeing the driveway to a one story motel she pedals in that direction. Not seeing a speed hump in the driveway her bike skids and she goes flying over the handlebars like a rag doll and falls on her back only feet from the motel entrance. For a moment she lies breathless, with the air knocked from her. Then she hears a concerned voice, a man with a middle-eastern accent who said, "Miss, are you ok? My wife and I saw you fly over the handlebars. He holds out his bronzed hand and she thankfully slips her scrapped hand into his. Slowly he helps her stand and she leans on him as she hobbles into the motel lobby.

They are met by a beautiful dark haired, dark eyed woman who with the man's help guide Flannery to an office behind the reception desk. Slowly the help her sit down on a cushioned straight back chair.

"Thank you. I didn't see the speed hump. Of course my mind was elsewhere so it is my own clumsy fault."

"Would you like for me to call the paramedics to check out your scrapes and to make certain that you haven't broken anything, said the tall, trim rescuer with true concern.

"No I'll be fine. I'm rather uncoordinated but also I have a mind that wonders hither and yon, so I'll be fine. Since I'm biking and the rain will soon be here I would like to book a room for two nights."

The man hands her purse to her that he rescued along with Flannery. While she looks for her wallet she said, "I'm Flannery MacDougall." She holds her hand out and he shakes it gently not wanting to hurt her.

"We have a first aid kit by the front desk. I'll bring it in and clean you scrapes."

"Thank you. That would help." Flannery tells the woman as she removes her bank card from her wallet and hands it to her rescuer.

"My name is Mo, short for Mohammad. My wife's name is Trish. She's second generation Iraqi so she has an American name. I'm first generation, so I have a Middle Eastern name. Your name is unusual although I have read a few of Flannery O'Connor's novels is that who you are named for?"

"Yes, my Dad liked her books and named me. I like it because he chose it and because it isn't used very often."

Trish returns with the first aid kit and a bottle of water which she hands to Flannery before getting on her knees in front of Flannery and checking her few scrapes. "How did you manage to scrape your palms when you fell on your back?"

Flannery winces when Trish begins to clean the dirt from her palms and seeing that Trish is expert with her aid tells her, "I started to fall on my face but stuck my hands out to stop the fall, and that move made me turn and fall on my back."

"Are you certain you don't want me to call the paramedics or drive you to the emergency room?

"Thanks but no I'm fine. I appreciate you helping me."

Mo watches the two for a short time and then said, "I'll book your room. There is one just across the way, not too far to walk."

Once her wounds are nurses Trish walks with her to her room. Mo has taken her bike and stored it in their supply room until she wants it.

"I guess I'll call a cab to take me to the mall. As you can see my jeans are torn and dirty.

"I can drive you there and wait while you shop or help you." Trish tells her with a friendly smile.

"I would appreciate that." Flannery said as she and Trish exit the room for Trish's small compact VW in the parking lot nearby. When they reach the mall which is only across the street and another parking lot away Flannery thanks Trish and tells her she will catch a cab back to the motel. "You may call if you can't find a cab and I will gladly pick you up."

Trish leaves Flannery standing at the entryway to the mall, she waves good bye and heads home. She likes the pretty, tall and slim woman that she has just dropped off and she wonders why she would check into the motel when she has seen the woman's, Flannery's wedding rings. The fact that she has no clothing with her but only her bike and purse tells her that Flannery has had an argument with her husband, got on her bike and rode farther than she should have. Why she doesn't have her husband come to her rescue is no surprise to Trish. Mo is an excellent husband most of the time but there have been times when she would have gotten on a bike and ridden away but she has no bike and so she bites her tongue and lets him rant.

Flannery decides to eat at the mall food court before she begins her shopping. There is a convenience store at the gas station not far from her motel and she will stop there on her way back and buy a few things in case she is hungry before she goes to bed. She knows that she will also need a few toiletries items.

The ladies clothing store that she chooses isn't far from the food court and has everything that she will need. Because the jeans that she wears now have the knees torn, and her jeans jacket is now minus the elbows she will have to buy one of each plus pantie's, a bra, a t-shirt and something to sleep in. Of course she can sleep in her undies but that idea is forgotten when she finds jersey sleep tees that fall to mid-thigh. As soft as Odie the kitten's tummy she holds one to her cheek and she knows she must buy at least one. With colors of old rose, buttercup yellow, delphinium blue and pale violet she cannot decide which to buy so she buys one of each. She will keep two and give the others to Nell.

She also buys black jeans, gun-metal gray jeans, a silk and wool jacket the color of the maple leaves that have suddenly popped up all over the Midwest. A soft pale pink long sleeved and a white t, plus three pair of satiny bikini panties and matching bras and several pair of dark socks she knows that her shopping is over, because she has more than enough to choose from and her knees, her elbows and her hips are aching from her fall off the bike. Her final stop at the mall is the book store where she buys several books. Only one is for her a romance set on her Isle of Skye. The others are gifts for Jack, Lucy, several books by an author that she met at a book signing in Edinburgh, Joanna Kelliher MacDonald is her name and Flannery loves her books. She'd bought two at the book signing and Joanna had bought several of hers but Flannery forgot them at the house on Skye. The other books are for her Granny Anne and of course Derek. He always enjoys John Grisham so she buys two that she knows he hasn't read.

Her face turns a little pensive when she thinks of Derek. She knows that she must stop her practice of running away whenever there is something confrontational that he wants to discuss. She loves him, knows he would never physically harm her and yet the heated temper scares her. She knows that he is trying to curtail that and she saw that he was trying to do so when he saw that she had gone against his wishes and deposited the check in the account for the building of their house and the purchase of the land. Though he takes his anger out on her, she knows that she isn't the issue. He is angry at himself for the wasted years with Chloe. She believes he needs counseling and has mentioned it but he gets extremely defensive and tells her that she can also use counseling because she doesn't handle confrontation well at all. He is right but so is she, so her next project is getting herself and Derek to see a counselor.

Once she has everything she needs she calls a cab. Trish had given her cards with the phone number for the motel, in case she wanted Trish to pick her up and one for a local cab company. Her cell phone is in her purse and surprise, surprise charged. Derek gets irritated when she forgets to charge her phone so he does it for her. She knows she can be scatter-brained at times and sometimes remembers to charge the phone but she doesn't feel that he should get all riled up when she doesn't. She knows that relationships are compromise most of the time but she feels that she does most of that compromise.

The cab driver comes to help her with her shopping bags, which she is grateful for. The load has made her hips hurt more. She is certain that she hasn't broken any bones, but maybe she will visit her doctor if the pain remains.

"Would you mind waiting while I go to the convenience store around the corner from the motel? I need to buy a few things. Do you have time to wait so I won't have to walk to the motel?"

The cabbie saw her limping towards the cab and that is why he helped with her packages, also he sees a sadness in her eyes that she tries to hide but her effort is futile in that attempt. She is near his daughter's age and he would want, hope that others would be kind to his daughter so he smiles at the beauty in the back seat and said, "I wouldn't mind at all. Actually I will come in with you and help you carry what you buy. I see that you have scraped you chin and nose and are limping. Were you in an accident?"

She gives him a sheepish grin and tells him, "Yes I was trying to beat the rain and was on my bike which I was riding too fast. As I rode into the motel parking lot I didn't see the speed hump and went head-over-heels over the handle bars. I'm sure I didn't break any bones but I am feeling the effects of the accident. I would appreciate you helping me shop. As soon as I'm finished I plan to go to my room and take a long, hot shower. Hopefully that will help."

"The owners of the motel saw my accident and wanted to call the paramedics or take me to the emergency room but I figured I can walk, though stiffly so I believe rest will be the best treatment." She isn't this open with personal information most of the time but she senses that Raj is truly interested in her plight so she feels at ease giving him the info that she has.

"If I were, you and the pain persist, I would see the doctor. Perhaps you should get some Tylenol for your discomfort. You also might want to get a couple of ice bags."

Yes, I'll do that. Thank you for your help and concern."

"That's why we're placed on the earth. We are here to be helpful to others." The cabbie whose name is Raj tells her. She knows he is the Raj on the visible cabbie license displayed for the passengers use because he looks exactly like his photo.

"Are you from India? I plan to visit there one day."

Raj turns to look at her in the mirror smiles and said, "Yes I'm from Mumbai. Of course most people seem to remember it as Bombay but Mumbai it is. My birth country has many beautiful things about it but there are far too many people, especially in Mumbai. My wife and I immigrated to the States shortly after our marriage, that was thirty years ago. Our children, one daughter and two sons were born here and are all American kids."{

"I will give you my business card and when you decide to take your trip to India I will give you the low-down on the best place to visit and where to stay."

"Yes I would like that." Flannery said as the cab pulls in front of the convenience store. Raj parks, turns the cab off and helps Flannery out of the back seat.

"How will you know what the exact fare is, if the cab isn't running? I want to pay for the time you wait also."

Raj places her hand in his and said with a smile," There is no need to pay for the time in the store. I want to get a drink and a snack and would have stopped the taxi anyway."

"Well then let me pay for your snack and drink. It is the least I can do."

"Sweet lady, you don't have to pay for what I purchase. Being in your company is my payment. I see that you are married. Where is your husband? I know that is a personal question but I was wondering why you would be riding a bike and checking into a motel, and buying clothing. Have you had a spat?"

She keeps her eyes opened to what she needs and doesn't answer right away, so he thinks he was too forward with his inquire. When she hands him two packages of cookies, a bag of sour cream and chive chips she finally looks at him and said, “Yes Derek, my husband, and I have had a spat, or truthfully, he confronted me on an issue that I wasn’t prepared to discuss, so I did what I always do when confronted with distasteful issues, I ran away. He doesn’t know where I am, but I will call when I get back to the motel.”

When they get to the dairy case she chooses several yogurts and a bag of string cheese. At the deli case she chooses a turkey club sandwich. “Would you like a sandwich or something else?”

Raj chuckles at the amount of food that she is buying and decides that she is probably a nervous eater. Without an ounce of extra body fat he bets she could probably eat more than most men and yet her willowy figure doesn’t show proof of that.

“I’ll also have a sandwich but remember I will pay for mine.”

“You seem to read me easily. I was going to put it with my things and hope you’d forget.”

He studies her for a short time and to her surprise said, “I’ll bet your husband, Derek, is an extremely traditional man who has told you he will take care of the family finances, but you an independent working woman want to help with the finances so try to do so without his knowing.”

With surprise in her eyes she said, “How did you know? That describes Derek perfectly. He’s a wonderful caring man but he can also be relentless whenever I go against the unwritten rules of our marriage.”

“By the way I’m Flannery.”

“Well Flannery, that’s an unusual but beautiful name, one I’ve heard only in college. Were you named for the American writer Flannery O’Connor?”

“Yes my Dad loved her writing so named me Flannery O’Connor.”

“The name suites you, it’s uncommon yet lovely as you are.”

When he sees a soft pink blush on her cheeks he pats her shoulder and smiles happily.

Once she has a variety of foods to choose from Raj helps her put everything on the counter. When he adds his sandwich and drink she smiles thinking he will let her pay for his snack also. While searching through her purse for her money, Raj hands the cashier more than enough money for his order and hers.

“I will give you the money when we get to the motel.” she said thinking he was tired of waiting for her to finish so decided to pay himself.

"There's no need to repay me. It is a pleasure helping you and I am honored with your company."

"Thank you. You are extremely kind."

When they reach the motel, Raj parks right in front of her door and carries all of her purchases into the room. She pulls her wallet from her purse and hands him several big bills, he shakes his head no and tells her, "You remind me a great deal of my wife when we first married. The reason I know what Derek is like is because I was once exactly like that. Rose and I grew up together went to University and married. We moved here after graduation. I was hired for an engineering position by Motorola. Rose was hired by The Chicago Tribune to work as an office manager. We had our plans. We'd work for five years and then begin having our children. Then Rose found out that she couldn't have children and we split over that. It was her idea because she knew that I wanted children of my own. We were apart for over a year, an extremely long time."

"Would you like to sit down and eat you sandwich and have your drink. You must take a break and I would love your company while I eat my sandwich. We can also share the chips and cookies."

He hears a loneliness in her and agrees that yes he will join her while she eats her sandwich.

"What brought you and Rose back together?"

"I kept tabs on her and knew that she was working long hours and that she was still living in our apartment and I decided I would go and beg to come back home. She took me back after much sole searching and said that she wanted our marriage to be a fifty-fifty union. She would work but also contribute financially as I did. She would also like to adopt several children and if I didn't agree then she saw no future for us. She also said that I was to no longer control her, that she would respect my position as her husband but she also expected the same respect. We got back together and had numerous quarrels because I had a difficult time giving up control over finances and just about everything. The final showdown came when I was reluctant to adopt. She said if we didn't go to counseling and work on our issues she didn't see a future with me. So Rose and I went to counseling for quite a while. During that time I realized that she was far more important to me then my controlling everything."

Raj eats his sandwich and the shared chips and even accepts several cookies. The two eat in companionable silence, neither feeling the need to talk. When he's finished he smiles at her and said, "If you are wondering if Rose and I finally saw the light, yes we did. Of course she saw it before I did. She told me that there was no need for me to expect our marriage to last unless I gave up my antiquated ideas of who was in charge of finances and my steel hand of control. She said she loved me and didn't want to divorce but she wanted children and was truly sorry that she could give me my own blood, but she had a childhood friend in India who was raped but wanted to carry her baby full term and she offered her friend a place with us and that she wanted to adopt that baby. I knew that she was serious about everything and decided that whatever it took I would become the man that she deserved. We brought her pregnant friend here. We were with her when her daughter was born. We adopted the baby girl and she is everything that a father could want in a daughter. This same friend stayed in the United States, decided that she would give us more children, which she did two times more, and that is how we adopted our two sons. By then she had married a wonderful man and he wasn't opposed to her giving us two more children. They now have several of their own."

Raj stays for another hour and Flannery tells him the story of her romance with Derek, about his marriage to Chloe and about their children. Because he is the father figure that she would have loved in her life, she also tells him that she cannot have children. He agrees that Derek was to marry Chloe so that she and Derek could parent Jack and Lucy. When he gets up to leave he gives her a fatherly hug and a kiss on the cheek and he tells her before returning to his cab, "Don't give up on Derek. From what you have told me he sounds like a keeper. Perhaps the two of you should try counseling, if he is apposed put your foot down hard, as Rose did and tell him that he has a choice. That choice would be you and counseling or you will rethink your marriage to him."

After Raj leaves Flannery decides it is time to let Derek and her Granny Anne know that she is fine. The phone rings only once and Anne answers, when she hears Flannery's voice her first question is "Granddaughter are you ok," Her second question asked before Flannery can answer the first is, "Where are you?"

"I'm fine and I will be staying here tonight and until Saturday morning. "

Apparently Derek is standing nearby and next she hears him say, "Flannery where are you. I'll come and pick you up. I know you won't be riding far in the rain."

She hesitates only a moment then tells him, "Derek I need a little time to myself. I'm booked into a motel until Saturday morning. I will let you know on Friday evening where I am staying."

When he says nothing at first she thinks he's through talking and she adds, "I'm sorry that I ran away when you asked me about the money I deposited in the account for our house and the land. Why I run I'm not sure, except I don't like being treated like a child and an air head. I also don't like being the brunt of your anger. I love you, always have, always will but we need some counseling."

Just when she decides the conversation is over he tells her, "I know we can use some counseling and I want to apologize for treating you like a child, and as you say an air head. I don't consider you either. I would love to come and drive you home tonight but if you feel you need time alone I will honor your wishes. Don't forget to call me on Friday and I will gladly come and get you. Good night Flannery."

"Good night Derek. Please tell my Granny good night. Don't forget I love you and Granny. One question how are Jack and Lucy. I hope they are having fun with Bing and Stella."

"Our kids are having a great time." She always smiles when he says our kids, and she knows that he and they consider her their Mommy.

"My Mrs. MacDougall, don't forget that I miss you and am looking forward to seeing you." This also brings a smile to her lovely face.

Her final words are these, "Good night my Mr. MacDougall. I'll see you soon."

Her night is restless because she aches all over from her biking accident. She took a long hot shower before bed and downed two of the pain killers that Trish had given her but not matter how she lies she hurts. All night long she moves around the bed. By morning she is exhausted but decides she will get up and walk across the parking lot to the motel office and find out where breakfast is served.

Rain had fallen throughout the long night and the parking lot looks like it has been cleaned by a street sweeper. The air is fresh and a weak sun is trying to force its way between the remaining clouds. Because she listened to the news before leaving her room she knows that more rain is predicted for later in the day.

A tall dark young man, who looks a great deal like Mo is working on the computer at the check-in counter and he looks up and smiles then said, "Good morning, if you are looking for breakfast it is served in the dining room around the corner." Here he waves his hand to the right of where they stand.

"Thank you. You must be a mind reader."

He studies her closely and knows that she is in room number two. He knows because his parents Trish and Mo have told him of their beautiful patron. He believes he has seen her before and searches his mind trying to remember where. He thinks of this the entire time that she is in the dining room eating and just as she enters the lobby he remembers where he has seen her.

"Aren't you the children's fantasy book writer?"

Surprised, yet pleased that he would recognize her she stops in front of the counter where he works and tells him, "Yes I'm Flannery O'Connor Larkin, although I go by Flannery MacDougall since my wedding in August." She has written for several years and though she is well known and recognized at times, she is still surprised and pleased that her readers recognize her.

"Are you Mo and Trish son? The reason I ask is because you look like Mo."

He smiles and holding out his hand said, "Yes I'm their youngest son. I help out most mornings when I am not at school."

She grasps his hand and said, "Your parents are sweet and kind. Will they be here this evening?"

"Yes, they'll be here from three to eleven. We live only a few miles away."

"Maybe I'll come by and visit them. Of course only if they aren't busy."

"They would enjoy your company. It's nice meeting you Flannery O'Connor Larkin MacDougall. My name is Tate."

"Tate, I like that. It's short and easy to pronounce. It was nice meeting you also."

He watches her walk away and notes that she is limping. His parent's told him about her accident and he will have to tell them of her limp.

The rain starts around noon and Flannery is much too tired to leave her room and so she naps most of the day, reads her book, eats and watches television. Daytime television leaves much to be desired and after several hours she shuts the television off and calls Derek.

She calls his cell phone and he picks up instantly. Because she's using her cell phone he knows he won't find out where she is by the phone number. He was hoping she would call on a landline and that that number would show on his phone.

"Hi Derek It's me."

"Hi Flannery, will you let me come and get you?"

"Saturday you may come, I need time to think about things." To change the subject because she knows if he asks enough she will let him come and get her, she said, "The rain is nice, don't you think. I saw on the news that it's supposed to last for several days."

"Ok, I will honor your wish and not mention coming for you until you are ready to come home. I want you to know that I miss you. Our bed is far too big when you aren't there with me."

When she doesn't respond to this very personal information he decides to talk about other things.

"This morning Granny Anne, Virginia, Nell's kids and I went and found your apple tree. We were able to save lots of apples and we kept a few but the rest are now being delivered to the food bank by Granny Anne, Virginia and Nell's three. I can see why you wanted them picked. Granny Anne saved enough to bake a cobbler for your return home. She said that she wants you here before she bakes so that the cobbler will be fresh."

"Thank you for picking them. I was going to have you help me with them. That was before I ran away. I really don't know what comes over me. My first thought whenever I am confronted by you is to run."

"I know, and I'm sorry that you feel that way. We will talk about things when you come home. I will patiently talk and will not get angry, I promise."

"I know you will. I trust you. I'll call tomorrow evening."

Chapter Fifty-five

By Friday afternoon Flannery is tired of her room and decides to go out for lunch. There is a restaurant across the street from the motel and she walks there. On her way back to the motel she crosses at the red light and passes right in front of Sean sitting at the light in his pickup. She wears sunglasses although the day is cloudy so she pretends that she doesn't see him. From the corner of her eye she sees that he is talking on his cell phone. When he stops talking and looks in surprise at her she knows that he will call Derek and tell him where he saw her. Once he knows that he will more than likely be coming to the motel to get her. This irritates her for a moment, but only that because she does miss him.

When she gets to the motel she sees Mo, Trish and Raj in the lobby by the desk and goes to talk with them.

"Hello lovely lady." said Raj as he smiles at her and gives her a fatherly hug. "Had I know you wanted to go out I would have gladly driven you there."

"Thank you but I needed the walk. It has helped greatly with the stiffness in my body. I was in the room all day yesterday, except for coming here for breakfast and my body isn't used to being idle for long. Besides I don't see the cab."

"I'm not driving today. Well, not driving the cab. My car is there in front." Here he points outside, to the drive in front of the motel to a silver Lexus.

"So your friend doesn't need you to fill in tonight?"

"No, he's driving the cab himself and so I decided to come by and visit with Mo and Trish and find out how you are doing."

"The first thing Raj asked even before he said hello, was, how is the lovely Flannery?" teases Mo who winks at Flannery.

"What would Rose think of your interest in our new friend/" teases Trish who walks around the counter and hugs Flannery.

"I know that my Rose would be just as concerned. I will bet Flannery makes friends wherever she goes."

Flannery blushes, and as the blush of rose paints her cheeks Trish also kisses her cheek.

"Have you let you husband know where you are?" Raj asks as a friend who wants to take care of her.

"I've talked with him but I saw his brother when I was crossing the street only minutes ago. I pretended not to see him, but when he saw me he had a look of surprise on his face so I can guarantee that Derek, my husband, will be coming soon." When she says his name the three new friends see the look in her eyes that can only be described as love.

"Please send him to my room when he arrives. Here is what he looks like." she said this while pulling her green wallet from her tan leather purse and pulling a photo from the wallet hands it to Trish.

Trish looks at the photo closely then hands it to Raj who also looks at it closely before handing the photo to Mo.

"He's an extremely handsome man. Isn't your married name MacDougall?" Flannery nods yes and waits for Trish to continue. "He appears to have a good deal of Indian blood, from the country of India. Was he adopted?"

"No Derek's fraternal grandmother came from a Romney family. Bing, Derek's father had their heritage, family linage traced and Charlotte, Bing's mother's family originated in northern India. His fraternal grandfather is Scottish, born and raised as was Bing, but his heritage is Scandinavian. Derek brother Sean has the dark Indian eyes like Derek and Bing but his hair is blonde because his mother is blonde and of Irish heritage. I believe he also gets the lighter skin from their grandfather MacDougall. Derek and Sean have different mothers. Hanna Derek's mother died when he was four from cancer. Stella, Sean's mother and Bing married when Derek was five."

"Bing MacDougall, I know him. For years we would team up and play charity golf." Raj reaches to take the photo of Derek from Mo, looks at it closely and adds, "I have met your husband and his brother. They came with Bing several times and caddied for us. They are wonderful young men. I haven't seen Bing for several years. The last time was shortly after Derek married a woman named Chloe." Raj is well aware who Chloe is but doesn't feel it's place to tell. If Flannery wants Mo and Trish to know her history she will tell them.

"Yes he was married once before but divorced Chloe. I guess they couldn't see eye-to-eye on most things." He knows he was right not to spill the beans on Derek's past marriage, when Flannery says no more on that subject.

Raj hands her photo back which she looks at for several moments before returning to her wallet. "Derek is a wonderful man, but as you know no two people always agree so that is why I am here and he will be coming to get me." She smiles a soft smile and adds, "Actually I'm looking forward to seeing him."

"I'd better go and order something to eat. I don't know why I've been so hungry this past three days.. I'll see you later and thanks for your kindness."

"You're welcome. Don't forget to call and let us know how you're doing. Now that we know you we would love for you to stay in touch." Raj tells her before giving her another fatherly hug and an added kiss on the cheek.

"Yes please let us know how things are going with you and Derek." said Trish who also hugs Flannery. Mo follows suit and kisses her cheek and hugs her tightly.

The three watch her walk away and note only a slight limp. Her walk has apparently taken care of some of the stiffness. They are certain that once her Derek arrives he will take care of any remaining stiffness.

Though the room is setup like nearly all motel rooms in America Flannery likes it. It is extremely clean and comfortable. She has always favored a queen sized bed over king-size, like Derek, and knows that he likes the queen size because she isn't too far away from him.

Chapter Fifty-six

Flannery takes a shower and washes her hair. Then she dresses in the black jeans and the pink long sleeved t that she bought at the mall only two days before, days that seemed more than twenty four hours to her. She looks through the take out-menus kept in the drawer of the desk and decides she will order pizza. She doesn't know anyone who doesn't like pizza. Next she checks the small frig to see what is left to drink. Bottled water and bottled tea are what she has so it will have to do. Of course she also has the packets of hot chocolate that she bought her first night in the motel and tea bags and packets of coffee. There is a carton of milk saved from her breakfast so now all she has to do is wait for Derek.

It is an hour and a half before she hears a knock on her door and hears Derek say, "Flannery its Derek may I come in?"

It has also started raining which had started right before the pizza was delivered. It sits on the rooms table still covered because as predicted Derek has come for her.

With the rain behind him and the dark stormy sky she cannot see his face clearly but she smiles and said, "Please come in before you are soaked."

"Thanks." he said as she steps back and opens the door widely for his entry. He carries a huge bouquet of wild flowers which he presents to her. He also carries a box of dark chocolate, raspberry filled truffles which he sits on the edge of the long dresser nearby.

"I hope you're hungry. A pizza was delivered only a few minutes ago. I also have some drinks in the refrigerator. If you would like something hot there is tea, coffee or hot chocolate." Because she isn't sure of his reception and because he hasn't utter a word since entering her room she begins to feel nervous.

She takes her bouquet and filling the ice bucket with water places them there to lean against the mirror above the sink. When she turns, he is behind her, and he removes his black wind breaker, and hangs it in the wooden wardrobe. Then he turns to her tilts her chin so she is forced to look at him and he said in a whisper, "Flannery, my Mrs. MacDougall, there is no need to be anxious or worried. I am not going to bite, at least not until we are in bed and making love, so relax and lets go and eat the pizza before it gets cold."

With his strong warm arm around her shoulder they walk the short distance to the table and Derek opens the pizza box, places two pieces on the paper plates she has for that purpose in the middle of the table. He hands her a plate with a napkin sits across from her and enjoys her company and extremely tasty meal.

They eat in silence for a short time and he smiles at her and said," I talked with your fan club in the motel office, Raj, Mo, and Trish, they think you are wonderful." He waits for her to respond when she shrugs her shoulders and looks more at the pizza than him he said, "I told them that they are right, you are wonderful, sweet and kind and that I am extremely proud of my Mrs. MacDougall."

At his words she raises her head and looks at his warm and welcome smile. Because the smile is sincere she cannot help but smile back. "I am also proud of my Mr. MacDougall, and I am extremely happy that you are here. Will you spend the night with me?"

He grins and tells her, "My dear wife, now that I know where you are there is no way that I would spend my night anywhere but with you. Our bed seems far too big without your presence and since we haven't made love since Monday evening, and this is Friday, I know that you will not deny me your sweet and lovely self. For a moment, while you were away from me and refused to tell me where you were I thought of buying a pack of cigarettes and a bottle of whisky, the Scottish whisky, but then I talked myself out of it. The reason being I want to spend a long lifetime with you, fighting, making up and definitely making love. And I have a full proof way to make sure you won't run away when I want to discuss things with you."

He waits for her to ask what the method is, but when she doesn't he tells her his plan.

"My method is this, before I even bring up a discussion on anything I will invite you to our room, strip you naked, make love to you, then tie you to our bed, hands and feet and you won't have a choice but to listen."

Her eyes light by degrees, she smiles a come hither smile and said, "So in other words you will placate me with sex and while I am under your spell you will set down the rules. You will make certain I know which side my bread is buttered on. You will make certain I know which way the wind is blowing and weather it is a soft wind or a chilly wind."

He smiles a crocked smile and with a wicked laugh tells her, "When I am through with our discussion you will be under my spell and be willing to do whatever I ask."

"Isn't there an international law against sex slavery?"

"Because you will willingly participate and you are legally my wife there isn't a law anywhere that I know of that won't favor my treatment of you."

"So, if I don't go along with this plan what will you do?"

"You see the plan is foolproof. I know that you will never turn down my sexual advances because you enjoy our encounters as much as I do, Actually I have a feeling that if we were to strip right now you would be more than ready and willing to surrender to me."

"Is that right? So you think that at the drop of hat, or in this instance when you drop your drawers, I will turn into a sex slave." He knows her well because she can feel her lady parts stirring happily at his words, but she doesn't plan to give in too easily.

He watches her eyes which are an open book and he knows that all he would have to do is go to her pull her close, kiss her and caress her and she would be undressed and waiting on the queen sized bed before he could remove his t-shirt.

"I'm hungry so the lustful part of your libido will have to put the brakes on. Once I have eaten and had my drink and a few truffles I might consider your offer but by then I might be too tired to participate in your sexual fare."

Derek raises his brows gives her a sexy white toothed grin, sets his nearly finished pizza aside, gets up from his chair, walks the short distance that separates her, lifts her from her chair, throws her over his shoulder and dumping her in the middle of the bed, kicks his sneakers off, begins to remove his long sleeved t-shirt, then his jeans and before she can move he removes his briefs and is beside her and removing her clothing also. She is surprised yet deeply excited by this daring move and she hurriedly helps him with her pink t-shirt her new black jeans her new pink bra and new pink bikini panties.

When he lowers his mouth to hers she pulls him tightly against her breast and kisses him as deeply as he kisses her. Everything is forgotten while they make sweet, long drawn out love. She was hungry for the pizza but she was much hungrier for him and their mating.

Several hours later, once they are totally sated, they lie side by side wrapped in the moment and one another's arms, with contented smiles playing on their faces, as they think of the amazing time that they have shared. Flannery turns to look at Derek and is rewarded with first a huge smile and then a long kiss. When the kiss is over she runs her fingers through his crisp short cut dark as black as licorice hair and said, "My Mr. MacDougal you certainly know how to make your Mrs. MacDougal extremely happy, excited and I feel as though I am the most blessed woman anywhere on the earth, or in the universe."

He brushes a stray strand of dark brunette hair from her long dancer's neck and plants a kiss where the stray strand once lay. He looks into her smiling eyes and tells her, "My Mrs. MacDougal you make me feel like I can conquer the world although you are my world so I guess I have conquered it."

"I have definitely been conquered and you may hang your flag anywhere you choose."

He grins and said. "I won't be hanging flags from you but I will be tying you up with silk scarves whenever I want to discuss anything of importance with you. You Mrs., wife, will no longer be free to run away from me."

She grin's thinks of his threat for short while and said, "What will you do if you want to discuss an issue and Granny Anne and our kids are at home with us?"

It doesn't take long for him to tell her, "When Granny Anne and our kids are at home I will wait until we put the three to bed, lock our bedroom door and then have my way with you. If I need to discuss an issue and they are still up I will wait for bedtime or come here and rent a room. There is always a way and always a place so don't think that I will forget our new plan."

Her smiles widens as she listens to him act all tough and controlling and when she giggles at his now fierce frown and arched brows she kisses his cheek and said, "I cannot wait until you tie me to our bed or a bed. I have a drawer full of silk scarves so you will not run out."

"I have seen the drawer filled with lovely scarves and that is where I got my idea."

"I don't wear them often so feel free to use whatever you choose. Maybe you would like to give me a preview before Jack and Lucy return from your parent's house. If I remember correctly My Granny, our Granny is going out with Virginia tomorrow evening to a movie and dinner and we will be home alone, except for the pets."

"Perhaps we will have a preview. If so you will have to be totally submissive to me. You will do whatever I say and let me treat you to whatever comes to my mind."

She raises her eyebrows, and with a twinkle in the green eyes pulls him close, and whispers in his ear. "You may do to me whatever you choose. I trust you and know that you will not harm me. May tomorrow come quickly."

He pats her fanny and whispers back. "Never will I physically harm you and hopefully I won't mentally harm you either."

She moves from his arms and sitting on the side of the bed said with sincerity. "I will never harm you physically and hopefully nor will I harm you mentally. When we are through showering I'm heating the left over pizza in the rooms microwave because I'm starving, are you?"

He moves to sit beside her and tells her, "When I first arrived it was you that I was starved for, now I agree that I too am starving for food, which reminds me I need a toothbrush. I saw a convenience store around the corner. After we shower would you like to go with me? I'm guessing that you will also need some snacks for later."

She stands, takes his hand and with a satisfied smile said, "I took care of everything. Wednesday evening Raj stopped there after he picked me up at the mall and I bought two toothbrushes, toothpaste, mouthwash, deodorant and snacks, You may use my deodorant, if that's ok."

He stands with her hand still in his and placing his arm around her shoulders walks with her into the bathroom and the shower. "I should have known you would have a supply of food. You are a forger and a gatherer, a true pioneer, just the kind of wife any man would adore. I do have a question, how did you know I would come for you. You apparently felt secure that I would or you wouldn't have bought a tooth brush for me."

"Derek, you and I have changed a bit, and you more than me but there is one thing I know for certain you would search to the ends of the earth to find me and bring me home. You are relentless or as some may say a hard ass when you want something or someone."

"That's true but would you please not use the phrase hard-ass. Chloe called me many rude and crude names and that was one of her favorites so I don't like the word."

She is washing his chest and focused on that beautiful sight until she hears his first admission of Chloe's cruelty to him. She knew from others that Chloe was unkind and mean to him, from Jack and Lucy and also from his parents and Gus and though she wondered what Chloe had said and did she has waited for him to tell her.

"Ok, I promise I won't call you that again. Are there any other words off limits not that I plan to belittle you."

He washes her breasts and turns her so he can wash her back before he tells her, "I don't like dumbass, shithead, asshole, the f word to name a few. I also don't care to hear undersexed, eunuch, nor do I like ugly as sin and twice as stupid. When he sees a look of disbelief and then sadness he knows that she needs some cheering up, so he said, "I also don't care for Scooby Doo, Wylie Coyote, Brutus or Goofy. His face is dark and serious when he tells her this and then he laughs outright and she shakes her head and smacks his taunt tightly muscled backside.

"You little devil you, were you kidding about the dirty names as you were the cartoon names. I hope so. I would hate to think that anyone would call you such hurtful and untrue things."

Flannery moves to wash his back when he is through with hers and as she washes she tells him, "To me you are kind, sweet, sexy as hell, so handsome that I still want to swoon when I see you, you are intelligent, a true gentleman, that's except in bed, and thank you that the gentleman stays out of our bed. You are a born father and a, as my Granny and Bing would say a grand man and a terrific husband. And to top it off you ring my chimes and keep my lady parts in a tizzy. Also you smell wonderful, kiss me in a way that makes me want to shed every stitch and I am proud to be your Mrs. MacDougall."

He turns her towards him tilts her chin and with a little smile said," you are wonderful for my mood, my libido and my heart. If you a wondering who called me those dirty and crude names it was Chloe, although I think you already knew that."

"I suspected so, but seriously hoped not. Apparently Chloe and I do have something in common." He looks at her puzzled at the statement because he knows for a fact that the sisters are nothing alike. They may have the same biological mother but that is where the likeness ends.

When she sees the puzzled look on his face she clears the doubt up. "Chloe swears and so do I although I have been trying to curb the urge to spew the curse words."

"I've noticed that you rarely curse. That's something that I tried not to get into because of Jack and Lucy, and as you know cursing sounds worse when we hear another using those words. I won't tell you that I have never cursed but I curb the desire to do so."

"I will admit, since we are apparently clearing our slate, that I still swear in my head and under my breath, but I'm seriously working on my horribly naughty habit."

"I've heard you swearing under your breath. It seems you do that only when I control you, so I will work on the control issue.'

He takes her hand in his and said, "So what do you say we shake on it. I will work on the control issue and you continue working on the not swearing issue."

She grins and shakes his hand, then she goes to the dresser nearby and pulls four sleep-tee's out. She holds them out for him to see and asks, "Which color do you like best with my coloring, I needed something to sleep in but got carried away by the beautiful colors so bought four. I will keep two, this here she holds out a shirt of delphinium blue. Then her second choice, one the color of a wild pink rose. The other two I will give to Nell."

He studies the shirts and her closely and said, "I think you should keep all four. The pale yellow and the light purple will also look lovely on you. Tomorrow before we go home we will go to the mall and you can buy more for Nell."

"Thanks. We can do that although I don't want to be greedy and materialistic."

She lays the pink shirt on the bed and puts the others back in the dresser. Then she pulls the shirt over her clean and showered body, and goes to the refrigerator for the milk. “I’m going to make a cup of tea, would you like one?”

Derek, whose now dressed in his jeans only goes to the table, places two pieces of the now cold pizza on two paper plates and follows her to the microwave on a shelf near the bathroom.

“Tea would be good.” She fills two hotel white generic mugs with tap water, adds tea bags and waits until he has warmed their leftover pizza.

The two eat silently for a time and then he tells her, “I don’t see you as greedy or materialistic. I know that you would much rather buy gifts for others than buy for yourself. I want you to feel free to buy the things that you need but also many of the things that you want because they are pretty or just please you. I will also continue to buy nice things for you, because you are my wife and because you have a huge and giving heart and I want to reward that wonderful trait in you.”

She sips her tea and looks shyly at him from beneath her long dark lashes. She bites a piece from her pizza and gives him a tiny smile before saying, “I love being your wife, not because you buy me beautiful gifts, which you do, but because I care for you, and love being your Mrs. MacDougall.”

Because she blushes a tad when she tells him this, he reaches across the table, takes her hand and said, “I also love being your husband, your Mr. MacDougall.”

“Good because now that we are husband and wife I intend to do many wonderful things for and to you.”

Before he can respond she gets up from her chair and goes back to the dresser, opens the long bottom drawer and pulling out two books hands them to him. She forgets to shut the drawer and he sees several more books stacked inside.

“These are for you. I stopped at the mall bookstore to buy a book to read while I was here. I saw the John Grisham’s and know you haven’t read these.”

He takes them from her, then pulls her to stand near the table, pushes his chair back from the table and pulls her onto his jeans glad lap. He smiles into her eyes and kisses her mouth, not once but two times. Then he picks the books back up, and affirms that he hasn’t read her selection. He opens each book and finds that she has also bought bookmarks for each book.

"Thank you. You are very thoughtful and sweet. I will read these at night after or before making love with you. *Mother Teresa* once said, *it's not how much we give but how much love we put into giving.* I once wrote the quote down because it definitely applies to you and the giving that you do. Your love shines through whenever you buy gifts and also by your treatment of others."

She is pleased by his assessment of her, but once again is slightly embarrassed also. To get the subject off of her she teasingly said, about the books she given him. I know you love to read but don't have much time with our kids needing our attention. Maybe you can do both, you know read while we are making love."

He narrows his eyes shakes a finger at her and said adamantly, "Loving you will always come first. I may enjoy reading, as you do, but there is nothing that will come before our love making. Do you have that straight my dear?"

"Just checking, I know you have many talents."

"Yes and you will be the one that I show or use those talents on."

She laughs and tells him happily, "I cannot wait to be the recipient to those talents."

"Good." is all he said before kissing her again.

Chapter Fifty-seven

The next morning, after breakfast in their room, food which he went to the motel dining room to get, so that she could sleep in, they pack their few things, putting them into the trunk of Anne's car they head for the mall to buy the sleep tee's for Nell.

"Derek I forgot to pay for the room. Of course Mo and Trish have my bank card number so I hope that is all they need."

"Not to worry my dear, I paid for the room on my way to pick up our breakfast. It's on our bank card so in theory you have paid for the room."

She is irritated for a moment that he didn't let the bill go on her credit card. She pays the balance each month, but then she knows he paid because he has old fashioned ideas about marriage and finance.

He figures she is irritated that he paid but is sweetly surprised when she kisses his cheek and tells him, "Thank you for paying. I appreciate everything that you do."

"I know that you appreciate me and all that I do, but it wonderful to hear the words also."

Anne is sitting on the back porch when they return to her house or home as he and she think of it. Anne is adamant that they feel welcomed in her home and tells them every day how much she enjoys Flannery, Derek, Jack, Lucy and the pets. Because Anne was an only child who married an only child and gave birth only to James, Flannery's father, she loves having people in her home and in her everyday life. Because he was an only child James her son went out of his way to make friends, and though he had other friends Bing was the one that became his brother of the heart. Anne considers Bing, Stella, Derek and his children and Sean family. Virginia, Nell and Nell's three children are part of the family circle and are always included in every celebration big or small, birthdays or holidays, they celebrate as a family unit and if any of them needs help in any way, everyone in the unit is there to comfort and help in any way possible.

Because she is in deep thought Anne does not hear Derek open the garage door and put her car away. The now barking dogs running to the side gate alert her to their arrival. She gets up from the patio chair and follows the dogs to the gate. It isn't long before Flannery and Derek walk through the gate that she holds open for them. When she sees their arms loaded down with shopping bags she knows that opening the gate was a wise move.

Though her arms are loaded with mall shopping bags Flannery manages to kiss her sweet Granny Anne's soft though slightly wrinkled cheek. Anne smiles at her granddaughter and said, "Welcome home granddaughter, it is wonderful to see you as always. Let me help you with your bags. I wasn't aware that Christmas is so close."

Derek leans towards Anne and also kisses her cheek. "Flannery and I decided to do a little shopping before are return. She had to buy some clothing because her jeans and jacket were ripped, and there was a sale at the mall so I thought, why not be more like Flannery and gift everyone that we love. So you see, not only are we gifting but we are also gifted by the Lord's gift of our loved ones."

Because they have been inside for several days, because of the rain that has now made its exit to the east, the three sit the bags on the patio table, on the porch, then sit down so Flannery can show Anne her gifts and the gifts for the others. While Flannery searches the bags for a jacket that she has bought Anne, Anne tells her, "I love your jacket. The burgundy goes nicely with your dark hair. The black jeans are nice. I guess you can wear those lots of places because they can be casual or dressed up."

When Flannery finds her Granny's gifts she smiles at her at said, "These are for you, because I love you and just because I knew you would look beautiful in them."

Anne takes three gift boxes from her and opening the top box sees a jacket like Flannery but in a beautiful royal blue. "This is beautiful." Before opening the other boxes she pushes her chair back and slips her arms in the silk and wool beautifully fashioned jacket. It fits perfectly and she bends down to where Flannery is sitting and gives her a kiss. Next she goes around the table to where Derek sits and gives him a kiss also. "Thank you. I will wear this tonight. Virginia and I are splurging and going to a nice restaurant where there are candles on the cloth covered tables. A place where the wine cost more than the dinner but Virginia has finished her computer class and received an A for her efforts. Now she can send email and get a Facebook account if she likes. Or as she has said, she now lives in the communication age not the Dark Age."

When Anne sees the black jeans and the white silk shirt in the other boxes she is speechless. She once more gives Flannery and Derek a kiss for their sweetness. Little tears spring into her eyes, tears of happiness that her granddaughter is safely home, that Derek and Flannery appear to be on the same page, and because she loves them and their generous gifts.

"Well now, won't I look all dolled up? Where did you buy the jacket because I would like to give one to Virginia?"

"No need for that." Derek tells her as he hands her two gift cars for the store where they shopped. "These are for Nell and Virginia so you may give one to Virginia tonight and she can buy what she wants."

"Goodness Christmas has arrived early. Thanks for the card but I will be sure Virginia knows that the card is from you and Flannery."

"Would the two of you mind if we go inside. I need to pee and take some Tylenol."

"Do your hips and back still hurt? If they do I'm taking you to urgent care after lunch."

"Flannery have you fallen? I see that your nose and chin have been scrapped."

"I didn't actually fall. Wednesday when I saw the rain coming I rode my bike into the parking lot of the motel where I found a room. There was a speed hump that I failed to see and the bike stopped but I went head-over-heels over the handlebars. There is a little pain but I think a bath will loosen my muscles. Derek I would rather try the bath first, after lunch of course."

"If you are still in pain tomorrow you will be going to the doctor even if I have to tie you up to get you there. Is that clear my Mrs. MacDougall?" Though his words are pointed, they aren't fierce and because he has called her his Mrs. MacDougall she knows that he is serious that she will go to the doctor but also that he cares a great deal about her wellbeing. She notes that he has been curtailing his bossiness and need to control her since her bike escape, and though she knows he is happy to have here safely home she wonders what is going on. She will make a point to ask him later when her Granny is out with Virginia.

Once inside Derek lets the ladies check out all that has been purchased for family and friends and he happily makes lunch. Flannery loves cheese, any kind of cheese, at any time of the day, so he makes grilled cheese sandwiches, plus heats up the homemade tomato soup that Anne has so generously cooked just for their return. He sets the kitchen table with an autumn patterned, cotton table cover. With napkins to match, and a pot of burgundy asters to adorn the center, the table is set for a welcomed lunch. When everything is on the table he calls two of his all-time favorite ladies to join him for a hearty lunch.

"Wow, this looks so pretty. The food looks wonderful and my mouth is watering so we best sit and enjoy. Thank you for this lovely lunch."

"Our little welcome home for you, Granny and I did the food shopping yesterday morning and we got carried away buying all the things that you love to eat. We knew that eventually you would return home."

Anne said the blessing and then she and Derek raise their mugs of tea to Flannery and toast with, "Welcome Home Flannery."

Flannery raises her mug to touch theirs and said, "Thank you, it is always wonderful to come home."

While they eat they talk about what Anne has been doing, about Jack and Lucy and that they are looking forward to their return home from Bing and Stella's on Sunday after lunch and church. Flannery doesn't say much, but is enjoying the conversation and the food equally. Derek and Anne watch her pleasure at eating but say nothing. Everyone who knows Flannery, know that she loves to eat. That she doesn't seem to gain an ounce is no puzzle. Flannery is not one who sits still for long. There are times, at night while they sleep, that she awakens Derek when she moves her limbs in her sleep. He has yet to awaken her but knows from what she tells him that she dreams of running and dancing quite often. With this nervous energy he and Anne know that Flannery will never be overweight.

She is so in-tuned to the meal and the conversation that she is unaware that she has tomato soup on her upper lip and on her right cheek. Derek looks at Flannery, then smiles at Anne. Anne smiles back because she has finally, after many years told Derek about why Flannery has an obsession with food and why she runs from any confrontation. Anne knew that Derek had trouble with giving Flannery too much freedom and that his control and anger at her asking about his marriage to Chloe had to be addressed. On Wednesday evening, the evening that Flannery disappeared on her bike

Anne, Stella and Bing intervened at Anne's and talked with Derek. Jack and Lucy were having dinner with Gus and Rena at their house so it was the opportune time for the intervention.

Derek said little while the three talked with him but once they were through he knew that he had to get counseling for his issues.

Anne was first to talk. She began with Flannery's time in Rena's care, her biological mother. "Derek I believe that you will be more understanding of Flannery if I tell you about Flannery's years with Rena. I believe Rena had Flannery only to insure that James wouldn't leave her. I also think that is why she had Chloe after marrying Gus, of course that is another issue that should have been addressed long ago also. When James was at work or traveled for his job Rena was very neglectful of Flannery. Flannery often had diaper rash because Rena didn't want to take the time to change Flannery's soiled nappies, diapers. James found out only when he decided to check on Flannery because she also had head colds quite often. James was the one who took Flannery to the doctor numerous times for the rash and colds. The doctor told James that he believed Flannery was being neglected by Rena. He felt that the colds were caused because Flannery was left to her own devices even as a baby. He told James that when a child is denied human contact for long periods that the child will become ill, because of the neglect and the stress put on the child both physically and mentally.

James would confront Rena and things would improve for several months. James wanted to hire a nanny but Rena wouldn't have it. This went on for several more months so James would bring Flannery here to stay while out of town. When he was home he took care of Flannery. So that James wouldn't quiz her about the day to day care for Flannery, Rena would do only the minimum required in raising a child."

"So, Chloe comes by her neglectful ways from Rena." Derek said with ire

"I know that Rena has finally seen the light. Gus was fed up with her and her neglect of Chloe when she was a baby. He finally put his foot down when Rena left Chloe in her car, asleep in the car seat, so that she could have lunch with her friends. He found out when one of Rena's friends called him about Chloe being locked in the car. Of course Rena tried to deny any wrong doing. When several workers from the restaurant were questioned they too had seen Chloe sleeping in the car. They did tell him that the day was cool and the car parked in the shade. With this information Gus confronted Rena. He told her she had a choice to make. If she stayed with him and Chloe either he hired a nanny or Rena had better accept her position of Chloe's mother. If she didn't he was divorcing her and she would no longer live in their house nor spend freely. Mild mannered Gus had finally reached his patient limits and Rena knew it. After that Rena took much better care of Chloe. Gus said he prayed it was because she loved Chloe, but also knew that Rena was a woman who married into wealth so that she would never have to work again."

The four sit quietly in Anne's comfortable living room and think of all that they have heard. They know that Rena has changed a good deal since Chloe dropped out of school and hung around home all day. Now Rena is a decent mother and an even better grandmother to Jack and Lucy.

"Granny Anne, I know that Flannery was here more then with Rena but when did she come here to live full time?" Derek asks with true interest.

Sorting her thoughts like she sorts her many dried flower seeds Anne tells the three sitting around the wooden coffee table in the center of the rooms muted colors area rug. "James brought Flannery here one night when she was three. I remember it well. He knew that he had to save the daughter that he adored from Rena and he and Flannery brought there things and came to stay, Flannery for good, James most nights although he would go home occasionally to talk with Rena about their failed marriage.

"What happened that night that he would bring Flannery here instead of confronting Rena?" Asked Derek who has not until this time heard about Rena's neglect. He now knows why Chloe was such a rotten wife and mother. With Rena as her role model she was programmed to believe it was acceptable to neglect ones children.

"James went home early that day. He was taking time off because he needed to rest from working too much overtime and because he was looking forward to spending time with Flannery. When he got there Rena was on her way to the Mall to shop with friends. When he asked where Flannery was she shook her head like she didn't know or didn't particularly care about her three year old daughters welfare. James refused to let her leave the house until Flannery was found." Though that day is still etched clearly in Anne's mind she still feels a bit of dislike for her ex daughter-in-law. That Chloe turned out as she has is no surprise to them or Gus.

"James found Flannery hiding in her closet. She'd been crying and her nose was running and she wore only a t-shirt. James helped her from the closet just as Rena sticks her head inside the room. She looks at father and daughter and said hatefully. "I see you have found your little princess. If you are wondering why she is wearing only a t-shirt it is because she was too lazy to come into the house and use the bathroom. When she came inside from playing she tried to sneak by me and go to this room. When she walked by I saw that the back of her shorts were wet and she smelled horribly. I knew that the lazy dirty girl had peed and soiled her panties so I made her remove the filthy garments in the laundry room. She was going to put on dry panties but I stopped that. I have informed the princess that I will not put up with that kind of behavior and that she will be going around without bottoms until she decides to use the facilities like a human instead of going in her panties like and animal."

"Stunned by Rena's treatment of her own three-year-old daughter James is speechless until Rena turns her back on him and Flannery and saying as she heads back down stairs, "I don't want Flannery here. Take her to your Mother. You're always telling me what a wonderful mother and grandmother she is. Let her train the little filthy animal. I want nothing to do with her."

James sits Flannery on her unmade bed and goes into the hallway. He tells Flannery he will be right back and then he closes the door takes Rena by the arm and as they go down the stairs he tells her, "You will never touch Flannery again. I should have you arrested for child abuse. I am taking my daughter, yes mine, because she is no longer yours and she will be raised as I was. You have six months to clear out of here and this house will be sold."

"He doesn't give Rena time to protest. He leads her by the arm down the stairs and out to the garage to her car. Then he tells her, you will never see Flannery again. I will be checking to see your progress on packing and finding a new place to live. You will get half the profits of this house and a lump sum a onetime check but that is all. If you protest you will receive nothing."

Derek knows what James felt to find the mother of his child, or children, neglected by the one person who should have taken quality care of them. How wise it was for James to bring Flannery to Anne to rise. He knows it is because of Anne's loving that Flannery is the kind and caring woman that she is, but he also believes that Flannery is programmed to be kind, caring and compassionate towards others. He knows that she, if raised by Rena after James died, would still have been kind, and sweet, and good.

"James also found out from Flannery that Rena would feed her when she had the time or was in the mood to do so. That is why Flannery started hiding food in numerous places around her parent's house and also here."

Hearing this makes Derek want to go to Rena and thrash her. Despite the fact that Rena has changed a great deal he would still like to thrash her. "How could a person deny their child food? That is extremely difficult for me to grasp. I cannot imagine denying my kids food."

Bing sees the spark of anger in his son's dark eyes and said, "Son I also can't grasp the reasoning behind that. We know nothing about Rena's upbringing except that she was raised by a legalistic grandfather and grandmother. James found out from her family acquaintances that Rena's mother had her at the age of fourteen. She left Rena when she was only two to be raised by them. I guess they were extremely strict with her. She was censored for the way she dressed, the way she talked and everything that she did. Her mother came back when Rena was in high school and by then it was too late to form a relationship. When Rena turned eighteen she left her grandparent's home and never looked back. I truly feel that the entire family should have had counseling. The reason Rena has changed is because Gus insisted she go to a counselor. It was a counselor or a divorce. Rena apparently loves Gus so she has taken giant steps to change. It is extremely sad that she was raised as she was, and also that James wasn't able to get her to counseling."

"Yes, it is sad for all those involved. James tried to convince her to get help but Rena had apparently had enough censoring in her life. James loved her in the beginning but I know her treatment of Flannery turned that love to disgust." Anne said with a shake of her head.

"When you asked Flannery why she hid food all over this house, here he waves his hand around the room, what was her reason. I know that you never let her go hungry." Derek said with great interest. He wants to understand his wife and he feels that this info will help.

"James and I found out because ants kept coming into the house. We would find them in every room. We would track where they were going and it was to Flannery's hiding places. In her room she hid food under her bed, in her dresser and the drawer of her night stand. She even stashed food in the bathroom linen closets. She would hide it behind the towels and sheets. Food was stashed under the sofa and chair cushions in here. Somehow she managed to open the bottom of the grandfather clock and store food like a squirrel for the winter."

Now that Derek knows her secret he also remembers seeing her hiding half a hot dog and bun inside her little jewelry box. He asked her what she was doing, which seemed to surprise her because she wasn't aware he had come up the stairs to her room to see if she wanted to play outside. "I'm just putting the food here so that when I get hungry during the night I can eat it." He reasoning made sense at the time, they were six that summer, so he had forgotten the incidence.

"James and I took her for counseling and her obsession stopped for a while. Then her father died and it started again. This time it took several years to convince her that she would always be fed when she was hungry. I asked her why she needed to hide her food when she knew that I would never let her go hungry and she said that if God could take her daddy then he could take me and the food was saved for when she was all alone. Although it has been a number of years since that happened, it still breaks my heart to think that my granddaughter was afraid that no one would be around to feed her."

When Derek, Bing and Stella blinks tears from their eyes Anne knows that they, like she, are truly saddened by her story.

"To my knowledge Flannery hasn't hidden food for a number of years but she checks the pantry and cabinets every day to make sure we won't run out of food."

"I wondered about that. I would find she in the pantry with a note pad and she would have everything listed in alphabetical order and would cross off the number used and then in on second notepad would write what needed replaced. I teased her the other day and asked if she is using the Mormon method of keeping supplies. She said that the Mormons are extremely smart to do so. I was kidding but I knew from her serious face and words that she was not."

Derek and Anne remember that conversation and he smiles at Anne again. Flannery wonders why they keep looking at her and said, "I notice that the two of you keep looking at me and smiling. Do I eat too much, and too often? If I do please let me know and I will pay more for my share of the food."

She pushes her half-finished bowl of tomato soup to the center of the table and then the half that is left of her grilled cheese sandwich. Derek and Anne see her move from one side to the other, like she is in pain and they know that she isn't upset about food and what she eats or how much but that her back and hips are paining her.

"Would you mind if I went upstairs and lay down for a little while? My back and hips hurt."

"What do you think would work best for relief, heat or cold?" Here she looks from Derek to Anne for the best method.

"You could try both, a little cold pack to begin with and then the heating pad."

"Flannery, are you in a lot of pain? When you don't finish a meal I know you aren't feeling well. I can take you to the emergency room if you like."

"I think rest and the cold and heat will do wonders. I'll also take a pain med and I should be fine."

When she places both hands on the table to get up from the chair Derek is up and beside her instantly. He picks her up in his strong arms and turns to Anne assures her that he will return to help clean up the lunch dishes as soon as he carries Flannery upstairs to their bed.

"I'll find the cold pack, the heating pad and a bottle of pain meds and will bring them to your room. As for cleaning the dishes up I will also do that. Take care of our girl. That is most important."

Derek tells Flannery if she isn't better by evening she'd going to the emergency room

Flannery asks Derek why he isn't balling her out about running away and not wanting to face confrontation as she lays on their bed later that night. He tells her what Anne, Bing and Stella have told him and also that he will be going for counseling every Wednesday for his anger, controlling and bossiness. She listens to all that he tells her about her time with Rena she takes it all in and then tells him something that only she, James and Rena know.

"The day that my Dad took me to live with Granny Anne will always be a memorable time for me. That day, before Dad came home I was playing outside because Rena said that she didn't need me hanging around bothering her. My friend from next door Julie and her family were away on vacation and I didn't have anyone to play with so I sat on the back porch steps and made up stories in my head. My creative talent began then. I was hungry and knew that I had some cheerios hidden in my night stand. I had to go through the kitchen but Rena was there so I waited until she had left. I also needed to go to the bathroom and didn't get there soon enough. Rena saw me sneaking down the hallway from the kitchen. She saw that I'd wet my shorts and I knew I smelled because I had also pooped in my pants. She took me by the arm and drug me to the back yard where she made me take my bottoms off, and then she took the hose and hosed me off. I was crying because the water was cold and I was afraid that the neighbors would see me without bottoms. She didn't care and once she was through threw my shorts and panties in the trash. She took me into my room where I was going to get panties and clean shorts. She refused to let me dress and took my clothes from my room and put them in trash bags and then into the garage. Before she left the room I told her I was hungry. I hadn't eaten since the small lunch she gave me the day before. She said food is a reward for good behavior, and that I was an animal who soiled my clothes, so I would not get to eat. After she left my room I looked for the Cheerios in my night stand but then remembered I'd eaten them the night before. I didn't want her to find me so I took my comforter and pillow and my stuffed dog and cat and hide in my closet. That is where my dad found me."

Derek cannot believe that anyone would treat a child so harshly and though Rena has changed he would love to tell her off. What he sees in Flannery's eyes surprises him, she appears to be at ease with the telling of such a sad tale and he knows that she has indeed forgiven Rena as the Lord would choose. Now he knows why she hates confrontation of any kind. He is lying beside her on the bed and pulls her into his arms. He kisses her softly and said, "I know that you have forgiven Rena, but I also think that you should be commended for not hating her, or having anything to do with her."

She knows that her father knew of that incident and many others, because she told him once they were living at Anne's. She and James were sitting on the backyard swing listening to the songs of the resident Mocking bird. Her Dad told her about birds and how they fed their young and also how they taught them to fly. He also told her that most animals were excellent parents and role models, although there were a few who had parents who didn't take good care of them and that those animals sometimes weren't good parents either. Then he told her what he knew of Rena's upbringing and that he prayed that she would forgive Rena for her neglect. Flannery listened to him and knew that he was sincere in wanting her to forgive her Mom. It had taken years but she has forgiven Rena and in her heart she knows that her Dad would be proud of her decision.

Chapter Fifty-eight

First Week September- the Abduction

Flannery goes to the mall to buy another cell phone thinking she will always have one that is charged and ready for use. She is there only half an hour, buys the phone she wants then heads back to her car. As she walks to where Anne's car is parked she is trying the apps on the phone.

Because the day is sunny but cool Flannery decides she will take her sketch pad and stop by the parcel of land that Derek and Sean want to buy. If they get it the five acres will be split and they will build themselves a house. Flannery has a few ideas but wants to see the sight to be certain her choice will suit the area. When she looks at the time on the car dash and sees that it is only four p.m. and figures that since the property is only half a mile from her Granny Anne's that she can do her sketches and be home before dinner.

The property is off the paved road and she drives slowly so she won't damage Anne's car plus she loves the sounds and colors and the scents of the fast approaching autumn. Autumn is one of her favorite seasons, a time to reflect on the year that has passed and a time to look forward to the winter months not far behind. Autumn in Scotland is similar but not quite as long. Princess Street Park in Edinburgh is one of her favorite places to spend an autumn day. With the car windows rolled down she breaths in the scent of falling leaves and autumn wildflowers. Although the parcel isn't near the river there is a little brook that flows freely near a grove of oaks, maples, and sumac and blackberry bushes. A few berries remain and Flannery parks nearby to pick a few to try. She parks the car at the end of the dirt road, pick up her sketching pad and pencils from the front passenger side seat and walks towards the blackberries. She tries several which are sweet and juicy and warmed by the sun. She looks around for the spot where a house would look best and begins to sketch. She and Derek have similar taste and she considers this while sketching.

The beautiful autumn colors distract her for a while and she enjoys the gold's, mauves, burgundy' and browns of the season. Because the leaves are turning early she knows that winter will more than likely be long and cold. Because she writes from home and doesn't have to worry about driving on the wintery roads she doesn't mind winter. With Derek home until the following year he won't have to drive the wintry roads either. She wasn't sure if she would want to have a man around all hours of the day, only because she has never had a man around all day, every day, but to her sweet surprise she and he get along well most of the time. He is also helpful and doesn't mind cooking, shopping for the groceries or doing any of the domestic chores that a house and family require. The fact that when he was married to Chloe, who wouldn't lift a hand to do anything, and that he did all the food shopping and cooking and laundry he is a great helpmate and she won't mind him being there every hour of the day.

When she begins her new book she will make sure he knows that he can come to her even when she is writing. Using a computer makes it easy for her to stop and start her writing. He has told her he will be working from home also, that won't be for at least another year so she is sure he will be hanging about while she writes. The thought warms her heart. Her years without him were long and extremely lonely. He may try to control her and he's definitely opinionated but she has resigned herself to being a submissive wife. She loves him enough to know that his controlling and his opinions she can live with, not having him in her life she can't.

Chapter Fifty-nine

Her head thumps, which awakens her, this and a huge gray stripped tabby that is lying on her chest and kneading her shirt. She opens her eyes slowly and looks around. She is in what appears to be a living room. As her eyes travel around the room they land on a young man with dark brunette hair. He appears to be sleeping, so she keeps her eyes peeled to him. She remembers that she at the property making sketches then someone coming up behind her, put a funny smelling cloth over her nose and mouth, that is all she remembers.. How long she watches him she isn't sure. The sky is golden, this she sees through the tall windows across from where she lies. There appears to be numerous trees but no other houses or buildings so her guess is that she is in the country. When she turns her head to look at the young man, he is watching her. His eyes are a dark midnight blue and he studies her as she studies him. He is extremely handsome in a Hollywood super star way.

"Hi, I'm Michael. You look familiar and now I remember who you are. You are the author of the children's fantasy books. I have everyone. My twin Patrick bought them for me. I can read most of the words, what I don't know Patrick tells me. He, Patrick was given most of the brains when we were born, but that's ok. Patrick helps me whenever I need help."

She knows from his voice and the way he tells her about Patrick that he probably needs special education classes. He seems extremely sweet and she has no fear of him so she tells him, "I'm Flannery Larkin MacDougall and I do write fantasies for young people. Where are we and why am I here?"

"You are at my Granny's farm, and me and Patrick brought you here until someone gives the lady who hired us some money."

Just then another man comes into the room from somewhere in the house, he is identical to Michal, tall, slim, handsome with the dark brunette hair and the midnight blue eyes, and he stands next to Michael, and shaking his head, looks at Michael and said, "Michael I told you not to give out any information on us, so why are you talking with the lady like she is a friend?"

"She's the author the one whose books you buy for me. She's very beautiful and nice so I don't see why we can't talk."

"Her name is Flannery, isn't that a nice name?"

Patrick goes to sit in a rocker only feet from Flannery and he studies her as she did his brother. "So, your Flannery O'Connor Larkin, I thought you looked familiar. I guess you want to know who we are and why we abducted you, and how did we know where to find you"

"Yes to all of that, plus who hired you?"

"As to who hired us, we don't know because we were hired by a third party."

While he tells her that she is indeed on a farm, his and Michael's Granny's farm and that they followed her to the vacant property because they had put tracking devices on Anne's car and Derek's van one evening when they were left outside. She notes that Michael is right about Patrick, he is intelligent, and she can see that he like Michael will not harm her.

"What time is it, and do my husband and Granny know what you have done?"

Patrick who is not only intelligent but also kind by nature decides that he will give her whatever information she wants. He and Michael hold no grudge against her, so he will not harm her in any way."

"It's six p.m. and yes your husband and Granny know that we have you. I'm not the one who called them but know from the man who did that they know."

"Do the police know that I was abducted? Also is there ransom involved?"

"Yes to both questions. You probably wonder how I know. Before I came into the living room to see how you are doing I got a phone call telling me all of this, the man who hired us once lived around here. He knew that Michael and I were having financial problems and need money not only to keep the farm but also for the care of our Granny who has Alzheimer's and is in a care facility. Without the money we will get from abducting you we lose the farm and will not be able to help our Granny."

Flannery can hear concern for their Granny but she also hears desperation and frustration.

She wants to know all she can about them, not because they are holding her against her will but because she can hear love in Patrick's voice for the farm and especially for their Granny. She understands love and what a person might do if they have no other choice offered to them.

"I was raised by my Granny also. When my Dad died Granny kept me with her and I know how you must feel that your Granny needs care. I would want the best care for my Granny also. "

"May I ask why the farm will be taken?"

Patrick hears genuine caring in her words so tells her, "We, I took out a home improvement loan on the house and land which was a huge mistake. The money was for our Granny's care. I keep the payments up until I lost my job and then I had no choice but to use my unemployment so that Michael and I would have food. The little that was left went for the utilities. All that is left from the home improvement loan is going to pay for Granny's care. The people at the bank know our situation but they don't care and the farm will be repossessed by January."

Michael remains quiet for quite a while but wants Flannery to know what a wonderful brother Patrick is so he tells her, "Me and Patrick were also kids when our Mom and Dad died in a car accident. Granny Emma is our Mom's mother and she took us in and raised us. After she started forgetting things Patrick talked with his girl Cassie, she's a nurse, and he decided that Granny would do best in a care home. He also has me to take care of. I used to wash dishes at a restaurant in Lake Geneva but was laid off when people stopped eating out as much."

"I'm sorry to hear that. Patrick what kind of work do you do?"

He hears true empathy in her question so tells her, "I worked as a mechanic and went to college part time. After I was laid off I dropped out of school. Right now Michael and I work around the farm doing the repairs that are needed. This farm has been in our family for four generations and I will do whatever it takes to keep it in our family."

"We are O'Keefe's and Granny a Taylor. Our mom was Rita Taylor then Rita O'Keefe after she married our Dad Seamus Michael Patrick O'Keefe. That is why I am Michael Seamus Taylor O'Keefe and Pat is Patrick Seamus Taylor O'Keefe."

Patrick shakes his head at all the info Michael is giving on them. He looks sternly at his brother and said, "Michael I told you not to tell Flannery anything about us. While you're at it why not give her our birth date, our height, weight and our social security numbers." Though his voice is stern Flannery can tell that Patrick loves his brother and has probably been Michael's ally for most of their life.

Michael tells Flannery, "Our birthday is May twenty-eighth. Pat was born first. It took me longer because I wanted to come out feet first. Because it took so long some of my oxygen was messed up so that is why Patrick is the smart one and I am not."

Patrick stands, goes to look out the living room window and sees that the sun has nearly finished its day and that because it has been hours since he, Michael and Flannery have eaten he should go and make some dinner.

"Michael I'm going to make some dinner. You may talk with Flannery but don't give her any more info on us."

"Ok Pat I'll try to remember that. What are we having for dinner?"

"We have some left over ham and eggs and some bread so that will be dinner."

Patrick looks at Flannery who now sits with the huge cat on her lap. He can hear the cats loud purring from where he stands. Apparently Flannery loves animals as much as Michael, so he tells Michael, "Mike why not tell Flannery about Harry and the chickens and the two cows."

"Sure I'll do that."

As he walks from the room to prepare dinner he hears Michael telling Flannery about their animals.

In the kitchen he pulls a cast iron skillet from the huge walk-in pantry. Next he goes to the refrigerator and pulls a bowl with eggs, a pitcher of milk, butter and the remaining ham out. He'd bought the ham on Monday, this is now Friday, and they have had ham every day. The ham was the best buy for the little money that they have. With only two hundred dollars left in the bank he hopes that the ransom money will be given to them soon.

Patrick and Michael have never been arrested nor have they ever taken something that is not theirs. Abducting Flannery is not something he would ever have thought of doing. Desperate times can change a man's thinking. He is well aware of the fact that if he and Michael are caught, that they will go to prison, but he hopes they won't be caught. He also knows that if they come up with the thousands of dollars that they owe the bank they cannot pay it all at once. Because he's tired of thinking and hungry he leaves thoughts of the ransom and the repercussions for later.

"I see you have a wedding band. When did you get married?"

"Derek and I were married in Early August."

"Do you have children?"

"Yes, Derek, my husband and I have a daughter and a son. They are from his first marriage."

"But you love them, the children. I can hear the love in your voice."

"Yes I love them and want to be at home with them."

They talk about her family until Patrick calls them into the kitchen for dinner. While they eat they say little. When dinner is over Flannery and Michael wash the dishes. When she goes to put the pitcher of milk in the frig she sees that there food supply is scarce so ask Michael about it.

"The eggs are from our chickens. The milk from our two cows and Pat bought the bread, ham and butter. We have a few things left in the garden and there is some in the pantry. I don't know what we'll do when Pat's unemployment runs out in December."

"Who milks the cows and collects the eggs?" she asks with true curiosity

"We take turns. I milked the cows while you were sleeping. Pat stayed with you. I guess tomorrow morning I will milk them and collect the eggs and feed the chickens."

"Maybe he will let you help in the morning."

"Yes maybe he will. I have lived on a farm. There are only a few animals there. It is in Scotland. It's my Granny Anne's farm but she is here in the states most of the time."

"Who takes care of the farm animals if no one is there?"

"My Granny has a nice man that lives nearby and he takes care of everything."

Patrick hears Michael talking with Flannery like she is an old and trusted friend. Although he'd told Michael not to give her any information on them he knew that his sweet and innocent brother would. Michael makes friends wherever he goes. Pat knows that if they are arrested for the abduction that Michael will also go to prison. He dreads the thought, but Michael has made it clear that whatever needs to be done to help their Granny and keep the farm he will also accept a prison sentence if they are arrested.

Their Granny brought them up to be law abiding and has taught them to go to God for all their decisions big or small. Everything would have been ok if he hadn't been laid off. When he worked he paid all the bills plus set a little aside each week. He even managed to take a trip with Michael and his girlfriend Cassie. They drove to Colorado and hiked in the Rockies around Aspen. He and Cassie shared a room, which Michael thought nothing about. Cassie is sweet, easy going and Pat wants to marry her. Now he knows that that dream is on the back burner for some time to come. If they are arrested he figures that there is no way that Cassie will marry him. So that he won't get any more depressed than he already is he pushes those hopes and dreams aside and sits quietly listening to his brother and their abductee talking in the kitchen..

Chapter Sixty

Derek arrives back at Anne's around three p.m. He's tried to get Flannery on her cell phone to no avail. He's left several messages since he left Anne's house earlier that morning to check out the building that Sean and his crew are now working on. They finished remodeling the two apartments above Nell's salon in record time and now are working on another building in the same area. Sean and his crew are making quite an impression with the excellent work that they do and Sean wanted Derek to see the building before they start the rehab.

Derek knows that Flannery is upset with his decision to not allow her to row on the Fox by herself. He is fully aware that she has done so for years but he doesn't want to take the chance of her having an accident or Heaven forbid, she be abducted. He cares a great deal for her, even feels love at times, although the love part he won't acknowledge yet.

Anne, Jack and Lucy are in the living room reading. Actually Jack is reading to Lucy while she colors in a coloring book with drawings of baby animals. Anne is reading a monthly magazine on Scotland, which she sets aside when Derek enters the room.

Derek goes to his children and kisses them on the cheek. They kiss him in return and give him a hug. Anne smiles when he also greets her with a kiss and asks, "Granny Anne have you heard from Flannery? I've tried calling her on her cell phone and have left several messages."

"She left it here to charge. She was going to lunch with Nell and then to the mall to buy a second cellphone so she will always have one available and charged."

At five Derek calls Nell and she tells him that Flannery was going to have a look at the land he and Sean are trying to buy after she bought her phone. At five-thirty he calls Sean to drive to the parcel of land with him.

Derek and Sean pass only one vehicle on their drive to find Flannery, a green Subaru station wagon. When they get to the dirt road that leads to the property they spot Anne's Honda sitting at the end of the road with the front driver's side door opened.

Derek reaches the car first and seeing Flannery's purse sitting on the front passenger seat and her sketch book and pencils sitting on top of the car he begins to worry. He and Sean search the area calling her name but no one answers. Derek calls 911 and reports his missing wife.

To their credit Derek and Sean don't touch anything in or on the car so the police are able to collect fingerprints. One set of prints didn't belong to anyone that Derek, Anne or Flannery knows.

Chapter Sixty-one

The Taylor-O'Keefe Farm

Flannery is once more in the living room of the antiquated farm house. The furnishings are clean and well taken care of but old. The floral sofa has a faded cover that at one time was dark rose, cream, blue and green. The colors are now faded to pale pastels. She isn't sure what time it is because the room is in near darkness and she cannot read the hands on the Grandfather clock across the room from her. The clock on the kitchen stove was at seven p.m. when they ate dinner. A full moon lights the outside acreage and she knows that it has to be at least two or three hours since their meal. She has seen the entire house. Michael insisted that he take her on a tour. Though small, with three upstairs bedrooms, a bath, which is off the kitchen, and living room, are clean, though could use a little sprucing up.

Michael is in his upstairs bedroom sleeping. Patrick is in the living room with her and is sitting in the rocker nearby. His eyes are closed but she knows he isn't sleeping. They are taking shifts to keep an eye on her. Where they think she will go is beyond her. She doesn't know what state the farm is in. It's possibly in Illinois but also could be in southern Wisconsin. She needs to pee so boldly asks, "May I go to the bathroom, if I don't I will wet my jeans, and I don't have anything else to wear."

Pat opens his eyes, stands up and waits for her to toss her blanket back and he walks her through the living room, across the kitchen and stands outside the bathroom door while she does her business. She would love to wash her face and brush her teeth so drumming up courage asks," Do you have an extra tooth brush, also may I have towel and wash cloth."

"Are you decent," she hears from Patrick who is right outside the door.

"Yes."

The door opens and in he walks. He goes to a wooden cabinet with doors and several drawers and he finds a new unwrapped tooth brush which he hands to her. "The toothpaste is in the medicine cabinet. If you want to bathe there are towels and washcloths in the linen closet." He goes into the hallway and comes back with a dark green towel and a matching washcloth.

"Thank you. I will bathe only if you aren't in the bath with me." He blushes big time, then leaves the room closing the door behind him.

She knows that the economy is not the best and empathizes with those affected. Although she and Derek and their families don't lack she knows many do. Though she doesn't know Patrick and Michael she can see that they are not a criminal element. Not once have they been unkind to her. True they haven't left her alone even once until now. She knows that Patrick is outside the door because she heard him when he brought a wooden chair from the kitchen to sit on while she bathes. It appears that Pat is the decision maker and she is sure he would not be holding her hostage if he weren't desperate. She can understand that he and Michael don't want to lose the family farm, and can understand that they want to take excellent care of their Granny. She would want the same for her Granny Anne. What can she do to help?

They are breaking the law in a big way and yet she wonders what she can do to help them. While she takes her bath and brushes her teeth she considers different things to do. When she is dressed in her clothing from the morning, a morning that started off with her argument with Derek as whether she should row on the Fox alone, she now knows how foolish that argument was. He said he wanted to keep her safe. She thought she was safe going to the property and making sketches and look at where she is now, somewhere in the U.S. being held for ransom.

When she opens the bathroom door after hanging her towels on one of two towels racks in the huge bathroom Pat is no longer outside the door. He is in the kitchen heating water in a stainless steel tea kettle. He turns from the white porcelain stove when she comes into the room, nods his head and goes to a built in wooden kitchen hutch with glass doors and pulls out two ceramic mugs with Colorado written in bold letters on their front. Could they be in Colorado is her first thought, no there wasn't enough time to go there.

"Would you like a cup of tea? I usually prefer coffee but tea is what we have."

"Yes, that would be nice."

He pulls a chair out from the big wooden table and pats it, then said, "You may sit here."

He said no more until they are sitting at the table, with Patrick on one side and Flannery on the other.

When she sees that it is eleven p.m. on the stove's clock she asks, "Have you heard from anyone what you are to do with me?"

He senses that she isn't afraid of him and he doesn't want her to be, then he tells her "No, we haven't heard from anyone. The last time I talked with the man who hired us he knew that we have you and he said to sit tight until further notice."

"You said you know this man that he is from here. Where are we, I mean what state are we in?"

"We're in Illinois. That's all that I will tell you. As for the man who set this up he once lived on a farm down the road. His father is also trying to keep their farm."

"Do you know anything about who hired him and you?"

"All I know is that the person who hired us knows the man that we call, the one who used to live around here."

"What if you let me go, and tell the man that I got away while you were sleeping?"

"That's not going to happen. Michael and I may appear to be country bumpkins but we aren't."

"What if I helped you and Michael save the farm and pay for your Granny's care."

He studies her and can see that she is desperate to return home but he can also sense that she is sincere in wanting to help so he tells her, "I'm sure you have the money but we both know that if Michael and I are caught we will go to prison."

"Yes unless we make a deal with the police. I will tell them that you didn't harm me, nor have a weapon."

"A deal huh, I guess you do believe in fantasy, maybe a little too much if you think the police will cut a deal."

"I watch Law and Order and love to read mysteries and maybe I do tend to fantasize more than most people but I will bet that if you and Michael set me free and turned yourselves in voluntarily without waiting for the ransom they would give you a break."

He doesn't answer so she continues. "I would put money into the account for your Granny and pay the farm off."_

"Law and Order, you know that they solve crimes faster than in the real world."

"Yes I know, still I know deals are made. For instance if you tell he police all you know I'm sure they would consider that."

Patrick drinks his tea and says no more about arrests or deals. He is a practical man and knew when he decided to go against everything he has been taught that he and Michael will probably get a prison sentence if caught, but he feels that there is no other way to save the farm and take care of his Granny.

Chapter Sixty-two

Derek paces the living room floor. From one end to the other he paces. Bing, Stella, Anne, Sean, Nell, and Virginia are with him, have been since everyone found out about Flannery's abduction. Jack, Lucy and Nell's three, Kristen, Tyler and Mary are sleeping in two of the upstairs bedrooms, so the house is relatively quiet. The television is on but turned to a barely audible level of sound. So far nothing about Flannery's abduction has been broadcast on the Chicago or national networks. It is now after midnight, and Sean is keeping an eye on any reports about Flannery. When he sees a news flash across the local stations screen, WGN, Chicago, he reads it to himself then turns to everyone and said, "It looks like the media has found out about Flannery." With this said he raises the volume with the remote he is holding.

Derek quiets his pacing and goes to sit beside Sean. When he sees a photo of Flannery, one taken for her last book, he takes the remote from Sean and turns the volume up another notch. He and the six adults in the room listen intently at the report, "*This afternoon, around four p.m. a local resident, Flannery O'Connor Larkin MacDougal was abducted from a vacant parcel of land near Geneva. She was there making sketches because she, her husband and brother-in-law are buying the land. There were no witness to the abduction, but tire marks were found on the dirt road leading to the property. Foot prints were found around the victims Honda Accord. Her husband and brother-in-law went there to look for her after a friend told them that she was going to stop there on her way home. Her purse, with money and I.D. were left on the front passenger seat along with Flannery's cell phone and her sketches were lying on top of the car.*"'.

Derek says nothing, gets up from the sofa and leaves the room. When the back door is heard opening, then closing, Bing excuses himself and goes to talk with his son.

Derek is sitting on the back porch steps wishing he had a cigarette and a huge glass of whiskey, because he has neither available, nor has he used the two since his trip to Galena, he sits there trying not to think the worst about Flannery's abduction.

Bing sits beside him and waits for Derek to speak. It is several minutes until he said, "Dad who would want to harm Flannery, she is kind, sweet and selfless." Into his mind pops the name Chloe, then he tells Bing, "I hope it isn't so, but do you think Chloe might have something to do with this?"

Bing's heart goes out to Derek. Finally after his dreadful marriage to Chloe and then the divorce, Derek has the marriage and the wife that he should have had for the past six years. When Bing sees Derek and Flannery together he cannot help but thank the Lord for giving them another chance. When Flannery is with Jack and Lucy everyone knows that she is the mother that they need.

"I don't know son. The last I heard from Gus she is still in Hawaii, not that she couldn't have hired someone from there. I think one of us should call Rena and Gus before they hear it on the news. Of course they probably already have."

They can hear the phone in the kitchen ringing and then hear Granny Anne's voice, she talks for a short time and then with phone in hand walk out on the porch and handing he phone to Bing said, "Its Gus."

Bing takes the phone from her and listens to Gus, "I saw the news and want to know if you have heard any more on Flannery. The newscast didn't say if ransom was asked for, but I'm guessing that it was." said Gus with genuine concern in his voice."

"Someone called Derek on Anne's landline and asked for fifty million dollars. We have until Sunday evening to pay what is asked." Derek is taking it all in and would love to know about Chloe's whereabouts.

"Dad asks Gus where Chloe is. Have he and Rena talked with or have they seen her recently?"

Bing relays the message and hands the phone to Derek. Derek listens intently when Gus tells him, "Derek we saw her shortly after you and Flannery married. Rena and I flew to Maui to let her know, but someone already told her. Apparently one of the stylists at Nell's salon has told Chloe's friend Mia and Mia called Chloe and told her. She told me and Rena that we are traitors to go to your wedding and that she doesn't want to ever see us again."

"Gus, do you think she would have Flannery abducted to get even? I know how unpredictable she is, but would she commit a crime just to get even?"

"I would hope not, but she was extremely enraged when we told her that you and Flannery are married. I asked her why it would bother her, given the fact that she was a horrible wife to you and a horrible mother to Jack and Lucy. She of course put the blame on Rena and my shoulders. She informed us that we were no better at parenting then she was. She also said that you, Jack and Lucy are hers and that as long as she lives she will do whatever it takes to get you back. She's been off the drugs for over two months and my hope is that she stays off. The police haven't contacted us, but if they need anything that will help find Flannery Rena and I will let them know about our daughter."

"Thank Gus. You and Rena are welcome to come to Granny Anne's and Dad and Stella's anytime. You are family also."

Derek ends the conversation and hands the phone back to Anne. He gets up from the step, where he sits and tells Bing and Anne, "I'm going down by the river to sit for a while. You may join me if you like."

"I'll stay close to the phone. Maybe we will hear from Flannery." Anne said with all the faith and trust that she can muster at the moment.

"I'll go with you son. The river can soothe a person." Bing tells the two as he also gets up from the porch step.

Father and son, tall and broad shouldered walk in silence to the river bank where they sit on one of the two park benches at their disposal. The river moves lazily on its route downstream, but they can hear its gentle lapping as it passes them by. The moon is only a quarter visible, but the dusk-to-dawn lights give them enough light to see around them. In the distance they can hear a few birds that are late to settle in for the night. A motorcycle engine can be heard on the road across the river. A dog can be heard barking in someone's backyard a few houses down. The summer has been unusually dry so they have had few mosquitoes.

"Flannery and I came here after our senior prom. We talked about our future and it was here that I asked her to marry me. We were so darned naïve back then. We lived with blinders on. We would get married after we graduated from college. We would wait a few years and then have children. She wanted at least four. I was crazy for her, would have done anything she asked, but she became famous with her writing and stayed most of her time in Scotland. I thought her career was more important than our relationship, so when Chloe said she's slept with me and was pregnant with my child, I knew that I was going to change the course of my life, Chloe's life and most of all Flannery's life. I was angry with her and wanted to get even. Who did I hurt, everyone involved."

Bing can hear the fatigue and sadness in Derek's voice and without a word puts his arm around Derek's shoulders to comfort him. This one kind and needed gesture brings tears to Derek's eyes and he weeps as he did when his mother died.

"I love her Dad, but I have not told her. Even on our wedding night I didn't tell her. I'm such a hard headed fool. She loves me and shows me in so many ways and for that love all I have done is try to control her and bully her. She wanted to go rowing this morning while I was with you and Sean looking at the building he and his crew are working on. I refused to let her go. I did that because I didn't want her to go alone. I know she is more than competent and I know she was disappointed but she said she would find something else to do. If she'd gone rowing instead of looking at the property she would be here with me, with us instead of who knows where being treated like a prisoner."

Bing holds his grown son in his arms and lets him cry, when Derek quiets and wipes his tears with the back of his hand Bing takes one of Derek's hands and tells him, "Son we will do whatever we need to do to get her back. Flannery's return and her safety are far more important than the money her abductors are wanting. The president of our bank is working right now to get all the money that was requested. If the men, or the people who took her, get away with all that cash it doesn't matter, what matters is that Flannery is here with us. Because we know nothing about those involved we must pray that they will not harm her."

Chapter Sixty-three

Maui-The same evening

Chloe sits in her condo looking at a baggie filled with cocaine. She has had it since her parents came to visit and told her that Derek and Flannery are now married. She wants badly to use the cocaine but knows she needs to keep a clear head. What she has done is unforgivable and yet she went through with it anyway. She knows she is her own worst enemy but at the moment she doesn't give credence to that fact. Foolish though she is she held hope in her heart that she could get Derek back. Now she has no hope. Derek is married to Flannery. Flannery will be mother to Jack and Lucy. This thought enrages her and she tosses the baggie full of cocaine through the opened patio doors. She tosses so hard that the baggie hits the rail of her balcony and the cocaine falls across the patio like a snowfall in Chicago.

When she realizes what her anger has caused her to do she pulls at her blonde short cropped hair as hard as she can and then screams "I hate you Flannery, I hate you." She marches into the kitchen to find a broom and dust pan hoping that some of the cocaine can be saved and is usable. When she heads for the patio and is ready to sweep the cocaine up the wind begins to blow with such force that if there were no railing on the balcony she would have been blown off to her death. Even this angers her and this she also blames on Flannery.

"Flannery wherever you are tonight I hope and pray that you will never be found. Derek is mine, will always be mine."

With this rant over she sits on the balcony floor and with arms around her bare tanned legs, and cries her heart out. She cries for what seem like hours when she is brought to the present by the ringing of her door bell. She doesn't want anyone to see her tears so she ignores the ringing. When the person on the other side of the door knocks several times and she hears Diego calling her name, she wipes her tears in the hem of her t-shirt, blows her nose with a Kleenex from a box on the living room coffee table then goes to see what he wants.

With a worried look on his face he studies her. He's never seen her cry so knows that whatever is going on is something very personal but he needs to know why he heard her screaming. With his condo directly beneath hers, and with his patio doors opened, as were hers he heard her screaming, though not the words of hate for Flannery.

She holds the door opened for him to enter then goes and sits on her denim covered sofa. Diego sits beside her and because she said not a word asks, "Why were you screaming. I thought maybe someone had broken into your condo."

She hears true concern in his voice and because she does like him a great deal she tells him everything. He quietly listens without saying anything until she is through.

"I don't know your sister, but I am sure her family is wondering where she is. Do you know where she is? If you go to the police and tell them what you have done they may make a deal with you and perhaps you won't get as long a sentence as you would if you don't go to them."

"I don't think anyone would care if I'm locked up for good. My parents are traitors and against me. Derek hates me as I'm sure Granny Anne and the rest of the family does also. I doubt anyone would care what happens to me."

Diego pulls her into his arms and holds her tightly against his broad chest. He is warm and there and she knows that he likes her so she lets him hold her for a short while. When she pulls back to look at his face she is surprised to see a sadness in his dark eyes. She gets up from the sofa holding his hand and she guides him into her master suite. Neither said a word, they undress and crawl beneath her light summer quilt and make love into the wee hours. The phone in her living room rings several times but they ignore it. Her voice mail is full when she checks it the next morning. The messages are from Gus, but she erases each one listening to only the first one. She needs to think and what she decides to do will change her life forever, but for once her head is clear, and she knows that she will do what is best for all concerned. Diego stays with her and cooks her meals and loves her in a way that she has never known. She cares for him but she is hung up on her love for Derek.

Chapter Sixty-four

Flannery opens her eyes slowly. For a moment she forgets where she is, but then she sees Harry lying on her stomach again and she remembers she is with Patrick and Michael somewhere on an Illinois farm. It is late morning, she sees from the living room clock that she has slept until ten a.m. She and Patrick had talked late into the night and she wonders if he is still asleep also.

She picks Harry up and sits with him on her lap. While she pets him she wonders what her family is doing. They know she was abducted, she knows that they are terribly worried, if only she hadn't dropped her cell phone when she was taken. There is a phone in the kitchen only and she wonders if she should try to reach her family on that. She listens but doesn't hear anyone in the house. Perhaps they are outside with the animals. She sits Harry beside her, foregoes putting her sneakers on and walks to the kitchen in her stocking feet. She looks around the door frame and sees that the room is vacant. With caution she moves into the kitchen and lifts the phone from the wall. She keeps her eyes on the back door and dials her granny Anne's number. The phone rings several times and she hears Derek's voice, "Hello."

"Derek it's me Flannery. I'm ok. I'm somewhere on a farm in Illinois, but not sure exactly where."

"Flannery can you tell me who abducted you?"

"All I know is that the two men, Patrick and Michael were hired by a third party a man that used to live nearby but who now lives in Hawaii, on Maui. This man didn't tell them who wanted me abducted. They, Michael and Patrick are doing this because of financial problems."

She hears someone walking across the floor overhead and whispers, "I think someone is coming, I love you, Jack, Lucy, my Granny and all friends and family."

"I love you too. We will do whatever it takes to keep you safe and bring you home."

"I know that you love me but it is wonderful to finally hear those words."

"I love you," Flannery said kissing the phone, then hanging it up goes from the kitchen to the bathroom. Hopefully whoever was in the room above the kitchen did not hear her talking to Derek.

In the bathroom she pees then washes her face and hands. She would love to have her purse but it was in the car.. She wears jeans, a long sleeved t-shirt of pale blue and a denim jacket with several pockets. Earlier, the night before, while taking her bath she was pleased to find some cash in her jacket pocket. There are two hundred dollar bills and four fifties and she knows that she is going to give the money to Patrick to buy food for them and Harry. There is even enough for cat food and treats so she re-counts the money and goes into the kitchen where Michael is sitting at the kitchen table eating some Cheerios and milk. He smiles at her and gets up to pull the chair next to his out for her to sit down.

He has also placed a bowl, spoon and mug with Wisconsin Dells inscribed across the front. "There's enough cereal for you and milk. Pat is going into town to get some things. If there is anything you would like there is a list on the kitchen counter. I don't know how much money he has but he said to write down what we need."

Flannery pulls the bills from her jacket pocket and hands them to Michael. "Patrick may have this, since you will be feeding me it's only fair that I help out. There are three things I need, lotion for my hands and face, lip balm and soap for my face. Other than that I will eat whatever he buys." She knows it may be odd that she would help her abductors in any way but having heard Patrick and Michael's story she is truly empathetic to them. She has known them less than forty-eight hours and yet she can see that neither is violent or unkind plus they have not harmed her. True she would rather not be their prisoner but she is so she will make the best of the situation.

Michael counts the money and his eyes light up. He leans sideways and to her surprise kisses her cheek, grins and said, "This will help a good deal. Harry is nearly out of food and he loves his Temptation treats. Maybe we can get the good macaroni and cheese, not the generic kind."

"I know how to make excellent mac and cheese my Granny taught me. We'll have Patrick get the ingredients for that instead."

"Ok and maybe we can get some pudding, chocolate and butterscotch. I like to make both then layer it in my Granny's glass sherbet bowls. Oh, he said with happiness, maybe we can also get real whipped cream, the one in the can."

While they eat they discuss what Patrick can buy. When he comes downstairs and walks into the kitchen Flannery and Michael are talking like long lost friends.

"Look Pat money from Flannery's jacket pocket." Michael smiling a huge smile gives the much needed money to his brother who sees the shopping list lying on the table between the two.

He looks at what they have written and all he said is, "I guess the two of you are hungry."

When they grin at each other, then at him and say in unison, "Yeah!" he cannot help but grin back.

"I'll see what I can do. Flannery thanks for the money. I'll be gone for a few hours there are a few errands I need to take care of. Michael, don't fall asleep on the job."

"I won't Pat. Flannery and I will be here when you return. She's going to make homemade mac and cheese and I will make the pudding."

After Patrick leaves Flannery and Michael wash the dishes then Michael who doesn't like to be cooped up inside for long decides he will trust Flannery and they will go to the barn to visit the animals.

The two Guernsey cows have been milked and are grazing in a fenced area near the huge red wood barn. When Michael calls first Lily and then Poppy the cows raise their heads and come to stand beside the log and wire fence. Michael has two apples, a little shriveled and hands one to Flannery. He place the remaining apple on his opened palm and Lily sniffs it then gently opens her mouth and takes the apple in one bite. Flannery does the same with her apple and Poppy also takes the offered treat and eats it.

She and Michael go and visit the hens and the rooster. These too come at each name given them by Michael. "I have always heard that chickens are not intelligent. Is that true or not?"

"I've heard that too but I patiently work with each one until they know their name. For instance watch this, Rocky Ragu come to me, " he said and the huge Rhode Island Red rooster walks to stand in front of Michael.

Michael taps his shoulder and said "Up Rocky," and the rooster flies to roost on Michael's left shoulder.

"That's amazing. May I try?" Flannery asks with excitement.

"Sure, I don't know if he'll come to you but you may try."

Flannery tapes her right shoulder as she stands in front of Michael and said, "Rocky up." When Rocky does as she commands without delay the two humans laugh and dance a happy dance.

"You should become an animal trainer at a circus, or become a veterinarian."

Michael knows she is kind when she tells him he could be a veterinarian, something that he would have loved to be but he knows he isn't intelligent enough to do so. "Pat could be a vet but not me I don't have the smarts."

Flannery studies the handsome and kind man and said, "I believe you are more intelligent than you think. Has anyone done an aptitude test on you?"

"Yes several times. I'm not an imbecile but my I.Q. isn't very high."

"Do you remember what it was?"

"I believe it was in the nineties."

"Did you have any special classes."

"Some but once I turned sixteen I decided it was a waist of everyone's time so I stayed home and helped Granny. Our Grandpa Ned died the year before. After she was placed in the care home I worked at the Animal shelter in the mornings and the restaurant in the afternoon, but I decided to take a leave so I could take care of everything here. Pat had the good job making cars but as you know he was laid off. He was also going to the community college but had to drop out when Granny got the Alzheimer's. He has a girlfriend, her name is Cassandra, but we call her Cassie. Pat met Cassie at school she is one of the nurses who takes care of Granny."

For a moment he is quietly thinking and then he adds, "Pat loves Cassie and she loves him. They want to get married but now I don't know what they will do."

"Do you have a girlfriend?

"Kind of, her name is Bernadette but I call her Bernie. She also works at the animal shelter. She is a vet tech. We do things with Pat and Cassie, go to movies or eat out, but lately Pat and I haven't had the money for dates. The ladies offer to pay but Pat is a true gentleman and instead they come here and we watch television or one of them rents a movie. Popcorn is cheap so we do have that for them."

"They sound like very sweet ladies."

"Yes they are. Bernie lets me kiss her and hold her hand and give her hugs but Pat has taught me that we should wait until marriage to have sex. I agree, it is a good rule. It would not be good to have a baby before we are married."

"That is a wonderful rule to live by."

"How old are your children?" Michael asks as they check for eggs and then head back to the house where they sit on a wooden porch swing that is hung from the beans of the back porch.

"Derek, my husband, has a three year old daughter named Lucy and a five year old son named Jack. He has full custody of them so yes I have two children. They are wonderful, so sweet and they call me Mommy which I love." Apparently he has forgotten that she already told him about Lucy and Jack.

"Where is their biological mother?"

"She lives in Hawaii and didn't want them."

"That's not normal to not want your own children. Have you ever met their mother?

"Yes, I've met her, but haven't seen her in years. Her name is Chloe and she is my half-sister. We have the same mother but different fathers."

"Is your Mom alive?"

"Yes she's alive and though we didn't have a good relationship for a long time she came to my wedding to Derek and has apologized for not being a good mother. I forgave her because I know that my life with my Granny Anne was exactly the life I needed."

"Why did Derek marry her then you?"

"That's a long story and why don't we talk about that later."

"Sure. Would you like some popcorn? Pat won't be back for a while and I think there is a movie on television."

Chapter Sixty-five

Derek is at a loss as to what he can do to help Flannery. He is not a man who likes feeling helpless. He doesn't want to leave the house incase Flannery or her abductors should call but he needs fresh air. Jack and Lucy are at Virginias playing with Nell's three children and though he has told then some of what is going on they don't know everything. He's hoping his wife will be home before he tells them the rest. His Mom and Dad and Granny Anne are sitting in the back yard and he needs some time to think so he lets them and the police know that he will be on the front porch if he is needed.

He does feel relief that Flannery hasn't been physically harmed and that he has told her he loves her. When she said she knew but was happy to hear him say the words it has helped. When she comes home he will never fail to tell her how much he loves her and always has. He will be courting his wife.

It is too bad that the call couldn't be traced. If only she'd talked with him longer. Hopefully she will call again and then the police can trace that call.

Derek sits there for quite a while until Detective Czerwinski opens the front door and hands him Anne's house phone. He raises his eyebrows in a questioning way and the detective said, "It's your ex-wife's father."

Derek thanks the detective and said," Hello Gus."

"I haven't been able to talk with Chloe. The lady who works in the office at the condos said that Chloe is there because they have seen her. She is with a man named Diego, he owns the condo across from the one Rena and I have. I don't know if they are an item but apparently they are together most of the time. I've tried his number but get only his voice mail. I'm hoping that he will get back to me so I can see what my daughter has been up to."

"That's a start. Flannery called not long ago. She said she is fine but to tell everyone she loves them. All she could tell me was the first name of the two men who abducted her and that she is still in Illinois somewhere on a farm. She didn't talk long because she heard someone walking above her."

“That’s good to hear. Did she say why she was abducted and how the men knew where to find her?”

“She said that they were hired by a third party someone they know from nearby, but apparently the person lives in Hawaii. Does Chloe know anyone in Hawaii that is from Illinois?”

“I’ll call the condo office again maybe they know someone in the building that is from Illinois. No wait, the custodian is from Illinois though I don’t know where. Hopefully the lady at the condo office does. I’ll call when we hang up.”

“Thanks Gus.” Derek said as he goes into the house to tell the cops and the family what he knows.

Chapter Sixty-six

Chloe and Diego are in her living room watching a movie, and though they have heard her phone ring, which they ignore, Diego hasn't bothered to check his messages either.

They sit with their feet on her glass topped coffee table and holding hands. He knows everything that she has done and is trying to convince her to turn herself into the police. So far she has not decided her next step. He has listened to her but not once has he made her feel less than who she is. She knows he is right and that she needs to fess up but she isn't ready to go to prison. Because he sincerely cares about her she hasn't thought of taking drugs even once.

Chapter Sixty-seven

Patrick doesn't return to the farm until after five. Michael and Flannery help him carry the groceries to the kitchen. He goes upstairs to change his clothes and without more than a hello in greeting he remains quiet until he remembers that he has some clothing in the car for Flannery. "I'll be right back. I forgot something in my car."

Flannery who is putting the final touches on her homemade mac and cheese and Michael who is whipping the milk and pudding nod their heads in answer.

Flannery has the oven of the old stove heated and opening the oven door sets the casserole inside. "That will be ready in thirty minutes. How's your pudding doing?"

"Ready to layer and chill in the refrigerator. What else do we have? We have fresh tomatoes and cucumbers from the garden. I'll cut them in slices and that should be enough."

"Yes, that will do it. Pat's awfully quiet do you think he's ok?"

"Yeah, he's not a chatter box like me. He is normally quiet, you know tall, handsome and of little words."

"Is Derek talkative or is he quiet?"

"Derek is quiet for the most part, but we also have some lengthy conversations."

"You love him I can see it on your face and hear it in your voice."

"Yes, I love him. Actually I've loved him our entire lives. We were born on the same day, only an hour apart and because our fathers were best friends we have always spent lots of time together."

"How old are you and Derek. You look about twenty."

"We were thirty-one on the Fourth of July."

"You don't look that old, not that thirty-one is old."

"Sometimes I feel that thirty-one is old. Do you ever feel old Michael?"

"Not often but with the bills, our Granny needing care and the bank wanting to take the farm, yes I sometimes do."

Patrick walks into the kitchen carrying a box which he sits on the kitchen table. He holds up a few pieces of women's clothing and said,

"Cassie gave me these for you to wear. I have told her everything and she wants us to turn ourselves in to the police. She said that she will make sure the house, the animals, and the farm are taken care of. If she can, with permission from the bank she will stay here until everything is worked out. She will also make sure our Granny is taken care of and she will visit her and us."

"If we are arrested before the ransom is delivered she thinks we can maybe cut a deal. I have lots of thinking to do, so after I eat I'm going to decide what would be our best action."

Patrick sounds and looks exhausted and Flannery wants to help so she tells him and Michael, "I will have my husband and his father find a way to help save the farm and a way to pay for your Granny's care. Will you let me call them so we can get the ball rolling?" Although she knows their last name she forgets to give the information to Derek when she calls.

Chapter Sixty-eight

When Derek hangs up the phone his feelings are a muddle. He's happy that Flannery is ok, but upset and frustrated that he does not know where she is or how to help find her.

Detective Czerwinski is standing beside the man, David, who was tracing Flannery's call. "Were you able to trace the call?" Detective Czerwinski asks.

David shakes his head no then tells them, "I almost had it then she hung up."

"Is there anything that can be done with the info Flannery gave me. The men's names are Michael and Patrick, they are brothers and she is on a farm somewhere in Illinois. Also the third party who hired them lives in Hawaii. I'm wondering if he knows my ex-wife who lives in Hawaii and has threatened Flannery."

"At least we now have a starting point. I will tell the Captain and he can figure out the best way to handle everything."

Chapter Sixty-nine

Flannery, Patrick and Michael sit on the back porch of the farm house. Flannery and Michael share the wooden swing and Patrick paces before them. From one end of the porch to the other and then back to stand in front of the other two. "You're saying that you will make sure our Granny is well taken care of and that you will pay off the lean on the farm?"

Flannery who is in no way afraid of either man, now that she has been with them for several days, and can see that what they are doing is out of desperation and love for their Granny and the farm that has been in the O'Keefe family for several generations, nods her head yes. Then she tells the two "If you will let me I will call Derek on his cell phone and tell him what I want to do, of course he can't tell the police until everything is set up. Whether he'll agree I don't know?"

"Once we have the money in the bank for your Granny's care and for the farm, you will drive me to the nearest police station, let me go and turn yourselves in":

Patrick paces some more and then standing in front of Flannery again said with fatigue, "Ok, we'll do it. Cassie said she will come to live on the farm until we come home. I don't want her involved so would you find out how we keep her name out of this mess?"

"Maybe Derek or his father can have their lawyer come here or something. The sooner we call him the more we will know."

"Ok Michael, are you sure you're ready for what might happen? I can say I forced you to accompany me when we abducted Flannery."

"I'm in, whatever happens we are both to blame and since we have always been together in everything I will be a man and accept whatever sentence we get."

"Let's go then. Flannery I think we need to use a pre-paid cell phone, one that I keep for emergencies only. Hopefully the call won't be traced before everything is set up."

"So the call can't be traced here, why not leave the farm and go several miles from here. How far is the next county?"

"We're only a few miles from there. Ok, the pre-paid phone is in my car, in the trunk, so let's get moving. Let's see it's nearly eight p.m. We should be able to get the call made and be back here in a few hours."

"Maybe we shouldn't come back here. Could Cassie come here tonight to take care of things? If she can we can avoid the farm for now."

"If the police do find out anything Cassie can say she is a friend and keeping an eye on things."

The three get into Pat's old Caddie, Flannery sits in the front with Pat, Michael sits in the back seat. They say little on the drive to the next county. When they get there Pat gets off the main road and follows a remembered road to a fishing and camping area, one where they once fished and camped with their Grandpa. The campground is quiet because no one is there. Because the area has been neglected for several years it appears that no one has used the spot for quite a while. The slowed economy is one reason the area is forgotten but also the availability of better campgrounds further away.

There is a quarter moon which lets them see somewhat. Little critters can be heard scurrying in the near overgrown bushes. Water in the lake appears silver beneath the moons light.

Pat had called Cassie who will stay at the farm until further notice. Pat didn't tell her where they will be so she won't have another piece of info to give the police.

He pulls the pre-phone from his pocket and hands it to Flannery. She dials Derek's cell number hoping that he is alone in their room. The phone rings only once and he answers, "Hello." he said not recognizing the number.

"Hi Derek it's me Flannery. Are you alone where we can talk for a while? I have something important to tell you and I don't want anyone but you and Bing to know for now."

"I'm all alone, in our room. The kids are sleeping but the cops are downstairs. What do you want to tell me? Before you do are you alright."

"I'm fine. How is everyone there?"

"We're ok. Of course we will be much better when you are safely at home."

"I have a plan. Please listen before you say anything. If we can get this plan in action I will be home soon."

"All right I'll listen. I love you."

"I love you too. Now here is what I need to do, because I want to help Patrick, Michael and their Granny."

"You want to help your abductors. That's rich? Have they brainwashed you?"

Though she understands his amazement she wants him to hear her plan first. "Let me tell you what I want to do, and no I've not been brainwashed. As foolish as this may sound I believe that I am supposed to help Patrick, Michael and their Granny. We know that the Lord works in ways that are not our ways, well I think with all my heart that this is one of those times. If you talked with Patrick and Michael you would do exactly what I am doing."

"Ok, I'll trust you. Tell me your plan."

Flannery tells Derek what she has told Patrick and Michael. She will pay off the lean on the farm and put money in the account for their Granny's care. She isn't sure how it can be done legally but knows that the MacDougall lawyers will know.

When she is through with her story about the hard times that Patrick and Michael have faced and their bad luck at Pat losing his job Derek decides he will talk his father when they are through talking. "I'll talk with Dad now. He and Mom have been staying in the quest room here at Granny Anne's since your abduction. Can I call back on this phone? I don't know but I think we will have to let the police know."

He hears her asking someone if he can call her on the phone and then hears a man say," we will call him. I'll make sure we call back."

"Derek we'll call you by midnight. If you see a number that you don't recognize it will be me. If the police have to know, I guess that's out of our control. Michael and Pat are going to take me to the police station and turn themselves in as soon as we know that the farm will be saved and that their Granny will be given the best care."

"Yes I trust their word on that. They are desperate but are not criminals. Neither has ever been in trouble with the law nor any of their relatives past or present."

"Flannery I know your heart, it is huge and you want to help everyone and believe every sob story that you hear."

"I'm a little naïve at times but my spirit tells me to help them."

"Al right, I will talk with Dad, and see if we can help, if there is no legal way to do this, then what?"

"We'll cross that bridge when we come to it."

Suddenly a scripture comes to his mind and Derek knows that what Flannery is doing is probably what should be done. she is a little naïve and yet when he thinks of her he remembers *Psalm 106:3, Happy are those who do right, who do what is fair in all times.*

Derek reluctantly hangs up and goes to the guest room at Granny Anne's and awakens his father.

The two talk in Derek and Flannery's bedroom. Bing listen to Flannery's plan and then calls the MacDougall family lawyers and once he talks with them he tells Derek what they can do.

"Son we have to tell the police what is going on. If there is a way we can help with the care of the Grandmother we will. The men will be arrested no matter what we do, but if it is possible the lean on the farm will be paid."

Derek knows that Flannery is a wonderful judge of character, but he worries that the same desperation that got Patrick and Michael to abduct Flannery will cause them to go against her plan. He prays that what she has said about them is true and that they will in no way harm her. She means far more to him and the families then any amount of money and he will do whatever he must to keep her safe and bring her home.

Chapter Seventy

At midnight as promised she calls. She, Michael and Patrick are back at the camp sight, after eating a fast food dinner and buying another pre-paid phone. "What did you find out?" is Flannery's first question.

"Dad has talked with the family lawyers and they are working on a deal. They need the name or names on the deed for the farm and the name of the bank that has the lean. They also need to have the account number of the account where the Granny's money is kept, plus the bank routing number."

"Ok, hold on."

He listens and hears not one but two male voices answer her bank questions. Then she is on the line and said, "Pat has the bank numbers. We brought all the important paper work with us. How long before everything is done? If we know, they will have me and themselves at the police station as soon as we hear."

"You know that the police need to know?"

"Yes, we figured that. Just do what you can and I will call back in the morning."

"Ok, I love you. Stay safe."

"I love you too. I know this is an extremely unusual way to settle this but as I said earlier I feel with everything that is in me that I must help Pat, Michael and their Granny. One question, was the ransom ever paid?"

"No it wasn't because we never heard where to leave it. The man who called didn't call back."

"That's odd. Do criminals ever ask for ransom and then not pick it up?"

"The police have said that it is rare but now and then the criminal decides not to carry through."

"I'll call in the morning. I love you."

Chapter Seventy-one

Chloe, though scared at the consequences of what she has done sits on the balcony of her condo. Diego is in the kitchen cooking breakfast. Although he is an excellent cook and prefers eating at home, he doesn't care that Chloe has no interest in domesticity. Because she has opened up to him in a way she has never done before he knows that she trust him and he waits patiently for her to make the right and best decision for all who are involved in the abduction.

Although she comes across as a woman who doesn't give a damn about anyone or anything other than her own happiness, he has seen the real Chloe and is growing extremely fond of her, or more to the point Diego is falling in love with her. She has told him a great deal about her relationships with Derek and his brother Sean and though she hasn't admitted it to him she is in love with her ex-husband and has been so for as long as she can remember.

He vaguely remembers Derek, tall, dark, handsome and extremely intense. Only the day before he asked to see a photo of the brothers, Sean definitely has the coloring of the Irish, and Diego sees that Jack looks exactly like him. Derek is as he remembers tall, trim and with the dark handsome looks of his gypsy heritage. Derek is in a photo with Jack and Lucy and though the little blonde haired girl has a slight look of Chloe, she looks more like Derek. There is the wide smile, and the dark twinkling eyes.

When the omelets are done he finds a tray in the kitchen pantry and loads it with their food. It may be their last meal together for some time and he wants Chloe to know that he will always be there for her.

She is extremely quiet while they eat but eats as much as he. Because she doesn't appear to be ready he takes the empty dishes into the kitchen and rinses them for the dishwasher. The dishwasher is rarely used because Chloe eats either fast food or eats out. When he is finished he goes back to the balcony and taking her hands leads her inside to the living room. At first she looks at the beautiful morning just arriving with its golden light and soft breeze. She has always loved Hawaii and the condo. She knows why she loves the condo, it's because Derek bought it for her. She'd bulked at his selling the huge house in Illinois, not because she wanted it, but because that is where she, he and their children were a family.

Could she have been a model wife and mother, she doesn't think so. Derek will never love her but will always love Flannery. Now that she is away from what once was her family she has many regrets that she didn't at least try to be the wife that he deserved and the mother that their children needed. She knows that having Flannery abducted will make Derek and the family dislike her even more. Derek will never know that after their last phone conversation, she cried herself to sleep. Whatever happens now, she will leave in the Lord's hands. It has been over ten years since she last attended a church service and though she is not one to pray, she silently prays now. She prays that she will become the daughter that Gus and Rena deserve. She prays that one day Derek and their children will see the real, the vulnerable Chloe and she prays that Flannery is unharmed. Her final prayer is that Diego will remain her friend and visit her in prison whenever possible and that God will forgive her for the mess she has caused.

Diego holds her hand as they sit on the sofa. When she closed her eyes he knew that she was praying so he closes his eyes and prays that Chloe will make the decision to do what is right no matter the outcome. He also prays that he will be allowed to visit her in prison.

They end their prayers at the same time and then Chloe tells him, "I need to call Mom and Dad before I turn myself in. Hopefully Daddy can get a lawyer for me."

He starts to get up from the sofa so she can talk to her parents in private, but she stops him and said, "Please stay. I love having you with me besides you already know what a fool I have been."

While she talks with Rena and Gus and explains what she has done, Diego sits with his arm around her shoulders. When the conversation is through she hangs up and tells Diego, "Daddy is going to talk with his lawyers and they will recommend someone that is here on Maui. Until then let's go out for a ride. I will take my cell phone in case the lawyer or Daddy calls."

Once they are on the road to Hana, Chloe sits back and enjoys the breeze that caresses her cheeks and ruffles her short cropped hair. Diego drives a Mustang convertible and with the top down the sun soothes her stiff shoulders and in minutes she is soundly sleeping.

Chapter Seventy-two

Derek is on the phone with Gus and though he isn't surprised that Chloe is the one who had Flannery abducted he is empathetic towards Gus and Rena. "I'm sorry to hear that Chloe would take such desperate steps to get revenge on me and Flannery. I'm not surprised though. I just pray that everything is settled without anyone getting hurt, especially Flannery."

"Yes, that is my prayer also. I have found a lawyer for her in Maui and he will let my lawyer know when Chloe turns herself in. Have you heard from Flannery about where she is?"

"We've talked several times. Dad has found a lawyer to represent Michael and Patrick O'Keefe. He is also helping with the lean on the O'Keefe farm and with their Granny's care. There is a friend of Patrick's staying on the farm and a couple of the neighbors are going to help keep the place up. The man Nick, the custodian from Chloe's condo building is the only piece to the puzzle not heard from. His parents have tried to get in touch and get him to turn himself in also. I know the slowed economy has devastated numerous families and have empathy for the O'Keefe's and Nick and his parents, but to commit a crime is only making their lives much worse."

"Yes, and to think that Chloe is the instigator, I asked her why she would do such a thing and she admitted that she wanted revenge on you and Flannery for getting married. She did say that she regrets her foolishness and that she wants you to know that she prays that Flannery is unharmed."

"Should I buy that? She has admitted that she hates Flannery, so why all of a sudden does she want me to believe that she cares about Flannery's well-being. At the moment I have no forgiveness for her. Perhaps one day I can forgive her but it won't be now."

"I understand. I would find it difficult to forgive her also."

"Gus I know that Chloe hasn't been easy to raise, but I want you and Rena to know that you are always welcome to come and visit us and Jack and Lucy can spend time with you."

"Thanks, I appreciate that and I know Rena will too. I'll call as soon as I hear from Chloe and her lawyer."

"Thanks Gus."

Chapter Seventy-three

Nick, the one missing piece of the Flannery abduction is sitting in a rental car on a dirt road not far from his parent's farm. He flew back to Illinois only the day before and has yet to visit his parents and tell them what he has done. Like Pat and Michael he was desperate to help his father keep the family farm. He has listened to the messages that his Mom and Dad have left on his voice mail but hasn't called them. He'd slept in the car and now he knows that he must face the music of his desperation decision. Apparently the police know his part in the fiasco and his parents want him to turn himself in. He needs to talk with them first and would love to have a lawyer there with him when he turns himself in. He knows that his parents don't have the money, for legal representation if they did their farm wouldn't be going up for auction in only a few more months. He dials his parent's number and his father picks up the phone after only one ring.

Chapter Seventy-four

Flannery walks to the edge of the small fishing lake, and finding a smooth stone watches it skip happily across the still mirror of pale blue water. The sky overhead has been clouding most of the day and she can feel the rain that wants to visit. She, Patrick and Michael have eaten the last of their convenience store food and she is waiting for them to decide when they will turn themselves in. The men have called Cassie and Bernie and are glad that the two women will be staying on the farm for as long as they are needed.

She had talked with Derek only minutes before and knows that Bing's lawyers and accountant have put money into the account for Patrick and Michael's Granny's care. There is an organization that helps farmers who are struggling to keep the land that their families have owned for several generations and they have come to the rescue of the Taylor-O'Keeffe farm and the farm owned by Nick's parents. They have paid off the lean on the house and farm which are paid off free and clear and will be kept in a trust for Michael and Patrick until they decide if they will keep it to move back in one day or if they want to sell it. There is a stipulation that Michael and Patrick will pay back whatever they can once they are released from prison and find adequate work. A lawyer is waiting at the farm to go with them to turn themselves in. Now they have to drum up the needed courage to end a crime that should never have happened.

She needs to pee and sees an old outhouse in a grove of elms. She has tissues in her pocket and there are antibacterial wipes in the car so she decides she will go and get the job done. She has been urinating quite a bit in the past few days and figures that she has a urinary tract infection.

When she gets back to the car Patrick and Michael are standing nearby and when they see her Pat said, "It's time to end this. We are as ready as we will ever be. We want to thank you for all your help and we also want to apologize for abducting you. We pray that one day you will forgive us."

"Yes, we are sorry to have taken you away from your family. You are very sweet and kind and if the law allows we hope we can see you one day, and that you will write to us in prison." said Michael as he holds the back left passenger side door opened for her. She leans towards Michael to hug him and then goes to sit in the back seat. The back window is down slightly and she has her left hand, three middle fingers outside the small space to see if she can feel the raindrops that are beginning to fall. Michael is driving until they reach the outskirts of the town where they will turn themselves in and checks to see if all windows are up. Not checking Flannery's side window he pushes the electronic button and the window closes tightly on her three middle fingers.

"My fingers please lower the window. My fingers are caught." Michael quickly rolls the window down and he and Patrick turn to look at Flannery who holds her left hand closely to her chest in hopes to ease the pain. Huge tears are awash in her eyes and run down her cheeks.

Pat and Michael open their car doors and go to see if she badly hurt. Pat slips into the right side of the car and gently takes her left hand to see what damage there may be. When he gently tries to bend them Flannery grimaces because the pain is piercing. "That hurts, I think they are broken."

"Yes I also think so. Michael we have to take Flannery to the emergency room then we will turn ourselves in."

Michael who also has tears in his eyes said, "Flannery I'm sorry. I didn't know that your fingers were in the window."

"I know. It was foolish of me to hold them out the window to feel the rain drops. It was an accident and could have happened to any one of us."

"I hope they aren't broken. " Michael said as he looks from Flannery to Pat who lets go of her hand and slides out of the car and goes to sit in the front again.

"Maybe you should drive," Michael tells Pat as he hesitates beside the driver's side door.

"Michael it was an accident. Any of us could have done the same. You'll drive to the outskirts of town as planned and then we must take Flannery to the hospital. Ok."

Michael wipes the last of his tears away and then gets into the car to drive. Before starting the car he turns to look at Flannery, who once more holds her left hand to her chest, and he said, "Please forgive me Flannery. I didn't mean to hurt you."

Though her fingers are extremely painful she doesn't blame Michael and tells him, "I know you wouldn't hurt me or anyone else on purpose. I know that you and Patrick are kind and caring and there is nothing to forgive."

Chapter Seventy-five

Nick sits in his parent's farmhouse kitchen, when he arrived home only minutes before, the police were waiting, but also a lawyer to defend him. The lawyer he knows, Sam Nolan is a well-known lawyer in their state, and Nick used to date Sam's daughter Casey. The police read him his rights and then they leave him in the kitchen with Sam and Nick's parents.

Nick's first question is, "Who hired you? Whoever did, please thank them."

Sam has always liked Nick and knows that the man is of quality character or he would never have let him date his daughter Casey. When he was called by the MacDougall lawyers to represent Nick he jumped at the chance. Because Nick's parents have no money he is working on retainer, or that is what he'd planned, that was until the MacDougall lawyers said that the fee would be paid from an account run by the same organization that paid off the lean on the two farms.

Chapter Seventy-six

Although her three broken fingers hurt and she hasn't been able to do more than rest since being admitted to the hospital Flannery is relieved that she is finally free. Patrick and Michael didn't keep her locked up nor were they unkind to her. She is truly grateful that they let her go. True it was in the hospital emergency room and not the police station, where they had originally intended to set her free and turn themselves in, but they knew she needed medical attention. Not only are her fingers broken, she also has a gash and a goose egg sized knot on her forehead where she hit her head getting out of the car at the hospital. This also pains her, but she keeps her focus and waits for her family to come to get her. She knows that Derek and Anne were called from the hospital, and though she didn't talk with them personally she was told by the evening nurse that they are on their way.

While she waits she prays for all those instrumental in her abduction. Chloe is who she prays for first and longest, next she prays for Patrick and Michael and finally Nick. She figures all have been arrested and yet she prays that they are safe and will be able to handle their time in prison. They have thrown her and her families lives for a loop and yet she knows the four are in for a huge eye-opener.

Then she turns her thoughts to her family, especially Derek. The time away from him has shown her that no matter how bossy he is she knows that he is perfect for her. She has missed him terribly and is anxious to see him, her Granny, Jack and Lucy and all family and friends. As she lies in her hospital bed waiting, she finally falls asleep. For several hours she sleeps, until she awakens to find Granny Anne and Bing beside her, smiling softly at her.

"Hello sweet Granddaughter. How are you feeling?" asks Anne as she leans towards Flannery and plant's a kiss on her cheek.

Next Bing does the same and said, "It's wonderful to see you Flannery. Everyone, family and friends are relieved that you are finally free. Everyone sends their love."

"Thank you for coming," she replies while looking towards the door to her room. Tears fill her eyes which she blinks away only to have more tears appear.

"Did Derek not come with you?" tears fill her words and she wipes them away with here uninjured hand.

"Granddaughter, of course Derek is here. He's talking with your doctor. He'll be here soon."

"Ok" is all she said before he walks into her room and comes to stand beside her bed.

"It is wonderful to see you and have you safe." are what he tells her.

When he leans towards her and kisses her lips her tears slide down her cheeks to her chin and then onto his hand when he cups her face in his hand. "Everything will be fine Flannery. Granny Anne, Mom and Dad, our kids and I plus our friends are going to get you through this. We love you and will help you in any way that we can. You just need ask and we will be there with and for you."

She smiles through her tears and said, "I want to thank everyone for their love and caring. I thought I wouldn't cry because I didn't want you to think I wasn't happy to see you. You must know that I am truly happy that the three of you are here."

Anne and Bing know that the two need time alone so Bing said, "Anne and I are going down to the cafeteria to eat. Derek would you like for us to bring something back, and Flannery I will ask the nurse if you may have something, if so what would you like?'

"I'm not hungry, but thanks for asking." said Flannery to everyone's surprise. Flannery has never been known to turn down food and everyone hopes she will be back to her food fetish soon.

'Ok. Derek what do you want. I'll choose if you like."

"I'll have whatever you are having and a cup of tea, and maybe a yogurt and fruit. While driving here Flannery was all that I could think of, but now that my sweet wife is here and safe I'm suddenly famished."

While Anne and Bing are in the cafeteria a hospital janitor delivers a recliner, plus a pillow and blanket. An older man with a huge smile he stops for a few moments to talk with the couple. The news of Flannery's abduction and her liberation has been all over the local and national news and Sterling knows who she is but decides to keep that to himself. He is a very discreet man who knows that the family has been through enough so he chats about the weather and the political scene in Washington D.C.

Flannery doesn't interject much to the conversation that he and Derek are having until she sees his name badge. She wonders if Sterling is his first or last name so ask." Is Sterling your first or last name?"

Sterling notes a slight Scottish burr in her speech but knows that she is American and having a grandfather from Scotland he answers, "Sterling is my first name. My fraternal grandfather was from Sterling, Scotland so my parents named me for the town in Scotland. My last name is Wallace and middle name Bruce so I guess the family named me for Robert the Bruce and liked that it went well with Wallace. Young lady I hear a slight Scottish burr in your speech, why is that?"

"I like your name. My Granny and my father, plus Derek father are from Scotland. I have lived in Scotland although I live here now so that is probably why I have a bit of a burr."

"Have you been to Sterling?"

"Aye, I have. I try to go in August every year for the Tattoo. I play the bagpipes. My grandfather taught me. I'm now teaching my grandson Sterling the second."

"It has been nice talking with you. If there is anything you need ask the ladies at the nursing station and I will deliver your request."

"Thanks." Derek said as Sterling takes his leave.

"You're going to stay the night with me, thank you." Flannery said as tears spring into her eyes once more.

Derek goes to her, sits next to her on the bed, takes her face I his hands and tells her, "Of course I'm staying the night. If I could I would be sleeping with you, but the nurses frown on that, so the next best thing the recliner"

"I will stay here for the next three nights and Monday morning we are going home to our kids. They miss their Mommy terribly and wanted to come with us. Why don't I call them now so you can tell them goodnight." He takes his cell phone from the pocket of his light weight black jacket, dials Anne's home phone and once he has their kids on the line he hands her the phone.

Flannery and their kids smile through their tears as they talk. She kisses the space between them and her, and satisfied for the moment that they are well she hands the phone to Derek. "Thank you. They sound wonderful. I have missed them and you, my Granny and everyone terribly."

She wipes her tears away and smiling a tiny smile said, "Monday won't arrive soon enough. Why must I stay here so long?"

"Your doctor wants to make sure you don't have a concussion and also wants to make sure your meds are right for you. I hear you also have a urinary tract infection and that you were dehydrated. Are you feeling any better?"

She gives him a thoughtful smile and said, "I feel much better but I believe it is due not only to the drugs but because my family has come for me."

Chapter Seventy-seven

Flannery comes home two and a half weeks after her abduction and release from a four day stay in the hospital. Jack, Lucy and Stella wait excitedly in the back yard when they see Derek drive up in Bing's Honda Accord.

Jack and Lucy know from Stella that Flannery has three broken fingers and that they must be careful not to hurt her left hand. The dogs are also waiting excitedly. When Flannery walks through the side-yard gate she is surrounded by dogs and children.

She bends down to kiss first Jack and then Lucy. They kiss her back and Lucy's bottom lip begins to quiver and then she wraps her arms around Flannery's thighs and begins to cry like her heart is breaking. This brings tears to Jack's eyes and he wraps his arms around Lucy and cry's with her.

"I missed you Mommy. I missed you." said Lucy with tears running down her cheeks."

"I missed you too," adds Jack not caring if everyone sees his tears

Everyone wipes away tears when Derek said, "Kiddo's let's let your Mommy sit until lunch is ready." Then he looks towards Stella for a lunch conformation time.

"We'll eat in thirty minutes. I'm waiting for the macaroni and cheese to bake."

"I'll come in and help." adds Anne who wants Flannery and the kids to share some needed quality time.

"I'm right behind you." said Bing who ruffles first Jack and then Lucy's blonde hair.

"Why don't the four of us sit on the swing? That way Mommy can sit between the two of you." Derek tells his sweetly smiling children.

Flannery sits in the middle of the swing as Derek suggests, and then Derek helps Lucy sit on her right and Jack on her left. Derek sits beside Jack.

Lucy holds Flannery's right hand and shyly ask," Mommy did the bad men hurt you?"

"Yes Mommy, did they break your fingers on purpose?"

Flannery hears the caring, love and concern in their question and answers truthfully, "Michael and Patrick, those are their names, didn't hurt me on purpose." Here she explains about her hand being in the way of Michael closing the electric car window.

Jack thinks about her answer and then asked, "You talk like they are nice men. If they are so nice, why did they take you away from us?"

Once again she explains about their grandmother and that the family farm was being repossessed. Jack considers this also and said, "I guess they felt they had no other choice but I wonder if they did? "

Derek takes over and tells his children, "Apparently they felt it was all that could do, and even though it was a crime they went along with the abduction. I believe as your Mommy does that they aren't bad men but it is too bad that they will be in prison, and who knows when they will see their Grandmother Emma again."

Quietly the four think about Michael, Patrick and their Grandmother. They say little more and before long Stella is calling them inside for lunch. It is a celebration for Flannery's return home.

. After lunch, Flannery decides to rest for a while. Derek helps her get comfortable on the living room sofa. Lucy through with helping clean up the lunch dishes comes to sit behind Flannery on the bottom step. Flannery turns her head and asks, "Lucy Hanna, sweetie would you like to come and snuggle with me?"

Lucy shyly moves from the step and comes to stand next to Flannery. Flannery rolls to her side, and taking Lucy's tiny hand smiles and said, "There is always room for my sweet Lucy. We can rest for a while and maybe sleep a bit. I'm tired, are you baby?"

Lucy snuggles her back against Flannery making certain she doesn't hurt Flannery's hand. Flannery kisses Lucy's neck and Lucy laughs her sweet little girl laugh. Derek who is supervising the entire act covers the two with the Lucas tartan afghan hanging on the back of the sofa. He kisses Flannery on the forehead and Lucy on the cheek then leaves the room to go and talk with the others. Then breath's a sigh of relief, and fatigue on his way to Anne's kitchen.

Jack loves having Flannery for a Mom and is very comfortable with her and her hands on mothering. Lucy is the one that desperately needed her unconditional love and caring. Lucy is a hugger and a kisser, and a cuddler and she needs the one on one that only a mother's love can bring to her. A little shy by nature, Lucy isn't as outgoing as he and Jack. She is more reserved and an observer like Flannery and the two get along amazingly well, as all mothers and daughters should. He loves Flannery for many reasons and especially because she definitely loves their children.

When his parents leave for home a little while later he goes into the living room to check on his girls and they are sound asleep. Tralee sleeps next to the sofa only inches from Flannery's hand. She opens her eyes slightly when Derek enters the room only to close them again when she sees who it is. Derek knows that Tralee considers herself Flannery's pet. He will have to clue Flannery in on this fact.

All the pets missed her but it was Tralee who searched for her several times a day, in the house and the yard. At night she would sleep beside Flannery and Derek's bed. He'd thought it was to keep an eye on Jack and Lucy because they insisted that they sleep with him. Now he knows that protecting the kids was only part of the reason, the other reason being Tralee missed Flannery as much as all those who love her.

At seven p.m. after an early dinner Flannery decides it is time for her to take a bath.. Her broken fingers hurt and she knows sleep will help. Derek goes with her in case she needs help since she can use only one hand to bathe or dress. He lets her have privacy using the toilet. When he hears her say, "Ah darn." then hears her crying so he knocks on the bathroom door and asks,

"Flannery what's wrong? Did you hurt your fingers?

"No my fingers are fine," she said with a teary voice. "I have started my period and I have ruined my new panties and the pants you bought for me to come home in. I'm embarrassed for you to help me."

When she cries even harder he decides he needs to reassure her. When she sees the door opening she said with tears now rolling down her cheeks, "Please don't look."

He goes to her and sitting on his haunches in front of her said, "Baby I need to help you. Let me pull your pants and panties off and I will rinse them and then will take them to the laundry room to soak overnight. Though her eyes are focused on his feet and she is still crying she lets him take her soiled garments and rinse them in the sink.

Next he quietly, diplomatically helps her remove her shirt and bra and climb into the garden tub now filled with warm, comforting water. He pulls a plastic bag around her injured hand then he slowly helps her wash her face and her body. When they are through he helps her dress in long pajama bottoms and a long sleeved pajama top. While he is attaching her sanitary pads to her clean panties Flannery looks everywhere but at Derek. He has empathy for her situation but wants her to be comfortable in his presence so he finishes ministering to her needs, then with teeth brushed, hair combed and moisturizer on every visible area, helps her into their bed for the first time in nearly three weeks.

It is here that she finally looks into his eyes. When she sees caring, concern and much love she tells him, "Thank you for helping me. I am truly thankful to be home and with you, are kids and my Granny. I'm tired so I'm going to sleep."

He gives her a loving smile, kisses her cheek and said, "There is no need to thank me for helping you, you are my wife, and I know that if I needed you, that you would help me. Actually you have helped me. I no longer have a need to smoke or drink the Scottish Whisky, your love has cured me."

She gives him the shadow of a smile and shyly said, "I'm happy to help you in anyway and I am also glad that you no longer have the desire for smoking and the Whisky."

"I'm going to take my shower so that I won't awaken you later. Then I'll check on our kids and our Granny and once that is done I will be joining you for a much needed night of sleep."

Chapter Seventy-eight

Her second full day home is much easier. A fall rain started during the night and is predicted to hang around for the remainder of the day and evening. Because she needs something to do Flannery volunteers to do all the laundry. Derek, Anne and the kids carry the soiled laundry into the laundry room for her and once Derek and Anne see that she can handle the chore easily, even with one hand they let Flannery do her duty and take care of other daily chores. The four are never far from her and for that she is thankful, and once the laundry is washed dried and folded with her one hand, the others take the clean wash to their designated drawers and closets and put them away.

Because Flannery hasn't eaten much since her return Derek and Anne and the kids make some of her favorite meals for lunch and dinner. She is grateful for their thoughtfulness but eats very little. That night, several hours after the family has gone to bed, Flannery wakes because her stomach is killing her. She goes into the bathroom so she won't awaken Derek, but the pain is so intense that she decides she better go to him for help.

He is out of bed and half-way to their bathroom when she finally decides to ask for help. He sees the pin in her eyes, plus she holds her stomach, and he sits her on the side of their bed and said, "Honey I think your problem may stem from the fact that you aren't eating enough and you should be taking your meds with food. Let's go downstairs and I will make you some tea, toast and oatmeal. If that doesn't help I'm taking you to the emergency room."

Anne, the light sleeper, hears them in the kitchen and comes to investigate. One look at Flannery's face and she tells Flannery what Derek has told her. Anne prepares the tea and toast while Derek cooks her oatmeal with raisins. Because the toast smells so good and the tea Derek and Anne join Flannery for her middle-of-the night meal. Actually they eat with her so she won't feel out of place. The three talk little at the late hour but words are not needed. That her Granny and Derek would take time to feed her at such a late hour is words not needed. Love is what they speak to her and she is blessed.

The next morning Derek lets Flannery sleep in. He and Anne get up with Jack, Lucy and the pets, have breakfast, and then Anne takes the kids to Virginias to play. They haven't played much in days and Anne decides that they need time with their friends.

The rain ended during the night, and though the day is cold, it is sunny with the promise of better weather in the forecast for the remainder of the week. When Flannery awakens at ten, goes into the bath, washes her face with one hand and brushes her teeth she notes the quiet of the house. Because she'd slept soundly after her late-night feast she didn't hear Anne, the kids, Derek or the pets earlier. Because the dogs are also at Virginias the house, yard and surrounding area are extremely quiet. When she comes out of the bathroom she goes to the bedroom door and listens intently for human sounds, when she hears none she panics that she is alone and running down the stairs to the living room cries out first, Derek, Anne and then Jack and Lucy's names. At the bottom of the stairs, she cries out from fright and starts walking towards the kitchen. Derek meets her in the hallway between the rooms and when he sees her tears and the fear in her eyes he pulls her into his arms and holds her until she stops shaking. Then he takes her hand and leading her to the now sunny kitchen pulls a wooden chair from beneath the table, sits down and pulls her to his lap.

"Flannery, you will be fine. I want you to know that Granny Anne the kids and I have a pact not to leave you alone until you are ready." As he talks with her she leans her head against his shoulder and won't look at him. When she continues to avoid his eyes he tilts her chin to look at her face.

"Why are you hiding from me? I know that you have been through a great deal and even though Patrick, Michael, Chloe and Nick didn't harm you physically they have harmed you mentally."

She looks steadily at him taking in each word and then tells him, "I know that I have some issues that need to be address and I am hoping that I can go with you when you go for your counseling. Will your therapist see us together?"

Though he is surprised by her question he is also pleased that she wants to go with him so he said, "I've not been there since before your abduction but have an appointment a week from today. I've have already asks if you may come too and my therapist is all for it. So next Wednesday morning at ten, you and I will go together. Meanwhile do you want some breakfast?"

"Yes may I have scrambled eggs and an English muffin? I don't want to eat too much since we are going to your Mom and Dads at four. I know Stella will make a huge meal. I'm surprised that she stays so slim. She eats nearly as much as me."

"She does like her food but she swims three to four times a week with Dad and once a week she plays golf with him even though she doesn't really considerate golf exercise since they ride around in a gold cart."

"I see us with a marriage like there's. Growing old together and loving each other like the first day that we recognized that love." Flannery said with a yawn.

"Me too, I see us that way as we age. They have a beautiful relationship, although I know that no relationship is perfect. I do know that compromise goes a long way in keeping a marriage strong. Being away from you has taught me that." Flannery at ease with Derek and their decision to seek counseling together has given her renewed confidence and she smiles her pretty smile and slipping from his lap lets him make her breakfast.

Chapter Seventy-nine

Thanksgiving dinner will be held at Gus and Rena's and the two are truly delighted to have the meal at their house. It has been years since they have had a big holiday meal and happily make the plans. Diego will be with them and he and they will see Chloe the day before. Diego will finally meet the rest of the family. Although he has seen Derek and Jack, at the condo when Jack was a baby, they were never officially introduced.

Because the abduction took place in Illinois Chloe was brought back to the Chicago area for the trial. Because of this she is imprisoned in Illinois so Diego will visit whenever he can.

They have also been invited to Sean and Nell's wedding the day after Thanksgiving. Chloe knows of the wedding and is actually pleased for Nell and Sean. Chloe knows that she took advantage of Sean's good nature and used him sexually and she is sorry for doing so. She has sent Nell and Sean a card and hopes that Sean will forgive her. She also has a card to send to Flannery and Derek and hasn't drummed up the courage to mail it although she knows she will soon. In her heart she always knew that Derek and Flannery were meant for each other and she has now resigned herself to that fact. That she has been blessed with Diego's love and loyalty still surprises her, but she has thanked God for His grace, His love and His forgiveness, and for Diego.

Thanksgiving dinner is held at noon so that everyone will be ready for the wedding the next afternoon at two. The meal is wonderful and mostly cooked by Rena who to everyone's surprise has discovered she loves to cook, and excels at making each tasty dish. All in attendance bring a side dish, but the main meal is cooked by Rena. Joe and Minnie are in attendance, and everyone who was at Derek and Flannery's August wedding are at the dinner also. Diego is easy going and accepted with open arms by everyone.

Diego and Derek find time to talk away from the others after dinner and Diego said, "I know that there is no excuse for the crime that Chloe committed, but I want you and Flannery and your families to know how truly sorry I am and that Chloe has told me to tell you that she is extremely sorry for the trouble she has caused. She admits that she was wrong and would like for you and Flannery, Granny Anne, and your children to try and forgive her. She has told me everything that has happened between the two of you and what a horrible wife and mother she was. She also prays in her heart that you will one day see that she wanted your marriage to work but didn't know how. She also said that she knew in her heart that you will always love Flannery and that she is sorry that you can never make up for the lost years."

Derek listens to Diego and hears the sincerity in his words. He knows that he needs to forgive her but so far hasn't. He also knows that he wasn't an innocent victim in that marriage and that if he'd not married Chloe he and Flannery would not have their children. With this in mind he tells Diego, "I know that Chloe was wrong in all that she did, in all the problems that she caused and yet I understand why she acted as she did. Please tell her I haven't forgiven her yet, but am working on that. Also please thank her for Jack and Lucy and that Flannery is home. After all it is Thanksgiving and we are together as a family. I pray for you and Chloe, that you will have a future and that it won't be too long before she is home with you."

"Thank you. I feel that the future is bright for me and Chloe and that she is the one I have been waiting for. I will tell her of our talk and let her know that you are thinking of forgiveness. That will bring her some peace. She also wanted me to tell Flannery that she has never hated her. She was jealous of her for many reasons but never really hated her. She also said that she knows that you and Flannery are wonderful parents and that she is happy to know that Jack and Lucy are in your care. She also wanted to ask Granny Anne for forgiveness. She now is sorry that she didn't know her better because she knows that Anne would also have been a wonderful Granny to her."

Before Anne and Flannery leave Gus and Rene's later that day Diego also talks with them and gives them Chloe's message of remorse. Anne is first to respond and said, "Please tell Chloe that I am also sad that we didn't get to know each other. If possible and she would like and with Flannery's approval I would like to send her letters. Then we can begin a new and improved relationship." Here Anne looks from Flannery to Derek waiting for a response.

"It's fine with me if you write to Chloe." Derek looks from Anne to Flannery and is surprised by her response.

"I think writing to her would be good. Chloe doesn't know her own grandmothers, so I'm defiantly ok with anyone who wants to write to her. Jack and Lucy have made cards for Chloe which I also approve of. It is after all Thanksgiving, and I have recently read *1 John 3:21* and in case you don't remember the scripture it says,

Beloved, if our heart does not condemn,

We have confidence towards God.

Anne pleased that her granddaughter's faith is growing hugs Flannery, Derek and Diego and said with a smile, "Flannery is right it is Thanksgiving and we must be forgiving and open our hearts to all possibilities."

Chapter Eighty

Nell and Sean's wedding is small yet beautiful. Flannery is her friend's made-of-honor. Derek is Sean's best man. Tyler and Virginia walk Nell down the aisle, and Tyler as proud as a five year old boy can be smiles happily at everyone as he and Virginia walk Nell the short distance from Virginia's entry hall to give her hand to Sean who stands in front of the gas logged fire place with Derek.

The room is decorated with an autumn theme, and the gold's, burgundies and berry colors give the room a rich and beautiful light. The afternoon is sunny yet cold and snow is predicted for the weekend, but those in attendance feel only the warmth from the gas log and the people around them. As with Flannery and Derek's wedding all pets are included in the celebration. The dogs on leashes, including Rena's surprisingly calm terriers, have bows on their collars. In a variety of autumn colors the dogs seem to know that this is a special day, a time to remain calm. The cats also have bows but are nowhere to be seen, although Odie is watching the scene from her vantage point at the top of the stairway.

Nell's dress is lovely. Long sleeved in wool and silk, the white below the knee scooped neck dress with a cinched waist, with sparkly belt is lovely on her very womanly figure. She carries a bouquet of autumn flowers and her smile is so radiant it alone warms the room. As she walks to Sean she remembers the first time he invited her on a date. It was April, one month after he and his crew began remodeling the two apartments in her building. She thought he was kidding and turned him down. After that he asked her every day to go out with him. Her excuse was that he was like a brother to her. Sean, sweet Sean made a deal with her. They go out on seven dates one date per day for a week. Her children were included as well as her Granny. By the end of that week she couldn't turn him away. Not only was she smitten by his kindness and gentlemanly ways so were her Granny and her kids. Now seven months later she is marrying him and couldn't be happier. She asked him if he purposely invited her entire family on those dates and his huge sexy smile told her that it was his fool-proof plan to win her over and her family. What a man. Nell hasn't thought of Sean as a little brother since their first date. The fact that he definitely loves her, her children and Granny is more than she could have ever prayed for and she will forever be thankful that it was Sean and his crew that renovated her building.

They like Derek and Flannery will honeymoon for four days and nights at The Palmer House in downtown Chicago. Their trip to California in early August with Virginia and the kids was fun but they are waiting until Derek and Flannery plan another trip to Scotland because they will go also as a family.

Nell knows that Sean wants more children, three more is his request. She loves him and has agreed to at least two more. When she tells him two more will be enough he grins, pulls her close and said, "You are a wonderful Mom and I know that three more would fit in Virginias house. Actually I have asked your Granny's opinion on this subject and she like Granny Anne has said the more the merrier. So, Eleanor, my love do you want to disappoint our Grannies?" She dislikes the name Eleanor, even though it was her great-grandmother's name and has requested that no one use it. Sean likes her name and uses it to get her goat. So she lets Sean call her Eleanor and she is certain that he will get his three babies.

Chapter Eighty-one

Second Week –December

With only two weeks until Christmas Flannery, Derek, Jack, Lucy and Granny Anne are decorating the beautiful Douglas fir in Anne's living room. They have the tree positioned in front of the four windows facing the front yard and the road. A few pieces of furniture had to be placed elsewhere and they had to clear a path to walk around the tree. They'd gone to Wisconsin to a tree farm and cut the tree only two days before. The day was cold but snow has so far not materialized in the Chicago area.

Jack and Lucy and Nell's three want snow for Christmas and pray every night that it comes soon. The gifts have been bought and are wrapped and hidden in the attic. Jack and Lucy are filled with excitement for many reasons. The number one reason is that they know this Christmas is special. Jack and Lucy love having Flannery for a mother and call her such. They also know that Derek is happy in his marriage to Flannery. To them their now parents are the ones they have always wanted. Living with Anne, who they have always considered their Granny, and living next door to Virginia, Nell, Sean and Nell's children is ideal. They always have someone to play with.

They are half through decorating when the phone in the kitchen rings. Anne goes to answer it and brings the phone back to Derek. He takes it from her and said, "Hi Gus. How are you?" Gus apparently has asked Derek to speak with him in private so he leaves the living room and goes into the kitchen. He is gone several minutes then returns with the phone and hands it to Flannery. She looks puzzled and whispers, "Who is it?"

"It's Gus he has something he wants to ask you. I have told him that once we talk over his offer we will get back to him, but he also wants to tell you what he has told me."

Flannery takes the phone, and talks for a short time, and she too goes to the kitchen to talk with Gus. She is gone longer than Derek but when she returns she said to Derek, "Would you mind coming outside with me so we can talk about Gus's news?"

Next she turns to Granny Anne and said, "Gus said that you, Bing and Stella know of this newest situation with Chloe." Anne nods yes.

"Gus called earlier while you and Derek were out with Nell, Sean and the kids. I know the decision is yours and Derek's, but Bing, Stella, Gus, Rena and I think it would be wonderful if you agree to Chloe's offer."

"The two of you go and discuss the offer. Jack, Lucy and I will finish up here and go and make some hot chocolate and popcorn. There is a Christmas movie coming on soon and when you are finished you may join us."

"Thanks Granny Anne. Flannery and I will go for a walk down by the river.. We always make the best decisions there."

Jack and Lucy are so involved decorating the tree that they aren't even a bit curious about what's going on.

They take their winter jackets from the living room closet and head outside and to the river. The benches are in an area protected so they sit side by side and Derek is first to speak, "What do you think? We want more children and as Gus has said Chloe's baby has your blood and also Jack and Lucy's. I guess he's told you that Diego, Chloe's friend is the father. Diego has four children already and has agreed to the adoption. Gus's lawyer has papers ready for us, Chloe and Diego to sign. I ask Gus if there was a catch and he said no that Chloe and Diego know that you and I are wonderful parents and would be grateful if we adopt their child. I would love to do so, but only if you are in agreement."

Flannery takes his cold hands and studies him for a while and then said just what he knew she would, "I would love to adopt Chloe and Diego's baby. I know that Jack and Lucy would love having a baby in the house. I'm puzzled as to why Chloe would choose me. She knows for fact that you are an amazing father, but she hasn't seen me with Jack and Lucy to know what kind of mother I am"

Derek squeezes her hands to warm then smiles at her and said, "Gus and Rena know what a wonderful mother you are and they have told Chloe as much. Gus said that because Chloe wanted her baby adopted by family, and not strangers she asked how you are with Jack and Lucy. When Rena and Gus said amazing Chloe knew that she would ask us to be the new one's parent. She is four months pregnant and won't have a sonogram for another month so then we will know if the baby is a boy or girl. It doesn't matter to me if it's a boy or girl, I will be happy to claim the baby as a MacDougall."

Flannery studies this man, the love of her life, and knows that he adores children, as does she, and so she lets her heart take the lead and smiles then said, "I agree with you. Having another child will be perfect. It doesn't matter to me if the baby is a boy or girl. Just think in five months we will have a tiny baby to love." She claps her hands to his and the beautiful smile that she gives him lights up the late afternoon.

"We will get to choose names." Flannery said excitedly. "What would you choose for a girl and what would you choose for a boy?"

"I will give you the privilege of naming the new one. I named Jack and Lucy, so it would only be fair that you name the new one."

"I already have two names "

He is certain he already knows her choice, but asks, "What names will you use?"

"I will name a son James Derek, for my Dad and Grandpa. Derek for you because we will nick name him Jamie Derek." She grins at the nick name but he knows that James will probably be called Jamie Derek by Flannery and Lucy who carries the dolls Jamie Derek and Anne Hanna everywhere and has said that one day she will name her son and daughter after the dolls.

"Ok, so James Derek it is. What name have you chosen for a daughter? Anne Hanna I guess."

"No I thought I would use Larkin for her first name and Anne Marie for her middle names. We can call her Lark or Annie."

He thinks of the names for several minutes even said them out loud and then kisses her and said, "Larkin Anne Marie is a beautiful name. Lark or Annie would be great for a nick name. Once we see the child then we can decide which nick name would fit. Maybe Chloe will have twins. Gus has said that Diego has a twin sister named Alicia, so there is a chance that we may get two for the price of one."

"Oh, yes that would be fantastic. You and I can share taking care of them. Let's pray that Chloe carries twins. Oh, before I forget I would have chosen Hanna as one of the names but Lucy already has it. I also thought of Charlotte Rose for Bing's mom but I have a feeling that Nell and Sean will be having at least two children and maybe they will use Charlotte Rose. Of course they have Stella for Sean's mom.

Derek grins at the happy woman beside him. After her abduction Flannery rarely smiled but three months have gone by and with love and counseling she is the loving, happy playful woman that he adores.

Derek wraps his arm around her shoulders and pulls her close. He kisses her cheeks and her lips and smiling said, “So you're already planning names for Sean and Nell. How long have they been married?” He counts on his fingers two weeks and kisses her again.

“You know as well as I that Nell is a fertile Myrtle like Chloe and she has told me, just yesterday after Zumba that she and Sean aren't using birth control so my guess is she will be announcing a pregnancy shortly. Tyler has told her and Sean they need another boy. Sean agreed and asked Tyler what he will do if a girl comes first. Tyler with a straight face said that he would love a sister but really wants a brother.”

“I can understand Tyler's thinking. I loved having a younger brother.”

They sit quietly taking in all that has been said and then Flannery said with a grin, “What if Chloe and Diego have more children. We can put our application in first for any and all children that they have.”

“Gus has told me that Diego loves Chloe and Chloe feels the same about him so who knows maybe they will have more, Of course Chloe will be in prison for quite a while Diego flies to Chicago for a week every month, stays with Gus and Rena and visits with Chloe. Diego and Chloe are allowed private time alone so who knows, maybe they will produce more children.”

“It does my heart good to know that Chloe is truly remorseful that she had me abducted. Gus has said, as you know, that she has also said that she never hated me, she was envious because you love me and she loved you knowing that those feelings would never be returned.”

“Yes, it appears that Chloe has finally grown up and has stopped being her own worst enemy. I forgot to tell you, Gus said that Chloe has gotten her G.E.D. and that she aced every question. Determination is its own reward, and Chloe was determined to prove to herself, no one but herself, that she is smarter than she thought. Diego was cheering her on and I know that this also helped her reach her goal. I feel that once she is released from prison that she and Diego will live in Hawaii. They can sell the two condos that they own and build a house. Whether they will marry is yet to be seen, but the love is there so who knows.”

"She can receive time off her sentence with good behavior, can't she?" Flannery asks then bites her lip.

"I'm sure she can. Prison has helped her admit to herself how self-destructive she was. She gets along well with the other inmates and goes to the Sunday church services. She has asked for a Bible for Christmas and Gus has had one sent from a publisher. He's also given her several Joyce Meyer and Joel Osteen books. These she shares with the other inmates. She has a daily job working in the prison kitchen and loves it. She has told Diego, who loves to cook, that he will have to teach her how to make the food delightful. Diego has agreed whole-heartedly. He may be twenty years older than her but his maturity serves them both well."

"Diego's children and his parents know about Chloe and are corresponding with her. His daughter Nicole, the daughter from his second marriage lives in Hawaii and has met Chloe and likes her a great deal. Claire the oldest, from the first wife is engaged and her fiancé and his family know about Chloe. His son's Seth and Zane also like her, and send her cards."

"I'm happy for them. I'm all for second chances. Without them you and I would be lonely and miserable. With them I can attest that I feel extremely loved and blessed."

"I feel the same, my Mrs. MacDougall."

"Let's go in the house and call Gus. Then we will tell Granny Anne, who is all for the adoption and has told me the house can hold as many babies as we bring here to live."

They call Gus who is ecstatic at their choice. He and Rena are looking forward to spending time with all their grandchildren no matter how many Diego and Chloe decide to have for Derek and Flannery and hopefully one day for themselves.

Chapter Eighty-two

Christmas Eve is celebrated at Anne's. Everyone comes for an early dinner and gift giving, except for the gifts from Santa. Rena, Gus, Diego and all from the August wedding and Nell and Sean's wedding are in attendance.

Everyone brings a dish but Derek and Flannery cook the main meal. The evening is slow-paced and sweet. After everyone goes home to get themselves and their children in bed, Derek gives Flannery a gift that makes her cry. They are ready for bed and sitting against their headboard talking when he pulls a wrapped gift from beneath his pillow. The paper on the square box is jade green foil and tied with royal blue ribbon. He smiles at her, gives her a lingering kiss and said, "This was my Mom's, Hanna's."

Flannery slowly opens the gift wanting to keep the beautiful wrappings and when the wrap is off and the lid removed she is speechless. She looks at the contents of the box several times and at him before she holds a cameo necklace, cameo earrings and a ring to study closely. When she looks at him there are tears awash in her eyes. Happy tears because she remembers plainly Hanna wearing the cameos on special occasions. Even as a child she would sit on Hanna's lap and Hanna would let her try each piece on. She even remembers Hanna saying that one day when Derek and Flannery got married she would give the Cameos to Derek so he could present them to her.

"Their beautiful, are you sure you don't want to give them to Lucy when she is bigger?"

He takes the necklace from her hand and lifting her long hair from her neck he hooks the necklace and smiling said, "Dad kept these for me. If you are wondering why I didn't give them to Chloe it's because she wasn't sentimental like you beside I remember Mom, Hanna, telling you that one day I would present them to you. She was a romantic and knew that one day you and I would marry and that is why I had my Dad keep the set. When we married in August everything was so rushed that Dad and I forgot the cameos. It was Stella, Mom, who reminded them, so I decided to wait for Christmas because I know how much the kid in you loves Christmas."

Flannery slips off the bed and walking into their walk-in closets comes out holding a sweater type dress with long sleeves. It is the color of an old rose and she holds it to her chest so Derek can see how lovely it goes with the Cameo's.

He's off the bed in a jiff standing beside his animated wife, studies the dress, the jewelry and her and said, "The dress is the perfect color. So you like the gift?"

She wraps her arms around him and the dress and smiling into his eyes said, "I love your gift. I love you and our kids and our families and friends and I will proudly wear Hanna's cameos. If I recall correctly didn't Bing give them to her the mother's day after you were born, not that I remember that day, but I recall her telling us that he did."

"Yes, it was then and she wore them with such joy. They were a gift that she always wanted and had told only Granny Anne about. Anne told Dad and he ordered them from a jeweler in Italy. The old rose color was one of her favorites."

She hangs the dress back in the closet, removes the cameos and lays them gently in the square box. She sits them on top of her dresser and they crawl beneath the covers and they snuggle against each other for warmth and comfort. They talk quietly about the day and their children and how much they loved their gifts.

"You would have thought Lucy and Mary won a trip to Disneyland they were so delighted by the doll clothes and the furniture. It was sweet of you to go on line and find the dolls for Mary. They may be used but so much like Jamie Derek and Anne Hanna that she didn't care. I love the fact that Sean had the foresight to put her choice of names on their bibs. Sean Bing and Ella Virginia are perfect and I know that Stella, Bing, Sean and Virginia are pleased with the name."

"Yes, Mom's eyes were filled with happy tears when Mary told her that she wants Nell and Sean to have a little Stella. Tyler of course put a baby boy on his wish list."

"Babies, how sweet they are and to think that in May we will have a new baby in this house."

When she grins he kisses her cheek and said, "I don't know

who's more excited, us, Jack and Lucy, Granny Anne or the baby's grandparents."

"I would say the happiness is equal all around. I'm so happy for Gus and Rena that Chloe no longer blames them for her problems, also that they will always be included in every family gathering. Gus is such a sweet man and he loves Rena, and it is good to know that she honestly loves him. It is wonderful to let the past go, I know that for fact."

"Yes, and I know that too. It is wonderful to look back and see that we have moved on and changed for the better. I for one have taken the ashes of my once broken life and tossed them to the winds of time. Now it is time to sleep," Derek said as he reaches to turn the lamp off on his bedside table.

"The ashes of our broken lives, I like that and it is definitely appropriate in our circumstance." said Flannery with a yawn as she snuggles against Derek and goes to sleep.

Chapter Eighty-three

Second Week January

Flannery and Derek know that Chloe has gone for her sonogram. She is now five months pregnant and they will hear from Gus if she carries a girl or boy. They don't care which and are definitely ready to adopt the baby no matter its sex. Flannery has the name chosen, James Derek for a boy and Larkin Anne Marie for a girl. Their families and friends are anticipating the news with as much excitement as the soon to be adoptive parents Derek and Flannery

It's nearly four p.m. and Gus should soon be calling with the much anticipated news. Derek, Flannery, Granny Anne, Jack and Lucy are in the living room at Anne's watching a movie. '*Brave*' is one that Jack and Lucy love and it was a Christmas gift. . Their personal movie collection is growing because when asked what they would like as a gift for any occasion they choose movies. They were delighted, by their unexpected Christmas gift from Chloe and Diego. Diego discussed with Derek and Flannery what movies they love and don't have and he bought them two dozen. Chloe also bought movies for Nell and Sean's delighted children. With winter upon them and colder than usual temperatures the movie gifts are quite a blessing.

The children are engrossed in the action flick because they haven't been told that the important test has been done. Anne and Derek wait calmly but Flannery is up off the sofa several times because the movie can't keep her attention. Finally she gets up, whispers to Derek and Anne, "I'm going into the kitchen. I'm going to make a cup of tea does anyone else want one?"

Derek excuses himself and follows her into the still sunny kitchen. Though the winter has been snowy and cold the snow hasn't stuck to the brown grass or anywhere else. Flannery turns on the stainless electric kettle, a Christmas gift to Anne from them and the kids, a gift that she personally requested. Dinner will be a little late because they drove to Minnie's for a late and huge lunch of Joe's famous chili, corn muffins and apple pie with French Vanilla ice cream.

Derek collects a tea pot that holds eight generous cups, a cream pitcher and sugar bowl plus three matching china mugs white with hand-painted thistle on the sides of each mug, teapot, creamer, sugar bowl and each sandwich, or desert plate. The tea service was also a gift but for Flannery from Gus and Rena for Christmas.

Flannery fills a huge tea ball with loose tea, the way she prefers over tea bags, which she will use in a rush, warms the pot with some of the now heated water and drops the ball inside. Derek loves to watch her no matter what she is doing. In the first few months of their marriage it drove her to distraction but she has resigned herself to the fact that her, tall, dark, handsome and sexy as all get out husband is making sure she is doing ok. For the first months after her abduction she was terrified to go out of Anne's house, even to the river. With weekly therapy and his love and that of family and friends she now can walk down to the river alone. Though she won't row alone nor shop alone or stay in the house alone everyone gives each new feat applause.

While Derek fills the teapot with hot water, Flannery fills the creamer and the sugar bowl. Then she turns to him, grins and said, "I'm going to fill two glasses with milk for Jack and Lucy plus I'm going to fill a plate with cheeses and crackers, another with grapes and sliced apple and a plate with cookies. Is there anything else you might want?"

Derek walks up behind her, where she stands at the green granite counter top and wrapping his arms around her waist first kisses her neck and then he said, "My Mrs. MacDougall you are what I have a taste for but I will wait until I can properly show you just how much."

He nibbles her ear which makes her laugh a happy laugh and she said in a whisper, "I am looking forward to your offer. I think you know that I crave you far more than food, and you know how crazy I am about food. If I had to choose between food and physical love from you food would lose out."

"That's good to know, although we do need food for the energy to carry out the physical loving."

"Yeah, we do. Can you think of anything else to add to our snack?"

"I believe you have it covered. If we eat all of this we won't need dinner."

"That depends on what time we eat dinner." she said with a twinkle in her eyes."

For several weeks after her return home Flannery didn't eat much. She would pick at each meal but finish nothing. Finally Derek and Anne ask her why and she said that she considered herself a glutton and that many people in the world were lucky to have even one meal a day, so she was giving up her food fetish and was sending the money to food banks. Derek and Anne told her they already give to food banks and Christian outreach which also gives people daily meals. She thought about it but was only convinced to eat more when her doctor told her she was far too thin, and needed to eat to stay healthy, with his words, and the agreement of her therapist, her family, and friends she started eating more. It was when Jack and Lucy became concerned that she didn't eat much she decided to ease their minds and makes a point to eat whenever they do and whatever they eat. She still could use at least ten pounds on her thin frame but she at least eats more than before.

They carry everything into the living room where they sit the two well filled trays on the coffee table. Anne smiles at the abundant snack but says nothing. Flannery and food will never be an issue in her house. Her granddaughter's food fetish will always be a part of her and Anne loves to see those around her enjoying food and life in general.

The five eat and finish watching "Brave" when the phone in the kitchen rings. Flannery gets up from the sofa then sits back down, then gets up once more. Derek, who knows she is excited to find out about Chloe's sonogram stands and taking her hand walks with her to the kitchen and the ringing phone.

Derek picks the phone up, says hello, listens to the person on the line and then smiling a huge smile hands the phone to a very excited Flannery. "Hi Gus," She said and then listens while he relays the news about the test. Her mouth opens wide, she smiles a big smile and then she said with happiness, "Twins, a boy and a girl. That's wonderful news Gus. Please thank Chloe and Diego and thank you and Rena for giving us this wonderfully amazing news. I'll call you tomorrow and I love you."

She hangs up the phone and taking Derek's hands in hers dances with him around the kitchen, down the hallway and into the living room.

"I guess the news is good." said Anne who is as excited about Chloe's test as Derek and Flannery.

"Oh yes. We will have two babies, a boy and a girl. I can use both names. Isn't that wonderful?" Flannery said as she leans down to kiss her Granny Anne's cheek.

"My loves that is definitely wonderful news, two babies, how grand."

Jack and Lucy finally in the real world now that their movie is over look at the huge smiles on the adult faces, and Jack ask, "Did you say that Chloe is having twins?"

"Yes Jack you and Lucy will have a new brother and sister in May. How do you feel about that?"

"Two babies, oh I think it's great. Mommy can use both names that she and I like." said Lucy with glee. "I will help you take care of them, Jack are you going to help too?"

"Sure, I'll help. There will be lots of diapers to change and tons of bottles to fill but I will help also. Lucy you and I will have to teach the babies what we know, the good things of course."

"We will need your help and it will be good that you and Lucy will teach them the good things that you know. Hopefully they won't learn too many bad things." Derek tells everyone as he ruffles Jack and then Lucy's blonde hair.

Chapter Eighty-four

In April Nell finds out that she is two month's pregnant. She has told everyone in the family except Flannery. She and Flannery are sitting in Virginia's kitchen drinking mint tea without caffeine. Nell's excuse for the tea is that she has a stomach ache. Flannery has seen Nell in the early months of each of her pregnancies. Nell shows all the signs of being pregnant and Flannery wonders why Nell has not told her. She sips her tea and they talk of many day to day things and then Flannery said, "Nell when are you going to tell me that you and Sean are going to have a baby. You know that I love the two of you and have seen you pregnant three times already so tell me please."

"I haven't told you because I feel guilty that I'm a fertile Myrtle and you can't get pregnant. I was going to tell you eventually but I guess you know me so well that you see can the signs."

"Nell, I am extremely happy for you and Sean, I knew that you and he would have a baby or two. I have seen the lustful look in his eyes and yours whenever you are in the same room. He loves children as much as you and when he is with Kristen, Tyler and Mary he shows them the love of a father. Have you and Sean told everyone but me for fear I would be jealous. You are my sister of the heart and Sean is like a brother and I will not be jealous. Maybe I can't give birth but the Lord is going above and beyond in giving me children to love."

"I knew you wouldn't be jealous but I still feel sad that a loving woman like you will never give birth. Of course you won't lose your lovely figure either, although I do know that you wouldn't care if you did."

"Your right, I wouldn't care. I would love to have your womanly breast. Derek never complains that my boobs aren't the biggest so I feel he is satisfied."

"The baby boobs can get in the way but Sean loves them. He's like a babe when he's nuzzling my boobs. If he had to carry then around he might think twice about big boobs, but he's a man so he would probably love having big boobs."

The friends grin at the thought of Sean with Nell's generous chest then laugh outright because they know that Nell's words are true. Nell was once a small busted girl but with each child she has grown by inches. Her thirty-eight D's are a feast for the eyes and Sean, totally uninhibited in bed, loves his wife's generous D's.

Chapter Eighty-five

May-First Week

Flannery, Derek, Anne, Jack, Lucy, Bing and Stella wait anxiously for Gus and Rena to arrive with the twins. Chloe and Diego's twins were born only two days before. Diego and Gus and Rena were permitted to be with Chloe when the babies arrived. James Derek was born first and weighed five and a half lbs. Larkin Anne Marie was born shortly after and weighed five pounds even. Because the babies weren't early, as twins can be, and because they are healthy Gus and Rena are allowed to take them to Derek and Flannery.

When the dogs, who are outside bark, this includes Charlie, Shane, Yates, Tralee and Rena's two Stanley and Lacey, plus Anne's little white Highland terrier named Skye and Stella's Highland terrier named Iona, gifts from Santa only five months before those waiting inside know that Gus and Rena have arrived with the much anticipated twins. Derek answers the front door when Gus rings the doorbell. Anne has blocked the doggie door to keep the rowdy canines out for a while so that everyone can see the twins in a peaceful atmosphere.

Gus holds a small bundled little one, wrapped in a royal blue blanket. Rena holds a tiny bundle wrapped in strawberry pink. The two are all smiles and walk with Derek, Jack and Lucy into the living room. Flannery, Anne, Bing and Stella are waiting patiently in their seats. He goes to Flannery and carefully hands her the bundle of blue. The others gather around her while she unwraps a tiny little baby boy with black hair and olive skin like Diego, Derek and Bing. She said, "Hello James Derek it is wonderful that you have finally come home."

His eyes were closed until he hears her voice and then he opens eyes as dark and mysterious as Derek's, he yawns, then watches Flannery's face while she introduces him to the others. When the introductions over, she kisses his tiny cheeks and he smiles showing his new family a dimple like Derek's and Lucy's. Diego also has the dimple.

Rena hands the bundle of pink to Derek who now sits beside his happy wife. He pulls the pink blanket back and they meet Larkin with dark brunette hair. Her complexion is much lighter than James' and she is a tad shorter. Derek says her name only once and blue-green eyes open to look at him. When Flannery said her name she turns her head and looks right into Flannery's moss green eyes. Larkin's eyes roam from face to face until she gets back to Derek. She purses her pretty lips and frowns.

"Would you look at that, little Larkin is already frowning at us, we must show her how much we have been wanting to meet her, then maybe she will smile, "adds Derek with a happy laugh.

Next Granny Anne meets her newest great-grandchildren. Lucy and Jack she has considered great-grandchildren since their birth. First she holds Larkin enjoying the warmth of the tiny bundle of joy. Lucy and Jack stand beside her rocking chair hoping they will also get to hold their new brother and sister. When Derek takes Larkin so Granny Anne can see James, he calls Jack and Lucy to come and sit between him and Flannery. Larkin is placed in Lucy's arms first. Lucy kisses the baby's soft cheeks and said with a happy smile, "I will be a really good older sister." then she turns to look at Flannery then Larkin and adds, "Mommy I love the dollies Jamie Derek and Anne Hanna but the real babies are wonderful and so tiny and cute. Hello Larkin Anne Marie you have a beautiful face and name. I love you."

When Anne gets up from her rocker to place James in Jack's arms, Jack's smile is so huge it seems to light the room. "Hi James Derek, I'm your big brother Jack. You are very cute and I will take care of you, Lucy and Larkin. That's what big brothers do, and I love you." Then he kisses James' cheeks and Flannery and Derek help switch the babies so Lucy can hold James and Jack Larkin.

Bing and Stella also have a turn meeting the newest MacDougall's. Rena and Gus sit down with the others and Gus tells them about Chloe and Diego.

"Chloe was a real trooper giving birth. She and Diego each took turns holding the twins. They kissed them and then the nurses took them to be cleaned up. Chloe said that letting Derek and Flannery adopt them was the best start in life that she could give them. Diego is in full agreement. Diego's four children are getting to know Chloe and like her. They know that the babies would be adopted and were happy to hear that the twins are related to Jack, Lucy and Flannery because of their connection to Rena."

"Also Diego has asked Chloe to marry him and she has agreed. Once they get everything worked out with the judicial system they will be married. As we know The Lord's ways are not our ways, but he always amazes."

Chapter Eighty-Six

End of June

The twins are thriving and extremely easy to take care of. Although they each have a crib Flannery and Derek decide to let them share while they are so tiny. The two sleep peacefully most nights and they believe it is because the twins enjoy being together. They sleep in the room that Derek once shared with Jack and Lucy. The big bed remains in the room so that Flannery and Derek can lie there during the night to feed Jamie and Larkin. Anne is always available when they need a break. Lucy and Jack help in any way that they can and Derek and Flannery are relieved to see that the two aren't jealous of the attention given the twins.

All is well the first month and then Anne notes that Lucy has gotten extremely quiet of late. Lucy is not one that is jealous by nature so Anne keeps a close eye on her. She also takes it upon herself to give Lucy extra hugs and kisses which helps for a while and then Anne decides she needs to talk with little Lucy Hanna. She and Lucy are walking back down the road from a visit with Virginia and Nell and Sean's children. Lucy played with Mary for several hours and seemed to enjoy her friend, so when Anne decides to go and help Flannery and Derek with the babies so that they can go to the market she is pleased when Jack asks to stay with Tyler for a while longer. She assumes that Lucy will being staying also to play with Mary so tells Virginia good bye and heads down the road. She is only a quarter of the way there when Lucy comes running as fast as her little legs will let her calling, "Granny Anne please wait for me. I want to go and help with the babies."

Anne waits for the breathless little girl and taking Lucy's tiny hand studies her as they walk. She smiles at the sweet little girl and asks, "Lucy is something bothering you?"

It is several moments before Lucy shyly tells Anne, "I don't want to be jealous of Jamie and Larkin. I love them but I am jealous because Mommy doesn't have any time to cuddle with me. I should probably ask but I don't want to be selfish. I'm four, so I guess I'm a big girl, but I miss my cuddles with Mommy." Her bottom lip begins to quiver and she bows her head and Anne sees the tears flowing down Lucy's cheeks.

Anne stops at the side of the road, pulls Lucy into her arms and tells her, "Lucy you may be four but you are still a little girl and no matter how big a person is, or how old everyone needs to cuddle, especially with their Mommy. You need to tell Flannery your Mommy, or would you like for me to do that while you are with me?"

Lucy blinks her tears away, and looks at Anne's kind face and tells her, "I can tell her if you are there. Do you think she will think I'm selfish?"

Anne wipes the last of Lucy's tears with a lace trimmed hanky carried for such a time, kisses her cheek and said, "Lucy honey your Mommy will understand perfectly. I want to tell you a little about Flannery when she was small." Lucy nods and as they walk home Anne tells Lucy a bit about Flannery's life with Rena. When they get to Anne's house, the sun is brushing the front porch steps, and kissing the porch swing so the two sit there for a while longer as Anne eases Lucy's worry. This is where Flannery finds them half an hour later when she goes to the mailbox at the front gate to check for the day's mail.

Anne knows that Flannery is alright with her telling Lucy about her childhood and also knows that the story has eased Lucy's worry because Lucy pats the swing beside her and begins to tell her Mommy that she loves the twins but misses cuddling with Flannery.

Derek hears them talking from the living room because the front door is opened and their voices float on the breeze into the room. He knew that something was bothering Lucy and was waiting for her to tell him or Flannery what it was. Now that he knows he feels that Flannery and Lucy have reached a new place in their relationship. Jack tells him what bothers him, and now Lucy has someone, actually two female allies to confide in.

Flannery is exactly the mother that his kids need, their kids need and she is exactly the wife that he needs. He waits for the ladies to come into the house because he doesn't want them to think he was eves dropping on their conversation.

Flannery smiles at him and walks to the sofa where he sits reading a book upside down and she grins, "Now aren't you talented, reading your book upside down."

He gives her a sheepish grin and said, “Well I didn’t want my ladies to think I was eves dropping so the book is my cover.”

She kisses him and said, “We’ll talk later. Now that our Granny is back to keep an eye on the twins you, I and our sweet Lucy Hanna are going out, Not only to the market but to the mall.”

“Are we Mommy? Oh, I can go with you and Daddy without anyone else?”

“Yes Lucy your Daddy, you and I are going out and you will be the only child with us.”

“Oh good,” she said with a smile which turns sad for a moment and then she adds, “I love Jack, Jamie and Larkin and will miss them but is it selfish to want to be the only one going with you?”

Flannery lifts Lucy to ride on her hip as they go up the stairs to change Lucy’s slightly soiled shorts and t-shirt. As they walk Derek, still in the living room smiles at Anne when they hear Flannery say, “Honey, my Lucy Hanna everyone needs their special times with the people that they love, even I enjoy my special times when I’m alone with Derek, Granny Anne, you kids and our friends and family. So in answer to whether you are selfish, no you are not. Cuddles and private time are needed even by the pets.”

Derek smiles at Anne who agrees whole heartedly with Flannery.”

Jack returns from Virginias two hours later and looks for Lucy. When Anne tells him where she is he smiles and said, “Good, Lucy needs special time with Mommy and Daddy. She’s little and I love the cuddles also but she really needs them”

Anne and Jack are sitting in the back yard with the twins who are awake and lying in their stroller. They are mesmerized by the breeze brushing their face, the leaves dancing in the trees above them, and the sounds of the birds singing all around. Jack and Anne sit side-by-side on the swing nearby. Anne takes his hand and said, “You are a sweet and kind boy. You are a wonderful grandson, son and brother, may you always love your sister as you do now.”

Jack squeezes Anne’s hand and thoughtfully said, “Lucy is easy to love. She wanted to tell Mommy and Daddy that she was jealous of the twins but was afraid to. I told her that they would understand, they did, didn’t they?”

Anne nods yes and tells him, “Yes they understand, especially your Mommy. Remember that she was raised by me not Rena.”

Jack purses his lips scratches his nose and replies, “Yes Daddy has told me some about that. Grandma Rena has changed, which is good for all of us. She’s a good Grandma.”

“Yes she is and people can change.”

The four sit in the sunny back yard enjoying the summer day until Flannery, Derek and Lucy return. Lucy goes to Jack and hands him a wrapped gift. He asks what it’s for. She kisses his cheek and said. “It’s for you because you are a good brother and you were right. Mommy and Daddy and Granny Anne understand about being jealous and needing cuddles.”

Jack opens the gift and his mouth is agape with sweet surprise, “Oh, how did you know I want an E-reader. We can use it everywhere, in the car, on the plane, everywhere. After dinner and we clean up may I show Lucy how to use it and I will read to her or do we still need to put books on?”

“That’s all taken care of so yes you and Lucy may use the E-reader after dinner, your Mommy and I will clean up so you and Lucy can enjoy reading.”

Derek also has a huge wrapped package that he’d placed beside the swing. This he pushes towards Anne and said, “For our Granny Anne, a gift of thanks for everything that you do for us.”

Anne removes the gift wrap and her mouth is agape also. “Wow, new luggage. I really need this. My old bags are on their last leg. The color is perfect, who chose it?”

Lucy shyly smiles and said, “I picked the color. I know that you love Royal Blue.”

Anne pulls Lucy to her lap and kisses her sun warmed cheek and said, “You have wonderful taste.” Then she looks from Derek to Flannery and then to Jack and adds, “Your gift is much appreciated. Thank you.”

Chapter Eighty-seven

July moves along like a ride in a surrey with the fringe on the top. Granny Anne always has things to do around the house and in her yard and huge vegetable and herb garden by the backyard fence. Anne is definitely a country girl. Flannery, Derek and the children help Anne with whatever they can. When not gardening, mowing, tidying the house or cooking meals they find time each day to have fun with Jack and Lucy. The twins are easy-going and extremely easy to take care of. The two are just what Flannery needed to heal from her abduction, plus the unconditional love from family and friends, especially Derek. She is their old silly, sometimes childlike woman that Derek, Anne and the kids adore.

Anne's garden is an oasis for humans and the birds. With bird houses and feeders plus several bird baths the yard and garden are always pleasantly visited by numerous birds. The favorites remain the Mocking birds. Most neighbors are respectful of the birds and keep their felines inside. When a rare cat appears the dogs chase them off. Tralee, with the herding instinct tries to herd any animal that may enter her yard.

The tree house is a favorite playtime spot for Jack and Tyler. Because Lucy and Mary are small Derek and Sean have built a little house for them near the tree house. The set-up is ideal. When the kids play they can be seen from the kitchen, enclosed porch, living room and upstairs windows. Not only does this ease Flannery's mind, who still doesn't want to be alone, it also eases all the minds of the adults.

Their trip to Scotland has been cancelled again but Derek knows that one day Flannery will want to take their kids there and she will also go because her Granny hasn't been to her country of birth in over two years. If all goes well they will go in one year with Sean, Nell, Virginia, Bing, Stella, Gus, and Rena. For now the family is settling in at Anne's, where they will live because Anne's loves having them and because it is home. They may eventually add on to the house, with Anne's approval already given. Though Jack and Lucy still share a room, this will change before Christmas because Jack and Lucy have requested that Jack share with Jamie and Lucy wants to share with Larkin. As long as Lucy has her one on one with her parents and Anne she is fine. Not a selfish girl by nature she loves her brothers and sister. Anne is always available to sit with the grandkids and volunteers several times a week so that Derek and Flannery can have a date night or so they can do big kid things with Jack and Lucy.

As for Sean and Nell they will remain with Virginia. She too has requested that their stay be permanent and has given approval to add on to her house when needed.

Chapter Eighty-eight

On Monday, late afternoon, Derek, Flannery Jack and Lucy take one of the two boats out of the boathouse and with fishing gear and they and the children spend several hours fishing on the Fox.

The four wear life jackets which is a must even though the four can swim. With a breeze blowing off the water they are not uncomfortable with the weight of the life jackets.

Flannery does her best to try and hook a worm to her hook, but cringes each time she picks one up then drops it back in the worm container between her long tanned legs. Derek laughs, Jack grins, but it is sweet Lucy who said, "I'll do it for you Mommy. Not everyone likes to touch them."

While Lucy hooks the worm, Flannery looks at Derek over her blond head of hair and nods her head with approval.

"You're a brave girl Miss Lucy Hanna MacDougal. You're brave and beautiful and smart."

Lucy smiles her sweet smile and said, "Thanks Mommy, you are also a sweet and smart girl." then Lucy looks to Derek for confirmation and ask, "Mommy is like a girl sometimes, isn't she Daddy."

Derek studies his smiling happy wife and said, "Yes Lucy your Mommy can be a girl, but for the most part she is definitely my woman."

"Ugh, Daddy I know why she is your woman. The two of you kiss so much I'm surprised that your lips haven't fallen off." said Jack with a little bit of disgust although he does smile.

"Jack, my friend, the day will come when you will no longer think kissing is uck. When the love of your life comes along you will be kissing and hugging too,"

"I'm staying away from girls except for those in the family which includes Virginia, Aunt Nell and her girls."

To change the conversation from the distasteful discussion Jack asks, "Do you think Aunt Nell and Uncle Sean will have more babies. I can't believe Aunt Nell is having only one baby, she is huge."

Derek laughs and said, "I wouldn't be telling Aunt Nell that she is huge. She thinks the baby, their son will be huge and she may be right.

Uncle Sean weighed over ten pounds when he was born. I think that is why Mom and Grandpa Bing had only Sean."

Jack thinks about this and calculating in his head said, "That means that Uncle Sean weighed almost as much as the twins together, Wow, that's big."

"Yep, that's definitely big." Derek tells Jack who has left the conversation behind for a moment because he has a fish on his line. Once the fish is set free he ask, "Daddy did you weigh a lot and did I and Lucy?"

"I weighed eight and a half pounds. Lucy was small at only six pounds and you weighed a little over seven. Compared to Uncle Sean we were light weights."

While Jack thinks of this Lucy looks at Flannery and ask, "Mommy how much did you weigh. You are tall like Granny Anne, not short like Chloe or Grandma Rena, so did you weight more and is that why you are tall?"

"I'm tall because my Dad was tall like your Daddy and Grandpa Bing and Granny Anne. Granny Anne has said that her family the Lucas' and my Grandpas family, the Larkin's were all tall, so I guess that is why I am. Granny Anne said that I weighed only six and a half pounds but was long and thin."

Next Lucy looks quizzically at Derek and then at Jack and ask, "Daddy do you think I will be short like Chloe and Grandma Rena? I would rather be tall like you and Grandpa Bing."

"Well Lucy girl there is a chance that you could be tall, my Mom Hanna was taller than Rena and Chloe and my Granny Charlotte Rose was also tall, so you just might be tall."

"Oh good Chloe and Granny Rena are pretty but I'd much rather be tall then I can eat whatever I want and still look like a model like Mommy."

Derek's dark eyes, usually unreadable smile into Flannery's and what she sees there is love. She smiles back and tells Lucy, "Honey it isn't height that makes a person who they are it is love. In our family we have tons of love and we never judge others, we accept everyone for who they are, After all it is God who made us and if any changes are made we pray and if it be God's will he will change us."

"Those are words to live by Lucy and Jack. Listen to Mommy she is a very intelligent and loving woman."

"Yeah," Jack and Lucy said in unison.

Chapter Eighty-nine

September is upon them and Jack and Tyler start kindergarten. Derek drives them there every morning and Anne or Virginia drive to get them every afternoon. Lucy spends a lot of time helping Flannery with the twins and she, Flannery and Anne are choosing colors for the rooms that Lucy and Larkin will share and that Jack and Jamie will share. She misses Jack but knows that he needs to go to school and she also knows that he will teach her whatever he learns at school. He is the best brother around and she loves him. Even though he is busy, he always finds time each day to spend with her.

He has given her permission to choose the colors for the boy's room and has approved the royal blue, red, black and green that she has chosen on her own. Jack has the talent for sketching, but Lucy has the talent for color so they work on art projects together. Jack has bunk beds in the room and Jamie sleeps in his crib, but when bigger will sleep on the bottom bunk.

Lucy and Larkin's room will be decorated in shades of green, pink and lavender. Colors that she, Flannery and Anne all agree are perfect for a girl, and to Lucy's delight she will sleep in the double bed that was Flannery's as a child and was stored away in an attic closet. The bed has a canopy and a bed-skirt. Flannery has sewn sheer panels that hang from the canopy to give the bed a hide-away effect. With plump pillows and a downy comforter Lucy feels like a princess in her beautiful bed, Larkin will sleep in her own crib for now. When she is big enough Lucy wants her baby sister to share the bed that was once Flannery's.

Though the house overflows with people and pets Anne is extremely happy and feels extremely blessed. The once lonely widow no longer worries about growing old alone. She and Virginia have gone above and beyond in raising their granddaughters and are willingly helping raise their great-grandchildren and couldn't be more delighted. The two travel now and then and go out at least once a week for dinner and movies and of late go out to dance. They have met two widowers and go out just for fun.

Nell and Sean's son Ethan Cole, for Nell's father and grandfather, is born on Thanksgiving eve, one year after Sean and Nell's wedding. He is a big boy at ten and a half pounds and twenty three inches, everyone is surprised that Nell had a natural birth. Sean may be younger than Nell by six years but he has finally grown into a wonderful husband and father. He still wants two more children and Nell knows that he will eventually get his way, After all there are girls names not yet used, Charlotte Rose, for his and Derek's gypsy Granny and Stella Leigh Morgan for his own mother.

Chloe and Diego were married the June after the twin's birth. It will be several years until she is free from prison but they know that one day they will share a life. Chloe has sent several cards to Derek and Flannery to tell them how pleased she is that they have adopted James and Larkin. Jack and Lucy make cards and send them every week. Chloe is delighted by this and sends them cards also. Everyone is surprised, but delighted that Chloe also has a knack for sketching. They see Diego on a regular basis at Rena and Gus' and at all family functions and he is well liked by all who meet him. His daughter Nicole visits with him and is enthralled by the Larkin's and the MacDougall's and tells Diego she wants a family just like theirs. He prays that one day she has one.

Flannery's first adult novel is a hit and she will begin her next novel in the coming year. She has not gone on a book signing tour for the new book but will eventually. Derek will travel with her. Derek works from home and he and Flannery have their computers in a nook under the stairs where they work face to face nearly every day. There is a huge window beside them that faces the back yard so they can watch their children. It is rare that he goes on the road, when he does Flannery goes with him and Bing and Stella, or Rena and Gus stay at Anne's to help with the kids. It is rare that they disagree and if they do they step back and listen to the others thoughts on whatever the issue is. He has grown beyond needing to pay for everything. Their money is in two accounts, one a general fund and one for the future. That she makes more than him is no longer an issue. She loves him and he loves her. They are sharing a life and that is most important. Everything else can be resolved in a civil manner.

They talk about adoption from time to time and wouldn't mind having at least two more children. Two and a half years down the road they get another call from Gus. Yes Chloe is again pregnant and wants Derek and Flannery to adopt. Diego is in complete agreement and Derek and Flannery adamantly agree to the adoption. To their surprise and that of all concerned they are gifted once more with twins. Callum Lucas and Flannery Catriona are born the October the year that Jamie and Larkin are three, Jack is nine and Lucy seven. Chloe gets her tubes tied and Diego has a vasectomy because Diego is now nearly fifty and he and Chloe don't want any more surprises.

Sean has also gotten his dark haired, dark eyed gypsy daughter named Charlotte Rose, named for Bing's mother, and his Stella Leigh Morgan, blonde, green eyed and named for his mother Stella. Sean has also bravely had a vasectomy. Nell loves him dearly but six children are plenty in her opinion. Had it been Sean's decision they would have had several more.

As a gift to Flannery Derek has given her a beautiful framed wall hanging with one of her favorite quotes by Oscar Wilde. Whenever she is happy, which is nearly every day she goes around their house quoting her favorite poets. The one by Oscar she has quoted so much, that even Jack and Lucy know the words by heart. They are working on a Friday afternoon, and she is totally into her writing. They have an agreement that work on Friday ends at two. It is three and she is still in her fantasy world so Derek walks around his desk to hers, turns her chair around, wraps his arms around her, picks her up and sitting her down near the sofa takes her hand and quoting Oscar said,

"It is sweet to dance to violins
When Love and Life are fair:
To dance to flutes, to dance to lutes
Is delicate and rare:
But it is not sweet with nimble feet
To dance upon the air!

She laughs and taking his hands they dance through the house and out the back door to the sunny day filled with family and friends and the promise of a peaceful afternoon and evening.

When they reach the yard Flannery takes one of Jack and Lucy's hands in hers and as they dance around the shady, fragrant, flower scented back yard she and they quote the poem for Granny Anne, Jamie and Larkin, Callum and Catriona.

Anne sits in a wooden rocker beneath a maple tree holding the newest twins and no one has to ask if she is happy. Anne now has the huge family that she has always wanted. That Flannery and Derek are in a happy loving marriage is a grand thing and Anne never fails to pray where ever she is for all the blessings that she and her family receive every day of their lives and the greatest of these is love. She also knows that prayers are answered, maybe not the way humans expect but she knows that the Lord hears our prayers and while she sits holding Callum and Catriona enjoys her family she remembers the words of Luke 11: 10, *God, I know that you are faithful and that if I ask and keep on asking I will receive from you. If I seek and keep on seeking, I will find. If I knock and keep on knocking, the door will be opened."*

That Derek and Flannery now attend church services with the family and read scripture every day is also a prayer answered. Forgiving Chloe for having Flannery abducted and for her past actions wasn't easy but all involved have done so. It took Derek longest to finally forgive that Chloe and Diego have let him and Flannery adopt their children was a huge factor in that forgiveness. He and Flannery took the ashes of their broken lives and have made a better life for all of them. For this he thanks the Lord. The faith that he considered dead during his years away from Flannery was only dormant because he needed to feed it with prayer, trust in God, and letting go of the hurtful past. Derek never thinks of smoking and may have wine for celebrating but his need to smoke and drink whisky no longer tease him. He is in the marriage that he needs and cannot thank God enough for the second chance with Flannery. She is his mate for life and he knows that she always was.

Flannery writing comes second to her family. Though she writes most week days for numerous hours, she always sets the writing aside to give Derek, her Granny Anne and their children her attention and time. Everyone calls Tralee Flannery's dog because she is always with Flannery unless Flannery tells her to keep an eye on Jack, Lucy, Jamie, Larkin, Callum and Flannery Catriona, who has been nicknamed Catriona (Catrina). Tralee is the perfect watch dog although she at times tries to herd her six charges into a corner of the house or yard.

The family tries to go to Scotland at least a few weeks every summer and some Christmases. Anne's farm now belongs to Flannery and Derek. A trusted family friend has been hired as care taker and does an amazing job of keeping thing up and in perfect shape. Anne's Geneva house and townhouse in Edinburgh will also go to Flannery and Derek when Anne is no longer with them. She has told the two of her wishes and they are pleased but don't want to think much about a life that no longer includes their Granny Anne.

Anne is the anchor of the family and Flannery and Derek never fail to tell her how much she is loved and needed.

They as a family know that life may sometimes take them down unplanned paths but with faith in God they will get through and become better people because of this.

For You, O God have tested us. You have refined us as silver is refined. You brought us into the net, you laid affliction on our backs. You have caused men to ride on our backs. We went through the fire and through water, but you brought us out to rich fulfillment.

– Psalm 66:10-12

ROBERTA KENNEDY

Coming Soon…

Where the Lovelight Gleams

Prologue

For you are the fountain of life, the light by which we see.

– Psalm 36:9

The Village of Rowan Tree
Scottish Highlands
In Ancient times the people of The Scottish Highlands believed that the Rowan Tree with its red berries kept evil from their doors. For this reason, every house had at least one Rowan tree planted in the front yard.

There is a village in this area where the Scots of old decided not only to plant Rowan Trees in the front yards but they also had the foresight to plant groves of these red berried trees throughout the village and around the countryside which gives the area great beauty. Throughout history those who live in the village of Rowan Tree or the surrounding area believed in this myth. Because they are Christians who have always believed in and worship the Lord they no longer believe in the protection of the Rowan Tree. Through the teachings of the vicars who came from elsewhere, that it is only a false belief, the villager no longer believe it is the Rowan trees that keep evil from their doors. For the most part the villagers trust God but being human they still sometimes have their doubts. When an American, of Scottish blood moves to the village and brings her deep faith in God with her the villagers learn the true meaning of faith and never giving up nor giving in to any doubts they may have about God. They learn the true meaning of love and the light which gleams when love surrounds them.

Jesus said, "Do not let your hearts be troubled. Trust in God and trust in me."

–John 14:1

Chapter One

First Day of November

Rowan sings Christmas carols as she crosses the border between England and Scotland. It is still several weeks until the magical day but the snow puts her in a holiday mood. Everyone that she knows in Phoenix, Arizona and elsewhere thinks she has lost her mind moving to Scotland in November. She bypasses the exit for Edinburgh and drives northwest to the Scottish Highlands and home. Snow is falling at a steady pace and she shivers beneath her fleece lined coat so she turns the heat up in the compact rental car. She is happy by nature and normally very positive so sings quite often, then there is also the thought of Alex Corbett, her childhood friend who has moved back to Rowan Tree her destination.

She and Alex have known each other since the summer that they were three. That is the first of many summers that her father Finlay brought her and her twin brother Jason to his birth place to stay with his own twin sister Grace. She'd seen Alex in February when he came to Arizona for a four week visit. That was the first time they had seen each other since the summer they were eighteen. Because Alex has an August twenty seventh birthday and she and Jason an August twenty ninth birth day they would celebrate together on August twenty-eighth.

They are now thirty-four and it was on his thirty-third birthday that they started communicating again. Jason and Alex had stayed in touch since that eighteenth summer and he knowing Alex is divorced wants to get Alex and Rowan together. She knew from Jason when Alex married a local village girl Pamela Smyth, the daughter of the town's eye surgeon. Although Rowan's heart was bruised by their marriage she knew that she didn't interest Alex in the romantic way. For the past fourteen months they have sent each other emails, cards and had even talked on the phone twice monthly.

Her father, Jason and Jason's partner had spent the past Christmas and New Years in Scotland. She'd been invited but decided to stay in Phoenix using the excuse that the dogs, cats and birds that they owned needed her undivided attention. When the three returned home the beginning of January and told her that Alex would be there for the month of February she knew that she would finally have to see him in person.

Because Jason and her father had used up their vacation time for the trip to Scotland Rowan asked for the four weeks of his visit off at the animal shelter where she worked. She picked him up at Sky Harbor airport in Phoenix the morning he arrived and to her surprise he and she renewed their close friendship. She made certain that he had a lovely time and took him to the Grand Canyon, to the mountains in Flagstaff to ski, plus they stayed in Sedona for four days. Then she ventured south to Tucson where they saw Kitts Peak and the observatory, Old Tucson and the Desert Sonoran Museum. They saw most of the tourist attractions in the Phoenix area and hiked in the Superstition Mountains. They enjoyed their time together, and he convinced her to come to Scotland for a while. Her Aunt Grace had been asking her for several years to come and stay so that is why she is moving to Scotland in November.

The two passengers riding in two cat carriers and sitting behind the front seats begin to meow impatiently when she stops the happy singing, so she talks with them for several miles to

Soothe their spirited souls.

"Don't worry, it is less than an hour before we reach the village and Aunt Grace's house is only three miles from there," she tells Greer a calico and Vivian a gray striped tabby. A lover of black and white movies from the forties and fifties she found it easy to name her girls. "I know it has been long journey but I want to thank you for being such good kitties on the plane from Phoenix and the drive through the tunnel from France. I didn't want you traveling with the baggage, and that is why we flew the extra miles to France. The other route from Phoenix to Chicago, Dublin and Edinburgh was shorter but you would have been beneath the plane where it is very cold."

"Meow, meow." she hears again and she talks some more.

"You will love Aunt Grace and her Scotties. She also has a cat named Merlin. Merlin keeps Angus and Sheila in line so I doubt they will bother you. You will also enjoy Aunt Grace's house. It is huge with many rooms to explore. We will have a suite all to ourselves. We will have the bedroom of course, but also a sitting room and bath. I think that is where I will keep you for the first few days until you feel at ease in a new place. When the weather is warm we will also be able to sit on our balcony. It looks out over Aunt Grace's beautiful garden."

Her heart fills with love when thinking of her Aunt Grace. Grace is Rowan's father's twin sister, the one Rowan feels very close to, never married because her fiancé Alexander Ross Grant died from cancer only months before the planned wedding, Grace is a handsome woman and has had several proposals over the years. Loyal to those she loves and extremely practical Grace will always love Ross her fiancé, and knows that she will never love another man as she does him.

Rowan's father hasn't lived in Scotland for many years and though he would bring Rowan and her twin brother to spend the summers of their childhood with Aunt Grace he would stay for only a few short days. Her father Finlay Graham Brown loves a warm climate and is much happier at home in Phoenix where he and the twins have lived since they were five. He is also one who no longer believes in the protection of the Rowan trees. He may have named his daughter Rowan, because the name is unusual and pretty, but to him the myth is just that.

She will miss her father and brother and her half-brother Jeff and half-sister Patricia, they have the same mother but that is a story to cover later, but she is ready to start a new phase to her life. Thirty-four and divorced Rowan is more than ready to start a new life in her father's country. From the age of three until the age of eighteen she and her brother Jason learned to love Scotland. Although they have travel many places with their father she always planned to move back for good. Jason has other irons in the fire namely his partner.

With spirits high that she has finally drummed up the courage to move here she starts to sing Christmas carols once more. The snow is falling softly all around and she feels like she has driven into a beautiful Christmas card.

Lightning Source UK Ltd.
Milton Keynes UK
UKOW01f2126290615

254311UK00005B/610/P